PRAISE FOR THE NOVELS OF
PATIENCE GRIFFIN

"Heartfelt and homespun! Curl up under a quilt and escape into this hopeful read."
—*New York Times* bestselling author Lori Wilde

"Stitched through with heart and hope, *One Snowy Night* is a story that will renew your faith in love, family, and the possibility of fresh starts. In short, this is the novel we all need right now." —*New York Times* bestselling author Marie Bostwick

"Pulls readers into an enchanted frozen land filled with people with warm hearts. So curl up with your favorite quilt and read Patience Griffin's newest book."
—*New York Times* bestselling author Jodi Thomas

"Griffin's lyrical and moving debut marks her as a most talented newcomer to the romance genre."
—*Publishers Weekly* (starred review)

"Griffin gets loss, love, and laughter like no other writer of contemporary romance."
—*New York Times* bestselling author Grace Burrowes

"A captivating story of four friends, two madcap romances, an idyllic Scottish town, and its endearingly stubborn but loyal inhabitants. . . . Witty, warmhearted, and totally charming!"
—Shelley Noble, *New York Times* bestselling author of
A Resolution at Midnight

"Griffin has quilted together a wonderful, heartwarming story that will convince you of the power of love."
—Janet Chapman, *New York Times* bestselling author of
Call It Magic

ALSO BY PATIENCE GRIFFIN

Sweet Home, Alaska Series
One Snowy Night

Kilts and Quilts Series
To Scotland with Love
Meet Me in Scotland
Some Like It Scottish
The Accidental Scot
The Trouble with Scotland
It Happened in Scotland
The Laird and I
Blame It on Scotland
Kilt in Scotland

Once Upon a Cabin

Patience Griffin

JOVE
New York

A JOVE BOOK
Published by Berkley
An imprint of Penguin Random House LLC
penguinrandomhouse.com

ISBN: 9780593101490

First Edition: November 2021

Printed in the United States of America
1   3   5   7   9   10   8   6   4   2

Book design by Alison Cnockaert

For James. Thank you for your everlasting support.

And for my readers . . . thank you for following me to Alaska. I'm so glad you are along for the adventure.

Chapter 1

TORI ST. JAMES gripped the chair in the lawyer's office as she and her sister McKenna glanced at each other nervously.

Terrence, their great-uncle's lawyer, opened the door and wheeled in a big-screen TV.

"Please tell us what's going on!" Tori implored. "Is Uncle Monty okay?"

The sisters feared the worst. Uncle Monty was their last living relative. He meant so much more to them than the large inheritance they were to receive when he passed away.

"Montgomery is well." Terrence plugged in the television.

"Then why all the secrecy?" McKenna asked. "Why were we *summoned*?"

"All will be revealed on the recording," Terrence said calmly. He stood back and hit play.

Uncle Monty appeared on the screen. "Hello, girls."

They were hardly girls. Tori was twenty-eight and McKenna was twenty-nine; they were only eleven months apart.

"I've made plans for the both of you," Uncle Monty continued.

Tori's worry turned to excitement. The last time Uncle

Monty made plans, she and McKenna were whisked off to Monaco for a month.

"I've rented out your condo. Make peace with it." Uncle Monty's voice had a steely edge.

"Wait a minute." Tori was confused. This wasn't the uncle they knew. "Pause the video."

Terrence clicked the remote.

"Is our uncle ill?" McKenna asked.

"He doesn't seem like himself," Tori added.

"He's fine and of sound mind," the lawyer said. He turned the video back on.

But Uncle Monty looked a little strained as he glanced down at his desk. It was like he was referring to a script. "Neither of you girls have any long-term goals because everything has been provided for you. You expect nothing of yourselves. I've decided it's time you both stood on your own two feet."

"I bet it was *Peggy* who decided," McKenna said under her breath. Peggy was a therapist and Uncle Monty's latest girlfriend. At least she was fiftysomething instead of the thirtysomethings he usually dated, and this one seemed to stick around for more than the money. Peggy had been shocked when she found out that the St. James sisters didn't work. *And why should we?* Tori thought. Uncle Monty had the means and allowed them to enjoy life without a budget.

On the screen Uncle Monty was wearing a stern expression she'd never seen before. "You both need to change. This is your notice: I've put your trust funds and credit cards on hold."

"You've what?" McKenna complained to the screen. "I have a climbing trip at the Grand Canyon coming up."

"Go home and pack," Uncle Monty said. "You'll need clothing for four seasons, but especially for cold weather. No Dallas winter for you girls this year. You're headed for Alaska."

"Oh, that's not a bad idea," McKenna said, smiling. "There's plenty of outdoor activities there."

Tori frowned at her sister. "Sure, Alaska is great for you. But what am *I* supposed to do there?"

Uncle Monty continued, looking increasingly grim. "I really hate to do this to you, but I'm going to split you up. One in the city, one in the wilderness."

"Sounds good to me," McKenna said cheerfully.

This time Tori glared at her. "I don't think Anchorage, Fairbanks, or Juneau is the size of Dallas. They probably don't have a single Galleria among them."

"And here's the hardest part," Uncle Monty said. "I've tied all this to your inheritance. If you complete your respective stays, the money will be yours. Terrence has your assignments."

The lawyer passed a folder to each of them. Tori flipped hers open but couldn't believe what she was seeing. "One year on a homestead *in the middle of nowhere*?"

"He can't seriously put me in a bank in Anchorage and expect me to survive," McKenna said at the same time.

Uncle Monty was talking again. "You've both heard me speak about my time as a young man living in Alaska near the small town of Sweet Home. Well, I've spoken with Piney at the Hungry Bear grocery-diner and she's found some local gentlemen to help you settle in and adjust to life in Alaska."

But Tori wasn't really listening at this point. "Why is he doing this to us?" she asked Terrence. "The Spring Fashion Show Gala is next week and I have responsibilities." Her job that night was to make sure every model was perfectly dressed and styled before walking the runway. It had taken her months to pick just the right outfits.

Uncle Monty was waving. "See you both in a year." The screen went blank.

"This is a disaster," Tori grumbled.

"He can't split us up, Tori," McKenna said fiercely.

McKenna had always watched out for Tori, as she was the younger and weaker of the two. *Fragile* was the word everyone used to describe her. Just like their mother, who had died during an asthma attack, Tori had weak lungs, too.

She looked back at the screen, about to let her uncle have it, only to be reminded he was gone.

As if choreographed, she and McKenna pulled out their phones at the same time.

"It won't do any good," Terrence said, pointing to their cells. "Monty is on a trip around the world for the next year. You are welcome to email him, but he'll only have limited access."

"He can't do this to us." Tori wanted to scream. "He can't make us go to Alaska!"

"True," Terrence said. "Neither of you has to accept your assignment."

"Really?" McKenna said.

"Yes. You can stay here, get jobs, and pay your own way in the world."

He didn't say the rest, but Tori could read his expression: *Pay your own way in the world, just like the rest of us.*

Terrence continued. "All assets are frozen except a modest allowance for incidentals, nothing like the unlimited access to cash and credit you had before."

"What about Tori's medication? Her inhaler?" McKenna looked as worried as she always did where Tori's breathing issues were concerned.

"Of course," Terrence said, giving Tori a pitying glance. "I'll have all of her prescriptions sent to Sweet Home."

McKenna didn't look satisfied.

"Fine," Tori said, tired of always being the sickly one. "We'll do it."

"We will?" McKenna said. "We'll stay here and get jobs? Do it on our own without the trust fund? If you say so, but I don't think your bachelor's degree in fashion management and mine in parks and rec are going to pay enough to feed us, let alone make rent on an apartment."

"No, silly. We're going to accept the challenge and go to Alaska. Uncle Monty wants us to get out of our comfort zones, and we will."

McKenna shook her head. "Alaska is a good fit for me, but I don't think it's a good fit for you. Remember when I took you to Thailand? You hated roughing it."

Tori was determined to prove her uncle—and that snooty Terrence—wrong. "Come on, sis. We can do this. A year will go by quickly," she added comfortingly, but she didn't actually believe it. The year would drag on. It would be miserable. But they'd survive.

Seven days later, she and McKenna were on a plane to Anchorage, both of them still shell-shocked from uprooting their life in Texas. When the pilot announced they would be landing soon, they reached for each other's hand and held on tight. Not because they were afraid of a bumpy touchdown, but because they would soon be separated.

"We've never been apart for more than a few days," Tori whispered.

"I know." McKenna's voice was filled with worry. "Did you pack your nebulizer?"

"Yes, for the millionth time. I have it packed along with my EpiPen."

"I can't stand it that I won't be there with you," McKenna said.

"Stop worrying." This was something Tori said often to her overprotective sister. "Besides, you made me research the allergens near Sweet Home that might trigger an asthma attack."

"I'm worried about the other triggers, too. Like cold air," McKenna reminded her.

"You were there when my allergist laid out a plan for me. I'm going to be fine." But then it all overwhelmed her again. "A homestead! It sounds dreadful. Like living in *Little House on the Prairie*." It rang of hard work and broken nails. She glanced down at her perfect manicure, knowing it might be some time before her hands looked this nice again. Glancing out the window, she saw her reflection and thought dejectedly, *No highlights or shopping malls.*

She knew most people saw her as pampered and shallow, but she wasn't as self-centered as she let on. Sure, she liked to buy clothes for herself, but not even McKenna knew the joy Tori found in shopping for the women's shelter. After all, every woman—homeless or not—deserved to look good when interviewing for a job. Tori's other clandestine pastimes included stocking the local food pantry and paying random people's utility bills through the Pay It Forward Organization. Why did Tori keep her charitable acts a secret from everyone, even her sister? A long time ago, Uncle Monty gave her some sage advice: when you do nice things for others, do it anonymously; never toot your own horn.

But how was she supposed to do those nice things now, when her accounts had been frozen and she was banished to a homestead?

"Tori," her sister said, squeezing her hand. "Don't worry. It's all going to be okay."

Tori gave her a sad smile.

When they got off the plane, Tori headed straight to Starbucks.

"What are you doing?" McKenna said.

"Getting my last latte for a year."

They took a couple sips of their coffees and headed for baggage claim. When they arrived there, two rather attractive men—one in a suit, the other in jeans and sporting a beard—were holding up signs with their names. As expected, the suit was holding McKenna's name and the mountain man was holding Tori's. The girls turned and frowned at each other.

McKenna looped her arm through Tori's and muttered, "What if we just switch places? No one would ever know."

"Yeah, but *we* would," Tori sighed.

"I know."

"Let's get this over with so we can get back to our normal lives," Tori said firmly. She set her sights on Mr. Mountain Man, walking straight to him. "I'm Tori St. James."

His eyes widened in surprise. "Jesse Montana." He scanned the sleek black sheath she'd bought at Nordstrom. He took in every inch of her with his eyes and seemed to appreciate the view, but at the same time, he looked like he was biting his tongue about something. He glanced over at McKenna and nodded as if *she* knew how to dress properly. McKenna was wearing her L.L.Bean flannel shirt, Levi's jeans, and Merrell hiking boots, looking like the next wholesome cover model for an REI ad.

Tori clipped her next words. "Is something wrong?"

"Are you really up for the challenge? You do know, don't you, that I'm taking you to a cabin in the woods?"

"Of course," she said, steeling herself while maintaining eye contact.

He broke away first and gestured to McKenna's handler, Mr. Business Attire. Tori's kind of guy. "Okay, well, this is my friend Luke McAvoy. He works at First Regional Bank here in Anchorage."

Luke gave her a sparkling smile. "Nice to meet you, Tori." His voice was deep and rich. She couldn't help but smile back.

But the frown on McKenna's face displayed her unhappiness. Not because Tori was smiling at him, but because she was stuck with a banker, dashing though he might be.

The baggage claim horn blew and the conveyor belt motored on. Jesse tilted his head toward the carousel. "Let's get your bags."

Tori stared at him for a moment. If there were any way she could've survived without Uncle Monty's gold card, she would've grabbed her sister and hopped on the next flight back to Dallas.

Jesse raised an eyebrow. "Point out your luggage. We'll follow you."

As luck would have it, their luggage was first—McKenna's brown duffel bag and Tori's three oversized Louis Vuittons.

"That's McKenna's and those are mine." Tori stood back and waited. McKenna reached for her duffel, but Luke grabbed it first.

When the men had their luggage beside them, Jesse nodded to Tori. "Say your good-byes."

Tori felt like she might cry, which would be utterly humiliating.

McKenna hugged her. "I need you to take care of yourself, Tori." She squeezed her tighter. "I'm going to miss you so much!"

"I'm going to miss you, too." She didn't want to let go, but she finally stepped away. "I'm going to text you a thousand times a day."

"You better!"

Reluctantly, Tori walked away with Jesse. "What was that all about?"

"What?" he asked.

"I saw that look you and Luke gave each other."

"Yeah, well, texting your sister a thousand times a day won't be possible," he said, looking down at the tile floor.

Tori clutched her bag with her cell inside. "I won't let you take my phone."

"Calm down." He'd motioned with his hands as if tamping down her distress. "I'm not going to take your phone. It's just that where we're going there's poor cell reception."

Tears threatened once again. She followed him with her rolling carry-on, trying to pull herself together. He might be right—she might not be up for the challenge, but that didn't mean that she had to show how weak she was in front of this mountain man.

When they walked outside, she glanced around. "No limo?" she joked.

"Not where we're going, princess," Jesse replied. "Your chariot needs four-wheel drive."

A dark cloud settled over Tori. *And so my year of misery has begun. Yippee.*

• • •

"CHEER UP." JESSE felt sorry for Tori. She clearly didn't belong in the wilds of Alaska. She looked more suited for the concrete jungle of New York or L.A., or some other big city. He'd bet his hard-earned money that she wouldn't make it a week in the little cabin outside Sweet Home.

Tori straightened her shoulders and stared him straight in the eyes, which was a little unnerving since hers were a vivid green. "I'm fine," she declared.

"Wonderful. I just hope you have some good utility clothes in these suitcases." He glanced at her cute black dress, tights, and silly short boots one more time. When they arrived at the homestead, she should soak her sophisticated clothes in kerosene, light a match, and incinerate them to a crisp in the burn barrel. "What you're wearing isn't going to work for homesteading."

"McKenna packed some of her jeans and a couple of chambray shirts in my suitcase."

"Good. Would you like to stop at Walmart on our way out of Anchorage, just in case? If not, the hardware store in Sweet Home might have your size."

She huffed. "No, thanks. Saks Fifth Avenue is more my style."

"Then you're out of luck." For his own peace of mind, he hoped the other clothes in her suitcase didn't hug her body the way this dress outlined her curves.

He pointed to his new blue Ford F-150. He glanced over at Tori, but she didn't seem keen to climb up into the cab. "Need some help?"

"Hm?" she answered distractedly.

"My truck. Do you want me to give you a boost?" He opened Tori's door and pointed out the running board. "Or use the step to climb up." She was tiny enough for him to lift her into the cab, and for a second he wondered if he shouldn't speed up the process by doing so. She was probably hesitant because her dress was so short. He looked away as she maneuvered her way up and inside.

He went to the driver's side and climbed in, trying to put himself in her shoes. *Displaced.* Piney had recommended Jesse for the job, and he appreciated it. But he hadn't known, until he'd talked to Luke, what his new employer—Montgomery St. James—was up to. Jesse actually felt bad for both Tori and McKenna. And he was worried for himself. This was going to be one tough job. Maybe he should ask the old man for a raise now.

He put the vehicle in gear and drove out of the parking lot, deciding to give Tori the three-cent tour before taking her to the homestead. "Hey, look at that." He pointed to the moose in a crop of trees as they left the airport. "I bet you don't see that in Texas."

Her mouth formed into a surprised O, making him glad that he'd taken this route. She was more suited to delight than sadness. He began a running commentary on the highlights of Anchorage, starting with a drive by Lake Hood as two seaplanes took off. She looked at everything with interest, and he was glad to see her so animated.

"I've been working on your homestead this past week," he told her. *Trying to make it livable.* "The old place has been empty for as long as I can remember." But he was proud of the headway he'd made and wished he'd taken *before* pictures. "I had Piney, the owner of the Hungry Bear, stock your shelves with some staples."

Tori gaped as if he were speaking a foreign language. "Oh, I don't cook," she finally said. "I usually order in or eat out."

He was definitely in over his head. "You do know what a homesteader does, don't you?"

She gave him her stubborn stone face in response. Was it really up to him to make her understand?

He sighed but continued anyway. "Homesteaders live off the land. Grow their own food in the garden and either hunt or fish for meat or raise cattle, goats, and chickens. Then they preserve their food for when it's not in season. As a homesteader, you don't necessarily earn money; your job is to keep you and your family alive. That's it." He glanced over at her astonished face.

She was frowning now, and looked like she might cry.

"Besides, your uncle's homestead is eight miles outside of Sweet Home so you won't be able to eat at the diner every day. Eating out or ordering in won't be part of the deal." Especially since she wouldn't have a vehicle, but he decided not to mention that tidbit. "You really don't know how to cook?"

"I know how to work the coffeemaker, if that counts as cooking," she said with a hint of sarcasm.

What could he say to that? He went silent then, deciding not to explain anything more. Soon enough, she'd see what she was up against.

TORI SHOVED JESSE'S comments aside and enjoyed the scenery. Everywhere she looked, there seemed to be mountains. She'd traveled plenty, though mostly to warm climates with beaches and lots of parties. But this view was breathtaking, and she could see why people might want to live in Alaska.

They drove for several hours, passing through many small towns until finally they reached the city limits sign for Sweet Home, population 573.

"Sweet Home has the basics," Jesse said. "We have the Hungry Bear for food. And here's the newly reopened A Stone's Throw Hardware & Haberdashery, where you can find just about anything you'll need . . . like sturdy clothing. At each end of the town, we have our churches—Baptist and Catholic. The schools sit behind the old medical clinic, which is shut down now. The bank is over there, but it closed for good last month."

By the time he finished saying these words, they had already passed through Sweet Home and were looking at the wilderness again. *Who in their right mind would want to live in such a tiny village?* But she kept the sentiment to herself, especially since he seemed proud of his small-town roots.

After a few minutes, Jesse made a right turn down a gravel road and after another mile, he turned again and pulled between two trees, drove another two hundred yards over grass and then stopped the vehicle.

"Well, we're here," Jesse said cheerily.

Tori's stomach dropped. The log cabin looked smaller than the walk-in closet at her condo. If you could call it a cabin; it was as ratty as a shack. "You can't expect me to live here!" she cried in a high-pitched voice.

His pitying look really ticked her off. "It's not that bad. Really. Don't worry. My job is to teach you everything you need to know about homesteading."

But she was worried. She hated the thought that everyone was right about her. *Poor, fragile Tori.* Well, she certainly felt too fragile to live in a hovel like this! She liked the finer things in life, and this place appeared to have none of the comforts of home.

Toto, we're not in Dallas anymore.

He got out and went to the back to retrieve her luggage while she sat there trying to absorb this fresh hell. Jesse came to her side of the truck and opened the door. He might as well have dragged her out of the vehicle, for the look he was giving her.

He must've seen her gaze go to two buckets of water sitting by the front door. "I brought those from the spring this morning so you wouldn't have to schlep them yourself on your first day here." He pointed out the window on the left. "You have a water catchment set up for when it rains, but you really need a larger rain barrel." He didn't give her time to respond. "Firewood is by the stove, too, so you'll be warm tonight." He set the luggage down on the porch and opened the door.

Tori felt like she was having an out-of-body experience

but managed to say, "Water? Firewood?" She'd never given a faucet a second thought, but apparently here in Nowheresville, Alaska, running water was a luxury. And warmth? She'd been wearing shorts since early March but with the temperature dropping, April here in Alaska felt like it could start snowing any second.

He held the door wide, and she walked in to the eighteenth century, and not some plush English ballroom either. This place was Daniel Boone's cabin. Timber from the outside made up the walls on the inside. A full-size bed sat against the right wall covered by a quilt made out of colorful fireweed and blue forget-me-not print fabrics, interspersed with squares of the Alaska state map with sayings printed on it—the quilt the only cheery thing about the place. Another green quilt was folded at the foot. The kitchen, if you could call it that, was on the left. There was no refrigerator, no cooktop, only two shelves with an iron skillet, a Dutch oven like the one she'd seen in *Julie and Julia*, and cans of food from this Piney person he'd mentioned. And wasn't Piney a strange name?

Tori spun on him. "You've got to be kidding me." She was in shock. "If I *could* cook, there's no place to even do it."

He set her luggage by the bed. "Don't worry. You'll use the woodstove."

That must be the cast-iron contraption in the corner.

He continued, "There's a small oven area and two burners on top. It should be plenty for you."

She choked back a sob. *What a nightmare!* "Uncle Monty can't expect me to live here. You have to take me back to Anchorage. To McKenna." *Now.*

His face fell into a frown, as if he was concerned she might start wailing. Which she was trying hard not to do.

"Let's get you settled in. I'll show you how to get a fire going." He pulled the quilt off the bed and wrapped it around her.

She hadn't realized she was shaking. She grabbed the edges and tightened them around her neck, burying her chin into the cotton blanket, seeking comfort. But this homestead had none.

Jesse went into action over at the woodstove, crumpling newspaper and shoving it inside. "You'll be an old pro at making a fire in no time. I'm using newspaper for tinder but I'll show you how to find good tinder in the woods so you can make a fire by yourself anywhere." He pulled open a coffee can, retrieved a matchstick, and struck the match, lighting the paper in the bottom of the stove. "Next, you'll set a little kindling on the fire." He blew on the paper and twigs until the larger bit of wood caught fire.

"I hope there's a smoke detector," she said to herself, wondering just how safe it was to have a fire going when the place was made of logs. What if the smoke triggered an asthma attack?

"I'll let that sit for a second, then I'll set one of your logs in the stove." He pointed to the stack of wood next to him.

And how sanitary is it to have part of the forest in your house? What about bugs? Spiders? And other creepy crawlers?

She was paralyzed. He was acting like she was really going to stay.

He stood, shoving his hands in his pockets. "I promise it's going to be all right," he ventured. But his tone wasn't convincing.

And she agreed with his tone! She wasn't sure she could survive here ten minutes by herself. But his overall lack of faith in her was making her mad—mad enough that she decided she'd have to prove him wrong! "Where's the restroom? I want to freshen up." She scanned the room for a second door but didn't see one.

"Well, about that . . ." He raised an eyebrow and tilted his head toward the door. "The outhouse is east of the cabin."

She was horrified but managed to square her shoulders. "Thank you." She walked toward the door, but his words stopped her.

"Keep an eye out for moose, wolves, and you gotta know this is bear country, too."

She sucked in a breath and spun around to see if he was kidding.

"Just be careful," he said. He might as well have said, *Have you had enough yet?*

She gripped her hefty Louis Vuitton handbag, deciding it would make a good weapon, if it came to that. "I'll be back shortly." She marched out the door, her eyes darting this way and that, making sure some grizzly wasn't ready to pounce.

Once she was off the porch, she wanted to make a run for the outhouse, but first she turned back to make sure Jesse wasn't looking. But he was, standing there in the doorway with his arms crossed over his chest. She gave a little wave and proceeded toward the toilet, forcing herself to walk with slow, even steps. Then something occurred to her and she spun back around.

"If there's no running water in the cabin, how am I supposed to take a shower?"

Jesse shrugged like it was no big deal. "There's a basin under your bed. You'll get water from the catchment, the spring, or the river and wash up that way."

She glanced down at her long hair, holding up some for him to see. "How am I supposed to wash this in a basin?"

"Oh," he said, as if only just noticing she had curly blond locks almost to her waist. "There is another option."

"I'm not cutting my hair!" Tori exclaimed. Her hair was her best feature. McKenna was the one in the family who looked cute with short hair.

"You don't have to. Piney rents out showers at the Hungry Bear to homesteaders and truckers. I'll take you once a week, if you'd like."

"This just gets better and better," she groaned. Was this part of Uncle Monty's plan? Did he want her to reek like an animal by the time she got her weekly shower?

She stomped the rest of the way to the outhouse, not caring in the least if some wildlife did surprise her on the way there. Maybe it would put her out of her misery.

The outhouse was a rustic leaning wood structure with the classic moon and star burned into the door, which didn't quite close all the way. The handle was some kind of antler—moose, elk, or caribou—she didn't know which. She pulled open the door to find a dingy white Styrofoam toilet seat sitting on top of a plank of wood. A roll of toilet paper hung from a length of twine. She was surprised that the place didn't smell awful, but that was probably due to lack of use for many, many years.

As she closed the door, the scene of the guy on the toilet in *Jurassic Park* came to mind. Only it wouldn't be a *T. rex* but a bear that could come knocking. Even worse, what if the bear tipped the leaning outhouse over with her in it? She quickly did her business, keeping her ears alert for an impending attack.

And because she was out in the wilderness and away from Jesse's piercing gaze, she pulled out her inhaler and took a draw before hurrying back to the cabin.

Jesse was pulling a few cans down from the shelf, along with a can opener. "Beans and peaches for dinner?" he asked. He wasn't opening the cans for her, so he must not be planning to stay.

She felt too despondent to answer aloud and just shook her head. Her new home had quashed her appetite.

He was giving her that look again. "Okay, look, Tori, I understand that a woman like you is overwhelmed with what you're seeing. Let's get you settled in here, get unpacked. Then I'll take you to my mom's homestead—where I grew up. You can have dinner with us and then I'll bring you back here."

Tori was grateful for this small concession. "Thank you. That would be nice." Unless he meant to serve her Bambi for dinner.

But then she had a reassuring thought. She wouldn't have to stay here in this awful little cabin for the whole year because she'd probably starve to death before the first week was over. Then Uncle Monty would be sorry!

She pulled her suitcase to the bed, opened it, and retrieved her favorite dress. Not to wear now, but because of what was wrapped inside—the family picture of her parents, herself, and McKenna. This was the picture she kept by her bed at home, same as McKenna did. Tori pulled the frame out and set it on the primitive nightstand so she could keep McKenna and her parents close by.

At home, when no one was listening, Tori would sometimes talk to her parents. She wasn't crazy; it just made her feel better, feel more connected to them. And at the same time, the picture was a cautionary tale, a reminder that she could be gone in an instant, too, just like her mother, just like her father. Her father's accident was the reason that she'd never wanted to get her driver's license, though McKenna had forced her to. But Tori never drove. When others thought it was weird, she told everyone that she had no need because Uncle Monty kept a driver for her. For some reason McKenna loved to drive and owned a Jeep Cherokee, which was now being stored at a garage, per Uncle Monty's proclamation.

Tori realized she was just standing there looking at the photo, while Jesse was looking at her. She quickly pulled out her silk nightgown and laid it on the pillow for later tonight. Jesse's eyes grew to the size of her gold hoop earrings. Had he seen this very nightie in Victoria's Secret's newest catalog? Was that why he was gawking?

"What's the matter?" she asked.

"When we're at my house, I'll dig up flannel pajamas for you." He pointed accusingly at her sleepwear. "*That* won't do you any good here in Alaska. Especially if that cold front comes through tonight as forecasted."

She shoved her nightie under the pillow. "I'll put the rest of my things away later."

"Suit yourself," he said casually. He held the door open for her and followed her to the truck. "Actually, it's good you're coming to the house tonight. It'll give you a chance to get on the computer and get your hunting and fishing licenses for the year. Your uncle will reimburse me."

She stopped and gaped at him. "Why in the world would I need hunting and fishing licenses?"

Jesse raised one eyebrow and stared at her, reminding Tori of Mr. Messenger, the headmaster at her old boarding school in England. "You'll need to hunt and fish to survive."

She chose not to argue with him but instead climbed into the truck.

Once they were both buckled in, he inhaled, like he was about to say something. He hesitated, then turned to her. "Listen, I want to talk to you about my mom. I don't want you to think it's weird if she's not awake when we get there."

But it was only five thirty. "That's okay."

"She's been sick."

The flu had been bad this year in Dallas.

But Jesse looked worried. "To make sure she had a decent meal today, I got a venison stew going in the Crock-Pot this morning. I hope that's okay."

Ugh! Bambi *was* on the menu. She managed to lie. "Sounds fine." Her stomach growled at the mention of food—any food—surprising, since a couple of minutes ago, her appetite was gone.

When they arrived at his house, she was astonished that his cabin wasn't tiny like hers but gigantic in comparison . . . and pristine, not a dilapidated mess. Two freshly painted red barns sat off to one side. There was a fenced area that held long-haired cattle. In another enclosed area, chickens milled about, pecking at the ground. Surprisingly, the main house was lit up like the Galleria in Dallas.

"You have electricity?" she said accusingly. Which made her realize that her nebulizer would be useless in her cabin. She hadn't needed her nebulizer in a while, but she should be prepared. As soon as she could find cell service, she'd call Terrence and tell him to get hold of Uncle Monty. Or she'd email him herself. Either way, she had to have *some* electricity. What had Uncle Monty been thinking when he'd exiled her to the homestead?

"And we have running water," Jesse said easily, apparently not aware he was rubbing it in. "Just so you know, me and my brother—our whole family—grew up without both amenities. But when we learned that Mom was sick, we installed solar panels for the summer and a generator for the winter. She fussed, saying she didn't need them, but I'm glad we did it anyway."

"And your father?" Tori asked carefully. It was still painful when people asked about her mother and father, and she hated how she had to check her emotions before telling the truth—she and McKenna were orphans.

"Dad had a heart attack while running the trapline . . . six years ago."

"I'm sorry," she said genuinely.

"Thanks." He opened his door and got out.

She followed his lead and disembarked, too, trailing behind him up the large flat stone walkway—not the kind of paving stones that could be picked up at Home Depot either. These looked real, like they'd been recovered from a riverbed.

When he opened the door, there was the sound of whining and a scuffle of feet before two caramel poodle-mix dogs appeared—a puppy and a full-grown one. The puppy shocked her when he jumped up on her legs. As she reached down to pet him, or her, Tori was glad she'd used her inhaler earlier.

Jesse snapped his fingers and pointed at the dog, whispering, "Down."

The puppy immediately plopped his bottom on the floor. The older dog sat, too. Jesse leaned over and scratched both of them behind the ears.

"Poodles?"

"Labradoodles. My mom's allergic to most dogs so we've always had them. This beauty here is Checkers. She's the mother of Scout."

Tori couldn't help but smile. At one time she'd thought about getting a teacup-sized dog for her purse like some celebrities had. McKenna, though, had pooh-poohed the idea because of Tori's allergies—even the hypoallergenic breeds.

"Scout needs more training. The rest of his siblings have found new homes, but we haven't sold him yet because he's still working on his manners," Jesse said without a hint of rebuke in his voice. "He'll get there, though. He's got great genes."

The dogs followed them into the living room, which had a long couch, a coffee table filled with hunting magazines, and two rocking chairs. Bright blue curtains hung on either side of the picture window, which made the house warm and cozy. Tori would have to find some curtains for her own cabin, too.

"Your home is lovely," she said.

"Thanks," he said quietly.

"It's okay, Jesse." A frail woman appeared, standing in the entryway of the living room. Her illness was clear by her pallor and seemed more serious than the flu. "You don't need to be quiet on my account. I'm awake." Checkers went to her side and sat next to her. Scout ran over, too, but with less restraint than his mother.

Jesse's mom wore a long white nightgown under a white robe. She had dark cropped hair and was as pale as her nightwear. Maintaining eye contact with Tori, his mother reached down and rubbed Checkers's head. "Who's your friend?"

Tori opened her mouth, but Jesse answered for her.

"Tori St. James."

"Oh, yes. Tori, you're staying in Monty's old place," the unnamed woman said as she treaded toward her, holding out her hand. "I'm Patricia Montana. Jesse's mom."

"Nice to meet you. So you know my uncle?" *The old devil who sent me to the wilderness.*

"Yes. We're a close-knit community. Everyone knows

everyone in Sweet Home and in the surrounding areas, too," she said. "We all help each other out. My husband helped Monty build his cabin."

Tori had never been part of a community like the one Patricia described. It sounded like something she'd seen on *The Waltons* or *When Calls the Heart*.

Patricia continued on, "We were all sorry when Monty had to leave. We were quite fond of him." Her sallow face produced a genuine smile. "Apparently, he'd come here to get away from it all—or so Piney said." Her smile faded then. "But his father passed away suddenly and Monty had to leave Alaska to take over his father's business." She reached out and touched Tori's arm. "We're glad, though, you've come to stay. It'll be nice to have a neighbor again."

First, who said Tori was staying? She hadn't quite made up her mind yet. Secondly, Patricia made it sound as if Tori had a choice in coming to Alaska.

"I think it's great that Jesse is still here to give you some homesteading lessons," Patricia was saying.

"Still here?" Tori spun around to him. "Does that mean you won't be here to teach me the whole year?"

"I'm starting a new job in a few months." He looked at his mother, as if he didn't want to leave her.

Patricia beamed. "We're all so proud of him. He's going to be the host of a new show on HGTV, *Homestead Recovery*. Didn't he tell you?"

"No. Not a word." Tori didn't necessarily like Jesse . . . but the news of him leaving made her feel like he was abandoning her.

"As I said, the job doesn't start for a while." He was trying to reassure her but it wasn't working.

"What do you do for a living, Tori?" Patricia asked.

Tori didn't know how to answer. She didn't really do anything but shop and hang out with friends. But she had to say something. "My sister and I live in Dallas on a lake, actually it's a little northwest of the city." A luxury condo that overlooked Lake Grapevine—modern, sleek, and with an amazing view of the water—but now it was rented to strangers for the year.

Jesse's mom was ill, but she wasn't dumb. She raised an eyebrow, as if waiting for the rest.

"I like the city. I like to shop," Tori said, trying to make it sound as if browsing Macy's apparel were a noble profession. But then she thought about her other hobbies. She loved to flip through magazines and keep an eye on the latest fashions. She was constantly doodling pictures of outfits she'd like to wear. Actually, she dreamed of cute clothes night and day. "For the last couple of years, I've overseen the styling for the models at the charity gala and fashion show."

Patricia nodded and her expression transformed into pity and understanding. "Well, you're a homesteader now. It's a good path. It's been my passion for my whole adult life."

Tori wasn't sure what to say. It seemed impolite to argue with Jesse's mom, but she had no intention of becoming a real homesteader. She couldn't, especially after hearing Jesse's description of what a homesteader was. Tori settled on a slight change of subject. "McKenna, my sister, is in Anchorage. She's going to work at a bank."

Patricia nodded. "Yes. Luke called and told us. He said he'd be showing your sister the ropes. I assume your sister likes finance?"

Tori laughed. "No. Not really." McKenna was as much a banker as Tori was a hard-core homesteader. "She's a very outdoorsy person. The opposite of me."

"I see." Patricia's brows knitted together. Checkers lay down at her feet.

Tori would love to know what Jesse's mom was picturing. She decided to give her the truth. "None of this was our idea. Uncle Monty had this crazy plan to separate us and send us up here for the year. Actually, I think it's his girlfriend who has him all riled up."

"In what way?" Patricia said.

Jesse leaned closer as if he wanted to learn more, too.

"It's like he's making us trade places. To force us out of our comfort zones. He should've sent me to the bank. I'm the one who's good with money"—she liked a good sale—"and I don't mind being inside all day," Tori said.

Jesse gave a disapproving shake of his head, like she'd commandeered his mountain man knife and dulled it by scraping it against a rock to flatten the edge.

Emotion overtook Tori. "What Uncle Monty wants us to do is absurd," she said, frustrated. For the umpteenth time today, she wanted to cry. She was so exhausted—spent from traveling, spent from the drastic change in her life and circumstances.

Patricia leaned over and patted her hand. "How about some dinner?"

"Yes," Tori said appreciatively. "Food does sound good."

"Come, Tori," Jesse said. "Help me in the kitchen."

"I'm not sure how much help I'm going to be," she admitted, but stood anyway and followed him to the next room. Checkers and Scout did, too.

The kitchen was large, with a good-sized rustic table off to the side. The curtains on the three windows sported a print of red cherries.

"I think we should eat in here." Jesse pulled a couple of dog treats from a plastic container on the counter and tossed them to the dogs, who caught them in midair. "Want to help set the table?" he said as he soaped up his hands in the farmer's sink.

"Sure." She washed her hands and then took the plates from him as he pulled them from the cabinet.

"Silverware is in this drawer." He pointed it out, then went to the freezer and retrieved a bag. "Frozen homemade biscuits."

While she finished with the table, the oven was preheated and he popped them in. Then he snapped his fingers. "I'll be right back," he said, disappearing down the hall.

In a couple of minutes, he was back, holding out red plaid flannel pajamas. "As promised."

She was so embarrassed. She couldn't wear his clothes! It was too personal. But he was still holding them out to her. She quickly shoved them in her oversized purse, which sat in one of the kitchen chairs. "What are all those plants in the window?" she asked, trying to make small talk.

"Oh, yes, remind me to put those in the truck before we head back to your place," he said.

My place? The homestead was not hers. Just where she'd been banished. "Why are we taking them to *Uncle Monty's* cabin?" she corrected. "I'm terrible with plants. No green thumb here."

"Those are the seedlings for your garden. Cabbage, kale, cauliflower, Brussels sprouts. I pulled them from our greenhouse for you. We need to get them in the ground, ASAP."

"You didn't have to do that," she said.

"Yes, I did. You'll need a hardy garden to get you through the winter."

The thought chilled her. Alaska. Cold. Alone.

She needed to change the subject for her nervous system's sake. "The stew smells good."

"It's my mom's recipe. I'll make sure you get a copy."

She looked at the Crock-Pot on the counter. "It won't do me any good. I don't have a slow cooker at the cabin." And then she remembered. "Or electricity."

"You can adapt it for the woodstove."

"You act as if I'd know how to do that," she said.

"Don't worry. It won't take long for you to figure out how to cook. Especially with Piney's help and the rest of Sweet Home as teachers."

Patricia shuffled into the kitchen and eased into a chair. "I'll help you as much as I'm able, too, Tori. And you're welcome to all my recipes, if you'd like. I can copy them for you."

"Thank you. That's very kind." But Tori wasn't going to add more work for a woman who had so little energy.

In no time, the biscuits were done. Jesse brought them and the stew to the table. The dogs were very interested, taking up a spot on the floor between her and Jesse. He dished up stew for his mom first. Then he filled Tori's bowl. "I hope you like it," he said to both of them.

Tori pulled the small crock toward her, ready to take a bite. Before she could, Jesse grabbed her hand.

"Let's say grace."

Patricia took her other hand and bowed her head.

Tori shut her eyes out of respect, though she and McKenna never prayed, or went to church, for that matter.

When Jesse finished the prayer, both he and his mother squeezed her hand on the *Amen*. Tori's eyes shot open. Patricia laughed and Jesse let go of her hand. Was he blushing?

Patricia held on and squeezed her hand again. "It's our little tradition. Squeezing hands at the end of the prayer is how we send an extra blessing to those sharing our food. It's a family tradition. I hope you don't mind that we included you."

"N-no. Not at all," Tori stammered, overwhelmed that these two people would so readily and easily make her part of their circle. Also, her hand still tingled where Jesse's hand had been. But apparently he wasn't affected because he was reaching for a biscuit now . . . and seemed to be avoiding eye contact with her. Which was okay, since she didn't want to look into his brown eyes anyway.

Once again, Tori reached for her spoon and this time, she was successful in taking a bite. "It's delicious." Not at all what she was expecting. She had thought deer would taste awful . . . like guilt.

Jesse did smile at her then. "Everything in the stew came from the land. The meat. The vegetables."

"And the love in cooking it," Patricia added.

"We take pride in living a subsistence life," Jesse said. "I promise to teach you as much as I can so you can live as we do."

But it sounded like fiction to this city girl. If his sweet mother hadn't been sitting right there, she'd tell him so, too. Tori St. James wasn't equipped to survive in the wild. And she didn't even want to. She liked the comforts of her condo—electricity, heating, A/C, and especially running water! When this was over and she got back to Dallas, Tori swore to herself that she would never take modern utilities and her privileged life for granted again.

Chapter 2

McKENNA FELT MISERABLE as Luke drove them out of the parking garage of the airport.

Luke glanced over, then put his eyes back on the road. "We'll go to the bank first. I thought you might want to see it today before you start in the morning."

You thought wrong.

"I'd like to introduce you to everyone, too," he said. "Your uncle has outlined what you are to accomplish this next year. We'll need every second to check everything off his list."

"What list?" This was news to McKenna.

"He wants you to learn the ins and outs of every aspect of his banking company. From being a teller and opening accounts for customers to issuing loans." Luke glanced at her again. "I assume you have a degree in business or finance?"

"Heavens, no." McKenna laughed sardonically. "I have a degree in parks and recreation."

Luke seemed to deflate for a moment. "Great," he said under his breath. He continued. "Montgomery wants you to learn all the security measures that are involved in running a bank, too." He frowned at the road ahead. "I assume you didn't learn anything about bank security in parks and rec."

"Nope. Not unless it's to keep raccoons out of garbage cans at a state park." Her spirits lifted a little because she'd made Luke as miserable as she was. Yes, misery did love company. Since he was now quiet, she put her thoughts on the scenery.

Anchorage didn't have the high traffic and energy of Dallas, which was a plus in McKenna's book. She and Tori had both compromised when they'd picked out their condo. McKenna had agreed to live close to the action if she got to have a bit of nature nearby. They settled on a high-rise condo overlooking a lake that was surrounded by trees. For Tori, the Galleria was only a ten-minute drive, and for McKenna, the trails outside their condo helped her to breathe. Being near DFW airport was a plus, as she could hop a plane for a long weekend in Colorado to hike through the mountains or river raft the Colorado River . . . but only when she knew that Tori was being watched over by reliable friends who could get her to the hospital if she had an asthma attack.

"Did you bring any business attire?" Luke asked.

McKenna didn't have to look down at her clothes to know what he was getting at. "Tori made me bring some of her professional outfits." She wasn't happy about it. A business suit went against everything that McKenna wanted in her life.

"Good." He pulled into a parking lot. "We're here."

The building was a square two-story block of concrete, with no interesting architecture to make it inviting. McKenna unbuckled and got out, ready to get this over with.

"I don't know how much your uncle told you, but I've been the manager here for the past three years. Before that I worked at another of your uncle's banks in Seattle."

Yeah, good for you. She looked longingly at the mountains off in the distance.

He held open one of the glass double doors for her to walk in first.

The place was as sterile as a hospital—white walls, white tile floors, and a scattering of cubicles with plain black desks. She looked over at Luke with disdain. The man looked like the bank—hard as the concrete walls, stiff and professional. Nothing about him or the bank said they were in Alaska—the state that was supposed to be all about its outdoorsy appeal.

He took her over to the information desk and introduced her to Annabelle, a small-framed woman with a serious face, who brightened when he spoke to her. Actually, it seemed as if all the women in the bank had stopped what they were doing to stare. Not because McKenna, a stranger, had walked in, but because their handsome boss, Luke McAvoy, had graced them with his presence. He didn't seem to notice how the women undressed him with their eyes, but McKenna certainly did.

He swiped his key card through a boxed slot and led her through the door to the tellers behind the counter, introducing each one. Next he showed her the room where money was counted and then took her to the vault, which was kind of interesting. She met the woman in charge of mortgages—who shamelessly flirted with Luke—then she met the loan officers, and finally the on-duty security guard. The tour was over and they left the bank.

"Banking is an interesting business," Luke said as they walked out. "Yes, we have to be courteous toward the customers, but I liken us to surgeons."

"Oh, really? How?" McKenna asked, but she was already cringing inwardly and he hadn't even answered yet.

"Surgeons are immune to the emotions of their patients. Surgeons have to see them as objects or they wouldn't be able to be effective at their job."

"Surely you don't believe that. Banking is not a life-or-death job. You're not cutting into them and making them bleed."

"True. But as bankers, we have to be diligent about not empathizing with our customers and their plights. Banking is purely business; what we do is not personal. We have to make hard decisions sometimes. I've found it's best to keep an emotional distance from the customers."

Had Uncle Monty come to the same callous conclusion as Luke? She couldn't believe it. Uncle Monty had never been one to keep his distance—well, until what he'd done to her and Tori by forcing them here.

McKenna couldn't let it go. "Can I be straight with you?"

"Sure. I appreciate honesty," Luke said.

He wasn't going to appreciate this, but she was going to say it anyway. "I think you're really cold." And a snob. Did he think he was better than the people who banked with him?

He shrugged. "I can live with that." He checked his watch. "We better get going. I made dinner reservations."

"I'm not hungry," she said, feeling petulant.

"You have to eat, McKenna. Or can I call you Mac?"

A lot of people called her Mac—mostly her guy friends—but she didn't like how it sounded coming from Luke. "No, you can't call me Mac."

"Okay. McKenna it is. After we're done eating, we'll drop by a store so you can pick up provisions for the week."

She would need yogurt and coffee to start her morning. "Okay." But she only had a little cash with her since her uncle had frozen both Tori's and her bank accounts. "How often do I get paid?"

"Twice a month. The first and the fifteenth," he said.

She was really going to have to be careful to make it to payday. And she prayed that Luke didn't expect her to go halvsies on dinner.

She was surprised when he didn't take her back to his car but started walking down the sidewalk in the opposite direction.

"Where are we going?" she asked.

"The restaurant is down the street."

As they walked in uncomfortable silence, she didn't feel the need to fill the void. He was her keeper for the year and nothing more. When they arrived at the restaurant, the noise of the crowd made it impossible to make small talk. She was grateful. She ordered the halibut and he did the same. The table he'd reserved was by the windows with a view of the water, which gave her something to stare at other than his perfectly symmetrical face, while she waited for her meal to arrive.

When her fish was placed in front of her, she spoke to him. "So where am I to stay?"

"Your uncle has an apartment for you with all the amenities—laundry, gym, cable. You'll want for nothing." He dug in his wallet and pulled out a credit card and offered it to her. "This is for you."

"Why?" She turned the card over and saw her name spelled out on the back. "Uncle Monty made us turn over our cards to the lawyer last week." McKenna had felt stripped of all security and hadn't felt stable since.

"I don't know why. I was told to give this to you when you arrived." He pulled a piece of paper from his wallet. "And I'm supposed to give this to you, too."

It was a note.

My dearest McKenna,

This $1000 cash card is a loan with five percent interest on it. Use it wisely.

> *Love,*
> *Uncle Monty*

Well, at least with the loan she'd be able to eat until she got paid. Tonight, before she went to bed, she would write Uncle Monty and thank him for the *gift*.

She reached in her purse for a notebook and pen. "Do you mind if I work on a list for the store?" She only said it as a courtesy.

"Knock yourself out."

But as she poised her pen, something occurred to her. "Is the apartment furnished?" Or would she be responsible for buying furniture and appliances with her card?

"I assume it's a duplicate of mine so the answer is yes."

A sinking feeling came over her. "Why would you assume that?"

He gave her a superior cocky grin. "Because your apartment is right next to mine."

FROM THE MOMENT Luke saw McKenna, he knew that she wasn't going to fit into the banking world. He scanned her again, something he'd done a hundred times since picking her up. McKenna was a jeans-sweater-and-hiking-boots type of woman. She wasn't meant for business wear, and it was clear that she wasn't meant for the MBA lifestyle either. Being a river raft guide would suit her better.

He glanced over, knowing he'd shocked her, and it pleased him. "Something wrong?"

"My apartment is next to yours?" she sputtered.

"Yes. My apartment is a perk for being the manager of Montgomery St. James's bank." Or maybe it was a curse. Because now that he'd met McKenna St. James, he wasn't sure how he felt about living next to her either. "I'm sure your place is furnished with comfortable furniture and an outstanding mattress like mine. You'll sleep like a baby." He might as well break the rest of it to her. "My instructions say that you're to ride with me every day to and from the bank. I hope that's okay."

"No car," she muttered, as if it were adding insult to injury.

"I'm happy to take you anywhere you want to go." He

didn't know why he'd offered that. But the offer didn't seem to cheer her. "Or you can Uber."

She glanced down at the credit card. "I will appreciate getting a ride to work. For anything else, I'll figure it out." Then as an afterthought, she said, "Thank you."

They finished the rest of their meal without talking, which felt as awkward as a blind date that had gone south. But he reminded himself that it wasn't a date—he was her boss . . . period.

At the store, they split up and she was done before him. Based on the few items in her cart, Luke decided she must be a minimalist.

The only sound on the short drive from the store to the apartment building was the whir of the car's engine. When he pulled up to their building and parked, she said, "So this is it," sounding like a convict seeing the prison for the first time.

"It's one of the nicest apartment buildings in Anchorage," he defended. "I'm sure you'll have a mountain view from your living room windows . . . like I do."

"It'll be fine." She sounded resigned.

He got out of the car and retrieved her luggage from the back, letting her carry her sacks. They rode the elevator up to the top floor, where he produced her keys and opened her door before reaching in and hitting the light switch.

As expected, her apartment was decorated in the same style as his. When Montgomery St. James came to visit, this was where he stayed. The cleaning crew must've been through because there was a fresh pine scent in the air. He walked in farther and saw that a bouquet of flowers had been placed on the bar. He set the keys beside them and put her duffel bag on the floor.

McKenna turned in a circle. "Yes, it's nice, functional." As if he'd asked a question.

He suddenly felt self-conscious. "I usually leave at eight thirty in the morning. I'll text when I'm ready."

She picked up the key and studied it. "Sure. That works."

She looked up then, as if noticing he was there. "I'll walk you out."

Which was the polite way to say that he should leave. Once outside, he pointed to the doorway a few feet down the hall. "That's my apartment, if you need something. Okay?"

"I won't need anything," she said. "Good night, Luke." She didn't wait for him to reciprocate before she shut her door.

"Sleep well," he said to the empty hallway.

This had been the most awkward evening, which made him dread the next twelve months. If Montgomery hadn't insisted upon Luke overseeing McKenna's training himself, Luke would've pawned her off on one of his underlings at the bank. McKenna's reticence mixed with how she threw him off his game formed a foreboding lump in his chest . . . followed by anticipation. Maybe he was coming down with something. He hadn't felt this unsure of himself around a girl since before high school. But that was a long time ago, when he'd been living on a failing homestead outside Sweet Home. In those days he tried not to compare himself to Jesse—his best friend, then and now—but it had been nearly impossible. Jesse didn't have to get hand-me-down clothes from the nurse's office at school. Jesse didn't have to endure the pitying looks from the people of Sweet Home when they saw that his father wasn't taking care of him. Forget Christmases and birthdays, Luke would've settled for a stocked pantry at home.

During Luke's junior year in high school, their homestead had been repossessed by the bank and his father left Sweet Home to find a job in Oregon. There had been little contact between them since. To finish out school, Luke had moved in with Jesse's family, a real family. Though Luke hadn't had the greatest start, he never felt sorry for himself. Everything he'd been through had been a lesson, giving him the drive to do better than his dad and not fail. And he hadn't.

Luke was a well-respected businessman who had no trouble getting a date.

He stopped himself from going down that track any further. He had no intention of dating McKenna St. James. His job was to train her and then send her back to where she'd come from.

AS SOON AS the door was shut, McKenna pulled out her phone to call Tori. The phone rang and rang and finally went to voice mail. She knew talking to Tori would make her feel better. But now, she was more panicked than ever.

She opened her door and stared down the hall, wondering what she should do. She didn't want to talk to Luke again tonight, especially after she finally had some time alone.

But Tori had to be in trouble if she wasn't answering her phone. McKenna went back and grabbed the keys off the counter, left the apartment, and pounded on the door next to hers.

Luke answered immediately, as if he'd been waiting for her. He'd changed into a tee shirt, shorts, and sneakers, looking totally different than the stiff suit of a short while ago. "What's wrong?"

"It's Tori. She's not answering her phone." McKenna lifted her cell as if it were evidence.

He put his hand on her phone and lowered it. "I meant to tell you. Cell service is spotty everywhere but especially awful around Sweet Home. Don't worry. She's fine."

Don't worry? Was he nuts? "I need to talk to her," McKenna said.

"Is there something I can do?" he asked. "I'm happy to help."

The words flooded McKenna's brain but she bit them back before saying, *Would it be too much trouble for you to take me to Tori? So I can make sure she's all right?* She grasped for an excuse. "I just wanted to make sure that she has her inhaler with her." Which McKenna knew she did. She'd finally quit bugging Tori when she'd shoved it in McKenna's face that morning and then made her watch as she secured it back in her bag.

"I can text Jesse for you, if you like. He seems to get my texts when he's at home. He'll see Tori in the morning, I'm sure," Luke said.

"No. That's okay." McKenna felt deflated. "Good night." She walked back to her apartment and unlocked the door.

This was an impossible situation. There was no way she was going to make it here in Anchorage, especially since Tori was far away in some remote cabin without her.

But McKenna didn't have to be completely without Tori. She ran to her duffel bag and dug around inside until she found the framed picture she'd kept by her bed at the condo. She touched Tori's face. "I promised Dad that I'd look out for you. I'm not sure how I'm going to do that with me stuck here in Anchorage and you out there by yourself." It felt like she was breaking her promise. If only she could explain it to Uncle Monty, then maybe he'd let them be together.

McKenna's friends back in Dallas had always said she felt way too responsible for her sister. But they weren't in her shoes. McKenna gladly lived in the confines of a city if it meant that Tori was going to be okay, looked after, protected from the weakness of her own lungs.

They were both doomed. Uncle Monty had set them up for failure, and McKenna just couldn't see why.

Chapter 3

WHEN TORI ARRIVED back at her cabin, Jesse came in with her, carrying the tray of seedlings. He set them on the kitchen counter, then pulled a piece of paper from his pocket. "I took the liberty of making you a planting calendar. We'll go over it tomorrow."

She just stared as he lit the kerosene lamp. Even though it was still twilight outside, the corners of the cabin were filled with dark shadows, making it the perfect locale for a slasher movie.

"Is it safe here?" she asked.

"Bar the door when I leave." Which wasn't the answer she wanted. He demonstrated how to place the slab of wood in the brackets on either side of the door. "Let me show you how to bank up the fire for the night."

She followed him to the small woodstove and watched how he spread out the coals with the poker, then laid more firewood on top.

"If you get cold, just throw another log on the fire."

"Are you sure you can't stay here with me?" She would have liked a sentry sitting by her door.

"I'll be back at first light."

"What am I supposed to do now?" She had no electricity, no TV, no way to skim social media on her phone, no nothing.

He walked to the door, but turned back, giving her a reassuring smile. "I suggest you go to bed. We have a lot to cover tomorrow, and morning will be here soon." He gave her that worried look again, which didn't instill confidence in her. "Good night."

"Good night," she said, though she really wanted to beg him to stay.

He shut the door and she was alone. She stood there for a moment, staring at the empty doorway.

There was a knock that made her jump. "Bar the door," his muffled voice said.

She ran to the heavy piece of wood leaning against the wall, hefted it, and then slid it into place.

"Good night, Tori St. James," came from the other side of the door.

"'Night," she whispered. She peeked out the window and watched him walk off the porch and to his truck. After a few minutes, she heard the truck roar to life. He turned the vehicle around and headed back down her primitive driveway. She'd never felt so alone. She couldn't even call McKenna to hear her voice, which would make her feel better.

Oh, crud. "I have to pee. Why didn't I go to the outhouse while Jesse was still here? Why didn't he remind me?"

Putting her anger aside, she unbarred the door and reached for the ancient lantern. With trepidation, she held up the lantern and peered into the darkening sky, still able to make out the outhouse from where she stood. She scanned the area for animals before she rushed down the steps and across the yard.

She brought the medieval lamp inside and set it at her feet, telling herself that she was safe, but not really believing it. If it was possible, the outhouse was much scarier at night than it had been earlier in the day. When she finished, she repeated the process of carefully opening the door, looking for monsters, and then rushing back to the security of the cabin. Once she was inside with the door barred, she felt like she could breathe again. But she couldn't help but feel exposed, as any animal—two-legged or four-legged—could peer in the window while she slept.

Who was she kidding? She wasn't going to get any sleep tonight.

Taking the lantern with her, she went to the bed, staring at her bag, which held Jesse's pajamas. It felt way too intimate to slip into his clothes. Anyway, she felt too scared to take her clothes off, knowing that a Bigfoot-Peeping-Tom could be lurking outside. She set the lantern on the bedside table, slipped off her ankle boots, and climbed under the quilt, fully dressed. She stared at the window, trying to discern any shapes that had formed on the other side.

She must've fallen asleep at some point, because she jolted awake at a crashing noise. Someone was on her porch. Or something! She saw the dark blob as it crossed in front of her window. *Oh, no!* Was that a bear? With shaking hands, she reached for her phone, hoping God had given her cell service, but she had no bars. There was some heavy breathing coming from the other side of the door. She was petrified. And she had to pee again!

If she made it through this night, the first item on her shopping list would be adult diapers. And the first skill she needed to learn was how to defend herself!

Which made every movie she'd seen about bears play in her mind. She jumped up, ran to the open shelf in the kitchen, and grabbed a metal spoon and a cast-iron skillet. She clanked the spoon against the skillet and yelled at the top of her lungs, "Go away, you damn bear!" Then, "Damn bear, damn bear, damn bear!"

There was a crack from a gunshot, and Tori froze, cutting off her frantic bear chant. She heard the animal lumber off the porch. She knew it was gone but she couldn't stop her heart from pounding, *damn bear, damn bear, damn bear!*

She held her breath, listening, hoping it was over. But then she heard a new sound on her porch. She was going to start beating the skillet again, when there was a hard knock.

"Tori? Tori? Are you okay?" It was Jesse.

She scrambled to the door and pushed the board out of its slats, letting it fall to the floor with a bang. Jesse pushed his way inside and she threw herself at him, wrapping her arms around him, clutching him and burying her face in his neck, but she couldn't stop shaking. She realized her arm was touching cool hard metal. Jesse's rifle was slung over his shoulder.

"Whoa." He clutched her back. "You're all right," he said into her hair. "You're all right."

"How did you know?" she asked. "How did you know I was in trouble?"

"I was sleeping in my truck to make sure you were going to be okay."

She pulled away slightly and whacked his chest. "You should've told me! I was scared to death!"

"I didn't know it myself," he said. "I pulled down the drive a bit and decided to wait until your light went out. I watched and watched but it never did. I guess I fell asleep."

Still in his arms, she asked, "Was it a bear?" It had to be a grizzly!

"I'm surprised the bear didn't run straightaway. I think your yelling woke the whole forest."

"Did you kill it?" she asked.

"No. Just a warning shot. I would never shoot at a cabin with you or anyone else inside." He let go of her suddenly, as if just realizing their faces were only inches apart.

"Will the bear come back tonight?" she asked.

"I doubt it," he said. But he looked worried. "If you want, I can stay to keep watch."

"I'd feel better, if you did," she said honestly.

"In the morning we're going to go over homestead safety. You're going to learn everything I know about keeping yourself safe. But most importantly, you're going to learn to shoot."

"A gun?" She'd never imagined she'd hold a gun . . . let alone shoot one.

"Yes, a gun. I'll teach you how to use bear spray, too. Then you and I are going to walk the perimeter of your property and fire warning shots at intervals to let the wildlife know that a human is living here again. My hope is that the big animals will get the message."

"And if they don't?" She wasn't sure she wanted to know the answer.

Jesse laid both of his hands on her shoulders and looked her square in the eye. His intense gaze almost made her woozy. "Then, Tori, you're going to defend yourself. Stand your ground. Just like any homesteader would do."

He scanned her head to toe and didn't seem happy. "Where're the pajamas I lent you?"

"In my bag." She wasn't going to tell him her quandary over his sleepwear.

His frown lingered for a moment, then changed, as if he understood why she hadn't put them on. He was gentleman enough not to call her on it. "You crawl into bed and I'll check the fire."

"Where are you going to sleep?" she asked.

"The rocking chair," he answered.

She stripped one of the quilts off the bed and took it to him. "Here."

"Thanks." He set it in the chair and then busied himself with the fire.

She propped herself up on the bed. "Your mom seems nice." Patricia could've easily judged her, but instead, she'd been welcoming.

Jesse closed the door of the woodstove before settling into the rocker. "She's the best." He laid the quilt over his lap and stared back at her for a long moment. "Tori, will you be okay if I turn off the lantern? To save kerosene?"

"Yes."

He blew out the flame and she settled down farther into her bed. "Your mom is really kind," she said, not expecting much of a response.

She was surprised when he spoke.

"My mom's been sick for quite a while," he said.

Maybe it was easier to talk about it with the light off. She didn't know what to say. "I'm sorry. It's great that she has you around, though." Patricia had a way of beaming when Jesse spoke.

"I know. My brother, Shaun, is moving home soon. He's been working in Houston in the oil fields. He's supposed to take over the homestead . . . before I leave for my new job."

There it was again—Tori felt abandoned, and he hadn't even left yet. She tamped down the feeling. "I'm sure your brother being here will be a comfort to your mother."

Jesse was quiet for a long moment. "What about your parents? Where are they?"

"Both gone. Uncle Monty is our only family now," she said honestly and succinctly.

He was quiet and she couldn't help but fill the silence.

"My mom died when I was seven. Asthma attack." Tori didn't tell him that she shared the condition. "My dad died when I was ten. A car accident."

"I'm sorry about your parents," Jesse said. "You were too young to have suffered so much."

Tori hadn't suffered. Not really. So many others had it much worse than she had. Tori always had a roof over her head, lots of beautiful clothes, food, and unlimited funds. Every day she was grateful she had McKenna and Uncle Monty. The women at the shelter had nothing. So Tori never considered herself a victim but more that there was a hole in her life that would never be filled by her missing parents. And she accepted that. She wanted to make sure that Jesse understood, too. "McKenna and I are okay. We miss our parents, but Uncle Monty has done a great job of making sure we felt loved and that we had everything we wanted."

Except for now. Where was the electricity and indoor plumbing when she needed it? But she wasn't going to whine to Jesse, who'd grown up without the same and seemed perfectly fine and well-adjusted.

"When do you have to leave for your show?" she asked. He would look great on TV. Just the right amount of ruggedness.

"The first week in August," he said.

That was only three and a half months away. "Do you really think you'll be able to teach me everything I need to know?"

"I'm going to do my best," he said.

But that wasn't reassuring. And she was sure she was going to hate every second of roughing it on the homestead.

Except she didn't hate this night. It might have something to do with not being alone. She wondered if anyone sitting in the rocker would do. Or if it was only Jesse who could soothe her.

"Well, if I forget to say it later," she said, "thanks for everything." She stared over at his figure in the chair, grateful he was here to watch over her.

"'Night, Tori."

Peace came over her and she drifted off to sleep.

WHILE IT WAS still dark in the wee hours of the morning, Jesse pulled two mugs from Tori's open shelf above the sink and quietly set them on the counter. If Sleeping Beauty wasn't up by the time he finished his cup of joe, he would leave without speaking with her first.

He lifted the percolator off the woodstove and poured a cup.

"That smells good. What time is it?"

He turned around to see Tori stretching like a cat, which was fascinating to watch. "Early. How did you sleep?"

"Fine." She glanced toward the window. "I assume the bear didn't come back?"

"No." He gestured toward his mug. "Want some?"

As if suddenly embarrassed . . . or maybe cold . . . she pulled the quilt around her and dropped her feet over the side of the bed. "That would be great. Do you have any fun creamer like peppermint mocha?" She glanced around, frowning. "But I don't have a refrigerator."

"Oh, but you do."

"Where?"

"I dug you a cold-hole."

"A cold-what?"

"It's basically an underground refrigerator that uses no power. You'll be able to keep perishables, like creamer, right here on the homestead. We'll pick some up at the Hungry Bear. I doubt Piney has peppermint mocha in the store's cooler, but you never know."

"A refrigerator in the ground?"

"I'll show you when I get back. I need to run home to take care of the animals." *And check on my mom.* "I shouldn't be long. Probably be back in an hour or so."

"Sure, I'll be ready to see this refrigerator hole and start my first lesson by then. I can't really fix myself up without water and electricity, now can I?"

He automatically opened his mouth but quickly shut it. He almost told her that she looked pretty darn good to him right now. To stop himself, he chugged down the nearly scalding coffee. He needed a bit of distance from Tori St. James. "I'll be back soon." He set his mug on the counter and rushed out the door.

As he hustled down the lane to his truck, he heard the cabin door open and shut. He glanced back over his shoulder and saw Tori standing on the porch, watching him.

He faced forward and picked up his pace to get home.

On the drive, he mentally went over the safety techniques he wanted to discuss with Tori today. At home, he would pick up a rifle for her and bear spray for practice. He probably should take something out of the freezer for dinner tonight, too. He wondered if Tori liked salmon.

But he stopped himself. She would need to learn to stand on her own two feet, which meant making her own meals. Montgomery wasn't paying him handsomely to entertain his niece.

When Jesse arrived home, his mother was still in bed but Scout and Checkers were awake, waiting for him. He fed the dogs and made tea for his mom, leaving the pot on the counter for when she woke. He retrieved the salmon steaks from the freezer, putting them in the fridge to thaw. Grabbing his work gloves, he went outside to take care of the chickens, feed the Highland cattle, and milk the goats.

The whole time he was doing his chores, Tori was on his mind . . . and not just what he could teach her today. He was attracted to her, but what man wouldn't be? She was gorgeous with her long curly blond hair and curves that had felt wonderful when she'd jumped into his arms after the bear episode. But Jesse shook it off. He had way too much going on to think of Tori as anything but another job for a few short months. Soon he would be out of here and on the new job.

He took a quick shower and left a note for his mother next to her tea, telling her that he would be back by five to start dinner.

"I've been thinking about Tori."

He looked up to see his mother standing in the doorway with both dogs by her side. "I didn't wake you, did I?"

She shook her head and waved off the question while making her way to the covered teapot. "It's Tori. I'm worried about her. Is she all right?"

Yeah, he'd been thinking about her, too, but certainly not in the way his mother apparently had. "Tori had a rough night." He told her about the visit from the bear.

Ten minutes later, he was headed back to the St. James homestead with his mother's idea of a gift for Tori. He wasn't sure she was going to think so, though.

When he pulled up, Tori was sitting on the front porch. She'd changed, all right . . . into mini camo shorts and a tight sexy top. What in the world was she thinking? She couldn't wear that skimpy bit of fabric on the homestead.

He left the present on the seat and stood outside the truck. "You need to put something else on," he said firmly.

She glanced down at what she was wearing. *Or not wearing!*

"What's wrong with my clothes?" She seemed honestly bewildered.

"We'll be heading to the woods and you'll have to be covered up or you'll end up scraped to pieces." He glanced down at her feet. *Good grief!* "Your sandals may be in style, but they aren't sensible on the homestead." He ran a hand through his hair. How could he teach her homestead safety while he was focused on her shapely legs and other parts? "Go change." He might have growled it; her glare said he had. He cleared his throat and revised his tone. "Your sister's jeans and a long-sleeve shirt will be fine. You'll thank me later."

Her expression said *I doubt it.* She huffed inside.

He grabbed the present and took it to the porch.

Five minutes later she returned, looking just as enticing in a chambray shirt and jeans.

"Sorry I barked at you," he said.

Her eyes dropped to the *present* at his feet, which barked at her. "You brought Scout with you?" There was that bewildered look again.

"He's a gift from my mom. She thought you needed a guard dog. Though I'm not sure he'll be much of that. He's kind of a coward." He waited for Tori to tell him to return Scout, like he was a pair of new shoes she didn't really want. "You don't have to keep him. As I said, he has a lot of excess energy and needs to learn his manners."

She smiled and knelt down. "Hey, cutie." She scratched Scout behind the ears but glanced up at him. "A dog of my own?"

"Yeah." Until Tori decided that Alaska was too much for her. He rubbed his neck.

She gazed at him with concern. "Crick in your neck from sleeping in the rocking chair?"

"Something like that." He noticed she didn't offer to rub it for him, then scolded himself for noticing. He unhooked Scout to let him run free, then handed her the leash before pointing to the west side of the cabin. "Let's check out the cold-hole. Scout, come."

Scout didn't heel beside him but frolicked like a cheeky puppy next to Tori. She followed him down the steps to the vertical post he'd planted. Jesse had also buried two fifty-five gallon drums to act as the outer casing for the in-ground refrigerator. Inside the drums, an "elevator" made of metal cables and five clear shelves could be winched up and out of the ground from an overhead beam with a crank attached to the vertical post. "Just grab the handle and turn. You'll see how your underground refrigerator works."

Warily she cranked the handle. Scout barked when the double-layered wood and polystyrene lid came off the top drum. When the shelves loaded with food appeared, the dog moved closer, sniffing the air. Tori looked over at Jesse in surprise.

"Keep turning. You'll see what's in there."

Shelf one had bags of vegetables he'd harvested from the greenhouse at home. The next shelf down held mason jars of canned salsa and canned meat. The next shelf had a half gallon of milk.

She secured the handle and touched the milk carton. "It's cold."

"The temperatures vary from shelf to shelf, but it all stays above freezing and below fifty-two degrees. It makes a great refrigerator. Shaun and I made one for our hunting cabin."

She beamed. "Ingenious."

He liked her smile. *Really liked it*. He was suddenly glad he'd gone the extra mile to make it for her, something that *wasn't* on Montgomery's list of requirements for the home-stead.

"It's not bad for the summer months as you don't have to worry about snow when trying to get to your fridge. For winter, though, we should think about digging you a cellar under the cabin."

"But you won't be here," she said defiantly. Scout barked, too.

"We'll work on it while I am." He turned the handle in the opposite direction and made sure the lid to the refrigerator was on tight before pointing up the hill to where the spring was. "Every day your number one concern should be water. People can go without food for three weeks but can't go without water for longer than three days. My suggestion is that first thing every morning you set yourself up with drinking water. Always have extra in case there is a day where you can't get out."

"What about getting water into the cabin . . . like you and your mother have?"

"I'm not sure that's feasible without your uncle's permission." It would cost a pretty penny to dig a well, and from what Tori said, she was currently without funds.

"Okay, water first. What's next?"

"Firewood. Every day you should gather and chop firewood to prepare for winter."

"But isn't there plenty already?" She pointed to where several cords of wood lay under the lean-to beside the cabin.

"The firewood we cut today isn't for this winter but for next," he said.

"But I won't be here but one year," she argued.

He blew past that. "This is how it works. You're always cutting wood for the next year or the year after that. New wood needs to sit for at least a year to dry out. Green wood will not do for your woodstove. I'll teach you how to use a chain saw and then how to split wood with an ax." He saw her glance down at her nails as if saying good-bye to the pretty polish.

"What other daily concerns should I have?"

"Food. Before I leave today, I want you to take an inventory of what's inside on the shelf and what's in your underground refrigeration. Your uncle has set up an account for you at the Hungry Bear. Piney, the owner, will be able to tell you the particulars." He didn't like the frown that crossed her face. "Come on. I'll show you where the spring is, where you'll get your water."

"But last night you said I needed to learn how to shoot."

"There's a lot I'd like to cover today. But remember: Water first." He went to his truck and grabbed two large jugs and handed one to her.

"Okay." She and Scout followed him into the woods. Not a minute later she spoke. "You were right."

"About what?" He glanced over at her as she moved a tree branch out of her way, her sleeve catching on another. "Ah, you're glad I made you change into something reasonable."

"Don't be such a know-it-all. It's not a good look on someone as nice-looking as you."

"So you think I'm nice-looking?" He was teasing her but if he was being honest, he really wanted to know.

She clamped her lips together, making it clear that he wasn't going to be privy to her inner thoughts.

He decided to put his mind back on homestead business instead of monkey business. "The stream isn't far, which is a plus for you." While he walked, he started scanning the area.

"What are you looking for? Bears?"

"No. I'm wondering if there might be a way to run the water down closer to the cabin."

"Really?" She sounded excited. "How?"

"We have some extra pipe lying around at home." Like most homesteaders, he kept everything in case he could re-use it later. He was pretty sure he didn't have enough pipe. "We won't be able to get it all the way to the cabin, but we might be able to get the water closer for now. Just a temporary fix and you could only use it during warm weather as the pipes would freeze during the winter months." He glanced over at her. "I'll have to think about it some more and possibly draw up a plan."

"Thank you, Jesse. Anything you can do will be appreciated."

He liked the lilt of her voice when she was happy.

When they reached the stream, he showed her how to gather water by laying the jar at the mouth of the spring. She leaned over him to get a better look and it was shocking how just being near her was suddenly intoxicating.

"Is it safe?" she asked.

No, he wasn't safe at all! He'd rather take his chances with an aggressive moose than get sucked into whatever spell she was casting over him.

"The water?" she clarified.

"Oh, yeah. The water is very clean from flowing through the rocks and sediment. Also, did you see that you have a Brita in your kitchen? I would drink and cook from that pitcher, if I were you."

Admittedly she had more than a little trouble schlepping her jug back down the hill. Though he wanted to come to her rescue, he didn't offer to help, as her uncle had been clear that she needed to learn to care for herself. Just when Jesse thought Tori might give up, she looked at him, seemed to steel herself, and then stoically kept walking. He had to admire her tenacity. Scout kept beaming up at her as if he admired her tenacity, too.

As they came out of the woods, his friends Hope Stone and her husband, Donovan, were getting out of their vehicle.

Jesse waved. "Hope, Don, what's going on?"

"Just coming to visit the newest member of the community." Hope held two brand-new milk pails, which were chock-full of stuff. "We come bearing gifts."

"Provisions. Lunch, actually." Donovan smiled and held

up one of the Hungry Bear cloth grocery bags. "Reindeer hot dogs, buns, and supplies to make s'mores." He glanced around. "Where's the firepit? It's a great day for a campfire, don't you think?"

Jesse had already scheduled Tori's busy day, but his dad always said that God laughed when we humans made plans. "A campfire lunch sounds great. Tori, come meet Hope and Donovan Stone."

Scout tore his way over to them first with his tail wagging.

"The welcoming committee," Jesse said, laughing.

Donovan reached down and petted Scout. "I assume this is Scout's new home?" He turned to Tori and stuck out his hand. "Scout will make a good companion for you. Hi, I'm Donovan Stone."

"Nice to meet you." Tori took Donovan's hand but seemed flummoxed, which bothered Jesse. "I guess Scout is going to stay here for now. I'm not even sure if I'm staying in Alaska, though."

"I see," Donovan said.

"Jesse will have to show me how to take care of him," she said.

Which was just one more thing on his list of things to do.

Jesse made further introductions. "This is Hope Stone, Donovan's wife. I went to high school with both of them. Donovan just recently returned to Sweet Home."

Donovan put his free arm around Hope and squeezed. "The best thing that ever happened to me."

Jesse continued on. "Tori, you saw A Stone's Throw Hardware & Haberdashery in town? That's his. It's been in his family forever."

Hope beamed up at her husband. "He's a hardworking man."

"They also own Home Sweet Home Lodge," Jesse added.

"Tori, you'll have to come by and see it," Hope offered.

"I'd like that," Tori said.

Hope held out both pails for Tori. "For you. Homestead housewarming gifts."

"Oh, thank you." Tori took the pails and gazed inside. It looked like there were a set of canisters in one pail, along with thick socks, soap, and lotion. The other pail held some girly work gloves, some sort of crafting kit, and other things. Tori beamed at Hope. "It all looks lovely. Thank you. Would you like to come inside while I set them down?"

"Sure." Hope and Scout followed her.

"The firepit is on the other side of the cabin," Jesse called to the backs of the women. "Donovan and I will get some wood."

Donovan followed him to where the logs were piled up. Once they were out of earshot, he spoke. "She looks like a fish out of water."

"She'll be fine," Jesse said, grabbing some logs. "She's still acclimating." *Why was he defending her?*

"I think you're going to have your hands full." Donovan grabbed a couple of logs, too. "Piney says she's supposed to live here for the whole year. Do you think she'll make it?"

Jesse glanced back. "I don't know." The truth was that he doubted it. But he didn't want to say anything bad about her. "She's got a lot to learn." He felt the weight of responsibility. He was afraid he didn't have enough time to teach her everything, especially if they had any more surprise visitors. But it was important for Tori to get to know the community and to become a part of it . . . before he left her to her own devices.

When he and Donovan arrived at the firepit with their arms loaded, Hope was instructing Tori on how to start the fire. Yes, he'd shown Tori how to start a fire in the woodstove, but he should've done what Hope was doing . . . *let Tori do it for herself.* He'd have to remember that technique.

Hope leaned next to Tori. "See? You may have to cup your hands around the flames to keep the wind from blowing it out."

"Like this?" Tori asked.

"Yes. That's good."

Yup, Montgomery St. James might've employed the wrong person to teach Tori.

While the fire came to life, and they sat on stumps and whittled branches to cook their hot dogs, Hope filled Tori in on the comings and goings around Sweet Home, like the Sisterhood of the Quilt.

"We meet the first Saturday of every month in the sewing studio at the lodge. If there's a quilting emergency, like a Comfort quilt for someone who's ill, we meet as much as we need. It would be lovely if you could join us. Do you sew?"

Tori's cheeks pinked up. "I do. McKenna and I both learned at boarding school as part of the life skills curriculum. I made costumes for the drama department, too. I especially liked making tops and skirts, but I never learned how to make a quilt." She glanced at Jesse and shrugged. "We also took woodshop, but it wasn't my thing."

"We can teach you how to piece and sew a quilt."

"It's been a long time since I sat behind a machine."

"It's like riding a bike. But it's fine if you don't want to sew. After the Sisterhood of the Quilt is over, we just hang out. Promise me that you'll join us."

"Okay." But Tori didn't look too enthused.

Hope continued. "We have so much fun! Everyone brings a dish to share, which turns our Sisterhood of the Quilt gatherings into a delicious potluck."

Tori put her hands up and shook her head. "I don't know how to cook . . . and that's the truth. Apparently, I'm going to have to live on canned beans and peaches." She gave Jesse a sorrowful look.

Before he could say anything, Hope jumped in. "I can teach you how to cook. Actually, Donovan is an excellent chef."

Tori seemed a bit startled. "I couldn't impose on either of you that way."

Hope smiled at her. "You won't be imposing. You know

what we should do? We'll all take turns teaching you our favorite dish. That way you'd get to know all of the members of the community and the Sisterhood of the Quilt."

"That's very generous, but—"

Hope cut her off. "I won't take no for an answer. I know all of Sweet Home is anxious to get to know Monty's niece—you're the talk of the town."

Chapter 4

LIVING IN DALLAS, Tori was used to a degree of anonymity and wasn't sure she liked being the *talk of the town*. Especially if that talk was disparaging.

She looked at Jesse to see if he was going to jump in and help her, but it was like she was carrying that massive water jug by herself all over again, except this time he was grinning.

"Then it's settled," Hope was saying. "We all get to play at being Rachael Ray or Jamie Oliver for a day. What about you, Jesse?" She was talking to the men now. "Will you each sign up to teach Tori how to make a meal?"

"Sure." Donovan was as tall as Jesse but didn't have that all-over rugged thing that Jesse had going on. "But you decide what I should teach her. Jesse, what are you going to do with Tori?"

Jesse seemed confused by the question.

"What *food* are you going to teach Tori to cook," Donovan clarified, chuckling.

"Oh, yes. Probably venison stew. My mom's recipe," Jesse said. "It's kind of my specialty." The guy looked embarrassed.

"It's very good, too," Tori interjected.

Hope's and Donovan's eyebrows rose in surprise, as if Tori had come to Jesse's rescue. Rescuing him from what, she didn't know.

Tori answered their unasked question. "I ate dinner with Jesse and Patricia last night."

"Oh. I see." Hope didn't give her the *ooh-la-la* look but instead turned to Jesse with concern in her eyes. "How is your mom doing? I was thinking about her this morning. When is a good time to stop by for a visit?"

"Probably sometime in the early evening. She's usually awake for a while then," Jesse said.

"And Shaun? I heard the engagement's off. I was sorry to hear it. He's moving home for good?" Hope said.

"Yes. He's winding things up in Houston now. He's not sure when he'll be here, but hopefully it'll be before I have to leave."

Tori really didn't like it when Jesse mentioned leaving; it made her want to put cotton in her ears.

"Does Shaun have any plans for when he gets here?" Donovan asked. "Is he only going to homestead, or is he looking for an outside job, too? I only ask because I could use him at the hardware store when the kids go back to school. If not full-time, then part-time, at least through the end of October."

"I'll let him know."

Tori was handed a stick and a reindeer hot dog, but she wasn't sure what to do with them. She watched while Jesse silently demonstrated how to skewer the hot dog and hold it over the fire, just out of the flames.

While they cooked their meal, Scout danced around as if they were preparing food for him.

"Sorry, buddy," Jesse said. "No reindeer hot dogs for you." He nodded to Tori. "Remind me to get the dog food out of the truck before I leave today, okay?"

"Sure," Tori said.

Everyone chatted about the milder-than-usual weather while they ate. It occurred to her that Hope and Donovan were probably going to ask her what she did for a living, as Patricia had. To circumvent the embarrassing question, Tori asked one of her own. "So do you two homestead, too?" Tori wondered if *homestead* was even a verb. "I mean, did you grow up on a homestead like Jesse did?"

Hope smiled. "No. We were townies, next-door neighbors as kids."

Donovan squeezed Hope's hand and gave her a loving glance, as if he were reliving a charmed past. "We grew up in town but we certainly spent a fair amount of time in the woods surrounding the lodge—fishing, camping—"

"Raising hell," Jesse added, and the three old friends laughed.

"Yes, that, too," Donovan said. "So how was your first night in the cabin? I expect it was quiet compared to your life in the city. I had a bit of an adjustment coming back to Sweet Home after living in San Jose."

"Quiet? Not even close," Tori said emphatically.

"She had a visitor," Jesse added, and then he told them about the bear who had come to visit, while the four of them roasted their marshmallows and ate their s'mores.

When he was done with the bear tale, Hope grabbed Tori's arm. "You poor thing! And your first night, too!"

Tori put on a brave smile, but she really hated it when people pitied her. She was grateful Jesse hadn't told them that he'd stayed in the cabin with her afterward. If the town was buzzing about her just coming to Alaska, she'd hate to think what they might say if they thought she and Jesse had had a sleepover.

Just then, the wind shifted and Tori was engulfed in smoke. She'd been careful up to now, trying to stay out of its path, but she hadn't seen it coming this time. She coughed, and then the wheezing began and her throat tightened. Her airway was closing. She ignored the others and stumbled away from the fire. But that seemed too much effort and she stooped over, trying to get a breath. She was in trouble. Frantically, she yanked her rescue inhaler from her pocket and took a long draw, but it seemed to catch in her throat and none of the medicine reached her lungs.

Her only thought—the EpiPen was in her purse! Staggering toward the cabin, she used her inhaler again, and thankfully, this time she got a little relief. She slowed down and realized Hope and Donovan were surrounding her, helping her to the porch.

"Tori? Are you all right?" Hope asked. "What can I do?"

Scout was barking and circling them as if he were her canine alarm.

As her breathing became less labored, the embarrassment settled in, and she was mortified as if she'd been bare naked and put on display. She'd made an utter fool of herself . . . again.

"We need to get her to the hospital," Donovan said.

"No. I'm fine," Tori managed through gasps of air. "Or I will be."

"What happened?" Jesse looked panicked.

"Allergic to smoke," Tori choked out.

"Why didn't you tell me?" Jesse had raised his voice and was rooted to the ground several feet away as if she had the plague.

"I didn't exactly know." But it wasn't surprising. The doctor had cautioned her about places that might be smoky, like parties, nightclubs, restaurants. Who would've thought that Tori St. James would ever be sitting around a campfire, shooting the breeze? Also, the allergist had said she was allergic to nearly everything under the sun. Which Uncle Monty knew! And yet . . . he'd sent her here anyway. What had he been thinking?

"Let's get you inside so you can lie down." With eyes filled with sympathy, Hope put her arm around Tori and guided her toward the cabin. Donovan and Scout followed.

This whole debacle with the smoke made it clear that Tori had been kidding herself. She was as fragile as ever. *Fragile as the teacup.* A memory engulfed her, as surely as the smoke had.

Tori was only seven years old the day of that fateful tea party with McKenna and Mom, when Mom suddenly started wheezing. Mom's fragile teacup slipped from her hand, shattering into pieces. McKenna grabbed one of Mom's many inhalers and handed it to her. But Mom didn't get a chance to use it before she crumpled to the floor, gasping for air. The memory haunted Tori, on constant replay. She wondered if the memory was like a crystal ball, foretelling her own future.

Jesse cleared his throat and brought her back to the present. "I'll stay here and take care of the campfire." She turned around and saw that he hadn't budged from his spot.

And dang it, Tori felt betrayed. Apparently he didn't care whether she could breathe or not. But who could blame him? She'd never looked in a mirror to see the horror show that was one of her asthma attacks. So what if Jesse kept his distance? Why should she care anyway? There wasn't enough oxygen going to her brain right now to sort out her own feelings, let alone what was going on with him.

Hope was talking to her. "I'm concerned. At first I was happy to see that you had Scout as company, but now I'm worried. Are you allergic to dogs, too?"

"Most of them," Tori admitted. "But I seem to be fine with Scout and his mom, Checkers. I guess it's because he's a labradoodle."

"Oh, yes," Hope agreed. "Hypoallergenic, good."

Tori glanced back again and Jesse was standing as still as a sentry, though there was nothing to guard at the firepit.

Hope must've known what was on Tori's mind. "You scared Jesse, that's all. Men can be funny that way. It's the reason he hasn't moved. Donovan, get the door?"

Donovan rushed around them and cleared Tori's path. Scout ran in first and jumped on the bed like he was pointing out where she needed to lie down.

But as she made her way over, she heard the porch steps creak.

"Looks like you're going to have someone to snuggle up

with." Her heart fluttered for a moment until she realized Jesse wasn't offering himself as the snuggler.

"We should leave you to rest," Hope said as she helped Tori into bed. At the door of the cabin she turned and gave Tori a sympathetic sad smile, the one she knew so well. "I hope you feel better soon."

Jesse remained just inside, looking disgusted, even angry, if she had to guess. Where was the friendly Jesse of earlier? Oh, she knew. He'd seen the *real* Tori. The weak one. Fragile. Certainly not anyone he could ever care about.

Realization hit as she heard Hope and Donovan's vehicle pull away, and Tori felt mortified. The buzz around town would certainly kick up several notches now that she'd made a spectacle of herself. Soon the news would spread that the newest resident of Sweet Home was nothing but a weakling. Too frail for Alaska.

At least she'd given the sleepy town something to talk about.

JESSE KNEW HE was being irrational, but he felt scared. Scared of what? He couldn't quite put his finger on it. And that made him mad. Right now, everything made him angry. His mom's illness. The fact that he would be leaving her soon. And Tori. At how helpless she'd looked as she closed her eyes. At how she had to work to make herself breathe normally again.

But mostly he was angry with himself. And frustrated! He'd frozen, hadn't jumped into action like he normally would have. Just thinking about Tori wheezing and stumbling away made him break into a cold sweat all over again. How had he come to care for her well-being in such a short period of time?

Jesse wanted to throw something. Montgomery St. James was crazy for sending someone like Tori to the wilderness! Someone who couldn't handle even a little smoke. Well, it hadn't been a little. It had engulfed her. The only other time he'd seen anything like that had been when he was ten and the flue on the woodstove had malfunctioned. The cabin had filled with smoke and his mom had run from the cabin, gasping for air. He and Shaun hadn't known what to do—it was the middle of winter and Dad was on the trapline. They had been completely helpless . . . just like Jesse felt now. His mom always kept an inhaler in her pocket, too. He hadn't seen her use it in years. But then again, he had been away so much.

Guilt and regret and fear piled up, and jumbled around his brain. He desperately wanted his mother to move to Anchorage so she'd be closer to the hospital, but he and Shaun couldn't convince her. Their mom was as stubborn as a musk ox.

A few things started to fall into place. He'd bet that some therapist somewhere might say that seeing Tori in distress caused him to relive the fear he'd had as a child. Maybe so. One thing was for sure, he would not put himself through it again. He vowed to keep his distance from Tori St. James. It wouldn't be an easy task, though, since she was his homestead student for the next several months. An even bigger obstacle was that since he'd met her, he'd been drawn to her—someone who was completely the opposite of the women he normally dated. What was wrong with him?

He turned halfway to Tori. "I'm going to get Scout's dog food from the truck. I'll be right back." He sounded cantankerous as if he'd whacked his thumb with a hammer.

"'Kay," she said, just barely above a whisper.

He started to tell Scout to stay but realized the dog was plastered against Tori's side and wasn't going anywhere. She had her arm around him, gently rubbing the fur on his back. The curly pup looked like he was in hog heaven.

The sight eased his anger a little, but he had a strong will. He wasn't going to let Tori pull him in. She was not the woman for him . . . even though she did like dogs. She was beautiful. And her tenacity made him smile.

He slammed the door on the way out.

As he stomped to his truck, he bolstered up his determination and tried not to feel so much. After high school, when he'd been offered his first construction job in Fairbanks, he'd been reluctant to leave Sweet Home and leave the homestead to his mom to handle. He'd said as much to her. She had insisted that he spread his wings and go. To ease his worry, Mom had also insisted she was like Teddy Roosevelt, who always said being active in the outdoors had strengthened him and curbed his asthma. Maybe it would do the same for Tori, too.

He grabbed the scoop from the cab of the truck, the big bag of dog food from the bed, and slung it over his shoulder before heading back to the cabin.

When he walked back in, Tori was propped up on a pillow with Scout sprawled across her lap. "What about my homesteading lessons for today? I think I'm able to continue, if you're ready."

He set the dog food in the front corner and handed her the scoop. "One of these in the morning. One at dinnertime." He frowned at the bag. "You're going to need a bear barrel."

"What's a bear barrel?"

"A plastic container that protects food from bears."

"Oh."

He was sorry he'd brought it up.

"You were going to teach me homestead safety today, remember?" She still looked weak from her asthma attack.

"I don't think so. We'll get a fresh start in the morning."

"But . . ." She nibbled at her lip. "The bear."

"Don't worry. I'll sleep in the rocking chair again tonight." He didn't want to linger around Tori, but what choice did he have? He had to make sure she had protection from the bear . . . and that she kept breathing.

Tori looked relieved for a moment, but then worried. "Are you sure?"

"Yeah. Also, I need to teach you how to take care of

Scout since you've never had a dog." He grabbed the lap quilt from the rocker and brought it over. "Cover up. I'll get a small fire going to take the chill out of the air."

Her eyes widened.

"Don't worry. My mom has issues with smoke, too. The number one thing you have to remember is to open the damper when starting a fire." He pointed out the lever on the side of the stove pipe. "Make sure it's parallel to the stove. If it's crossways, the flue will be blocked." He demonstrated with his hand how the internal valve plate opened and closed.

"Thank you," she said. "I can remember that."

As he started her fire, he periodically spoke to her over his shoulder. "I'll do a few chores outside. About four, I'll run home and make my mom dinner. When I come back, I'll bring you a salmon steak and green beans."

"I appreciate it, but won't you get in trouble with Uncle Monty for pampering me?"

"Actually, no." In fact, he was going to call Montgomery on his emergency cell and give him a piece of his mind. What if Tori was all alone and had an asthma attack and her inhaler didn't work? And the bear? How come *Uncle Monty* hadn't thought to have him make some anti-bear improvements to the place before his beloved niece came to stay?

Yeah, he had a few choice words for his employer.

"What kind of chores need to be done outside?" she asked.

"The old chicken coop needs reinforcing before your laying hens arrive."

"Won't they be in danger from the bear that was here last night?"

"That reminds me," Jesse said. "I'll walk the perimeter and make those warning shots I told you about, to let the wildlife know that you're here. As for the chickens, I think we should put up an electric fence to keep the predators out."

Her brow furrowed. "This may be a dumb question but doesn't an electric fence need electricity?" She'd been snarky about it but then she bit her lip again. "If I did have power, I could really use it for my nebulizer."

"Yeah." That was something else he was going to talk to *dear old Uncle Monty* about. Tori needed a couple of solar panels and a backup generator.

And if the old man wasn't going to spring for them, then Jesse would have to find the cash to make it happen. If only he hadn't splurged and bought himself a new truck with the signing bonus he'd received for the TV show.

Chapter 5

McKENNA HAD BEEN counting the minutes on her first day at the bank in Anchorage—a half day, since it was Saturday—but the day was only halfway through. While she was watching the clock, she couldn't help but see that Luke was watching her. Was he worried that she was going to rob the bank or maybe mix the ones with the fives? Who knew . . .

She'd had a hard time getting out of bed this morning. An even harder time putting on the pantsuit she'd brought. If it weren't for Tori and her business wear, plus her sister insisting all these years that McKenna own at least a week's worth of dress clothes, McKenna would have had to resort to dressing as Lumber Jill at the bank. She glanced down at the black suit. The suit fit fine, but she felt awkward in it. A fish out of water. McKenna missed her flannel shirt and worn jeans. Every time she caught her reflection in the windows, she almost didn't recognize herself. Her likeness wore the same surprised look that Luke had given her this morning when he came knocking on the door. It was an uncomfortable ride to the bank. He hadn't spoken to her since, except for assigning her to the tellers for the day.

Looking over the shoulders of the tellers had been a total

Snoozeville. The mountains outside the glass windows called to her. *Run to me*, they were saying. McKenna had thought about it nearly a hundred times today, but the price of running away from this concrete shoebox was too great. She didn't believe she needed Uncle Monty's money, but Tori certainly did, as she liked the finer things in life. Though it hadn't been spelled out explicitly, McKenna could only assume their two fates were tied together; if one failed, they both did. So McKenna stayed next to Nancy or Karen or whatever her name was and gladly suffered for her sister's sake.

Besides, everyone at the bank had been welcoming and nice to her. Except for Penelope, who flirted outrageously with Luke whenever he walked by. Luke smiled and chatted here and there with the other employees, but with McKenna, it was crickets. He seemed disgusted with her. Well, she decided, she didn't like him either.

"Miss St. James?"

She jumped and turned around to find Luke standing there with a notebook and keys.

He nodded to the other tellers, then turned his focus back on her . . . which was intense. "I thought you might need a change of pace. I'll give you the rundown on the safe-deposit boxes."

"Lead the way. I'm up for anything, especially if I get to mosey on to a different locale."

He raised his eyebrows.

"What's wrong?" she asked.

"Nothing," he answered.

He probably thought she wasn't taking her job as seriously as he thought she should. And rightly so. But it wasn't her idea to work at a bank . . . Luke's bank.

She frowned at his backside. Not that it wasn't an impressive backside, but because she was being held hostage—well, sort of. "You should call me *McKenna*. You singled me out just now when you called me 'Miss St. James' in front of the others."

He stopped and turned around. "Yes. You're right." Then he kept walking. "What do you think so far?"

"The truth?"

He used his key card to go through to the vault. "Yes, the truth."

"I'd rather be hiking," she said. "I don't know how you can stand to be cooped up all day, day in and day out."

He gave her a condemning glance, which made her want to take it back. "Banking provides a service to others."

"But what do *you* get out of it?" she asked.

He shook his head as if he wasn't going to answer. Finally he said, "It's a good way to make a living. Satisfying. Stable. Steady."

The way he said it made her wonder if he'd seen rough times. Yes, she and Tori had been put through the wringer when their parents died, but they'd never wanted for money.

Luke set the notebook on the counter and opened it, all business now. "I'll walk you through the process of letting someone access their box."

But the room felt . . . tight, and she was distracted. For some weird reason, it was like electricity was pulsing within the vault in time with her beating heart. She kept her uneasiness to herself, worried she might be imagining it.

Luke looked uncomfortable, too, but he was able to go over each detail . . . twice, as though he thought she was thickheaded. Which was annoying. She'd gotten straight As in math all the way through school. Though in college, a parks and rec degree didn't require much math and she'd had absolutely no accounting.

"Okay," he finally said. "Do you think you've got it? If a customer walked into the bank right now, could I trust you to handle this?"

"Yeah." And if she didn't, she'd ask Nancy or Karen to help her out.

She followed him out and he walked away to his office, shutting the door behind him. Suddenly she felt as if she could breathe again. She didn't have a good explanation for what had happened in the vault. She wasn't claustrophobic. After all, she'd been spelunking a zillion times and the closeness of the caves never bothered her. But then again, Luke hadn't been there rappelling into the darkness alongside her.

McKenna went back to the tellers and learned how to handle the drive-thru until it was time to close. McKenna joined Nancy to count the end-of-day money, thankful this half day was over.

But it wasn't really. She'd forgotten who was to drive her back, and only remembered when Luke came toward her.

"Ready to head home?"

The apartment wasn't actually home. "Yes. More than ready."

On the ride back to the apartment complex, neither said a word. It was awkward, but she didn't care. She was having trouble breathing again . . . which made her think of Tori. *Please keep my sister safe*, she implored the universe.

When he parked, she opened her door quickly. "See you later," she said as she hurried into the building.

Once her apartment door was closed behind her, however, she felt restless. She went to the dresser in the bedroom and grabbed her running clothes. Five minutes later, she was walking out of the building.

But what she saw made her stop short. Luke, who seemed to be in the middle of stretching in front of the stone benches, was staring straight at her.

His eyes skimming her, he sighed heavily, and frowned. "Go on and stretch and we'll run together so I can show you where the closest trail is."

She raised her arms above her head and then did a couple of lunges. "I thought you'd be a gym rat who bench-presses two-twenty-five with an entourage of females *oohing* and *ahhing* nearby." Yeah, she was poking the bear, so to speak.

"Yes, in the winter the gym is a godsend. But the second the weather warms up even a little, all Alaskans are outside." He raised his eyebrows. "It's the law, you know."

Was Mr. Serious making a joke? She hated to admit that she liked how the playfulness danced in his silver-blue eyes.

"I'm ready," she said, not sure how this was going to go. She'd tried to run with other people in the past, but it had never worked. First, there'd been the guy in the condo next to theirs who'd made it into a competition, who always made sure to stay five strides ahead of her. Then it was Tori's friend who'd wanted to tag along, but she was so slow that McKenna barely got a workout in.

But as she ran beside Luke, she was surprised at how he kept the perfect pace. Running with him felt . . . fun?

As her feet hit the trail, she mused to herself that all these years she'd never realized she was a bit like Goldilocks in running shorts.

This one ran too fast.

And this one ran too slow.

Ah, but this one was just right.

LUKE DIDN'T LIKE McKenna, but right now, it was hard to keep up his grudge. All morning, he'd watched her look longingly toward the window like a second-grader held back from recess. Yes, he loved the outdoors, too, but his first responsibility was the bank.

He pointed out the way. "Are you up for four more miles?" He knew the answer before she replied.

"Sure, city boy," she said. "But only if you can go the distance."

"I haven't always lived in Anchorage, you know." He wasn't sure why he was correcting her and defending himself. What did he care if she was mocking him for living in the city or not?

"Where are you from? Seattle?"

"Actually, no, I'm from Sweet Home."

"What? Where Tori is?" That seemed to stop her laughing.

"Yes. On a homestead, not far from Montgomery's." *On*

a dilapidated homestead that never grew a decent root vegetable.

"Then I did peg you correctly," she said. "The first chance you got, you hightailed it to the city." She didn't let him respond but went on. "That's completely okay. Tori is a city girl, too, through and through. Some people aren't made for the outdoors."

He didn't point out the truth . . . or his obvious tan. Instead, he grabbed her arm and pulled her to a stop. "Moose." He let go and pointed as the bull walked from the shrubbery into the trail.

"How did you know that was going to happen?" Her eyes were still on the moose.

"I keep a lookout. You should, too. Come mid-May the calves will be coming. Mama cows fiercely protect their young." The moose left the path and went down to the swamp. "Did you know that more people are hurt by moose than bears?"

"Really?"

"It's a fact. Promise me that you'll be vigilant and keep your eyes peeled."

Her eyebrows shot up as if he'd announced that he cared about her.

Instead, he clarified. "Montgomery would not take it well if his niece were to get trampled by a moose. Come on. I think it's safe." They started running again.

She looked at him. "I have to admit that for a city, this place has some stunning views."

That was when he realized she was looking at the mountains and not at him. But he was looking at her when he responded, "Yes. Very nice views."

She smiled then and it felt like the sun had come out from being tucked away all winter.

The rest of the run was very comfortable. Not like running with one of the guys, but not bad either. When they arrived back at the apartment complex, they both made a slow walk around the grounds to cool down.

McKenna glanced over and looked both hopeful and worried. "Since we're off tomorrow, I was hoping to go to the homestead and see my sister."

"Sorry. I should've told you. You and I are volunteering at the soup kitchen downtown."

"Normally, I would be all for it," McKenna started, "but Tori needs me. How about you volunteer and I find a ride out to the homestead?"

"You'll have to take it up with your uncle. He set your schedule. Next Sunday, we're washing clothes at the Shower House. Haven't you seen your itinerary? If not, I'll email you a copy."

"First of all, I can't take anything up with my uncle because he's on a round-the-world trip and can't be reached. Or apparently bothered."

Luke didn't know why Montgomery hadn't given his nieces the emergency number. But it wasn't his place to intervene.

"And second, no, I haven't seen the itinerary." McKenna was glaring at him as if it were all his fault.

"I don't know what to say," Luke replied honestly. This had to be hard for McKenna and her sister. He couldn't imagine being uprooted from his life like they had been.

But then, he realized that was exactly what he'd done to himself. He'd left everything he'd known—homesteading, poverty, and Sweet Home—to look for a better life. He glanced at the mountains, wondering if he'd accomplished that. At least he knew where his next meal was coming from. He knew the roof over his head didn't leak. And he could stand tall in clean, nice clothes when he saw the people of Anchorage. Which wasn't something he could say about his life in Sweet Home. He was lucky he'd gotten out.

But he still missed his life from before. God only knew why.

"Tomorrow be ready to leave by ten . . . for the soup kitchen." Luke held the door open for McKenna and they went inside the apartment building. He didn't know what she was going to do for the rest of the afternoon and he wondered if he should offer to take her out to dinner again or not. Probably not—he wasn't there to be her boyfriend. His job was to teach her about banking, watch out for moose wandering around town, and get them through this next year.

Chapter 6

TORI WAS FEELING much better, but . . .

"Scout, what am I supposed to do now? I'm bored. Your daddy left an hour ago and I'm already antsy without my phone to keep me company." She scratched him behind the ear. "So how am I supposed to spend my time when your daddy heads off in a few months to wherever he's going and leaves me behind? And you behind, too?"

Scout glanced up at her and licked her hand, probably to thank her for all the cuddles she was giving him. "I feel like it's happening again. I'm becoming attached to him . . . your daddy." She didn't want to admit this, but who was the dog going to tell? Isolation could make people do weird things. But even leaving that aside, she'd had a tendency in her past relationships to become attached too quickly. It was a common problem among her friends. Most women she knew, excluding McKenna, had the habit of reading more into a relationship, especially at the beginning, than was actually there.

Tori looked out the window and frowned. It wasn't fun examining her own flaws, but here in the silence they presented themselves with horrifying clarity. Maybe she should use this time alone to work on herself. There wasn't much else for her to do. But her eyes landed on the other milk pail that Hope had brought her.

Tori gently nudged Scout off her lap and got to her feet. The dog jumped to the floor excitedly as if something amazing was about to happen, which made her laugh. "It doesn't take much to entertain you." She retrieved the pail, brought it back to the bed, and tipped the contents out. The first thing she picked up was a packaged cross-stitch kit with the outline of Alaska. Around and within the image were different symbols of the state—a seal, a whale, forget-me-nots, Denali, a moose, a bear, a seaplane, and even a cruise ship—everything that Alaska was known for. Though the intricate details of the pattern's features should have intimidated Tori, she felt like she could tackle this project.

But instead of perusing the pattern right then, she picked up the sketchbook and colored pencils that had caught her eye. Since arriving at the cabin, she'd been getting ideas for practical pieces to wear while she worked on the homestead. She hated to admit it, but Jesse was right about her stylish clothing not being appropriate. But she couldn't imagine wearing jeans and chambray shirts for her entire stay in Alaska. Functional, but so boring.

Tori sketched a cute long-sleeved shirt as fit for the runway as for the homestead. "See, I'd make it from denim instead of silk," she explained to the dog.

Scout grabbed one edge of the pillow and tugged it.

"Drop it." But the dog kept on tugging. When she grabbed the other end to take it away, the dog seemed to smile because she'd joined the game.

"Oh, come on, Scout," she pleaded, trying to gain control over her pillow. By now, the corner was pretty slobber-ridden. "If you rip it, I won't have anywhere to lay my head tonight. It would be one more thing that I'd have to do without."

"Negotiating with a dog?" Jesse had let himself in. "Won't work. He'll win every time."

"But he won't let go." Now she sounded like she was whining. "And don't you knock?"

"I thought you might be sleeping. Or at the very least resting. I didn't expect to see you in an all-out tug-of-war with my dog—I mean your dog."

"How do I get him to let go?" she asked.

"Simple commands. Make sure your tone says that you're the boss." Jesse turned to the dog and his face became stern. "Drop!"

Surprisingly, Scout let go and plopped his butt down with his tail thumping against the quilt.

She frowned at Jesse. "You didn't have to yell at him."

"Tori, you're going to have to let Scout know that you're in charge."

"If you're saying that I'll have to be mean to him, then I don't think I can do it," she said honestly.

"That wasn't *mean*. Does Scout look upset?" he asked.

"No," she said begrudgingly. In fact the silly puppy was happily glancing from one to the other of them as if waiting for the next game to begin. "I guess not," she conceded.

"You have to remember that you're the alpha . . . as far as Scout is concerned."

But Tori wasn't buying it. Right now, there was only one alpha in the cabin and he was looking pretty hot in that sexy mountain-man thing that he had going on. That was when she noticed his hands were full. "What do you have there?"

"Scout's bed. I figured you wouldn't want him sleeping with you. And if you don't, you'll have to lay down the law now because he's looking pretty comfortable in your bed."

She leaned over and scratched the adorable puppy behind the ears. "As long as he doesn't snore, he can sleep with me." She was surprised at how quickly the dog had stolen her heart.

"Well, I'll leave this here in case you change your mind." Jesse dropped the bed in the corner.

Scout jumped down, barked at the dog bed, and then

jumped back up on her bed, peering down at the dog bed as if he was too good for the likes of it.

"Don't spoil him," Jesse warned.

But it was too late. Scout looked at her with big eyes and she melted. "I wouldn't dream of it."

Jesse frowned at her before walking to the door.

"Where are you going?" She hoped she didn't sound too clingy.

"To get your dinner." When Jesse said *dinner*, he frowned even more. She suspected it was because he wasn't supposed to be spoiling *her*.

"Do you want me to help?" she asked.

"Yes," he said definitively.

She and Scout followed him out of the cabin and down the stairs. Jesse stayed three steps ahead of them but spoke over his shoulder.

"It's okay to let him run free while I'm here. But if I'm not, it's important that he's on leash. At least until he's fully trained, okay?"

"Sure," she said to Jesse's back.

He headed to the truck bed. "Your plate is in the cab." Instead of reaching over the edge, he stopped and paused before turning around to stare at her.

"Is everything okay?" she asked.

"Are you feeling better?" His look was both irritated and concerned.

"Yeah, I'm okay. Usually after an asthma attack I feel a bit hungover, but that's passing." Thank goodness.

"Does it happen often . . . asthma attacks?" he asked rather straightforwardly.

"I don't have full-blown attacks very often anymore. I know my triggers and stay away from them."

"Which means?" He was leading her and she reluctantly played along.

"I'll be much more careful around smoke in the future."

Jesse nodded as if she'd passed the first of many tests to come.

But she was worried. Her only heat source for the cabin was wood, and eventually she would have to fix the fire herself. What would happen then?

Jesse lifted a cooler from the back and walked right past her to the cabin with Scout at his feet. She quickly opened the passenger door and lifted out the aluminum foil–covered plate resting on the seat. Then she hurried to catch up with Jesse. She was feeling a bit like Scout . . . wanting to stay close to the alpha.

When she got inside, Scout came to greet her, his nose sniffing the air.

"The dog only gets dog food," he said in the same tone he used for Scout.

"All right." Though she'd seen Jesse slipping bits to both Scout and Checkers under the table at his mom's house.

"You should eat while it's warm."

Tori pulled a fork from the tin canister on the shelf and took her meal to the tiny café table by the window. "Thank you." She nodded at the cooler he still held. "What's in there?"

"Dessert." He was frowning again. "I'll be right back." He left once again.

"What do you think that's about?" she asked the dog, and then took a bite of salmon. "Yum." Besides the promised green beans, he'd made her an arugula salad. Normally she wasn't crazy about the peppery greens, but she wasn't going to turn down real food. She glanced up and grimaced at her future of canned beans and peaches looking back at her from the shelf.

Jesse returned with a sleeping bag in one hand and a backpack in the other.

"For me?" she asked.

"No. The sleeping bag is for me. Unless I decide to sleep in my truck again."

"But . . ." She wanted to remind him that he'd promised to stay in the rocking chair, but instead she let it drop.

He dug in his pocket and pulled out a whistle. "For you."

"Thanks." He seemed to always be thinking of her. As she took it she wondered if he would even be able to hear a whistle if he was asleep in his truck. "What kind of dessert?"

"Ice cream."

Very thoughtful. She was really growing to like him, which wasn't a smart idea.

"I thought when you're done with your meal, we could sit on the porch and eat it."

"Sounds good," she agreed. The quarters were too close in here. Maybe it would be a good idea for him to sleep in his truck after all.

He pulled out two containers while she finished her plate.

"Chocolate or strawberry?" he asked.

"That's easy. Chocolate."

After she set her plate in the sink, she followed him outside. They positioned themselves on the edge of the porch with their legs dangling.

"You're going to need a couple of chairs for out here," he said, almost to himself.

She thought about a sleek modern set she'd seen at Glam Furniture in Dallas, which fit her city lifestyle to a T. But of course Jesse meant chairs that suited Alaska: rugged, perhaps homemade.

Once they were settled, Jesse spoke. "I've brought something else for you so you won't be completely without electricity."

"What is it?" She liked presents.

"My mom's portable generator for her nebulizer, now for your nebulizer, if you need it. The nebulizer is about all it can handle."

"I appreciate the loan. Please tell her thank you. But what about Uncle Monty? Will he be okay with it?" she asked.

"I don't care if he is or not," Jesse said angrily. "That man had no right to drop you out here with what I believe are severe allergies. And God knows what else." He said the last bit like an accusation.

She could've gotten mad, but instead her insides warmed because Jesse seemed to be on her side. She answered him. "Just allergies, nothing else."

"Well, your uncle is certifiable. My grandparents were crazy, too, for moving my mom to Alaska, given her asthma."

Tori wondered if that was what was making his mom so ill.

Jesse answered her unasked question. "What she has going on now has nothing to do with allergies or asthma. Just bad luck." Now he just looked upset.

Tori reached over and laid a hand on his arm, hoping to comfort.

He glanced down and seemed alarmed that her hand was there. He scooted away, which made her feel embarrassed.

Then he made it worse. "Listen," he said wearily, "I don't need any complications right now."

She slipped off the porch and faced him with her hands on her hips. "Yeah, neither do I. I was just trying to show you that you're not alone. I know what it feels like to have a parent in trouble and have no clue what to do with those emotions." *And to feel like you're drowning in loneliness in a sea of people.* She started to tell him that he was being a jerk but decided to save her breath. "Can you keep an eye on Scout?" She didn't wait for his answer but huffed off to the outhouse. Tori didn't know where else to go, but she had to get away from him!

JESSE WAS RELIEVED when Tori walked away. It would be even better if she would leave Alaska altogether. She disturbed him to his core. Yes, he needed the money, but he needed his peace of mind more. Why did she have to put her hand on his arm? He certainly didn't need *her* to comfort him. He was a tough Alaskan man, yet he could still feel her touch and how it had spread warmth throughout his body. She was beautiful, so of course he felt attracted to her. That was simple enough. He needed to remember that he was leaving soon so it made no sense to start something with her. Besides, the way her touch made him feel . . . it muddled up things. Before she arrived, he was clear about his future, but now . . .

He just didn't know.

Scout lay down beside Jesse as if he knew that Jesse needed companionship right now. Not the female kind either. Automatically he reached over and petted the dog. "Man's best friend."

Ten minutes later Tori returned. She didn't look any happier than when she'd stomped off.

She marched up the steps, passed Jesse without looking at him, and flounced inside.

From the doorway, she said, "Come, Scout." Scout jumped to his feet and ran inside. The door closed harder than usual.

So the silent treatment is how it's going to be. But wasn't this the way he wanted it? No budding connection between them?

He slipped off the porch and stood. "I'm heading home to get a bear barrel." He'd raised his voice to penetrate the oak door. "Knock once if you heard me."

There was a thump. He'd bet his best hunting rifle that she'd thrown his sleeping bag at the door.

He was back in fifteen minutes. Mom was sleeping, and apparently Checkers was in with her because the dog didn't come out to greet him.

He knocked on Tori's cabin door. "I'm coming in."

He waited for a response but didn't get one. Alarm rose up for a moment, but he quashed it down as he walked inside. Sure enough, Tori was sitting in the rocking chair with her sketchpad in her lap and Scout at her feet.

He set the bear barrel down and then filled it with dog food before putting it by the counter. He reached into the corner and picked up his rifle, knowing there were always things to be done on the homestead. He caught Tori's quizzical look. "I'm going to take some shots around the perimeter to let the wildlife know that you're here."

"Don't I get to come?" Tori said belligerently.

"I figured you weren't up for it," he said.

She stood and set her sketchpad on the table. "You figured wrong."

"Stay." He grabbed the rifle and walked out. He noticed that Scout sat . . . but Tori didn't.

"Come on, Scout," she said.

Jesse just kept on walking, hoping she'd take the hint that he needed his space. Once again, she didn't. He glanced back to see that she had the dog on a leash and was rushing after him. He would've picked up his pace except he worried it might spark another asthma attack.

"Did you bring your inhaler?" he asked, irritated.

"Yes, and my EpiPen." She sounded spitting mad.

Fine. That made two of them. He kept scanning the area as he headed deep into the forest.

"What are you looking for?" She sounded a little scared.

He slowed down so the two of them could walk abreast. "I told you before it's important to be on the lookout for predators. I promise that soon it'll be second nature to you, too."

"What should I be looking for?"

"Shapes, movements, sounds that seem suspicious. A branch cracking is either a moose, a bear, or another big animal." It was funny to describe the animals as predators, since he and Tori were the ones intruding on the wildlife. "It's especially important to be quiet when we're hunting. And to stay downwind. We don't want to give ourselves away when we're hunting. Right now it's okay to make a little noise, but at the same time, we need to listen, too, okay?"

She nodded.

Just then, there was a crunching noise off to the right. He

signaled with his hand to stop and she did. He peered into the thicket.

The noise became louder. And Scout started to bark. "Shttt," Tori commanded quietly, and the dog obeyed. Jesse was impressed that she'd gotten Scout under control. He also was glad Tori was stepping up and listening now, too. He'd been concerned she wouldn't listen to him when her life might depend upon it. Apparently she had better instincts than he'd given her credit for. He raised and positioned his gun while focusing his eyes on the source of the noise . . . and trying not to notice that Tori had laid a hand on his back. She was so close that he could feel her warm breath penetrate the back of his shirt. He shook the sensation away. The woods were tensely silent as they watched for movement.

A moment later, a deer came crashing through. He lowered his gun and at the same time pulled her close to his side. As it rushed toward them, Jesse ducked them back behind the nearest tree. But the doe suddenly stopped and lifted her head, sniffed, then snorted. She took off again, veering left away from them. Scout went crazy, barking like wild, as if to say *Jesse! Tori! Did you see that?*

Tori was trembling in his arms and Jesse tightened his grip. At the same time, he remained vigilant, his eyes peeled, ready to raise his gun again if something more threatening had been chasing the deer.

After a few minutes of continued quiet, he spoke into her hair. "All clear. Are you okay?" He wanted to make sure she was breathing okay, too, because he sure wasn't. Yes, a little spook from a wild animal always got the adrenaline flowing, but this time, it had been more thrilling because Tori was pressed up against him.

"I'm okay," she said shakily. His dog quieted at the sound of her voice and rushed to sit at her feet.

Jesse should've set her away from him then, but his arms wouldn't let go. Instead he pulled her closer and did the unthinkable . . . he kissed her. Not quickly either, but deeply.

And she kissed him back. Warning shots fired in his head—*danger, danger.* He finally regained his senses, summoned sheer willpower to drop his arms, and stepped away from her.

"Let me take you back to the cabin." His mind was racing as he tried to figure out why he'd done it. Was he trying to calm her down? Well, he'd only revved himself up. And complicated things more.

She touched her bottom lip with her index finger. "I don't want to go back to the cabin. I'm fine." She glanced down at her furry companion. "Scout doesn't either. Right, buddy?"

The dog jumped up and put his paws on her knee. She reached down and scratched him affectionately.

"Okay, then," Jesse said, "since the dog wants to stay." He pointed to the east. "This way." He waited until she was beside him before he started walking again.

When they got to the edge of the property, he had her cover her ears while he fired three times. He was proud that Scout wasn't gun-shy, which was important for a hunting companion.

They repeated the procedure three more times, going to the corners of the property and firing off more shots. "That should be a warning to the bears and other wildlife that you've moved into the cabin."

"So the bear won't be back?" she asked.

"I never said that. But this should help."

When they arrived back at the cabin, she lit the lantern all by herself while he pulled the portable generator from his backpack. "It's fully charged now. I'm looking into getting you a solar panel. Until then, I'll charge it at my mom's or in my truck. My mom keeps her nebulizer set up and ready." Though he hadn't seen her use it in a long time. He pointed to Tori's nightstand. "Is that something you want to do?"

"I guess I better."

He set the portable generator and the lantern on the nightstand while she unpacked her nebulizer.

"Thank you," she said when she had things arranged as she wanted.

He grabbed his Tom Clancy novel from his backpack and lit a second lantern for himself. The light cast a cozy flicker for them, which he tried to ignore. Before he settled into the rocking chair, he glanced over at Tori, whose sketchpad was once again in her lap.

"Do you ever get used to the quiet?" she asked.

"I don't think it's quiet at all," he said honestly. "If you listen closely, you'll be able to hear the homestead speak. The leaves rustle and the trees creak. You can hear the wood frogs, moose—"

"And bears. Yes, I know. But nothing sounds familiar here."

"You miss cars and sirens?"

"And the neighbors on either side of me." She laughed. "I never thought I'd say that."

"You'll get used to it here. Just give it time."

She looked at him as if she wasn't sure. He went back to his book. He wasn't here to coddle her. He was just staying tonight to make sure she was okay after her health scare. It was the least he could do.

An hour later, he closed his book. "I'll give you some privacy so you can get ready for bed." He prayed she wouldn't don that skimpy nightgown but wear his flannel pajamas instead.

"Thanks. I won't be long."

He took Scout out with him.

Ten minutes later, she came out on the porch with the lantern, wearing his flannel pajamas turned up at the cuffs, and headed for the outhouse. She gave him a look he could already interpret: *Keep an eye out for that bear, will you?* It was hard to believe that he'd become so in tune with her so quickly. And he was glad she'd decided to be sensible about her nightwear.

When she came back, he rolled out his sleeping bag. He was bone tired, mostly from the roller coaster of emotions today. He wasn't looking forward to tomorrow and how he would have to use his strength to keep his emotional distance from her again.

"Good night, Jesse," she said into the night. "Thank you for staying."

"Yeah. 'Night," he said. He fell asleep quickly.

The sound of an approaching truck woke him in the morning. He jumped to his feet and saw that Scout was on high alert, too, although Sleeping Beauty was out cold.

Jesse went outside with Scout at his heels. Two burly guys got out of the truck, one of them holding a clipboard.

"Morning," Jesse said, feeling a little suspicious. "What can I do for you?"

"I have a delivery for Tori St. James. Is she around?"

"Still sleeping." Jesse made his way down to them. "What kind of delivery?"

"Solar panels. Metal door. Electric fencing. Bear barrels. Bars for windows." The guy flipped a page. "And a portable generator. Sent by . . ." He checked his clipboard again. "Montgomery St. James."

Jesse wasn't entirely surprised after the harsh voice message he'd left for Montgomery yesterday. It was amazing the solar panels and other items could arrive so quickly. Definitely not typical for Alaska. But apparently in Uncle Monty's world with unlimited funds, the man could move mountains and get things done quickly.

The delivery guy flipped through the papers and pulled out an envelope. "Are you Jesse Montana?"

"Yes."

"A note from Mr. St. James."

Jesse took the note, which was probably his pink slip. He hadn't minced words when he'd accused the old man of not caring for his niece and insulted the old man's intelligence for leaving Tori here with no means to power her nebulizer— an essential medical device.

"Where do you want the solar panels?" the guy asked.

Jesse scanned the area and pointed to the front of the

cabin, the south side. "There will be fine." He tore open the note.

In the future, watch your language.

Yeah, Jesse deserved that. The next line, though, shocked him.

Text me a list of other essentials for Tori. I expect regular updates about her.

M. St. James

Jesse stuck the note in his pocket before heading inside to wake his student. But getting an early start today wouldn't make a difference in the long run. There was no way in heaven he could teach her all she needed to know in a few short months, especially if she was going to have an asthma attack every other day. Still, he was going to do his best to give her a solid foundation before he left . . . without pawing her and kissing her every chance he got. He knew he'd eventually have to find someone to take over the homesteading lessons, but the thought of basically handing Tori off to another man made Jesse's gut hurt.

Chapter 7

TORI WAS BY herself again with only a cuddly canine for a companion. Jesse had woken her with a little shake to her shoulder. "We have a lot to do today," he said brusquely before he stalked out to his truck. She had assumed they'd spend all day on homesteading lessons. But that was two full hours ago—way too much time to relive the amazing kiss that Jesse had given her yesterday. It was hands down the most passionate kiss she'd ever had. There was nothing tentative about Jesse! Compared to him, the guys at the country club or the galas were boys, mere children. She couldn't get enough of remembering how it felt to be in Jesse's arms, and her brain watched the kiss unfold on re-play until, finally, she forced herself to stop and come back to reality. The truth was that ever since the kiss, Jesse hadn't said a word about it, acting as if it had never happened.

Tori put her mind on other matters. With Jesse being gone so long, she worried something was wrong with his mother. Thinking of Patricia gave Tori an idea. She pulled out the cross-stitch project and looked down at Scout as if to get his opinion. "What do you think, pooch? Should I make this as a get-well present for Jesse's mom?"

The dog answered with a *yip*.

"Come on, you. Let's get on the bed and read the directions." Everything was included in the kit—the needle, floss, and printed cross-stitch fabric. She appreciated how clearly the instructions were written for beginners, down to detailing how to separate out the floss and how many strands she needed for each object and color. "This could be fun." Tori checked the basket for scissors. Sure enough, Hope had included those, too, along with another package of needles.

"I guess I'm all set." She glanced over at the new portable generator sitting on the small table and wondered for the tenth time in the last two hours why there was a new one when Jesse had given her his mom's last night. Plus, when she'd gone to the outhouse earlier, the yard was full of boxes. "I'll ask Jesse about them when he returns."

Scout went to the door and whined.

"But, of course, I'll take you out first." She grabbed the leash, clipped it to his collar, and went outside. She looked this way and that for anything dangerous, like a moose ready to charge her, but saw nothing. She looked down at Scout.

"So tell me . . . are you a good guard dog or will you be one of those mutts like on TV who hide under the bed at the first sign of trouble?"

Scout barked at a spooked rabbit and pulled on the leash, almost wrenching it from her grasp. To keep it from happening again, she wrapped the leash twice around her hand. "I can't lose you. You're all I have." Which made her think of Jesse sleeping on her floor last night . . . and Scout sleeping in the bed with her. When was Jesse coming back?

She and the dog walked down the muddy driveway. "I'm going to need a pair of wellies." The thought of wearing a pair of plain, boring black boots made her cringe. But then she had an idea—what if she painted a bright floral motif on each boot? That would give them some style. Tori couldn't wait to start designing the pattern in her sketch-book. She peered down the road and watched longer than necessary for signs of life, specifically Jesse, before heading back to the cabin as Scout ran back and forth between her legs, apparently trying to trip her.

Just as they reached the porch, Tori heard Jesse's truck and she turned around. Her stomach squeezed and she couldn't stop watching until he parked and got out. He'd taken a shower and seemed to be wearing a new shirt and new jeans. For a moment, she allowed herself to believe that he'd spruced up just for her.

Scout jumped and barked uncontrollably.

She rushed into the cabin and straightened the quilt on the bed so the place wouldn't look a mess. She knew it was ridiculous, but Jesse seemed to bring out all kinds of strange behaviors in her. She wished she'd been able to shower, too.

She undid Scout's leash and let him run free to jump on Jesse. Which the dog did. Until Jesse snapped his fingers. "Sit."

She needed to learn that trick.

Jesse patted the dog and looked at her. She wished he were as happy to see her as he was to see the dog, because she'd gotten a little light-headed at the sight of him.

"What's all this stuff out here?" She pointed to the load in the front yard.

"We'll talk about it while we get water from the spring," he said as if she hadn't heard a word from his first lesson.

"All done," she said proudly. She wouldn't tell him how many trips and how long it'd taken her, but the chore got done for the day while he'd been gone.

He pulled out his phone and spoke into it, though she hadn't heard it ring.

"What are you doing?" she asked.

"Making a list. You need a new rain barrel, mesh to cover it, and a strap to hold down the mesh."

She motioned to the yard. "I don't think Uncle Monty would be happy that you bought all those things for me, plus the new portable generator I found on the table."

"It wasn't me. Your uncle sent it all. He's aware that the

homestead needs some basics. He'll approve the expenditures." Jesse acted confident but Tori knew Uncle Monty was out to teach her a few lessons . . . in hard work, minimalism, and poverty.

She went on the offensive with Mr. Mountain Man. "Before you ask, Scout and I gathered firewood, too." It was mostly twigs and leaves but it was part of her homestead checklist to think about preparing for winter, according to Jesse.

He raised his eyebrow and shook his head. "You're going to have to learn to swing an ax and build up your wood supply." He put his phone to his lips again. "Chain saw."

"Can you add a couple of cute sweaters to that list?" she teased, then remembered the mud on the road. "In all honesty, I do need a pair of wellies."

He nodded at her suggestion.

"And some acrylic paint," she added.

He frowned at the latter.

"Where do we start today?" she asked.

"Go inside and change."

She looked down at her clothes—McKenna's appropriately rugged wear. "Sorry, I can't get any less cute, if that's what you're looking for."

"Catholic or Baptist?" he asked, a complete non sequitur.

"What?"

"Your choices for church today. Those are the only two in town."

"Neither." When Dad was alive, they'd gone to church, and for a while Uncle Monty made sure they attended, but they'd fallen off since. "I don't attend."

Jesse shook his head. "That's going to change now. Go put on some church clothes."

She stood her ground. Scout, her faithful little guy, came to stand beside her in solidarity. "Jesse, I'm really tired of you telling me what to do."

He sighed and sat on the edge of the porch where they'd sat last night. "I know you are. I'm not trying to boss you around, Tori. The whole church thing was my mom's idea. She had a lot to say about it this morning, which is why I was gone so long. She believes—and I agree—that if you get to know the people of Sweet Home you'll do better when I'm gone. You'll have a support system to rely on."

Well, that deflated Tori. She sat beside him. "If it's your mom's idea, which church should I choose?"

"The Montanas are Baptist, but I'll take you to either service. The catch is that the Baptist church starts in forty-five minutes. Catholic mass starts an hour after that." He chuckled. "I guess the two churches got together and decided to give the uber sinners a chance to hit both services in the same day."

"I guess"—she hesitated—"I'll do as the Montanas do."

"Can you be ready in time?" he asked.

"Sure. Without water to take a shower and electricity to straighten my hair, there's not a whole lot to do. I just hope no one expects me to look my best."

He looked at her as if he didn't understand the problem, but then finally answered, "You couldn't look bad if you tried."

Mixed signals much? Tori blushed and jumped up to go inside. Why did he say something so nice, when he'd been a little distant since yesterday? For a second she reveled in his flattery and the fact that he seemed sincere. And then she blushed some more, thinking about that earth-shattering kiss. Through the closed door, she said, "What qualifies as church clothes in Sweet Home?" Of course, she'd been to weddings over the years and she remembered dressing up for Easter and Christmas, but she suspected small-town churches might have a different dress code.

"Anything will work," Jesse said on the other side of the door. "You'll see dresses and jeans there. The only reason I told you to change was because I thought you might enjoy dressing up a little. It's certainly not a requirement."

She pulled her large suitcase out from under the bed and chose a yellow print dress. It was perfect for spring, and her sandals would look cute with it. But she'd need something warm to wear over it, as there was a chill in the air. She pulled out a cardigan and held the two together. *That'll work.*

From the safety of her cabin she yelled, "Can I ask a favor?"

"Yeah, go ahead."

"Can you try not to be so bossy?"

He didn't answer so she added, "At least work on your tone and maybe your choice of words?"

She heard footsteps on the porch and then a hand laid on her door.

"Yes. I'll try not to be so bossy."

"Thank you. I appreciate it. You were starting to sound like my sister." She slipped out of McKenna's clothes and then put on the dress and warm tights. Her toes were still cold so she retrieved the socks that Hope had given her and donned those, too, before pulling on her short boots instead of her sandals. She liked the stylish rustic look and she felt like, for today at least, she belonged here in Alaska. If she was going to stay at the homestead—she was still on the fence about it—she was going to have to be a little more practical, and the warm socks were a good start.

"By the way," she hollered through the door, "I think you look very nice today."

"Yeah, thanks. New clothes that I bought for the TV series." He chuckled. "All in vain and a waste of money. The same day I bought everything, the producer called to tell me they only wanted me to wear my old work clothes, saying it would be more authentic that way."

"Well, I think you look good." But *good* didn't exactly cover it. Sexy Mountain Man hit closer to the mark. She opened the door. "Come on in. I just need to brush my hair." She pulled the hairband from her hair and shook it out, laughing at Jesse's mesmerized expression. "What? Haven't you ever seen long hair before?"

He reached out a hand unconsciously as if to touch it, but drew back. "There's just so much of it."

"I know I said I wasn't going to cut it for the homestead, but I may have to. It's so curly and I can't use my straightener here." She brushed her hair, smoothing it as best she could, then pulled some back into a silver clip. "What do you think? Acceptable for church?"

His eyes took her in as if he were looking at a radiant sunset, which only made her face heat up again. He cleared his throat and shook his head as if to make himself stop staring at her. "You, uh, look fine."

His words weren't the compliment she was looking for, but his expression was.

"Good." She picked up her purse. "Do I just leave Scout inside?"

"He's coming with us."

"To church?"

"He'll wait in the truck."

Scout looked very excited to ride along.

This time, when they pulled into Sweet Home, Tori had a totally different impression. Apparently, isolation had worked on her—civilization had never seemed so sweet. The town had a charm she hadn't seen before, and there were so many people milling around, as though they were there for a tourist attraction.

Jesse pulled up and parked next to the church. Not one of the megachurches of Dallas but a quaint white building with a tall steeple and a cross on top. Some people were walking up the street—must be the townies that Hope mentioned—and others parked in the same lot they had. Tori was nervous.

When they got inside, though, her emotion turned to irritation. "I'm so overdressed," she whispered to Jesse. She saw lumberjack shirts, polos, jeans, a couple of women wearing bib overalls, and even a few men in hunting vests. Tori looked down at her outfit in dismay.

"You're fine," he said. "Here. Let me introduce you to Aberdeen North."

Aberdeen was tall, blond, and friendly, and hers was just the beginning of a long line of twenty-some introductions that Tori would never be able to keep straight. She had trouble concentrating, too, because Jesse had his hand on her back to move her along to the next person. Finally, he had her slide into the second pew. She told herself she could relax now, but she still felt all eyes on her.

Jesse leaned over and whispered, "Calm down. The service is about to start."

She hadn't realized she was wringing her hands. She stopped and looked up, only to admire the simplicity of the front of the church. Two empty antique chairs were off to the right, along with a short row of folding chairs. A wooden lectern was a little off-center, making the simple wooden cross hanging on the wall the star of the show. The cross was draped with what looked like a shawl falling from each crossbeam.

Quiet music began, and gradually breathed a calmness into her that she hadn't expected. But Tori was a pragmatic person and didn't believe for a second that something spiritual was happening. She was sure the peace that came over her had to do with getting a little distance from the onslaught of people.

Jesse stood and handed her a book. "Page three-fifty-seven."

She stood along with everyone else as the small choir, followed by the pastor, made their way up the aisle to the front. Jesse had a nice voice—and Tori suddenly remembered that she was holding the hymnal.

The calm she'd felt was gone. She was much too self-conscious to join in. As a kid, she used to sing in church, but now she didn't want anyone to hear her unused singing voice . . . especially Jesse.

He leaned toward her. "What's wrong?"

"Sore throat," she lied, a sin that must only be made worse by her sitting near the front of a church.

Scriptures were read, followed by more singing, and Tori felt totally displaced. Until something caught her attention. The pastor was speaking about community, specifically how uncomfortable the church community could sometimes make people feel.

Nailed it, she thought.

The pastor said he hoped the church community could better itself by making a concerted effort to get everyone involved.

Tori was touched. *But how can I get involved when I'm stuck out on the homestead?* she thought. The pastor didn't answer that for her, but Tori remembered what Hope had said about the Sisterhood of the Quilt, about making Comfort quilts for those in need. Tori didn't know how to piece a quilt, but she remembered the Alaska cross-stitch project she was going to do for Jesse's mom. She would work hard to finish it for Patricia.

There was more singing, and soon the service was over. Jesse took the hymnal from her and put it back in its slot. "Ready to meet Pastor Joe?"

Did she have a choice? "Sure."

Pastor Joe and his wife stood at the exit and shook their hands. Up close, Tori could see compassion in the man's eyes, and she liked him even more.

"It was a lovely service," Tori said honestly. "I especially enjoyed the sermon."

"We're so happy you joined us today," said Pastor Joe. "Are you going to stay around for the ice cream social?"

She glanced at Jesse and he nodded. "That sounds nice." But she silently hoped the people Jesse had introduced earlier didn't expect her to remember their names.

In fact the next hour proved to be relatively easy. Everyone reintroduced themselves, which put her somewhat at ease, and she enjoyed being around people after being isolated on the homestead. Several locals told her—proudly, it seemed—that Alaskans consumed more ice cream per capita than any other state, which seemed a weird factoid. She would have guessed Texas or Florida or some other hot state.

But there was something bothering her. People were giving her and Jesse sly glances, as if they were an item. No, it must be her runaway imagination. None of them knew about the kiss. Did they?

"I thought I might see Hope and Donovan here," she said, thinking how nice it would be to see at least one familiar face.

Jesse shook his head. "They're both Catholic. But we'll stop by the hardware store afterward to get you some wellies. They might be there." He took his last bite of ice cream. "Are you ready to go?"

Tori's strawberry ice cream had melted and didn't look nearly as appetizing as before. "I'm ready."

Pastor Joe caught up with them at the door. "Will you be joining us again next Sunday?"

"Yes," Tori said.

Jesse seemed to give her an approving look. In retrospect, church hadn't been awful, and Jesse was right—she did need to know other people, especially since he wouldn't be here forever.

When they were outside, she said, "You were right."

"I often am." He gave her a teasing smile. "What was I right about this time?"

But she decided to change what she was going to say. "The clothes. I did enjoy getting dolled up."

He smiled at her as if her hair weren't a wild mess without her straightener and her nails weren't wrecked from carrying water. "Come on. Let's get to the hardware store. We have a lot to do on the homestead and can't spend all our time in town."

"Shopping?" she nearly squealed. "Now that's an area where I excel."

He frowned as if that was the wrong answer. But she didn't care. Shopping would help her feel more normal, not so out of her element.

They headed to the truck to let Scout out for a drink of water and a run around the parking lot. When Scout jumped back into the cab, Tori slid in beside him. But Jesse didn't get in. "Aren't we driving there?"

"It's just a short walk," Jesse said. "After we're done at the hardware store, we'll stop by the Hungry Bear. Did you remember your grocery list?"

She lifted up her Louis Vuitton bag and patted it. "Right here."

He frowned at her bag. "Your purse isn't very Alaskan."

She shrugged. "Yeah, so, neither am I."

He chuckled, and it was good to see him smile again. When they arrived at the store, he held the door open for her, just like he'd done at church. The Dallas guys she went out with never opened doors for her. She had to admit that mountain men scored extra points for chivalry. Especially when that chivalry encompassed sleeping in her rocking chair or in a sleeping bag on her hardwood floor.

Inside A Stone's Throw Hardware & Haberdashery, Tori could do little but stand and gawk. She had never seen anything like it. This hardware store was more haberdashery than nuts and bolts. Dishes were an aisle over from the fishing rods. School supplies and uniforms had their own section. She saw lumber and Crock-Pots and board games . . . But the one thing that Tori was really interested in—besides a pair of wellies—was the area in the front corner where all the fabric and sewing supplies resided. Several women milled about, and Tori felt too intimidated to head over until she saw Hope with her arms loaded with bolts of fabric. She awkwardly waved Tori over with one full hand.

"Come here and see this cute camo fabric we just got in," Hope said, glancing down at her load. Nestled among the purple, pink, and delicate green fabrics was a bright psychedelic camo print. "I can think of a million uses for it but the first thing I'm going to make are purses for me and Ella. Ella's my daughter that I told you about."

"I can't believe all the beautiful fabric," Tori said. *In the middle of nowhere.* "The colors are so vibrant."

"We like a lot of color here in Alaska," Hope said. "I have the standard Alaska fabric for the tourist season, which is coming up. You know, the fishing, hunting, seaplanes, bear, moose, elk fabric. But the bright wild colors—florals, geometrics, and plaids—are for us locals. The winters are long and dark, so it's nice to have the color to fill our homes."

Tori thought about the cross-stitch project that Hope had included in her welcome pails. "Thank you again for all the thoughtful gifts." She lifted one foot. "I'm wearing the socks now. And I'm excited about starting the cross-stitch project." Tori glanced down at her dog. "Scout and I read the directions and I think we can manage it."

Hope laughed. "Yes, that dog comes from a long line of readers. Just know that I'm happy to help you, too."

Tori's eyes landed on a row of what looked like a new take on buffalo plaids—not just the standard red and black—lined up like colorful soldiers on the far wall. She walked over and touched several of her favorites, picturing them as curtains hanging in the windows of the cabin. Maybe even as a little shade in the dreaded outhouse to spruce it up, too.

"Those just came in yesterday," Hope said. "What are you thinking?"

"Curtains," Tori said on a sigh. "I love the fuchsia plaid. And the green, too." The whimsical fabric sure would soften her harsh cabin existence. But it didn't do any good to dream, because she was broke. Not something Hope could understand.

Hope pulled the bolt from the rack. "How much do you think you'll need?"

Tori shook her head and backed up. "Oh, no. Just wishful

thinking. I'm just here to get wellies." Which raised the question . . . how was she going to pay for them?

Hope gave Tori a sorrowful look.

Tori glanced around for Jesse, saw him, and rushed away, saying over her shoulder, "It was nice to see you." And if Tori was lucky, she'd never run into Hope again. She was so embarrassed. She thought about the promise she'd made to come to the Sisterhood of the Quilt's gatherings. Well, she'd suffer through the embarrassment of seeing Hope just once, and after that, Tori would hide out in her cabin forever.

"There you are," Jesse said. "What size do you wear?" He held up a pair of the depressingly standard black wellies.

"Nine," she said lifelessly.

"Oh, I got you eights." He held up a box for her to see. "And acrylic paints, paintbrushes included."

More wishful thinking. "I don't think so. I don't even know how I'm going to afford the wellies."

"Your uncle has set up a small credit account at A Stone's Throw. The paints, well, are on me."

"I appreciate the offer but I can't accept." For the first time in her life, she didn't want something handed to her, which was weird. She'd spent her life depending on Uncle Monty to pay for everything. "But I do need wellies."

Maybe she could figure out some way to make some money while she was on the homestead. Except she didn't have any real skills. Maybe she could get a job here at the hardware store? But she didn't have any way to transport herself to town. Plus, she couldn't bear to work where Hope worked because of the pitying looks Tori was sure to receive. *Poor Tori St. James needs a job.*

Speak of the devil, Hope was walking toward her and Jesse.

"I forgot to tell you. Piney wants the Sisterhood of the Quilt to meet tonight at the lodge. Can you make it?"

"No," Tori said. "Yes," said Jesse at the same time.

"What time do I drop her off?" Jesse added. He sounded eager to be rid of her.

"Six. Make sure to bring your Alaska cross-stitch project. Of course, we're doing a potluck," Hope said. "Can you bring a dessert? We have plenty of entrées and vegetables lined up. I know Ella is making chocolate chip cookies with her best friend Lacy. We have all ages, from teens up to Miss Lisa and her crowd."

"Sounds nice." Tori forced a smile. No doubt Hope would tell everyone that not only did she have debilitating asthma, she was also as poor as a church mouse. Tori wanted to crawl into a hole. Well, when the time came, she'd feign a headache and claim that she couldn't possibly go to the lodge tonight. Problem solved.

But that had Tori thinking about her other problem of the evening. Where was Jesse planning to sleep tonight?

Chapter 8

"HERE." JESSE TOOK Tori's hands, opened them, and handed over the too-small wellies. "Go find a pair that fits. Aisle eight. I'll be waiting for you up front."

He strode off. She couldn't stop him from buying the paints. He had no idea why she wanted them. All he knew was that her eyes lit up when she'd mentioned them, and dang it all, he wanted to see her that happy again.

He heard her say "Bossy" as she walked away.

Yeah, he'd have to work on that. When he got to the checkout counter, he laid the paints down and dug out some cash, bagged the paints himself, and shoved the receipt in his pocket. Instead of waiting like he said he would, he went to find Cinderella to see if she'd found a pair of wellies that fit.

Tori was standing in front of the rack of boots looking forlorn. "I can't decide. Black or hideous green."

"Would you rather get duck boots instead?"

"What are duck boots?"

"Here. I'll show you." He guided her to the other side of the rack.

"Well, those are just as ugly as the wellies. Not girly at all."

"I don't know about *girly* but you can wear duck boots

longer than wellies." He picked one up. "But you can't go deeper into water, mud, or snow than up to here." He pointed to the top of the yellow rubber.

"These would probably keep my feet warmer, too," she commented.

"Yup." He pulled out the box that had 9½ on it. "If you go up a half size, you can add an extra pair of socks. Which I think you might need. While we're here, let's get you a couple more pairs." Not only did he pull the duck boots from the shelf, but he grabbed the black wellies, too.

"What are you doing?"

"I'm making an executive decision. You need both."

"Are you sure I can afford it?" she asked.

"Yeah."

She looked unhappy not knowing anything about her finances, and he started to understand why she didn't want to accept the acrylics. It was too late for him to put them back now, though.

"Listen, from what I understand, as long as it's an absolute necessity, then Montgomery is going to pay." Jesse had gleaned that from talking with Piney.

Tori's eyes scanned the room and stopped at the fabric. "Who decides what's a necessity?"

That was where it got a little murky. "I guess, for now . . . I do."

She certainly didn't like that answer. "And what happens when you leave?" As they checked out at the register, she looked like she was calculating everything—the cost of food, clothes, maybe even allergy medication.

"Honestly, I don't know. But I promise to have some answers before I go." He felt genuinely sorry for her. Here she was in Alaska to learn how to be self-sufficient, yet she didn't have control over how her money was spent or the power to make her own choices. It wasn't fair, and Jesse suddenly wanted to dial up old *Uncle Monty* and give him another earful. "Come on. We still have a lot to do before you're introduced to the Sisterhood of the Quilt this evening."

"I don't want to go tonight." She glanced back at Hope over at the cutting counter.

"Well, I know the quilters of Sweet Home, and I don't think you have a choice." He was trying to sound light-hearted, but his words only testified to Tori's lack of control over her own life. "Listen," he added quickly, "I'm certain you'll have a good time. Getting involved in the community will be fun—and it will definitely benefit you later." Especially if she made some friends here besides him.

Were he and Tori friends? No. Not really. Putting the kiss aside, he was just her babysitter and teacher.

He grabbed her bags, showed her out the door, and then they dropped their purchases at the truck before walking down to the Hungry Bear.

Piney, the sixty-something owner and resident hippie, met them at the front counter.

"This must be Tori." Piney pulled her in for a big hug but let go quickly. She removed one of the long necklaces around her neck and placed it on Tori like she'd just arrived in Hawaii. Except this wasn't a lei but a gaudy necklace with a big crystal dangling from it. "I knew you'd be in to-day so I brought this special for you. It's to keep you safe."

Tori looked shell-shocked, whether from the hug or the necklace, he didn't know. "How did you know I was coming to the store?" she asked.

Jesse could've explained but he didn't. And Piney only answered with a knowing twinkle in her eye.

Sink or swim, Tori would have to get used to the quirky residents of Sweet Home on her own . . . or she wouldn't survive her year in Alaska.

Jesse was doing his best not to care either way.

"COME INTO THE diner and meet my daughter, Sparkle." With her Bohemian skirt and flowing top, Piney looked like an aging flower child. Tori liked her outfit but she wasn't so sure about the crystal Piney had hung around her neck.

Tori glanced at Jesse and mouthed *Sparkle?*

Jesse nodded.

Tori felt like she'd been dropped into the sixties. She followed Piney into the dining area of the grocery store but stopped as a magazine caught her eye: *Real Men of Alaska*.

Either Piney must've seen where her gaze landed or she had eyes in the back of her head because she stopped, too. "That's a bachelor-hunting magazine. The most popular magazine in the place, actually." She pulled it from the rack.

"A magazine for bachelors who hunt?"

Piney chuckled. "Not exactly. And it's funny that you would bring this up." She flipped it open to the credits inside and pointed her finger at a small picture in the upper corner. "This is Kit Armstrong, the owner of *Real Men of Alaska*. It's a matchmaking service. She started it here in Alaska and now has *Real Men of Scotland*, too, where she lives with her husband. She rang me up and said she's in Alaska right now, looking for a new manager and signing up bachelors, and she was looking for recommendations from Sweet Home." Her smile broadened. "Donna, her former manager, is a hometown girl and told Kit to call me." Piney tapped the magazine. "Kit started the magazine in order to reach more women, and it's been a huge success. Lots of women have found love this way." She flipped through the pages slowly for Tori to see all the rugged men looking for love.

Piney glanced over at Jesse, who wasn't listening but picking out gum. She tilted her head in his direction. "We do have a couple of eligible men who could do with some womanly taming and training." She laughed at her own joke and then put the magazine in Tori's hands. "You take this one. On the house. I have a few stashed in the back to re-stock the rack."

"But—"

Piney pulled her toward the diner. "You need to meet Sparkle."

Tori let herself be dragged along while she clutched the *Real Men of Alaska* to her chest.

Sparkle, a straight-haired strawberry blonde with a face full of freckles, came over to greet Tori with a brilliant smile. She might be Piney's daughter but she sure didn't dress like her; she was wearing a cute striped top and straight-legged jeans. "I'm so glad someone new has come to town." She stuck her hand out for Tori to shake but stopped when she saw what Tori was carrying. She lifted an eyebrow. "That's not a bad idea."

"What's not a bad idea?" Tori was confused.

Sparkle's eyes glinted with mischief. "It's not a bad idea to find a man to help out on the homestead. Especially since I hear that Jesse won't be around too much longer."

"Oh, this." Tori held it away as if it were a crying child. When Sparkle didn't take it from her, Tori clutched it to her chest again. "Your mom gave it to me."

Piney bobbed her head. "Sparkle, that's what I was thinking, too. Tori will need a man to help keep up the place."

This conversation was making Tori uncomfortable, and her mind scrambled for anything else to talk about. "Um, Hope said the Sisterhood of the Quilt is meeting this evening?"

Jesse ambled over to join them.

Sparkle beamed. "You're going to love the Sisterhood of the Quilt. They're anxious to meet you, too. We're all women except Mom's boyfriend, Bill." She turned to Jesse with another spark of mischief in her eyes. "Unless Jesse wants to learn how to quilt?"

Jesse put his hands up and stepped back. "Nope, that's okay. I've got my hands full with hauling firewood and swinging hammers."

And he has his hands full dealing with me, Tori thought. Thank goodness Sparkle took the bait. But the magazine felt heavy in Tori's hands, so she shoved it into her large purse before Jesse saw it.

Sparkle went on. "Anyway, men are welcome, like Bill, who's an amazing quilter. He specializes in Alaskan-themed quilts. They're fabulous. If he comes tonight, you'll see."

Tori didn't know what to say, but Jesse answered for her. "Tori's excited about meeting the Sisterhood. I hope that everyone will take it easy on her, though."

Tori's mouth went dry. "What does he mean by that?"

Sparkle squeezed Tori's hand. "I promise everyone will be on their best behavior."

Piney laughed. "Sparkle, you best not make promises that you can't keep."

Tori glared at Jesse, willing him to tell her what they were talking about.

"Get that worried look off your face, Tori," he said. "Meeting the Sisterhood of the Quilt is not like facing the Inquisition, even if you have to endure the third degree. Honest, they're mostly harmless."

She wanted to know exactly what she was up against tonight, but just then a very good-looking man with dark hair appeared through the swinging doors that probably led to the kitchen. He gave Sparkle an I-adore-you smile.

Sparkle waved him over. "Rick, come meet Tori."

Rick set down a plate of cookies and wrapped an arm around Sparkle, while he offered his hand to Tori to shake. "Rick Miller. Sparkle's boyfriend and Donovan Stone's business manager. Today, though, I'm on cookie-making duty for the after-church crowd."

Sparkle beamed up at him. "Grab a couple for Tori and Jesse."

First, Rick picked up the plate and held it out to Piney. "Ms. Douglas, would you like some?"

Piney slowly took one as if she were just tolerating Rick, and then ignored him altogether to turn back to Tori again. "I know it's been many years, but we've certainly missed Monty. He really livened things up around here. Never missed a church social or a town dance. And yet, he was a rascal, breaking hearts in Sweet Home and every surrounding town. No one could ever get him to settle down. Did he ever marry?"

Tori shook her head. "Still a bachelor." But Uncle Monty was sweet on Peggy and was letting her butt her nose into places it didn't belong. "However, he seems pretty serious about the woman he's currently seeing."

"Well, I told him when he called that he'll always be welcome back here in Sweet Home. You tell him that I mean it. He's been gone thirty-odd years, but he left quite an impression on us."

An elderly gentleman walked into the diner. "Who left an impression?"

Piney took the man's arm. "Never mind, dearest. This is Tori St. James. Tori, this is my beau, Bill Morningstar." Piney looked lovestruck, while Bill looked a little gruff and grizzly around the edges with his gray beard, bushy eyebrows, and scowl. "Tori is coming out to the lodge tonight to sew with us."

"Hm," Bill said.

Tori was shocked by Piney's certainty . . . *and* Bill's indifference.

"Don't worry about Bill," Piney said. "He has the best heart of anyone I know."

Tori wasn't sure that Piney was a good judge of character. She certainly thought Uncle Monty was the cat's meow, while Tori thought her uncle had rounded the bend and become a traitor for leaving her abandoned in this out-of-the-way town. "About tonight . . ."

Piney jumped in. "Hope said she gave you one of the Alaskan cross-stitch kits."

Jesse looked over as if this was news to him.

She gave him her best *you don't know everything* look.

"You could bring your cross-stitch project or let me get you set up on one of the sewing machines to start quilting."

"As I told Hope, I haven't sewn in a long time." And Tori knew nothing about quilting.

Piney waved her hand as if that were inconsequential.

"The most important thing is that you get to know everyone in the Sisterhood of the Quilt. I promised Monty that I'd welcome you to the community."

It would be even better if they gave her a ride out of the sticks and into Anchorage. Which reminded Tori: she wanted to try to call McKenna while she was in town.

But Piney tugged on her arm. "What's that in your hand? A grocery list?"

"Yes. I was wondering if you have any peppermint mocha creamer?"

"Ah, dumpling, that stuff is nothing but chemicals. Let me get you some local honey and goat's milk from Meyer's farm. Or Jesse might have extra milk, since he's got goats."

Tori didn't get a chance to decline before Piney dragged her to the back of the store. Jesse didn't follow.

Piney showed her where the fresh locally sourced eggs were and said, "Jesse says your chickens will be arriving any day. What do you think, will a dozen do?"

But Tori was waffling, still not sure if she would last the week. She looked down at her list: Peanut butter, bread, apples . . .

Piney handed over the eggs and patted her hand. "You know Monty has set up an account for you here, so you need not worry about paying."

Tori was so embarrassed, but she asked the next question anyway. "How much is in the account, so I can plan?"

"I don't know, dumpling. Didn't Monty tell you? I'm just supposed to invoice his lawyer at the end of every month."

Which was no help. Tori sighed, pondering which personal items she could cut from her list. All these years, she had been buying clothes for the women's shelter but never thought about what other necessities they might need, like soap, shampoo, toothpaste, moisturizer, tampons . . . the list went on and on. Uncle Monty's experiment had opened Tori's eyes. And not just to the physical needs of those less fortunate. After the frustrations she'd felt in the last couple of days, she could only imagine the emotional hardships they faced, too.

"Um, I better call Terrence, Uncle Monty's lawyer, to ask him about the budget. Excuse me." She pulled out her cell, not even certain it would work in town.

"Take your time. Holler if you need me." Piney went behind the meat counter.

Tori looked at her phone and the thought of contacting Terrence shifted to the back burner. Her phone was filled with messages from McKenna. A whole slew of them.

I miss you so much!

My apartment is lonely without you.

The bank is so boring that I want to scream.

Are you being careful and taking care of yourself?

Instead of answering the messages, she dialed McKenna.

"Oh my gosh!" McKenna answered immediately. "Are you all right?"

"Hi to you, too. I'm in town with only two bars so if I lose you, I'll call right back, okay?" Tori said.

"Tell me everything. How's Uncle Monty's cabin?"

Tori wasn't sure how to answer. If she told McKenna the truth, it would only make her worry more. "It's okay."

"How is your guy treating you? Jesse, right? Is he helping you at the homestead? Is he making sure that you're taken care of?"

Tori didn't want to discuss Jesse . . . mostly because she didn't know what to say. "He's okay. Tell me about your apartment." *Running water? Heat? Curtains?*

"It's all right. Pretty standard." Then McKenna whispered into the phone. "My apartment is right next to Luke's."

McKenna's clandestine whisper made Tori smile, as her

sister only acted this way if she was interested in a guy. McKenna was always levelheaded when it came to men, and never fell head over heels the way Tori was apt to do.

McKenna went on. "The strange thing is that after work, he was mysteriously outside just when I wanted to go running. Do you think Uncle Monty told him to do that?"

"I don't know," Tori said. "I wouldn't put anything past Uncle Monty at this point. So I have to know, do you have a crush on Luke? He's very handsome."

"No, I don't have a crush. What am I, a teenager? You know I don't care for men like him. He's too polished. His hair is always perfectly combed and he's probably had more pedicures than I have."

"Well, you sound like something is going on," Tori said.

"The only thing going on is that I don't have transportation and I have to carpool with him. And well, we went running together. He is so difficult!" She gave a miserable sigh.

"I don't believe you. Luke looked *very* nice at the airport." With his business suit, gorgeous eyes, and cleanshaven face, he didn't look difficult to Tori . . . unlike the man who had stood next to him.

"He's my boss," McKenna hissed.

"Calm down. I was just joking. Have you made any friends at the bank?" Tori asked.

"It's torture," McKenna groaned. "The walls feel like they are going to close in on me. I don't think I can make it a year, Tori." She sounded as if she were in genuine pain.

"It's Sunday. Tell Luke that you want to come visit me. Make something up, if you have to." Tori debated her next words. "Tell him I had a bad asthma attack and that I need you."

McKenna sucked in a breath. "Are you okay? What happened?"

"It's just an excuse. Nothing happened." Tori didn't like lying to her sister, but sometimes it was for McKenna's own good. She worried too much.

"Are you sure?"

"Yes." Then Tori remembered tonight's sew-in with the Sisterhood of the Quilt. Perfect. If McKenna came to visit, Tori could get out of it. "Talk to Luke and call me back. Where are you anyway?"

"We're just finishing up at the soup kitchen. Give me a few minutes, okay?"

"Okay. Bye." Tori hung up, feeling hopeful.

"Why?" Jesse's voice made her jump.

"Why what?" It was bad enough that he made her heart pound just by being near; she didn't need him startling her, too.

"Was that your sister? Why does she need to talk to Luke and call you back?" he asked suspiciously. He was acting like she was trying to make a run for it while keeping him in the dark.

"I thought McKenna could come visit today."

Jesse looked at his watch and frowned. "It's kind of late for them to start out."

"Maybe she can spend the night with me."

He nodded. Oh, he'd like that, wouldn't he? It would relieve him of the chore of staying with her. He opened his mouth to reply but his phone rang. He put his hand up as if to pause their conversation.

"Hey, Luke." Jesse listened for a second. "Yeah, it's true."

Oh, crud. McKenna would know the truth any second.

Another pause from Jesse. "See you when you get here." He pocketed his phone. "Your sister's on the way. They are both going to take off work tomorrow so they can stay overnight." He studied Tori for a moment. "I think it's good you let her know about the asthma attack. Maybe between her, Luke, and me, Montgomery will listen to reason and let you go back to the *comforts* of your home in Dallas."

Tori was surprised at how angry his words made her. "I don't need to go back to Dallas. I'm fine here." She slammed her hands on her hips. "I'm not some fragile china doll."

But he raised an eyebrow as if she'd only just confirmed it. "Come on, city girl, let's get your groceries so we can get back to the homestead." He took the list from her. "You have extra ground to cover today, since you're having company later and because you're not fragile in the least." He walked down the aisle, and then turned back, giving her a look of mock confusion. "What's a loofah?"

She grabbed for the list and pulled it from his hand. "Never mind. I can pick out my own things." She'd skip the loofah but she did need some dry shampoo. While she went in search of it, she checked out one of the showers at the back of the store. The room was clean and smelled of disinfectant, which alleviated one of her worries. But she added shower shoes to her list of things to look for at the hardware store before her first Hungry Bear shower.

She grabbed yogurt, cheese, oil and vinegar, lettuce, dog treats, and a loaf of bread before heading to the front to check out. She was glad Piney was there waiting because she didn't want to explain to a different clerk that her uncle was paying for her groceries. Tori had suffered enough humiliation for one day. Which reminded her to email Terrence about what her budget was for both the Hungry Bear and A Stone's Throw Hardware & Haberdashery. She hoped she hadn't exceeded it already.

After the bags were stored in the bed of the truck and Scout had gobbled up one of the dog treats, they headed back to Uncle Monty's homestead. "You go on inside. I'll be back soon. Can you be dressed and ready for your next lesson in half an hour?"

"Of course." With bags in hand, she walked up the steps to the porch. "Come on, boy. Let's prove your daddy wrong about me."

Scout followed her inside the cabin where she put her groceries away on the kitchen shelf, shoved the *Real Men of Alaska* magazine deep in her bag, and changed quickly into jeans and a OneRepublic tee shirt.

Jesse returned with a second rifle, goggles, and a head-set. "Eye and ear protection." He handed her the rifle. "Shooting lessons today."

The gun was surprisingly heavy, and she nearly dropped it. Even though she was from Texas, she was conflicted about using a gun. "I've never fired a shotgun before. I've never even held one."

"You're not holding a shotgun. You're holding a rifle."

"Is it absolutely necessary that I learn how to shoot . . . a rifle?" She was kind of terrified just holding it. "I saw bear spray at the hardware store."

He put his hands on her shoulders and held her full attention by staring deep into her eyes. "Yes, it's absolutely necessary." He looked at her searchingly for a long moment and she wondered what he was looking for. Probably her backbone.

She shrugged off his hands, finally remembering that she was tired of looking like a weakling to him and everyone else. "Okay then." She repositioned the gun but he quickly grabbed on to it.

"You have to be aware at all times where you are pointing it. If you're holding it in front of you, keep it pointed at the ground. And I beg you to keep from pointing it at me." He lifted the strap of his own rifle. "You can wear it over your shoulder like this and everyone will be pretty safe. Are you ready to head to the meadow?"

She noticed then that his backpack rattled when he moved. "What's in there?"

"Cans for target practice." He ambled away and she followed, secretly admiring the man hiking ahead of her.

Yes, she'd always found businessmen in a sharp suit appealing, but she had to admit that the suits had nothing on Jesse. *Wow!* He oozed sex appeal. A true mountain man. As rugged as the terrain surrounding her cabin.

"Are you keeping up?"

She jolted at his voice. The only way to recover was to

make small talk. Alaskan small talk. "So what's the difference between a shotgun and a rifle?"

"Accuracy. Rifles fire a single bullet, while a shotgun fires pellets encased in a shell. For me, shotguns are mostly for hunting birds, where my rifle is built for precision. And out here, precision and accuracy can be everything. Come."

She followed him into the woods, but this time they headed west. The woods here were thicker than on the route to the spring. But then the woods cleared and they were standing on the edge of a meadow with rough grass.

She saw Jesse scanning the area and realized she'd better practice scanning it, too. She didn't see anything dangerous, but she didn't move until Jesse started walking again. When they reached the other side, Jesse pulled out the tin cans and positioned them on a set of stumps.

When he passed her the goggles and the oversized headphones, she felt like she was dressing up as a fighter pilot. "Safety first," he said.

He reached out and gently removed the sling from her shoulder.

She stretched out her arm. "My shoulder thanks you."

He lifted one eyebrow. "Your shoulder will have to get used to it." He didn't wait for her to respond but started in on the different parts of the rifle, pointing out each piece. "The most important thing to know is that if you see red, the safety is off—*not safe*," he emphasized, "and the firearm is ready to go. *Red means dead!* Don't forget that, okay? I'm sure I don't need to point out, Tori, that you'd probably feel horrible if you accidentally shot me."

The thought of Jesse lying on the ground, bleeding, frightened her. What would she do in such an emergency? There was no one around to help. No way to call 911. "Okay. Red means dead," she repeated dutifully.

He took Scout's leash and then passed the rifle back to her. She nearly dropped it again. "Careful."

"It's not light," she complained.

"Good grief, Tori, you're not a wimp. That ginormous designer bag you've been lugging around has to weigh twice what your rifle does."

"True. But the gun doesn't *look* heavy."

He went through a thorough shooting lesson and she focused on every part as if her life depended on it. *The safety off-on. The trigger. How to line up the sight. Breathe evenly to steady yourself, then hold your breath. Be prepared for kickback.*

"Do you feel ready?" he asked, more patiently than she would expect of someone so experienced.

She nodded. But she wasn't.

"Take off the safety."

She did, and then she lifted the rifle and lined up the sight with the can just like he'd shown her. She took even breaths until she worked up the nerve to pull the trigger. She held her breath, tried to squeeze the trigger, but it wouldn't budge.

She put the safety back on and glared at him. "This is a prank, right? You've superglued the trigger? Well, Jesse Montana, that's just plain mean."

"The trigger is fine," he said placidly. "You have to squeeze harder."

"This is so stressful," she carped.

"It's going to be okay," he said soothingly.

In the end, it was his calming voice that had her turning off the safety and raising the gun again. This time she exhaled, held her breath, and squeezed the trigger. *Bang!* The kickback nearly knocked her backward but Jesse was there to steady her.

"Ouch!" She rubbed her shoulder.

"Come on and try again." But he was looking at her shoulder as if he was concerned.

With her second shot she nicked the side of the can and it slid off the stump.

"Good job," Jesse said.

"That was fun." She knew she was grinning at him stupidly. "Who would've thought that shooting a can could feel so satisfying."

"Put the safety on," he admonished. "Relax your breathing, then try again."

This time the can fell straight backward.

"Well, I'm officially impressed," he said. "You may have a gift, Tori St. James."

She'd heard this before. "A few years ago McKenna made me take archery lessons with her. The instructor said I had exceptional aim." She couldn't help sticking out her chin a little bit.

"Your instructor was right. How about you shoot the rest of those cans so I won't think it was beginner's luck?" Jesse said, egging her on.

Tori liked that he was challenging her instead of treating her like a delicate flower. She undid the safety, took aim, and fired four more times, knocking down three cans.

"Here, let me take that."

"Okay." Her arms were getting tired and her shoulder still smarted. And she was jittery all over. Sure, she was exhilarated from firing the rifle, but she also knew that part of the blame rested squarely on Jesse's broad shoulders. Just being near him gave her butterflies.

He checked to make sure the safety was on, then checked the chamber. "Okay," he said, "let's head back. You have plenty more to do today." He stepped closer and for a moment, she thought he was going to brush the hair back from her face. Instead he carefully slid the firearm's sling over her shoulder. "You carry it back. Remember, you're getting used to the weight. Your rifle is your friend. And?" He gave her a leading nod.

"Red means dead," she replied easily. He was still close enough that she could reach up and run a hand over his beard, which she longed to do. She was bewildered by her feelings. Back home in Dallas, men were a dime a dozen, hitting on her at the gym, trying to pick her up in restaurants, buying her drinks at clubs. It had always been such a game. But with Jesse, she felt different. He wasn't her type at all, yet her nervous system zinged this way and that just thinking about the man. Something was definitely up. *Is this what they call Stockholm syndrome?* she mused.

He reached over and adjusted the rifle sling again, as it had slipped a little, and their eyes locked. She had a front-row seat to his soul—or at least she thought she did. As his pupils dilated, her stomach did three twirly somersaults in a row. Subconsciously she licked her lips and waited to see if he would kiss her again. The way his eyes were devouring her, he certainly looked like he wanted to. And she wanted him to, likewise. But then the moment turned awkward and he stepped away.

He cleared his throat. "Next we'll talk about what to do if you encounter a bear—"

Suddenly, a drop of rain hit her. Then another. Then it began to pour.

"Come on! Back to the cabin," he yelled.

Scout led the way, thinking it was great fun to bark and frolic in the rain. Tori wished she'd braided her hair that morning because it was a tangled mess by the time they reached the cabin. She was soaking wet and seriously chilled. She couldn't stifle a shiver, and Jesse's eyes narrowed.

He gave her that accusing, worried look again, like she had the stamina of a squished bug. "I'll wait outside while you change into warm clothes. I suggest my flannel pajamas. Then I'll start the fire."

"Okay." But she had no intention of letting him start anything. Instead of changing first, she checked to make sure the woodstove damper was open, which it was. She sat on the floor and piled in some of the tinder she'd brought in this morning, which was a good thing, too, as the rest of it outside was surely soaked. She made a mental note to always keep a stash of dry tinder and wood indoors in case this happened again. She lit the match and held it to the dry grass and twigs, careful to keep her face away from the stove. It was hard to blow on the fire from a distance, but it was safer for her. She was pleased when flames sprouted from the tinder. She peeled off bark from the logs and put that in the stove to feed the fire.

"Is everything okay in there?" Jesse said through the closed door.

"Fine. But I'm not decent yet," she lied. Now her little fire was blazing enough that she added a skinny log. She was excited that she'd done this all on her own, but she was really cold now. She grabbed Jesse's pajamas from under her pillow and stood in the corner so no bear or *bearlike man* could see her change.

"It's safe to come in now," she said as she returned to the stove to put in a bigger chunk of wood.

Jesse stopped short. "What are you doing?"

"I made my own fire," she said proudly.

He looked astonished. "I can see that." He paused. "Well, that's the second time."

"The second time, what?"

"The second time today that you've nearly rendered me speechless."

"And the first time was?"

"You and your Annie Oakley shooting—you are full of surprises, Tori St. James."

"Get used to it," she said smugly. "I plan to keep you on your toes."

Chapter 9

LUKE WAS DRIVING as fast as the speed limit would allow, but that still wasn't fixing the furrow between McKenna's eyebrows. He couldn't help but glance at her more times than he should.

"What did he say exactly?" McKenna asked.

"I told you. That Tori had an asthma attack . . . the same thing your sister told you."

"But she sounded okay. I thought she was just making up an excuse to get you to drive me to her."

"Well, sometimes lies are based in truth."

Damn, that didn't help her furrow at all. He reached over and gave McKenna's hand a squeeze. "It's going to be all right." He started to withdraw his hand but she clutched him back. Well, he only needed one hand to drive, so he continued holding her hand . . . But it was a bit distracting.

"It feels like it's taking forever," she said.

"I know. Don't worry, your sister is fine. I'm sure of it." It started to rain, which he hoped wasn't a bad omen.

When they drove through Sweet Home, he said, "Just a few miles out to Montgomery's place." McKenna was on high alert and still clutching his hand.

She didn't say a single thing about the town. But for him, it was a fount of unhappy memories, of growing up poor and sometimes hungry. Back in the day, he couldn't wait to get away from the homestead and away from Sweet Home, but seeing it today, with its slightly less empty main street, he felt almost nostalgic. Homestead life had been hell, but high school had always been great. He'd been popular and successful, and he was grateful for the confidence it gave him, which had helped get him where he was today. If his dad had had his way, Luke wouldn't even have attended high school but would've stayed home to work on the failed homestead. Luke was relieved at the end of junior year when the bank repossessed the land and his dad moved away to work in Oregon. Luke had spent his senior year living with Jesse on their successful homestead. Living with a loving family like the Montanas had given Luke hope that one day he'd have his own loving family, too.

He pulled down the muddy driveway of Montgomery's homestead—he'd have to wash his Saab as soon as he got back to Anchorage—and stopped his car behind Jesse's truck. Before he'd even shut off the engine, McKenna let go of his hand and was out of the car, running through the mud to the porch.

Tori, Jesse, and Scout came out to meet her. Scout didn't stop at the top step but tore off to happily bark McKenna up the porch.

"That's Scout, the homestead's mascot," Tori hollered above the noise.

McKenna gave Scout a quick pat before pulling Tori in for a hug. "Are you all right?"

"I'm fine," Tori said. "I'm sorry Jesse frightened you." She glared over at him. "It was nothing. Just a little attack. Nothing to write home about."

McKenna let go and gripped her shoulders, staring into her eyes. "You and I know you can't take this lightly. Tell me everything."

Jesse interjected then. "Luke, come on up on the porch."

The rain had slowed to a sprinkle. "Tori just set the Dutch oven on the woodstove."

"Tori's cooking?" McKenna said incredulously.

"Learning," Tori said. "Jesse did most of the work."

"What are you making?" Luke asked.

"Brownies."

"My favorite," Luke said. "How's homestead life treating you, Tori?" If he kept up the conversation, McKenna might have time to settle down.

"It's fine, I guess." Tori looked disheveled, not the sleek, sophisticated woman he'd seen at the airport. Her wary stance said she enjoyed homesteading as much as he had. But he had missed Dutch oven brownies.

She motioned to McKenna. "Let me show you everything." The sisters and Scout went inside, which gave him a moment to speak to Jesse alone.

"The place looks good." A lot better than where he grew up, an eyesore with junker cars and trash littering the yard. "Solar panels?"

"Monty sent them. I kind of told him what was what with Tori," Jesse said as the rain stopped completely.

"So the asthma attack?"

"It was bad. Scared the hell out of me, and Hope and Donovan. They were here when it happened," Jesse explained. "I'm glad you brought McKenna. Tori really wanted to see her. Something bad could happen to Tori out here on the homestead . . . and I don't want that . . ." He cleared his throat. "I mean, I don't want to be responsible."

"Yeah, sure." But Luke knew something was going on with his friend. "So what do you think of her?"

"Who?"

"Tori."

"She doesn't have any skills . . . except she's a pretty good shot, especially for a novice. She has no clue how to dress properly. And she's as stubborn as all get-out."

"I see," Luke said.

"See what?" Jesse growled.

"You like her."

"No, I don't." Jesse looked like he might punch Luke. "She's a pain in the backside."

"And you like her."

Jesse stomped over to the solar panels. "So are you going to help me install these or not?"

"Sure."

The two of them broke open the first box and pulled out the instructions. Luke had helped Jesse set up Patricia's solar panels a few years ago. But Jesse had bought a whole array of panels to run Patricia's homestead, whereas Montgomery apparently only wanted his niece to have the bare minimum.

Tori stuck her head out the door. "How do I know when the brownies are done?"

"Oh, right." Jesse slapped the instructions in Luke's hands and headed up the porch steps.

Luke followed, certain that Jesse had turned into a lovesick pup. The last time Luke had seen Jesse this smitten was in middle school when they'd fought over Aberdeen North, who was older and way out of their league.

Jesse had been alone a long while, and it was good that he was thinking of something other than work. Luke could tell that Jesse definitely cared for this woman.

USING GIANT POT holders, Tori lifted the lid off the Dutch oven and waited for Jesse. She'd only called him in to stop McKenna from nagging.

"I don't think you've told me everything," her sister complained.

"I did. I told you about the asthma attack." An abridged version. "And as you can see, I'm perfectly fine now."

"You have to get out of here and come back with me to Anchorage," McKenna insisted. "I've said it before and I'm going to say it again: You're too fragile for life on a homestead. It's not your fault, but you're clearly struggling—"

"No," Jesse said firmly from the doorway with an expression that said he'd just surprised himself.

Tori was surprised, too. She felt herself go warm. Had there been something *possessive* in Jesse's exclamation?

McKenna straightened and Tori could tell she was going to tear into Jesse. "Excuse me, but who do you—"

Luke appeared in the doorway and cut her off. "Jesse's the expert, and he thinks Tori is doing fine and that she should stay."

McKenna glared at her boss and in return he gave her a big smile, shrugging as if to say *There's nothing you can do about it.*

Luke wasn't your average suit, Tori decided. Back home, McKenna chewed up and spit out men like him on a regular basis. But Luke was tough, with an edge to him. Most importantly, he didn't seem scared of McKenna at all.

Jesse had been glaring at Luke, too. He walked over and peered into the Dutch oven. "The brownies are done." He lifted it off the stove and put it on the counter. "So now you know how to make brownies." He said it like the brownies were a chore that could be crossed off the list. "Tori, you should take your sister and show her around the homestead. While I have Luke here, I'm going to put him to work putting up the solar array." He stomped out of the cabin.

Luke grinned and followed Jesse out the door.

"Come on," Tori said, heading for the door, too. "I'll show you my refrigerator."

"Hold up." McKenna spun around in a circle. "Where's your bathroom? You said you didn't have electricity but you didn't say anything about . . ." Her eyes swung to the kitchen. "No running water?" It was both a question and an accusation.

"Don't blame me. Blame Uncle Monty!" Tori pointed in the direction of her outhouse. "The *facilities* are that way."

McKenna put an arm around her. "I know you. You can't live without a proper bathroom with outlets, mirrors, and a hair dryer."

Ever since she got here, Tori had been wondering about how to fix her hair. The curls were turning into a tangled mess. "You're right." She pulled out the scissors Hope had left her and bravely held them out to McKenna. "While you're here, I need you to cut my hair."

McKenna backed away. "Absolutely not! The last time I cut your hair, I was five and I got a spanking for it."

"But you're right that I can't keep my hair cute without the proper amenities."

"You could keep it in a braid," McKenna offered.

"If you won't do it, I'll just have Jesse cut it when you leave, and you know you'll do a better job than him. Cut it like yours. Yours is so cute and easy to take care of." Tori felt like she was begging.

"Come back with me to Anchorage. That's the better solution. You'll be safe there and you'll be able to keep your beautiful hair."

Tori picked up her detangling brush and ran it through her hair while giving McKenna a sad smile. "Cutting my hair is just a little thing. I've always wanted to donate my hair to one of the hair loss charities and now I will."

McKenna shook her head.

"Please," Tori said.

McKenna took the scissors and stared while Tori pulled her hair back, wrapping it in a hairband, then added a second hairband an inch down.

She spoke while she made a quick braid and put another band at the end. "I've seen the videos. Just cut it between the two upper bands. When you get back to Anchorage, you can send it off to the appropriate place. You don't mind taking care of it for me, do you?"

"Are you absolutely certain?" McKenna asked.

"Positive." Tori really was at peace with it.

McKenna stepped up to Tori's back and gave a quick snip. She held out the braid. "You are so generous. You are going to make a lot of people happy."

Tori smiled. "Plus I won't have to worry whether my hair

looks decent. Now can you trim it up? Give me some bangs . . . but not like you did to me in preschool." Tori remembered her school pictures that year.

For the next fifteen minutes, Tori sat in one of the kitchen chairs while McKenna carefully fussed with each clip of the scissors.

"I think I'm done. Do you have a mirror?" McKenna asked hesitantly.

"Get my purse. I have a compact in there."

But the second McKenna picked it up, Tori jumped to her feet, remembering what she'd shoved in there earlier.

"No. Never mind. I'll get it." She reached out, but McKenna jerked Tori's purse away from her.

"Put my bag down!" Tori said.

"Why?" McKenna asked as she dug around in the bag. "What's in here you don't want me to see? Aha!" She pulled out the *Real Men of Alaska* magazine.

Tori lunged for it, but McKenna was too fast.

"What in the world?" McKenna studied the front cover. "He's cute." She began flipping through the pages. "Is your new hobby catalog shopping?"

Tori groaned. "No. It's not mine. Well, I guess it is. Piney, the store owner, gave it to me—correction, she *forced* me to take it," she said as she lunged for the magazine again.

McKenna ran to the bed and plopped down. "Ooh-la-la," she said, showing Tori the centerfold of a shirtless man standing in the river, with a fishing rod in his hand. "He is one hot tamale."

"Not my type. Now give it back so I can put it away."

McKenna glanced up again but this time with a serious expression. "Does Jesse know you have this?"

"Does *Jesse* know what?" Jesse said as he walked in.

McKenna grinned and held up the magazine. It might just as well have been Tori's bra, the way her cheeks reddened. "Tori has been browsing for a man."

Jesse took a step closer. "What the . . ." He shifted his gaze to Tori with a questioning look . . . but she had no idea what he wanted to ask. "I thought you were going to show McKenna around . . ." His expression suddenly changed. "What did you do to your hair?"

"I had McKenna cut it."

"Why?"

"Long hair doesn't work for me on the homestead." Unless she had a vanity, indoor plumbing, electricity, and hair appliances. Not to mention a lot of time to mess with it. "I'll let it grow back when I leave Alaska."

She might have imagined it, but he seemed to flinch at the mention of her leaving. It served him right. How many times had he reminded her that he was leaving? Every other second? It wasn't like she was leaving him alone to survive with the bears, wolves, and other beasties.

Jesse picked up the braid from the table and ran it between his fingers. "Just like that?"

"Yes, just like that." Tori ran a hand through her hair; it felt good, like a badge of honor. She felt as though a piece of her delicate façade had been chipped away. Because that was all it was anyway. A label that she'd worn for so long.

Jesse fingered the braid for one more second, then dropped it on the table. He shoved his hands in his pockets. "McKenna, come see the cold-hole." He walked out without waiting to see if she was going to comply.

McKenna raised an eyebrow as if he'd insulted her. "Wow," she said sarcastically. "Who is he to issue commands? I know you said he brought you a portable generator to use with your nebulizer, but I don't like this *Jesse*."

But Tori did. Liked him a lot. She didn't mind that he could be commanding. Jesse had been there for her when the bear came a-calling. Of course, Tori had no intention of telling her sister that harrowing tale, or about the other predators on the property. Tori wondered how long it would be before McKenna started asking questions about the wildlife around the homestead. "Jesse grows on you" was Tori's only explanation.

"How do you stand him? He's so bossy," McKenna complained.

Tori laughed. "Are you serious? That's like the stilettos calling the platform heels too high. Besides, bossy doesn't bother me. I'm used to it, my lovely sister."

McKenna air-swatted as if batting Tori's pointed look away. "I am not bossy. I–I . . . just know what's best for you, is all." She went to the door. "I guess I better do as your mountain man says and see this *cold-hole*. What is it anyway?"

McKenna walked to the door, then stopped. "All joking aside, Tori, I hope you're appreciating this view. It's amazing. You won't get this in Dallas. Or this clean, crisp air."

"I know." Tori came to stand beside her. She was torn—she missed the comforts of home—heck, she missed the necessities! But . . . "I agree, this place is kind of magical." Or it might just be that she was crushing on her homestead teacher.

"Hey, Jesse," Luke called, "am I supposed to put up the solar array by myself?"

"You're right." Jesse glanced back at Tori. "You two will have to go on without me."

Tori grabbed a pail and handed it to McKenna before getting one for herself. "First I'll show you the stream where I get my water. That's job one every day."

McKenna shook her head. "I can't believe you're living like this."

Me either. But she wasn't about to say it out loud. "It's not so bad," she said casually. "It's just a matter of getting used to something different, is all."

After they returned from the stream, Tori enlisted McKenna to pick up firewood around the cabin with her. She couldn't help but notice that McKenna's gaze kept wandering back over to where the guys were working, too. When they'd deposited the sticks and twigs in the basket on the porch, Tori showed McKenna the underground refrigeration. "Jesse said we're going to rig up something below the cabin so I'll be set for winter."

Once again McKenna shot her that look of astonishment, then an ironic frown that said, *Yeah, like you'll make it to winter.*

Jesse and Luke were putting things away as if they were done.

"I'm taking McKenna to the meadow to show her where we had target practice," Tori called.

"No time," Jesse said. "You have the Sisterhood of the Quilt meeting."

"I can't go, McKenna's here."

He looked at her as if she'd gone mad. "You promised Hope you were going to show up."

"No, *you* told Hope I would be there. I only said that it sounded nice."

"They're expecting you. And you're supposed to bring a dessert." He hooked a thumb toward the cabin. "That's why we made the brownies."

"Hey!" Luke said, pretending to be offended, "I thought you made those for me."

His attempt to cut the tension didn't work. Tori stood glaring at Jesse. *I can be just as stubborn as you, mister.*

"You're going," Jesse said.

"I don't want to go." And that was that.

McKenna touched her arm. "What's the Sisterhood of the Quilt?"

Luke, the peacemaker, jumped in. "The Sisterhood of the Quilt is like a sewing circle, a group of women—"

"Mostly women," Jesse interjected. "Bill Morningstar sews with the ladies, too."

"They make quilts," Luke finished.

"First Saturday of the month," Jesse added.

"Hmm." McKenna looked over at Tori with a wistful smile. "We used to sew the cutest things when we were at school, remember?" She wrapped an arm around Tori. "Come on. Let's go. It sounds like fun."

Tori didn't want to explain that Hope had probably told everybody in town by now that she was too broke to buy a bit of fabric.

McKenna gave her *that look*, the one that usually made Tori cave. "Please, Tori, do it for me. You know I'd feel more at ease if I knew you had someone other than Grizzly Adams watching out for you."

Jesse jabbed his finger into the air. "That's basically what I told her."

That got an approving nod from McKenna. And just like that, the two bossiest people Tori knew—the two bossiest people in the world!—had united against her, and she was ticked off at both of them. Darn it, all Tori wanted to do was get McKenna alone to ask her how she was handling things in Anchorage without Uncle Monty's credit cards. Maybe she had some tips Tori could use. Instead, it felt like she was being dragged in front of a firing squad—no, into the town square, buck naked!

"Ugh, fine. Let's get this over with." She ran inside to get the Alaska cross-stitch project. Then she took a moment to freshen up her makeup. She might not have any control over her money or her life, but that didn't mean she had to look like a hag to the rest of the world. Besides, she reasoned with herself, having McKenna as a buffer would help her feel less self-conscious around the women of Sweet Home.

"What are you two going to do this evening?" McKenna asked the guys.

"Get up to some kind of trouble, no doubt," Luke said.

Jesse didn't crack a smile. "Check in on my mom. Have dinner. Then head back over here and work on the solar array."

"What about Scout?" Tori asked.

"He'll hang out with us. He'll be excited to see Checkers, and Checkers will be excited to see her puppy, too."

They rode to Home Sweet Home Lodge in Luke's car, and Tori was surprised when the men came inside. Jesse carried in the brownies and made a big announcement that

Luke McAvoy was gracing them with his presence. All the
women gushed with glee. Funny, Tori had worried that she
and McKenna were going to be the gushees, but having
Luke around had taken the pressure off. Tori wondered if
Jesse had brought Luke in for just that reason.

She leaned toward her sister. "Did you know he was so
popular?"

"Yeah. He's like the golden boy wherever he goes. You
should see how the female tellers and other bank employees
fawn over him. Disgusting."

But there was something in McKenna's tone that said
there might be more going on than she was admitting.

Before she could rib her sister a little, Tori found herself
engulfed in a hug. "I'm so glad you made it," said Hope.
"And I love your new haircut."

"Um, thanks." Tori felt a little suffocated, still jammed
in the doorway with all the women surrounding Luke. But
at least Jesse was next to her to calm her anxious nerves.

Hope turned to McKenna. "You must be Tori's sister. I
see the resemblance. I'm Hope Stone." She pointed across
the room. "That's my husband, Donovan. Our daughter,
Ella, is in the studio with her friends." To Jesse she said,
"You can set the Dutch oven on the dining room table."

Jesse squeezed through the throng, and as soon as he left
her side, Tori instantly felt a chill of loneliness. Oh, this was
absurd. She'd become unreasonably attached to her mountain man. Maybe being here surrounded by other people
was a good idea after all. Her world had become small, she
conceded, and she needed to expand her horizons.

Hope took her arm. "Come on, you two. I want to show
you something before the rest of the quilters try to steal
your attention."

Tori couldn't help herself. She looked back at Jesse . . .
and sucked in a breath. He was looking at her, too. She
started to wave but made herself stop, telling herself that he
was just a man, like any other man. Flawed. And this time,

she was going to achieve something she'd never done before: she wasn't going to get hung up on him.

They followed Hope through the large living room, past the kitchen, and down the hall to the sewing studio. "This is where the Sisterhood of the Quilt officially meets."

The cheery room was large, with numerous sewing machines on expansive tables. Racks at the back of the room held bolts of fabric, and pieces of quilt blocks were stuck to white flannel panels hanging on the walls. In the center stretched a table almost the length of the room, with a line of irons plugged into outlets on the floor. A quilt hanging on the wall looked like an aerial view of a quilting bee, with the hands of quilters stitching a quilt. What really interested Tori, though, was the dress form in the far corner. She hadn't been this close to sewing notions since her boarding school days. She wondered now why she and McKenna hadn't continued sewing when they went to college and then moved into their apartment in Dallas.

Hope beamed at them. "Isn't it wonderful!"

"Yes, wonderful." Tori walked farther into the room to get a better look at the dress form, noticing all the adjustable knobs. It didn't seem to be in use as no fabric was hanging from it.

McKenna rushed to the closest design wall to get a better look at one of the quilts in progress. "This is great. I've always been fascinated by quilts." She turned to Tori. "Do you remember the sewing machines we had when we were little?"

"Yes. And all the Barbie clothes I made."

"I made pillows and blankets for them," McKenna said, "and my G.I. Joe. You know how I was never a fan of Ken."

"I remember."

Hope pointed to one of the tables. "These two machines are available. You're welcome to them while you're here."

The machines looked more sophisticated than the ones Tori had learned on. Hope must've noticed her hesitation because she said, "I know the bells and whistles can be intimidating, but don't worry; I'll show you how to use them." Hope picked up a Stone's Throw Hardware & Haberdashery tote bag and approached Tori. "I got you a little gift to welcome you to the Sisterhood of the Quilt. McKenna, if I'd known you were coming, I would've brought something for you, too, but you can help yourself to any of the fabric on the racks. You, too, Tori."

"But you already got me a housewarming gift." Tori held up the cross-stitch project, feeling embarrassed by all the attention.

"Just say *thank you*," McKenna prompted.

Tori took the sack. "Thank you." Before she could open it, Hope started listing the contents of the bag.

"It's the fuchsia buffalo plaid you were admiring at the store and the green, too. Once you mentioned it, I couldn't help myself. I cut enough for you to make curtains and pillow shams. Plus, I threw in some of the fireweed fabric to make pullbacks or ruffles . . . or both. There's still plenty on the bolts, if you decide you want to make yourself a quilt, too. Just let me know and I'll hold the rest back for you."

Humiliation returned in full force. She thrust the bag back at Hope. "I can't accept this."

"Yes, you can," McKenna chirped as she rushed over. She took the sack from Tori and pulled out the buffalo plaid fabric. "Ooh, it's gorgeous! Sophisticated but fun. It's really going to spruce up the cabin." She thrust the bag back into Tori's hands. "What else is in there?"

"Flannel lining and blackout material. The lining is to help insulate the windows during the winter and the blackout material is for the long summer days so you can block out the light at night. Trust me, you're going to need both."

Before Tori could respond, the rest of the quilters filed in and gathered around her. McKenna came to her side, and for once Tori was grateful for her sister's overprotectiveness.

Piney made the introductions and Tori recognized some of the ladies she'd met at church. She wished the townsfolk would all wear nametags, or at least the same clothes so she could keep them straight. Everyone had some comment to make about *dear old Monty* or the homestead or about her and McKenna. Her sister seemed to really enjoy the attention, but Tori was still shaken by Hope's gift of fabric. Fortunately not a single quilter brought up Tori's dire monetary circumstances. Yes, there were comments made about her clothes not being tough enough for the Alaska terrain or about how her new haircut was *just the thing for homestead life*. No one said a word about her finances. Tori was beginning to believe that maybe Hope *hadn't* told everyone how broke she was, how she didn't even have enough money to make a couple of curtains.

"Okay, everyone," Piney said above the din, "let's give the St. James girls some room to breathe. Besides, I know all of you have plenty to work on."

Hope was back at Tori's side. "Would you like me to get you started on your curtains?"

"Of course she would," Piney piped in. "You help Tori and I'll help McKenna figure out what she'd like to sew." She whisked McKenna away, saying, "First let me show you what everyone else is working on . . ."

Hope smiled after them. "Even though the lodge is my home now, Piney is in charge when it comes to the Sisterhood of the Quilt."

"Your home is beautiful," Tori said, trying not to compare her ramshackle cabin with Hope's lodge.

"Home Sweet Home Lodge belonged to Donovan's grandparents. I moved in here only recently . . ."

But Tori had been introduced to Donovan and their sixteen-year-old daughter.

Hope smiled at the confusion on her face. "It's a long story that I'll share with you sometime. But right now, let's cut out your curtains."

Hope and Tori guessed at the size of the windows, and then Hope showed her how to use the rotary cutter, not something Tori used when she'd made clothes for the drama department. Once the fabric was ready, Hope pointed out the extras on the sewing machine—like the automatic thread cutter—and waited while Tori sewed the top edge down.

Tori grinned over at her teacher. "I love this machine."

Hope got to her feet. "While you turn up the bottom edge for the hem, I'll look in the garage for curtain rods. I know I saw some in there somewhere."

Tori had the bottom and sides done before Hope returned.

"They look perfect," Hope said, bending closer. "Nice seams. This isn't your first rodeo."

"But they are my first curtains. You're a good teacher."

"Since you have this under control, I'll check on Ella and her friends to see if they need any help."

"Thank you again for the fabric."

"My pleasure," said Hope with a squeeze of her arm.

Tori zipped through making the other curtain panel. *This is fun! And a great distraction.* She started to imagine what else she could make. With this fancy machine, she bet she could make some cute clothes. She pulled out her notebook, flipped to a clean page, and sketched out a vest that was both stylish and functional for life in Alaska. Then she quickly glanced through the drawings she'd made earlier.

But fanciful thoughts would do her no good. She didn't have electricity or a sewing machine. Or money for fabric and thread. She sighed heavily, once again struggling to accept that she had no control over her life. To get her mind off her pity party, she looked over to see what was going on with McKenna.

She was standing at the cutting mat with Piney, who said, "Okay, just line up this line on the fabric."

"What are you working on?" Tori asked.

McKenna gave her instructor a mock frown. "Piney says I have to start with something small, so I'm going to piece together some blocks to make a pillow." She held up the fabric she'd just cut.

"Four nine-patch blocks," Piney interjected. She peered over at Tori. "What's that you're drawing?"

Tori shut the notebook. "It's nothing, just doodles."

"What does she have there?" asked Miss Lisa, shuffling over from her sewing machine.

Aberdeen and Lolly came over to see, too.

"Show us," Piney said. "We love to see what others are working on." She got a determined look on her face. "Besides, it's a requirement of the Sisterhood of the Quilt . . . show and share. Right, ladies?"

They looked like a group of bobbleheads with all the nodding they were doing. But Tori wasn't going to show anyone anything. She knew the drawings weren't good enough.

McKenna pushed her way through. "Oh, good grief, Tori. Just show them."

Tori didn't have a chance to think before her sister grabbed the notebook and offered it to Piney. This was the second time today that McKenna had interfered when Tori wanted—*no, needed!*—to keep something private. Later she would have a talk with her sister.

The other women moved closer, murmuring as they looked over Piney's shoulder.

"This is good," Piney said. The others were back to nodding. Piney tapped the notebook. "You know, we have patterns over there in that drawer. Mostly quilt patterns, but clothes, too. If I'm not mistaken, there's a vest pattern in there. You could use the pattern to make a rough outline and then add extensions and make nips and tucks as you see fit."

"No. That's okay." Once again, Tori was being put in the position of having to confess that she didn't have the money to buy fabric. "I just like to draw clothes. It's one of my hobbies." At least Uncle Monty hadn't found a way to take drawing away from her, too.

"It won't hurt you to look at patterns," Piney argued. Once again, the ladies were bobbing their heads, McKenna included.

Reluctantly Tori rose and followed Piney to the ornate antique chest of drawers with the marble top. Tori ran her hand over the cherubs carved around the pull handle.

"Go ahead and open it. The clothes patterns are on the right side."

The drawer was heavy and Tori had to tug hard to get it open. Dutifully she went to the right side, planning to give it a cursory glance to appease Piney. But the moment Tori caught sight of all the patterns, going back decades, she was enthralled.

"Aberdeen, bring over that laundry basket so Tori can pull out everything and look at them properly." Piney cleared off a table for her to spread them out. On her way back, she pulled a book from one of the shelves. "Here's a guide to garment fitting." She held it up to Hope. "Can Tori take this with her so she can study it back at the cabin?"

"Certainly. She's part of the Sisterhood of the Quilt now. What's ours is hers," Hope said.

Tori couldn't believe how nice everyone was, how inclusive. "Thank you," she said, genuinely touched.

Piney patted her on the back. "I'm going to help your sister but if you see a pattern that you'd like to practice with, let me know, and we'll grab some fabric from the rack." Yes, Hope had said she could use that fabric, but Tori wondered if the women paid dues or something to afford that luxury.

She opened her mouth to ask, but Piney had stepped away.

Tori picked up a vest pattern and set her drawing next to the pattern cover to see what changes had to be made.

Like a bee to honey, Piney was back. "I knew that was in there. Have you used a pattern before?"

"Yes."

"Good. You know it's important to have the weave go in

the right direction. Make sure the grainline is always parallel with the selvage."

"Yes, so the fabric will hang right," Tori said.

"You do know your clothes. Pull out the pattern pieces and let me take a look." Piney laid out the pattern. "Feel free to cut up the pattern any way you want." She pointed to the shelf near the rack of fabric. "We have brown paper and tape, if you need those for modifying."

"Oh, I couldn't cut up the pattern," Tori argued. "That would ruin it."

Piney laughed. "Look around. These ladies are more interested in quilting than messing with clothes. How do you think the studio ended up with all those clothes patterns anyway? No one wanted them anymore, so help yourself." She handed Tori a pair of scissors. "These are my *paper* scissors." A label was affixed to them—*PAPER*. "If you use any of the fabric scissors on paper, you'll have to answer to me."

"Got it."

Tori went to work redesigning the vest by adding length with the brown paper, then added tucks to make it more fitted, but it still wasn't right. Eventually she scrapped the pattern altogether and drew her own pieces onto the paper. She glanced up a couple of times to see McKenna bent over a sewing machine, looking so very happy, which made Tori happy, too.

Piney came back with a bolt of brown buffalo plaid. "I see you're about ready to make a test vest. I know cotton probably isn't what you're looking for, but it will at least give you an idea of what the final product might look like. We have plenty of this brown check."

But Tori had other ideas as she gazed at the bolts of fabric. "Um, would it be okay if I pieced a bunch of different fabrics together? I'm thinking I could mix those black stripes, an animal print, and some of the earth-tone florals together. And what do you think if I put a bold seam down the back?"

Piney chuckled. "I'm not the designer, dumpling. You are."

"I'm not." She was just plain Tori. "I think the earth-tone florals would blend in better out in the woods than the buffalo plaid."

Piney gave her a quizzical look. "The woods? I thought you were making something for church. Your drawing looks awfully fancy for hunting and fishing."

"Can't clothes be both cute and functional? At the hardware store, all the women's clothes looked the same as the men's. All function, no style. The colors were boring and there were no prints. Okay, yes, some plaid . . . but they looked like men's plaid. How's a girl supposed to look cute out here in the sticks?"

She finally noticed that the room had gone quiet. Some of the women were even looking down at what they were wearing. A couple were tugging on their hair. And Tori cursed her big fat mouth! Just because style was important to her didn't mean that she had to berate others for their lack of it.

She didn't mean that either. She had her own style, that was all, and she certainly hadn't meant to inadvertently insult them for theirs. Oh, why hadn't McKenna jumped in and made her shut up before she made such a fool of herself?

Tori put her hands out, placating. "I'm sorry. I shouldn't have said all that. I know I don't belong here. I know I'm too girly for Alaska. I just thought if I could wear something that was a little more *me*, while still suitable for homestead life, then maybe I could make a go of it here." *Fit in, even.*

But she'd blown it. When would she learn to shut up? She should've gushed over the quilts everyone was making like McKenna did. Yes, they were beautiful, but Tori would rather dress people than beds.

The air in the room felt awkward, suffocating. She didn't meet anyone's eyes as she took the bolt of brown buffalo plaid from Piney. "Thanks, I think I will use this after all."

The room was frozen. Piney stood there a beat longer before walking away.

Tori's face felt like she'd pressed a hot iron to it. As she spread out the fabric, she tried to ignore everyone in the room. She'd said she was sorry. What else could she do? She went to the fabric rack and pulled other bolts to lay on the table, planning to cut small pieces to sew together to make her fabric for the vest.

Before she could pick up the scissors, her sister finally woke up and ran over to her.

Tori leaned in and whispered, "I really messed up." She tilted her head toward the others. "I never should've implied that their clothes weren't attractive."

McKenna didn't reply, only turned around to the group. "Hey, everyone. Tori thinks you're mad at her. She feels really bad about what she said."

Tori yanked on McKenna's arm. "Stop it."

But McKenna shook her off. "She's offered to make everyone a vest like hers." With a grin as big as a Cheshire cat's, she picked up Tori's notebook and turned to a new page. "Just put down your name, your size, and your favorite color."

Chapter 10

TORI WAS SEETHING mad at her sister. As she carefully sewed fabric together for her vest, one by one the quilters came up to write down their name and size. Darn it! Tori hadn't even finished her own vest. She kept her eyes glued to what she was doing because she didn't want to see the glower on their faces. What if the vests turned out to be a horrible mess? It would be another mark against her with this crowd.

McKenna came over and wrapped an arm around Tori's shoulders, which she immediately shrugged off. "Was that really necessary?"

"What?" Her sister was playing innocent now.

"You *know* what. Putting me in this position."

McKenna dropped the act and looked a little hurt. "I was trying to *help* you. Fix what you did."

"By promising something that I can't deliver?" Tori hissed.

McKenna wrapped her arm around her again and squeezed. "I know you can do it, Tor. I believe you can do anything. Besides . . . how many times have you fixed me up and made me presentable when it seemed hopeless?"

"This is different. I don't have any experience designing clothes!"

"What about all those costumes we made?"

Yes, Tori had designed the costumes for *The Sound of Music*, *Oliver*, and *Anything Goes*.

McKenna gave her another squeeze. "Just pretend it's another play and you have to dress the cast members."

"Well, I guess I could do that," Tori said. "How am I supposed to buy fabric?"

"I talked to Piney about it. She said to use the bolts at the back of the studio." McKenna leaned her head against Tori's. "And it's all going to turn out great."

"We'll see." But what her sister didn't understand was that Tori was living a subsistence life. She had to provide for all her own needs, including collecting water and firewood every day. Where was she going to find the time to make vests for all these women? Her life felt like one unanswered question after another. Not knowing what else to do, she picked up the scissors and cut.

"Come sit next to me when you're ready to sew," McKenna said, and went back to her place.

Tori didn't answer but kept cutting until she had the three main pieces laid out in front of her. She'd added pockets to her drawing and she went about making pattern pieces for those, then cut those out, too. Finally she sat down next to McKenna and peered over at her progress.

"I've finished another nine-patch block." McKenna held up a block made from the same blue and pink flower print on Tori's quilt back at the cabin. "Forget-me-nots and fireweed. Piney says they're Alaskan favorites. What do you think?"

"Looks really good," Tori said.

"Piney showed me how to press the seam to the opposite side to make a perfect corner."

Because McKenna had been a pill, Tori pointed to a corner that was off. "What about that one?"

"Piney said something off here and there gives a quilt character," McKenna said grinning.

Tori wished she could be that nonchalant about her own project, but she couldn't, for surely the quilters would scrutinize her every stitch.

Hope interrupted her by holding out a box. "Donovan's grandmother had this great button collection that all the women contributed to. I thought I'd let everyone pick out the buttons for their own vests. But you choose first."

Tori raked through all the beautiful buttons, flashing back to her mom's own button box, a red flowered octagon with two metal handles that met at the top.

"Thanks," Tori said to Hope. She pulled out a button that would be perfect for what she was imagining.

"I know a few of the women were wondering if they could have a zipper instead of buttons?" Hope said it like a question. Or maybe a favor.

Tori's heart sank. "Zippers are not my thing," she admitted. "In the past, I've avoided them at all costs."

"How about this," said Hope. "The ladies who want zippers can either do it themselves or ask Lolly or Jilly Crocker to do them. Those two are geniuses with zippers and they won't mind at all." Hope pointed out the Crocker sisters. "When the linemen or lumberjacks ask for zipper mending at the Hungry Bear, we always send them to the Crockers."

"You work at the Hungry Bear?" Tori asked in disbelief.

"Not anymore. But I did for seventeen years," Hope said.

What a shock. Hope lived like a queen here at the lodge, so why had she worked at the Hungry Bear?

Hope laughed. "I told you I didn't always live in the lap of luxury. I lived paycheck to paycheck my whole adult life."

Just then Donovan stuck his head in the studio. "Hope, honey, you wanted me to tell you when it was time to break for food. I made my famous banana bread."

Hope beamed at her husband. "I knew I smelled something yummy coming from the kitchen. You definitely know the way to my heart. We'll be right there."

The women filed out, including McKenna, but Tori hung back. She figured she'd be better off if she stayed back to work some more. Hope gave her a look.

"Come on, Tori, everyone needs a break to socialize," she said.

Tori picked up her pencil, notebook, and signup sheet, and followed. Even if Hope insisted that she take a break, she'd work on refining the best way to put the vest together. Once she was happy with that, she'd sew assembly-style.

But when she sat down in a corner away from the dining room table, the quilters came up to her one by one.

"Do I get to pick out fabric?" Aberdeen asked. "Blue is my favorite color."

"I really like large florals," remarked Miss Lisa. "My eyes aren't what they used to be." Her old eyes were milky with cataracts.

Before the third person could say anything, Tori jumped in. "Everyone can pick their own fabrics. Choose three or four for me to piece together to create your unique fabric."

Piney stood and spoke above the hubbub. "I have a better idea. Since Tori is offering to make each of you a designer vest, I think everyone should piece together their own fabric before handing it off to Tori to sew." She turned to her. "What do you think? One and a half yards of whatever you want for the vest and the same amount for the lining?"

Everyone nodded in agreement, and Tori didn't have words. Weren't they supposed to be punishing her for calling their clothing unfeminine?

"That's an excellent idea, Mom," said Sparkle. "The burden shouldn't fall on Tori alone." She handed Tori a plate. "I was afraid you weren't going to make it to the table, so I got you a little of everything."

Tori felt choked up. Not only for the food but for Piney stepping in. This had to be the nicest group of women she'd ever met. "Thank you. That's very thoughtful."

While they ate, Piney and Miss Lisa took turns telling stories about the antics of the Sisterhood of the Quilt.

How they once took a field trip to a quilt show in Fairbanks and were nearly thrown out of the hotel for causing such a ruckus. How they'd held a piecing and quilting marathon for families who lost everything in a forest fire. How the Wines of Alaska wine tasting usually ended with quilters in the studio madly trying to finish their last-minute Christmas presents, only days away.

Piney held up her glass. "This lodge holds a lot of quilty memories for nearly all of us. Let's give a toast to Elsie Stone, our dear departed friend, who started us down the right path, the quilting path."

"Here, here," the women chorused.

Tori and McKenna looked at each other from across the room. Tori knew exactly what her sister was thinking. They'd never lived in and experienced such a close community.

Finally, Piney pushed back her chair. "We have about an hour left to sew. Let's head back to the studio."

Sitting behind the sewing machine, Tori stitched pockets onto her vest: one for a water bottle, several for bullets— with guidance from Hope—and even a place for lip gloss, her inhaler, and EpiPen. McKenna had finished her last nine-patch block and was starting to piece the four blocks together.

"Hurry up and get the piecing done." Piney was holding a square of batting and another piece of fabric. "I want to show you how to stitch in the ditch. It's a great way to quilt."

"What's the other fabric for?" McKenna asked.

"It's the backing," Piney answered. "Just something I had lying around. No one's going to see this anyway because it'll be inside the pillow. Now hurry up." She walked away.

"Sounds like you're going to be in trouble if you don't get a move on," Tori jibed.

"I—"

But Miss Lisa interrupted by sitting next to McKenna

and setting a shoebox beside her. "Piney told me that you live in Anchorage."

"For the time being," McKenna answered pleasantly, as though it had all been her own idea.

Miss Lisa opened the box. "If you want, I have a little project you might like to take back with you." The box held a stack of fabric that had been cut into circles. "It's to make yo-yos. You can do all sorts of things with them when you're done, like make a quilt to decorate a wall or a bed."

McKenna looked hesitant. "I don't have a sewing machine at my apartment."

Miss Lisa smiled sweetly. "Oh, you don't need a machine, just needle and thread." She dug in her sweater pocket and pulled out what looked like a poof of fabric joined in a circle. "This is a completed yo-yo. May I show you how easy it is to make?"

"Yes, please." McKenna now seemed intrigued.

The older woman demonstrated how to baste around the edge and pull the thread tight before knotting it off. "See? Easy as pie."

"I think I can do it."

Miss Lisa pushed the box toward her. "That should keep you busy until you can get back to us, don't you think?"

"Yes, ma'am. Thank you."

Miss Lisa rose and left them.

"What do you think?" Tori asked.

"I believe this shoebox is going to help me get through the long nights without you there," McKenna said as she picked through the fabric.

Tori hugged her sister. "I miss you."

"I know you do."

McKENNA WATCHED AS Tori worked on the vest. "You kind of went overboard on the pockets, didn't you?"

Tori laughed. "I kept thinking of more items I want to

have with me, just in case. This vest will basically take the place of my purse." She put two seams together. "Now that all the pockets are installed, I can begin the construction of the vest . . . shoulder seams first."

"Well, I just completed the top of the pillow." McKenna held it up.

"It's wonderful. I can't believe you made it."

McKenna gave her an offended look.

"I mean, I can't believe you sewed it in such a short period of time."

"That's better." McKenna looked around for Piney, but she wasn't in the studio. Probably in the kitchen. She went to the door to look for her and nearly ran into Luke, who was just coming in. He grabbed her shoulders and steadied her.

"Your chariot has arrived," he said, playing the part of a cheery taxi driver.

McKenna glanced back at Tori and saw that her sister was craning her head to the side as if to see around Luke.

Apparently Tori wasn't going to ask, so McKenna had to. "Where's your sidekick?"

He patted his pocket. "My phone? I have it right here."

Hope waved. "C'mon, Luke, where's Jesse?"

"At home, chilling," Luke said.

McKenna glanced at Tori to see her reaction, but, unsurprisingly, Tori was up to her old tricks. When she was upset about something, Tori worked hard to hide it . . . the opposite of McKenna. McKenna had hoped her sister was turning over a new leaf.

"We'll be ready in a second," she told Luke.

"Take your time."

Tori kept her eyes on her vest as if it were the most interesting thing in the world. She quickly folded the pieces and put them in a pile.

"Where are you staying tonight, Luke?" Hope asked. "We have plenty of space."

"Thanks for the offer, but I'm staying in my old room at Jesse's."

McKenna wondered why he would have a room at Jesse's house.

Piney came up behind Luke. "What's going on?"

"Our ride is here," McKenna said.

"But you're not done yet."

"Luke?" Hope was rifling through her things on the table. "If you can give us a little more time, I'm going to give McKenna a crash course on hand quilting."

"I'm not in any hurry. Jesse's the one who sent me. He said Tori needs a good night's sleep because there's a lot to do on the homestead tomorrow."

"It'll only take a minute." Hope apparently found what she was looking for because she held them up for McKenna to see. "A hoop, needle, and thread. Piney, where's the backing you had earlier?"

Piney handed it to her.

Hope demonstrated how to layer the fabrics before slipping the hoop over them. She threaded the needle and stitched about an inch. "That's a little guide to show you how big to make your stitches. Any questions?"

"It'll be fun," McKenna gushed, then saw Luke looking at her with a strange expression on his face, as if he didn't know her at all.

In ones and twos the ladies of the Sisterhood said "Good night" and "See you soon."

McKenna picked up the box of yo-yo material and her hand-quilting project, and as they left the lodge, she leaned into Tori. "I don't know why you didn't want to come tonight. I thought they were all very lovely."

Tori pouted. "That's because you got off easy. You don't have to sew a vest for practically every woman in town. I haven't forgotten who's to blame either."

"You? For letting your mouth get away from you?" McKenna offered.

"Har-har, very funny. You've always volunteered me for the craziest things. Like making Halloween costumes for everyone in our dorm when we were at boarding school."

"They wanted to celebrate an American Halloween." McKenna smiled sweetly. "I bet you're glad you have that experience now. Without me giving you a little nudge, you never would've become such an excellent seamstress."

"Sometimes your nudges feel more like you're pushing me off a ledge."

"All in the name of love, my sister," McKenna said.

Tori gave her a little shove and caught up with Luke. "How's Patricia feeling?"

"I think she's better. She definitely looks better than the last time I saw her. She was in good spirits tonight, too. She was happy to see Scout." Luke opened the back car door and Scout barked like he was saying *What took you so long?*

Tori slid in and Luke closed the door behind her. Before McKenna could go around to the other side, he said, "Sit up front with me."

"I should sit in back with Tori."

"There's no room. Scout's back there."

"He's not that big."

"C'mon, I just want to see what you made tonight. Besides it's only a short ride to Montgomery's homestead and you'll have the rest of the evening with her."

When they were all settled inside, McKenna held up the hooped pillow top for him to see.

"It was so much fun," she said. "Who would've thought I'd like something as girly as quilting?"

"Apparently you haven't met Bill Morningstar yet. And if I were you, I wouldn't let him hear you say quilting is girly," Luke warned, laughing. "He's as grizzly as they come and he's known statewide for his Alaskan quilts. He won first *and* second place in the last quilt show in Anchorage."

"How would you know?" McKenna asked.

"Sweet Home is my hometown," Luke said matter-of-factly. "And the quilters used my apartment to throw a party for Bill after the awards ceremony."

Tori piped up from the back seat, "I hope Bill will show us his work sometime."

"Ask Piney," Luke said. "She seems to be the only one who can get him to do anything."

For no apparent reason, Luke looked over at McKenna and held her gaze for a long moment, which made her stomach squeeze in on itself. She wasn't the type to crush on a guy like him. Maybe she was coming down with the flu. Or maybe she was the one turning over a new leaf. She hoped not.

Either way, Luke should keep his smoldering looks to himself and his eyes on the road.

He turned down a few more roads and finally they went up the gravel road to Tori's cabin. McKenna clicked open her seat belt and prepared to hop out of the car as soon as it stopped.

But Luke grabbed her hand. "Hold on."

McKenna started to jerk away but she saw that he was pointing with his other hand.

"There. A wolverine."

The wolverine, which looked like a short bear, was crawling around the outside of the cabin. It disappeared from view, but it definitely hadn't left.

Luke reached under the seat and pulled out a holstered gun.

"What's that?" Of course she knew what it was, but it was the first thing that came out of her mouth.

"Don't worry. I have a concealed carry permit."

"What do you plan to do?" McKenna asked.

"Make sure you two are safe tonight." Luke got out and made a warning shot.

The pop of the gun made McKenna jump. "Are you okay, Tori?"

"Yes. I'm just waiting for the all clear."

Luke motioned for them to get out of the vehicle.

McKenna was suddenly ready to head back to Anchorage. To her surprise, Tori scooped up Scout, opened her door, and bravely exited the car. McKenna had no choice but to follow suit, but in her case, she ran to Luke's side.

"Is he gone?" she asked.

"Yes. But I'd feel better if you two made your trips to the outhouse while I'm still here. Tori, is it okay with you if I get a fire going in the woodstove?"

"Yes. Thank you. That would be great." She hurried up the steps and lugged Scout inside.

Luke took McKenna's hand and guided her toward the cabin. That was when she realized she was shaking. How embarrassing! This was completely out of character for her. She usually had nerves of steel; everyone knew that. But Luke's firm grip was calming, and at the same time, his handholding kicked up her heart rate several notches.

"I've got you, you're safe now," Luke said quietly, soothingly.

Tori peeked outside. "Are you two coming in?"

Ugh, why did Tori have to see her clutching Luke's hand? Apparently she didn't have an ounce of dignity left. But Tori did. Her eyes darted to their clasped hands and she immediately looked away as if she'd seen nothing.

Luke led McKenna into the cabin, where Tori had lit the lantern and was now clipping a leash onto Scout. "Jesse fired warning shots around the perimeter, but I guess the wolverine didn't get the memo. I'll take Scout and head to the necessary first." She might as well have announced *I'll leave you two alone.*

McKenna dropped Luke's hand and said, "You're acting pretty calm for someone surrounded by vicious wild animals."

"I know." Tori shrugged as if she'd accepted it. "Jesse told me there's no record of humans being attacked by wolverines."

"Of course not," McKenna said sarcastically, "because none of those humans survived to tell the tale. Haven't you seen how vicious wolverines are on the National Geographic channel?"

Tori just smiled. "I'll be right back." She held the lantern high and walked back outside.

Luke, his pistol, and McKenna followed them to the porch and watched Tori walk her dog safely to the outhouse, tie Scout's leash to the handle, and go inside. He set his pistol on the little porch table, and in the same fluid motion, pulled McKenna into his arms and kissed her.

At first, she was so shocked that her brain couldn't latch on to what was happening, except panic that Tori might pop out and see them. But Luke's kiss brushed that thought aside and made McKenna's body come to life, and she kissed him back. Normally when she had the wits scared out of her, she craved chocolate to soothe herself, but now she knew the real cure for nerves—this man's kiss.

He pulled away slightly without releasing her. "I thought that might help you get your mind off the wolverine." He gave her another delicious kiss and let her go. He didn't say anything more, as though everything was perfectly normal and he was the same man who'd driven her to the cabin earlier today. Did he truly not have a clue that he'd just flipped McKenna's world upside down?

Tori and her lantern appeared as Luke holstered his gun at his waist. Mr. Knows How to Kiss a Woman seemed perfectly fine, while McKenna was still foggy from being grabbed and kissed . . . thoroughly. Was this one of Luke's duties as dictated by Uncle Monty? Keep her nerves steady by any means possible?

Wordlessly McKenna accepted the lantern Tori handed her, but she didn't move.

"It's okay," Luke said, "I'll make sure you're safe."

Her stomach did another delicious squeeze as Luke ushered her down the porch steps. She hurried across the yard, barely registering the charmless outhouse. When she returned, Luke was still manning his post. She couldn't meet his eyes and tried to walk past him without acknowledging his existence, but his hand caught hers and pulled her to a stop.

"You okay?" he asked softly.

"I'm fine," she said.

"Processing?" he asked.

"Yeah."

"Me, too."

He followed her in, and McKenna took her backpack to the far side of the cabin and fussed with the contents, while Luke made a fire—not unlike the one he'd started inside her. Afterward, he walked the perimeter of the cabin and fired two more warning shots.

"I better get to Jesse's," he said when he circled back. "He'll be wondering where I am. Are you two going to be all right tonight?" But his gaze was directed only at McKenna.

"We'll be fine," Tori answered.

McKenna managed a nod, not quite able to take her eyes off him now.

Smiling as if she had a secret, Tori walked to the door and slid the slat into place behind him. "Well, I like him. He's so obliging."

"What's that supposed to mean?" McKenna said.

"I like that he wants to take care of my sister. You should've told me that something was going on between you."

"There's nothing going on," McKenna lied . . . through her still swollen lips. And to divert Tori, she said, "What about you and Jesse? Something going on with *you* two?"

Tori shook her head. "Just like you, apparently. Nothing's going on."

But they both knew they were lying.

Tori set her purse on the table. "So tell me . . . have you gotten anything from Uncle Monty? You saw my solar panels." She tapped the box on the table. "And the portable generator."

"No," McKenna lied again. She thought it was nicer to keep quiet about the thousand bucks Uncle Monty had loaned her, as Tori's feelings would be hurt, especially as she was forced to live so primitively. "Not a thing. Well, he is paying for my apartment."

"Just so you know, I have a small account at Piney's grocery store and the bill goes to Terrence." Tori pointed to the black wellies and duck boots sitting by the door. "And Uncle Monty paid for those. I should've listened to you and brought more of your clothes with me." She pulled vest pieces from her bag. "But I guess I'll just make myself some appropriate clothing instead."

McKenna came over and studied all the pockets. "You did a really nice job. Are you going to hand-stitch the rest?"

"No. I think the sewing machine makes a sturdier stitch than I ever could. I'll just have to wait until the next Sisterhood of the Quilt get-together."

But McKenna didn't think that was good enough. She wondered if her thousand dollars could buy Tori some real electricity. She'd ask Luke what it would take to have a power line sent out to the cabin. And maybe Piney would let her sister borrow a machine from the lodge.

McKenna hugged her. "I'm really proud of you, you know." Out of the corner of her eye she saw the *Real Men of Alaska* magazine under Tori's bed. "How about we go through your magazine and rate the guys?"

"We shouldn't!" Tori squealed, but then she ran to get the magazine and plopped onto the bed. "It's been a long time since we shared a bed."

"Oh, we'll be fine. Now let me see those guys."

For the next hour, they debated and ranked the men on the page, until they realized that they were comparing every guy to Jesse and Luke . . . with the magazine men coming up short. They laughed late into the night as they lay in the cozy shared bed, and felt like they were twelve again.

Right before McKenna fell asleep, she thought about telling Tori about Luke kissing her. But then she heard Tori snoring softly.

Chapter 11

AT SEVEN THE next morning, Jesse pulled up to Tori's cabin with Luke in his car right behind him. The goal was to finish setting up the solar panels and have them running before Luke and McKenna headed back in the afternoon. Which would really help Jesse. The less time he had to work closely with Tori the better.

When Jesse parked and got out, he expected Tori to come out and greet him, but she didn't.

Luke came up beside him. "What do you think? Still asleep?"

"Yeah." Which was just as well.

As quietly as they could, they worked on the solar array. An hour later, Hope's SUV pulled up to the cabin, and Hope and a petite woman got out.

"Hey, Jesse. Hey, Luke," Hope hollered. She turned to her companion as they made their way over. "Jesse Montana and Luke McAvoy are two of Sweet Home's most eligible bachelors."

Startled by the strange introduction, Luke opened his mouth as if to contradict her, but Hope went on.

"Luke is the manager of First Regional Bank in Anchorage and Jesse is the soon-to-be host of a new show for HGTV—*Homestead Recovery*."

Jesse and Luke frowned at each other. Then Jesse turned back to the women. "Hi, Hope. What's going on?"

Hope smiled like she was delivering a lottery check. "I went by your place, and since your truck was gone, I knew you'd be here."

That still hadn't answered his question.

Hope gestured to the other woman. "This is Kit Armstrong, owner of *Real Men of Alaska*. You've seen the magazine in the Hungry Bear, right?"

"Yes." He'd seen countless women either flipping through the magazine at the Hungry Bear or buying it. But worst of all was when he'd seen the *Real Men of Alaska* magazine wrapped in Tori's arms.

The short woman took over. "*Real Men of Alaska* isn't primarily a magazine. It's a matchmaking service."

"Okay . . ." Jesse put an arm out to stop Luke as he stepped back as if to make an escape. "You're not going anywhere."

Hope jumped in like she knew Kit was going to lose her audience. "Kit finds matches for women who are looking for real men . . . like the men here in Alaska."

Nice try at flattery, Hope.

"And in Scotland, too," Kit added.

"Scotland?"

"Yes. That's where I met my husband," Kit said. "I'm just here temporarily."

"Her manager got married and recently moved to San Francisco. You remember Donna DeMarco, right? She's older than us and moved away to Fairbanks when we were in high school."

"So I'm in Alaska to find a new manager—"

Jesse started to breathe easier.

"—and to find new *real men* recruits. Like yourselves."

Jesse sighed and glared at Luke.

Luke shook his head. "Not my idea. I didn't tell her to come here."

"Actually, Donna suggested I contact Piney about bachelors around Sweet Home and also to see if Piney knew anyone who could take her place as manager." Kit chuckled, a tinkling kind of laugh. "I'm interviewing a few people tomorrow for the manager position, and Piney sent me out here to talk to you today. Didn't she tell you I was coming to meet you, Jesse? And it's just sheer luck when Hope told me you were going to be with him, Luke."

Luke's expression said Jesse was less rabbit's foot and more like a broken mirror.

"I offered to show her the way," Hope said proudly.

Jesse wanted to take back all the times he'd been nice to Hope over the years.

"Do you have a minute to talk?" Kit asked.

Jesse glanced back at the solar array, which still needed attention, but it was Hope who answered.

"Of course they do," Hope said.

Yeah, he and Hope would have a *talk* later. Just because she was newly married and happy didn't mean she had to make sure that everyone else was set up, too.

Then Jesse had a new idea, and made a quick decision. "Sure. We can take a few minutes."

Luke looked at him as if Jesse had lost it. "It's your dime, brother. You know I'm heading back to Anchorage in a bit, whether these solar panels are up and running or not."

Jesse would explain everything to Luke later. Kit's visit might just be the thing to save him. No, he wasn't looking for a date, but maybe Kit's deal would help him to keep his mind off Tori. Or at the very least, make Tori quit looking at him with her doe eyes and stop his heart from pounding so hard. The good Lord knew that chopping wood at the crack of dawn hadn't kept him from thinking of Tori. Or watering the Highland cows. Or repairing the bear fence around the chicken coop. Or the hundred push-ups he'd done in the middle of the night.

"Let's hear Ms. Armstrong out," Jesse said gruffly.

"Call me Kit," she said, as if alpha males didn't bother her at all.

"What's required of *us*?" Jesse said *us* firmly so Luke would understand that it meant him, too.

Luke looked as puzzled as if Jesse had caught the football and then run the wrong way on the field.

"I'm looking for men all over Alaska." Kit smiled. "You two will fill out my stable nicely."

"Excuse me?" Apparently Luke didn't like being compared to a farm animal.

"Sorry. Just a figure of speech," Kit said. "I had only planned on finding a new manager and possibly landing some new bachelors. But today, after sending out feelers to my clients and getting positive feedback, I decided to throw together a little soiree at a hotel in Anchorage. My clients are willing to fly up as soon as my plans are firmed up. They're anxious to meet all the new Alaskan men. You know, a get-to-know-each-other event." She beamed at Jesse and Luke as if she'd found the two best pumpkins in the pumpkin patch.

"Why Anchorage?" Hope asked. "Why not have your get-together at Home Sweet Home Lodge? We would love to host your event."

Jesse liked the idea, too. That way he could fulfill his responsibilities to Tori—to teach her all she needed to know about homesteading—and still get what he needed: the opportunity to be distracted by other women. He wasn't proud of himself, trying to use Kit's clients that way, but desperate times called for desperate measures. And man, was he desperate!

Kit nodded. "You know, having the event in Sweet Home makes perfect sense. That way my clients can get an idea of what it might be like to live in a more secluded area, when they find their match."

Hope smiled as if she'd hooked a big fish. "Yes, and during the day, Donovan could take the guys out fishing or hunting, while the Sisterhood of the Quilt keeps the ladies busy."

"Sisterhood of the Quilt?" Kit asked.

"It's Sweet Home's quilting group."

Kit's smile broadened. "That's fabulous. We have a strong quilting tradition back in Gandiegow, where I live. But what about accommodations?"

It was nice of her not to say that Sweet Home was the size of a gnat and couldn't compete with Anchorage.

"It won't be a problem for your clients. We have cabins as well as rooms at the lodge."

"The men who don't live nearby can be put up by other folks around town," Jesse added. "Of course, Luke, you'll stay at my mom's house."

"Of course," Luke said sarcastically.

Kit pulled folders from her messenger bag and handed one to Jesse and one to Luke. "There's a questionnaire for each of you to fill out."

Luke shot Jesse a panicked look.

"Listen," Jesse said, "if I'm doing this, then you're doing it, too."

The cabin door opened and Jesse turned around to see Tori dressed in jeans and a cute plaid shirt tied at her waist, holding two mugs. "I thought I heard voices out here."

"Tori, come here," Hope said. "I want you to meet Kit Armstrong, the matchmaker and owner of *Real Men of Alaska*."

MATCHMAKER? REAL MEN of Alaska? Tori was thrown completely off-guard. She had a crazy thought that she and McKenna had magically summoned this woman to her doorstep by poring over the magazine last night. "Um, nice to meet you."

Kit was all smiles, but Tori was distracted by the folder in Jesse's hand.

Hope must've read her mind. "Luke and Jesse are going to be Kit's newest bachelors. Isn't that great?"

No! Not at all! Jesse didn't need help to find a woman. *Look at him!* Tori wanted to scream.

But Hope was still talking, as if she hadn't just ruined Tori's morning . . . perhaps her year. "Tori is Sweet Home's newest citizen. Jesse is giving her homesteading lessons before he starts his TV show."

"I see." But Kit was studying Tori, seeming to sense a deeper meaning in Hope's words. Hope, on the other hand, was totally unaware of Kit's perception. Tori guessed that being happily married and having running water did that to a person.

Tori suddenly remembered her manners and held up the mugs. "Would you like some woodstove coffee?"

"Woodstove coffee?" Kit said.

"Yeah. Just a disclaimer. It's the first coffee I've made without the help of Mr. Coffee or Mr. Keurig." Tori passed the mugs to the women. "I promise it won't hurt my feelings if you hate it. Just pour it in the bushes when I turn around, okay?"

Hope gave her an understanding nod. "I'm sure it's great. Thank you."

Tori knew Jesse had been staring at her the whole time. She could feel his gaze as surely as if he touched her. But she refused to give him the satisfaction of glancing over at him. "I'll be right back with coffee for the guys." She rushed up the stairs and back inside.

McKenna, the bed hog, was still curled up on the mattress.

Tori shook her. "Wake up!" she whispered so the audience outside wouldn't hear.

"Go away. I'm tired."

Tori yanked the quilt off her. "Get dressed. Apparently Jesse and Luke are looking for a love match."

McKenna sat up straight, wide awake now. "Love match? What are you talking about?"

"Kit *Something-or-other* is outside signing them up for the *Real Men of Alaska* matchmaking service."

"You're messing with me, right?" McKenna glanced around the cabin. "You're recording me to see if I'll fall for this prank, make me rush outside and make a fool of myself." She dropped back onto the mattress. "I'm not falling for it. No one is out there."

Tori rolled her eyes heavenward, knowing she would have to prove it to her sister. She opened the door. "Oh, Hope, Kit, I didn't ask. Do you take sugar in your coffee?"

"I'm fine."

"Me, too," came through the door as well.

Tori shut the door and turned on her sister . . . whose mouth was gaping like a wide-open cosmetics bag. "Satisfied?"

"No!" McKenna shot out of bed.

"You better put your game face on," Tori warned. "You look mad enough to maim someone."

"Me? You should worry about *your* face."

Tori plastered on a smile and went back out with two more cups of coffee—which left zero cups for her and McKenna.

But when she stepped out on the porch, she worried she might have been away too long. Jesse and Luke both had clipboards and were filling out their paperwork.

Blonde, brunette, redhead? Tall and skinny? Petite and curvy? Tori could only imagine the questions on Jesse's questionnaire.

Kit pulled out a notebook for each of them and flipped one open. Tori could easily see what they were from her place on the porch.

"I thought you might like to see a portfolio of my female clients. All accomplished women, all from the East Coast from good families," Kit said as she turned the pages. "You can keep those to browse through."

Tori couldn't get a close look at the photos but she was sure they were all supermodel types. She was going to be sick.

"Tori, are you all right?" Hope asked.

Tori found her fake smile and slapped it back in place. "Fine. Thanks."

Jesse looked up at her, glaring. She glared right back.

Go ahead and answer the next question, Tori wanted to say. *Do you want a woman who loves the outdoors?*

Just then, McKenna stepped out on the porch, and Tori's thoughts came to a screeching halt as she tried to register what she was looking at. Instead of jeans, McKenna was wearing Tori's best dress, which perfectly showed off her toned arms and sleek body. Her sister was a panther and looked ready to pounce on the intruder.

Poor Luke was staring bug-eyed at her. Jesse rolled his. But it was Hope who spoke.

"Oh, hi, McKenna. Come meet our new friend Kit."

New friend, indeed! Tori was nothing but jealous of Kit, who had been able to take a real shower this morning and was wearing an adorable gray ruffle-back blazer and black slacks. Cute and classy.

McKenna sashayed down the stairs and joined them in the yard.

"You look great, by the way," Hope said. "Are you headed back to Anchorage now?"

"No. Just shopping in Tori's suitcase for clothes to wear to work this week."

With a pained expression on his face, Luke made a small groan that he poorly masked as a cough. Apparently McKenna's attempt to torture Luke was working.

Jesse tapped Luke's clipboard to bring him back to the task at hand.

"Well, you're going to knock them dead at the bank. Don't you think so, Luke?" Hope asked. She had a mischievous smile on her face as if it was fun to twist the knife.

Luke's reply was an unintelligible grunt.

Kit looked over at Tori. "You've got great taste in clothes."

Tori couldn't help but look down at the rodeo girl outfit she'd picked out today of jeans, plaid shirt, and duck boots.

She'd modified the shirt by cutting off the bottom hem into two strips and quickly hand sewing them into a ruffle, just to give it the *cute* factor. It was nice of Kit to notice, and maybe in another time and place, she and Kit would've been friends, but that wasn't going to happen right now, as Kit was putting Jesse on the market.

Kit pulled out her phone, scrolled, and studied it. "I was thinking to have the event in three weeks, the weekend of the fifteenth. Jesse, Luke, does that work for you?"

Both Luke's and Jesse's heads popped up. "We can't," they said together.

Hope frowned. "What do you two have going on?"

Yeah, Tori wanted to know, too.

"We're both signed up as instructors for the Women's Warrior Weekend," Jesse said.

"We put it on the books at least six months ago," Luke added.

"What's a warrior weekend?" McKenna asked.

But it was Hope who answered. "It's a survival course for women."

"We teach novices about hunting, fishing, cooking . . . everything they need to know to rough it in Alaska," Jesse said.

Suddenly Kit and her darn Real Men of Alaska weren't the only threat. Now Tori had to worry about Jesse spending a whole weekend with beautiful warrior women? This was too much. "Did you sign me up?" Tori blurted. "I want to be proficient in everything Alaskan. No. I *need* to be proficient. Extra lessons couldn't hurt, right?" *And Jesse, you aren't going to be here forever.*

McKenna jumped into the fray. "If Tori's going, then I'm going, too."

Hope put her arm around Tori. "You don't need them to sign you up. You can do it yourself. I'll give you the address of the website."

Jesse shot a few darts at Hope this time.

Finding a computer with Internet was only one hurdle in

Tori's mind. "How much does it cost?" Right now she didn't care if she did look stupid for being so poor. She just wanted the answer. But Jesse averted his eyes as if he had the answer but wouldn't give it to her.

McKenna touched her arm. "Don't worry about the cost. I'll get us both registered."

"You have the money to do that?" Tori asked, feeling bewildered. Surely McKenna hadn't been paid by the bank yet.

McKenna's guilty look spoke volumes. Tori glared at her sister, letting her know that she wouldn't soon forget the lie she'd been told earlier.

"Well, yes," McKenna finally confessed with an I-got-caught look on her face. "Uncle Monty sent me a debit Visa card . . . for business clothes." McKenna had brightened as if proud of herself for coming up with a good excuse. "Since you're letting me borrow your wardrobe, then I won't need the money for work clothes. See, it's all working out. I'm sure there'll be enough to pay for both of us to attend a weekend course."

But Tori had point-blank asked McKenna if Uncle Monty had given her anything, and the injustice of it was nearly overwhelming. Tori knew she was overreacting but for goodness' sake, McKenna had running water and could wash her hair any time she wanted.

Tori's face felt blazing hot. "Excuse me. I forgot to fix myself some of that yummy woodstove coffee."

She turned and hurried back to the cabin. She thought she was too infuriated to cry, but she was wrong. She tried not to slam the cabin door, but she was wrong about that, too. Not one minute later, she heard footsteps on the porch and the door opened and closed. She kept busy pouring herself a *bowl* of coffee and felt sure it would taste as awful as she felt.

"I don't want to talk to you," she said, not turning around to see McKenna's lying, deceitful face.

"That's okay." It was Jesse. "You don't need to talk." Tori

didn't get a chance to whirl around because he wrapped his arms around her from behind and pulled her back against his sturdy chest. "I'm just sorry that you're upset." He rested his head on top of hers.

"I'm mad at you, too," she said in a kind of whimper. But it wasn't a bad sort of whimper. Being in his arms felt so good and so steady. He was the only tree in the forest to lean against, solid as an oak. And since he'd offered, she didn't hesitate to lean back and soak him in.

"Why are you mad at me?" he said as if trying to coax the answer from her.

"I don't know." Of course she had an inkling of what she was feeling. She didn't want him signing up with the Real Men of Alaska, where women were going to be ogling him. Or worse, pawing him! She also didn't love the idea of Jesse working with all of those strong, powerful women warriors and realizing that she wasn't brave enough or competent enough for him. All things she couldn't say.

But she could give him one piece of truth. "I'm mad because you are the most confusing man."

"Sorry." He kissed the top of her head. "I don't mean to confuse you."

But more footsteps on the porch had them automatically separating. A knock came at the door.

"Come on in," Tori said in what she hoped was a cheery voice but afraid it would come out as wobbly as she felt. She wiped the tears from her face before Luke and McKenna appeared.

"Hope and Kit had to get back to the lodge to start making arrangements," Luke said, mirroring Tori's fake cheeriness as if she hadn't made it extremely awkward for everyone. "They're going to switch the date of the event to the weekend after the Women's Warrior Weekend."

Tori took a sip of coffee from her bowl without looking any of them in the eye. "Let me gulp down my coffee and then I better get my water from the spring, don't you think?" she said to no one in particular.

Luke set the empty coffee mugs on the counter and grabbed one of the water jugs. "Jesse and I will help with the water. You might as well take advantage of our strong muscles." He grinned and curled the empty jug as if it were a herculean effort. "After that, we better finish up with the solar panels before McKenna and I have to head back." Luke continued chirpily, as if he'd been appointed today's morale officer. "Tori, I'm sure you'll appreciate the solar panels. If the sun is a-shining, you'll get enough juice in your batteries to run a small appliance. Like a lamp or a coffeemaker."

"Her coffee wasn't that bad," Jesse said.

Not exactly an endorsement of her first attempt.

"How about a sewing machine?" Luke asked. "It might be nice if she had a sewing machine here at the cabin."

"That's a great idea," McKenna chimed in, as if she was going to pull out Uncle Monty's debit card right now and produce a state-of-the-art machine out of thin air.

"Don't waste your money. I'll just borrow one," Tori said.

Jesse grabbed the other jug. "How about we give you two some privacy." The guys left.

The second the door closed behind them, McKenna spoke. "I'm sorry."

Tori knew what those words cost her. McKenna, being the older sister, rarely fessed up and apologized.

"It's okay." It wasn't really okay yet, but it would be. They'd always found a way to get over their disagreements.

"I should've told you."

"Yeah. You should have."

"I promise to tell you everything from now on. *Sisters have to stick together.*"

Tori's hard feelings softened, not because she'd completely forgiven her, but because McKenna had been saying that since Mom died. Once again, Tori could feel the tears coming on.

McKenna hurried over and hugged her. "Don't cry."

"I'm not. It's just allergy season."

"That's right. It's allergy season." McKenna let go and smiled, her own eyes misty. "Now that we're okay, can we dish on the matchmaker? What gives her the right to come to Alaska and steal all the Alaskan men for her clients?"

Tori laughed at the comical indignation on McKenna's face. "You're right. Kit has no right at all." She plopped down on the bed. "I don't like what she's doing, but she seemed nice, don't you think?"

"Yeah. She was very nice." McKenna looked pained to have to admit it.

By the time the guys returned, things were back to normal with her and McKenna.

"Thanks for the water," Tori said. "My arms appreciate the break."

"Jesse tells me that you're looking for cooking lessons. How would you like to learn to make Luke McAvoy's famous scrambled eggs?"

"Are they really famous, Luke?" Tori asked.

"No. Jesse's just hungry."

They all worked together. Jesse built up the campfire outside. Tori and Luke pulled butter, eggs, milk, and cheese from the cold-hole. McKenna brought the cast-iron skillet and a bowl to their makeshift table by the campfire, which was nothing but a plank of wood sitting on two logs.

Luke was a patient teacher and Tori hoped that Jesse was taking notes because he still had so much to teach her about the homestead.

The outside breakfast was novel and fun and it made Tori wonder if maybe homesteading wasn't so bad. When breakfast was done, the guys returned to the solar array while she and McKenna cleaned up, then hung the curtains Tori had made last night.

She stood back and admired them. "I'm really happy with them."

"Tori, come out here," Jesse called.

She hurried out to the porch. "What's going on?"

"I want you to help with the final hookup so you'll know what to look for if the solar panels have a problem in the future."

Yeah, this part of homesteading didn't sound like so much fun. Fixing things. Being solely responsible. And being all alone.

For the next thirty minutes, Tori learned about her new source of power with McKenna leaning over her shoulder. Then the four of them took the seedlings and planted them in the garden.

"We're a little behind," Jesse said, "but at least they're in the ground now."

"You'll have fresh vegetables before you know it," Luke added.

Tori stared at her poor nails, not sure if the dirt would ever come out from beneath them. But she had to admit that working with her hands had felt good, and there was something satisfying about gazing upon her little plants.

McKenna put an arm around her. "I'm having the best time."

"I'm really glad you're here," Tori said.

Luke gave them both a regretful smile. "Unfortunately, it's time for us to head back. We can only play hooky for one day, and today was it."

Tori didn't want them to go. Scout didn't either; he began to bark incessantly.

Jesse looked torn. "Don't look so sad. You'll see each other in a few weeks."

"We will?"

"The survival course," Jesse reminded them. "I assume you both still want to attend?"

"Yes," they said together. This time when they hugged they were laughing. They went inside to gather McKenna's new clothes for work and put a little snack together of cheese and sliced vegetables for the road.

Tori, Scout, and Jesse walked Luke and McKenna to the car, then said good-bye with big hugs. Tori's throat grew tight and her eyes misted up as she waved and watched them drive away.

Jesse laid a hand on her back. "Come on, homestead girl. We have things to do."

Chapter 12

JESSE DIDN'T LIKE how forlorn Tori looked. "How about we run into town first and see about borrowing a sewing machine?"

She perked up but then she looked unsure. "Are the solar panels powerful enough to run one?"

"They should be. Hopefully, when we get to Sweet Home, I'll have enough bars to check the Internet for how many watts it takes to use one. It might depend on the model."

Tori nodded. "I'll never take electricity for granted again. I'm really grateful that you and Luke put the solar array together."

"Promise you'll keep your portable generator charged for your nebulizer." It was the whole reason he'd taken Montgomery St. James to task and put his job on the line.

"Yes. Of course. If I didn't, you know McKenna would have a fit."

He smiled. "Yes. I know. I like that about your sister." Knowing that McKenna was a taskmaster when it came to Tori eased the apprehension he was feeling about leaving her alone on the homestead.

When they arrived in town, Jesse pulled into the Hungry Bear. "You might want to restock your eggs while you're here, and whatever else you might need."

"I could use a Hershey bar," she said. "Actually it might be nice to have all the ingredients on hand for s'mores in case I have *s'more* drop-in visitors."

"That's a good idea, as long as you lock up your items in the bear barrel." He should pop over to the hardware store and get her another one. "I'll be right back."

Jesse was back in five minutes with Tori's new bear barrel in the back of his truck. Tori was making her way to the cash register.

"Hey, Piney," Jesse said. "You are just the woman we need to see."

Piney lifted her eyebrows. "Spit it out," she said matter-of-factly. "I can tell you want a favor."

"Tori is going to have a bit of electricity as soon as the solar panel batteries charge up. Do you have a sewing machine that she can borrow for the homestead? And if so, what's the make and model?"

"Stop looking around like I have one under the counter. Call Hope. She'll be able to point you in the right direction and give you the make and model number, too. Once you get it, just make sure to bring the machine with you for the Sisterhood of the Quilt, okay?" Piney shot Tori a piercing stare. "I hear you're going to the WWW."

"Excuse me?" Tori said.

"The Women's Warrior Weekend." Piney chuckled heartily. "You know what we call it, don't you?"

"No."

"How to Catch a Husband."

Tori looked a bit stricken. "Really?" She aimed that question at him.

"No comment." Jesse decided to get back to their initial purpose for being here and pulled out his phone to call Hope. He scribbled down the info she gave him, hung up, and did a quick search. Unfortunately the juice from the solar panels wouldn't cover the sewing machine for very long, but he kept his disappointment from showing.

"Well?" Tori said. "Will my solar panels do the trick?"

"It's borderline," he lied. He'd have to make *another* call to Uncle Monty. If Monty saw how Tori's face lit up over sewing, surely he would want to keep that smile on her face, too. "But I'll rig something up to make it work." There was an old solar panel that wasn't being used on his homestead, just sitting around in the barn as a backup. That might do the trick until Monty came through with more panels. "Should we head out to the lodge now and get the sewing machine on our way home?" *Home*. Now, why would he use that word? Probably because he'd been spending so much time at Tori's homestead and working on it that it felt like sweat equity. Of course, it had nothing to do with its female occupant.

Tori's eyes squinted like she was examining his *home* slipup, too.

Piney's head had been swinging from one to the other as if watching a tennis match, but now she stopped on Tori. "Don't worry. I put your groceries on your tab."

"Thanks," Tori said, not meeting either of their eyes.

Jesse was determined to ask Monty why his niece couldn't be allowed to manage her own money. How else was she going to learn to live on a budget?

Piney tapped the counter. "Oh, yes. It's good you came in to remind me. Lolly says she wants you to come by her house soon for a baking lesson. She makes the most amazing cookies and cupcakes."

"Okay," Tori said hesitantly. "Thanks."

They drove out to Home Sweet Home Lodge in silence. Jesse was trying to figure out how he was ever going to get through the list of things he wanted to teach Tori. She really needed to be ready to stand on her own. Thank goodness the days were getting longer. When he pulled up to the lodge, there was a car in the driveway he didn't recognize. Probably the matchmaker's rental.

"We shouldn't dawdle too long," he said. "We still have a lot to cover this afternoon so I want to hurry back, okay?"

"Sure." Tori opened her door and got out.

He hopped out and walked up the stairs with her, fighting the urge to put a hand on her lower back to guide her in the right direction, something he'd gotten used to doing.

Hope opened the door before he could knock. "Come on in and pick out a machine."

But before they could take one step away from the entryway, Kit appeared.

"Oh, good. You're here to drop off your paperwork?" she said.

Tori went still and stiffened. Jesse imagined that if she were a cat, the fur on her back would be raised.

"No, we're here to get a sewing machine," Jesse said.

Kit started toward a large tote on the sofa. "Here, let me get you a new packet and you can fill it out now and leave it with me."

"No, no, that's okay," Jesse said hastily. "I was nearly done with it. I'll get it to you later." If he could remember where he left it. Probably in Tori's cabin when he went after her.

"Okay," Kit said. "Let me know if someone sparks your interest."

But Tori was the only woman he found interesting, for some inexplicable reason.

He must've paused too long because Kit said, "From the portfolio?"

"Oh, yes. I haven't had time to look through it." He remembered his mission. "But I will."

Tori muttered something under her breath that sounded like a death threat.

"Good. Can you get the paperwork back to me this evening? I'd like to put your info online so my clients can see it as soon as possible."

Man, he regretted getting involved. And what kind of name was *Real Men of Alaska* anyway? What a mess.

"Well, we have to pick up a sewing machine and head back to the cabin now. Then Tori has homestead lessons for the rest of the day. Just trying to make up for lost time."

Kit stood out of their way. "Yes. Of course."

When they got to the studio, Hope went to the middle of the room. "I know we talked over the phone, but really, you have a choice of several machines." She pointed out which ones were available to borrow.

"If it's okay," Tori said hesitantly, "I'd like to keep using the one from before."

"Oh, yes, that's fine." Hope walked over and unplugged it.

"Let me take a look at that." Jesse examined the power adapter's specs. "Yes, I think we can make this one work." Until he could get a better solution installed.

They loaded up the machine and, once they were in the truck, Tori spoke. "What is it that you're not telling me?"

"What?"

"Why are you worried?"

"I'm going to have to finagle things a bit."

"What does that mean?" she asked.

"The sewing machine will power up, but you won't be able to sew for very long. I'm working out a way in my head to make sure you have enough power to sew for long periods of time." What Jesse was really trying to do was to figure out how to approach Monty again so Tori could get what she wanted . . . *What she needed.*

"Oh. I see," she said. "Thank you."

"Don't be thanking me yet. I'm not sure it's going to work."

"I have faith in you."

Her words shouldn't make his chest feel warm like that.

Not a minute later, she spoke again, and the warm feeling drained. "Do you need help going through the portfolio?"

"What portfolio?" he asked. But the second he said it, he remembered. "Um, no." Absolutely not.

"I could help you narrow down your choices. I think I have pretty good taste."

Why was she suddenly being agreeable to the whole Real Men of Alaska thing? He liked it much better when she seemed angry about it. "Listen, Tori, I only did it on a lark." *And to distract myself from thinking about you nonstop.*

"Really. I could help you find someone good."

"No." The word came out harsh, and he wasn't surprised when she bristled next to him in the cab.

"You have to admit"—her voice was high and mighty—"that you're rough around the edges. Maybe I should give you lessons on being civilized. You've been on the homestead too long. I'm sure Kit's bachelorettes won't put up with you biting their heads off all the time."

He rolled his eyes and sighed. "Sorry. I shouldn't have agreed to be part of her dumb Real Men of Alaska event."

"It's not dumb. There are a lot of women out there who are giving up hope of ever finding the right guy."

"What about you? Have you ever found the right guy?" He wasn't sure why he asked, but now that he had, he certainly wanted to know the answer.

She was silent for a long minute. He finally glanced over to make sure she hadn't swallowed her tongue.

"Have you?" he asked again.

"No. Of course not." She sounded mad. "But I wouldn't mind if Prince Charming showed up at my doorstep to take me away from all this."

Her words were like a sledgehammer to the chest. And frankly, an insult to his way of life—just another example of why he had to forget about Tori St. James.

He said nothing as he pulled up her lane and the cabin came into view. What could he say? Sweet Home didn't have the nightlife that Dallas had, and Prince Charming wasn't coming here to rescue her from her misery.

He parked the truck and thought about all the men who happened through Sweet Home and who stayed at Home Sweet Home Lodge. Fishermen and hunters—mainly sportsmen from the Lower 48 who booked cabins—would be there when Tori came to sew with the Sisterhood of the Quilt. Lumberjacks came through town all the time; what if she was showering at the Hungry Bear when one of the burly men came in to have Piney make him a sandwich? There were linemen. Tourists. Heck, his own brother would be in Sweet Home soon!

Jesse felt sick. Lots of men came through town. And any man who laid eyes on Tori would want her.

Stop being ridiculous, he told himself. It didn't matter who wanted her. Jesse had a new job that was taking him away. A dream job. A new direction. A whole new future.

In that moment, Jesse renewed his decision to embrace the distraction of Kit's bachelorettes. When he was done with the homestead lessons for the day, he was going to finish the Real Men of Alaska paperwork, drive back to the lodge, and deliver it to Kit with a bow on top. Really, it would be a present for himself for relegating Tori to the back of his mind. Unfortunately, it wasn't going to be easy. Especially since they would be working closely together for the rest of the day.

He jumped out of the truck and grabbed the borrowed sewing machine from the bed. "Let's go, Your Highness. I hope you're prepared to act like a real homesteader today."

FOR THE REST of the afternoon, Jesse ran Tori ragged. She was more tired than she'd been in her whole life. Today had been a whirlwind of lessons, from mulching the new garden to building a chicken coop. Then Jesse taught her how to use the anti-bear spray, which turned out to be harder than spritzing her hair in the morning. But just knowing how to use the spray made her feel safer.

Next Jesse rushed her off to the meadow for another round of shooting lessons. She was proud of how well she'd done and he seemed proud of her, too.

After that, they cleared brush and trees from around the cabin as Jesse pointed out which trees were in danger of falling on the roof. He also showed her the healthy trees that would have to go to make a firebreak—a gap between the forest and her cabin—to ensure her safety if a forest fire broke out. He was very serious and stern as he showed her the angles of the trees and where to cut so she wouldn't get hurt or wind up with her cabin crushed.

Once she got over being scared of the chain saw, she discovered how useful and quick it was to clear trees. Having all the dead trees downed made the homestead look better, more appealing.

Because they'd worked so hard, she assumed homestead lessons were done for the day. She was wrong. They spent the remaining daylight hours cutting logs with the chain saw, splitting them with the ax, and stacking them into two different piles—one for dead wood, one for green.

"You'll use the dead wood this winter," Jesse reminded her. "Next winter, the green wood will be seasoned and ready to put in the woodstove." Tori didn't say that she had no intention of spending a second winter in the cabin. She wasn't even sure yet if she would make it through the first one.

Jesse handed her a split log. "That'll be the last one for the day. We'll get the rest cut up later."

"Thank goodness." She laid her last log on the ever-growing pile. "My arms are killing me. My legs, too. I don't think I even have enough energy to make it up the steps and into the cabin." She briefly fantasized about Jesse chivalrously scooping her into his arms and carrying her inside.

It didn't happen. Jesse only gave her that you're-a-lightweight look. "You'll be grateful for all your hard work today when it's the middle of winter." Which did nothing to ease her fatigue or give her peace of mind. Winter meant Jesse would be gone.

She didn't like the I'm-all-business demeanor he'd had all day. He seemed to put distance between them physically and verbally. She missed the Jesse of yesterday, the one who'd pulled her against his chest and let her lean against him.

She dragged herself to the cabin, went inside, and fell on the bed. All day she'd been thinking about her offer to help Jesse pick out a woman from Kit's portfolio. She wished that Kit's bachelorette stable was filled with bucktoothed, frizzy-haired, obnoxious women. The thought made Tori smile and she closed her eyes, relishing the notion.

The next thing she knew, she heard knocking at her door. She opened her eyes, expecting to see twilight, but the sun was morning-bright.

"Tori, it's me," Jesse said through the door. "It's a new day. Are you ready to get to work?"

Chapter 13

FOR THE NEXT couple of weeks, Jesse kept Tori busy. So busy that she'd fall into bed at night exhausted, without the energy to dream. Or to be scared. If the bear had come around, she wouldn't have noticed. Surprisingly, though, during the days she felt very rested and alive. It was weird how hard work could do that to her, make her feel like she could tackle anything and everything.

And tackle they did. She admitted to herself that Jesse might be one of the reasons she was bright-eyed and bushy-tailed every morning. But she was also coming to enjoy the lessons, taking pride in her accomplishments. Jesse seemed proud of her, too, but he was stingy with his praise. It felt like he was keeping his guard up on purpose. She could almost hear him counting the days, anticipating the moment when his time as her homesteading teacher would be up. So she resolved—repeatedly—to push him out of her mind.

They spent time every day cutting up more of the downed trees and adding them to the woodpiles. They bearproofed the chicken coop and finished up the day before the laying hens arrived. He taught her how to use a rod and reel—she couldn't lay a fish net in the river, he explained, because she hadn't lived in Alaska for twelve consecutive months. Jesse even mapped out where they were going to put a hole in the floor of her cabin to build the cellar he'd promised. And they constantly added to her food reserves for winter. Like they did this morning.

She'd been so excited to catch five large fish. Jesse stood over her, issuing instructions as she scaled and gutted the fish, a nasty job. But when he showed her how to fry them in the cast-iron skillet in the firepit, it was the best-tasting fish she'd ever eaten. After that they smoked the leftover fish and put it up in jars, using the pressure cooker. Not some fancy electric pressure cooker, but a big old-fashioned pressure cooker to use over the fire.

When they were done, Jesse pointed to the jars of fish sitting on the counter. "You're going to thank me for this in January and February."

Oh really? she thought. *You'll be nothing but a faded memory by then.* At least she hoped so. If he was still on her mind then, she would be in big trouble—an emotional wreck. But she did find immense satisfaction in placing the jars on the shelf and standing back to gaze upon them, her hard work made tangible.

"In June," Jesse said, "salmon will make their way up-river and give you lots of fish to put up for winter." Preparing for winter was Jesse's big thing. So she decided it was important to her, too.

Most days he took her to the meadow for shooting lessons, and he would praise her keen eyes.

"What about rabbit hunting? To get some real practice," she asked one day.

"We wait until winter to harvest them. The cold weather cuts down on the diseased animals."

Her head buzzed with all the information he threw at her each day, and she wondered if the homesteading life would ever become second nature to her like it was for Jesse.

When she finished sewing her vest, she gleefully donned

it to model for him. "What do you think? It's not perfect. I would've made it a little longer"—she pinched the fabric at the waist—"and added a couple of tucks here and here."

"It's so girly," he declared.

"That's the whole point," she shot back with loads of sass. "Would you like me to make one for you?"

"No!"

Tough. She wanted to do something nice for him, and his vest wouldn't be girly in the least. She'd already nabbed some of the extra camo fabric from the back wall of the studio to fashion him a manly version of her vest as soon as she finished McKenna's. Back at the cabin, she cut out the pieces by lantern light, hoping she'd gauged his size correctly.

The next day, more solar panels arrived, and this time, she helped him install them. When the batteries were charged, the sewing machine whirred to life and she stayed up late to finish his vest and work on the vests for everyone in the Sisterhood of the Quilt. McKenna had thoughtfully tacked the list of the other vests to her kitchen wall. Now that Tori had refined the vest, she put extra time into working on the Alaska cross-stitch for Patricia. But most of Tori's creative energy went into drawing new homestead clothes; her drawing hand could barely keep up as she sketched every night.

During their baking lesson, Lolly taught Tori how to use the Dutch oven without a kitchen. They started a fire in the firepit and made a delicious peach cobbler over the coals. It wasn't even that hard. Others from the Sisterhood of the Quilt taught her techniques and recipes, too. Miss Lisa invited Tori to her house, showed off her vast array of quilts, and then showed her how to make salmon with thyme and butter.

Every morning, Tori checked on her vegetable garden; she couldn't believe how much things had grown. Tori mused that she was kind of like her vegetables and had grown, too. She'd gotten used to not taking a full shower every day but certainly luxuriated in the times Jesse had taken her to the Hungry Bear with her shower shoes and shampoo in tow.

Another thing she'd gotten used to . . . was working side by side with Jesse every day, having him near, talking with him, sometimes laughing with him, and being able to gaze upon his face for most of her waking hours. She couldn't help but wonder what it would be like to spend all her days with him . . . forever. As she glanced at the calendar that Jesse had thoughtfully hung next to her vests-to-make list, she realized that the most magical and unexpected thing had happened over the last few weeks. She had settled in . . . and her days seemed to have a comfortable rhythm to them. If she stood still and closed her eyes and concentrated, she could almost feel the beat of the earth through her boots. She wished she could tell Uncle Monty what had happened . . . for she wasn't nearly as angry with him now as she had been. She wondered if he, too, had felt the heartbeat of Alaska when he was here.

Tori had tried so many new things, one of which was praying, which the pastor talked so much about on Sundays. When she went to bed each night, she said a little prayer for Uncle Monty, for McKenna, for Luke. She prayed for Patricia's healing and expressed gratitude for Piney, Hope, and the other members of the Sisterhood of the Quilt. She even prayed for Jesse . . . okay, especially for Jesse. And she offered up a prayer for herself, too.

"Please keep us healthy, safe, and stress-free." It was simple and basic . . . and it came from the bottom of her heart.

FOR THE PAST few weeks, Luke had been putting McKenna through her paces by teaching her every aspect of banking. Honestly, she was surprised he hadn't yet given her a uniform and had her act as the security guard for a day. In the evenings, though, they ran when the weather was good.

And for the past two Wednesday nights, they'd ordered a pizza and watched a movie. It had come about organically, and she hadn't questioned why they were spending so much time together, after being together all day. The strangest thing was that being with Luke felt comfortable and at the same time disconcerting. She just couldn't make it add up in her brain.

But during the day, when dealing with numbers, everything did make sense. Numbers came easily to her, though she just wasn't interested in the big picture, which, according to Luke, was profits. It wasn't until he placed her in the loan department that she got jazzed about the banking business. It was like a switch had been activated and her mind lit up at the possibilities.

When Luke wanted her to start foreclosing on individuals and businesses that were behind on loan payments, McKenna instead spent long hours trying to figure out a way for them not to lose their homes or the businesses that they'd built. One by one, she called the people on the foreclosure list to brainstorm ways for them to make a payment, like sell some kind of property or draw up a budget. Then she helped them come up with ways to cut future costs. Luke had asked her several times how the foreclosure paperwork was coming, and she'd put him off. So when she saw him heading her way she shoved her latest project under her legal pad and pretended to review her notes.

"I just got a strange call . . . from the CEO of Alleviate Industries. She wanted to thank the bank for going the extra mile to help save their business. What do you know about this, McKenna? Because I sure as heck didn't know a thing and felt pretty stupid on the phone. They were on the foreclosure list. How were they suddenly able to make up all their payments?"

"I don't understand why you sound unhappy, Luke. Didn't you want them to get caught up?"

He glowered and towered over her desk. "I don't like

being left in the dark. And I don't like it when my employees don't follow directions."

She stood to oppose him. "Can we talk about this in private?" She wasn't keen on being yelled at in front of everyone. Maybe she could get him to pull the blinds in his office. Was his office soundproof?

"Yes. My office. Now." He pointed the way as if she hadn't spent a good amount of time watching him while he sat at his desk or paced while he talked on the phone. Or at the end of the day, when he'd gaze out of his window. She often wondered what he was thinking about at those times.

"Are you coming?"

"Oh. Yes." She trailed after him across the bank as all eyes followed them to his office.

Once inside, he shut the door but not the blinds. He walked around to the other side of his desk. She assumed he was going to sit, so she took the chair.

He remained standing. "What did you do with Alleviate?"

"I met with their CFO and helped them figure out how to make all the back payments."

"You did what?"

"They had other property they owned outright, property adjacent to Doughton Fur Distributors that I figured Doughton could use." She straightened her shoulders, proud of the digging she'd done to get that information.

He frowned at her. "Okay. That's fine and good. I'm glad they are caught up. But what about the future? From my experience, by this time next year, they'll be in the same boat . . . *behind*. Did you consider it might be better to put them out of their misery and not let them go further into debt? Or do they have even more property just sitting around waiting to be sold to a willing customer?" He sighed heavily and ran a hand through his hair. "Who knows what Alleviate is putting on credit elsewhere."

"Oh, I know."

"What do you mean *you know*?"

"I told you I met with their CFO. We went over the books very thoroughly—assets and liabilities. We pinpointed cuts they could make elsewhere to get in the black long-term. I think things are looking bright for them."

Luke was silent for so long that she was beginning to think it might be better if he yelled. Finally, he shook his head. "It's good that you helped them. It's good for business if our customers are doing well. But how have you had time to do this? You have a stack of foreclosures on your desk that are being . . ." He trailed off and gazed at her. "You have been taking care of the foreclosures, haven't you?"

"Yes," she said confidently. "Well, sort of."

"What does *sort of* mean?" he said, sounding exasperated.

"The Petersons were behind on the mortgage because he and his wife were laid off from the hospital. She's a nurse and he's in janitorial services."

"And?" Luke prompted.

"They were able to make a payment."

"I'm glad—how were they able to do it? Did they have something lying around that they could sell, too?"

"Cash in." She'd picked their brain until they remembered.

"What did they cash in?" Luke asked.

"A stack of savings bonds that Mrs. Peterson had gotten as a gift at her high school graduation twenty years ago."

"And what about the next payment?" Luke asked.

"I helped them apply for unemployment, which they'd never done because they insisted they wouldn't take a handout. It wasn't easy to change their minds, but when I showed them how much they'd paid into unemployment insurance over the years, they acquiesced. Mrs. Peterson called this morning to tell me they'd both qualified. Plus she has a job interview next week."

"And the rest of the foreclosures?" he asked, as if he already knew the answer.

"Most of them are not going to lose their homes or businesses. There are a few exceptions. The Lyles abandoned their home and left Alaska. It's sad because there might have been a solution there, too. And Tortellini's restaurant has decided to close its doors for good."

Finally, Luke sat down at his desk and wrote some notes.

"Surely you're not upset that I helped these people."

He looked up at her. "No. But you should've let me know what was going on. It's my job to know and it's your job to discuss these things with me." His gaze dropped back to his notepad. "You can go. Close the door on your way out."

His dismissiveness reminded her of every movie she'd ever seen where the boss treated his employees as minions instead of people. She wished she could call Tori right that minute and tell her what a jerk Luke had been. McKenna angrily got to her feet and made her way to the door. He should've congratulated her on a job well done, but instead she had the awful feeling he was going to tattle on her to Uncle Monty for not being a proper banker.

As she reached for the doorknob, Luke's voice stopped her. "Wait."

She turned around to see that he had risen and was looking uncomfortable. "Yes?" Was he finally going to praise her?

"Do you want to go to a concert tonight?"

LUKE COULDN'T BELIEVE what had come out of his mouth. Had he actually asked her on a date?

"Excuse me?" McKenna said.

Apparently she couldn't believe it either.

"Um, Last Call is playing at the Wild Frontier tonight," he said. "I thought you might like to go." What was wrong with him? Montgomery would kill him if he knew that Luke was hitting on his niece or that he was asking out an employee.

"I'm, uh, flattered," she said, obviously uncomfortable,

"but I don't think it's a good idea, the two of us going out on a d—"

"I meant as friends, of course." *Who are you trying to convince?* he admonished himself. He didn't want to be just friends. He wanted more. But that could never happen. Bank rules were clear: fraternizing among coworkers was forbidden, especially bosses and employees. Yes, he'd kissed McKenna, but that was only to calm her down after the wolverine frightened her.

How had he gotten himself into this mess?

He wished he could talk to Jesse about McKenna. She was so genuine, and he liked how she stood up to him instead of simpering and agreeing with everything he said like some of his dates. Plus it was so refreshing that she wasn't coming on to him every second of the day . . . like most of the women he knew. He liked running with her after work. He liked her companionship. And he liked looking at her, too.

Why *didn't* McKenna ever flirt with him, anyway? Was it because she wasn't attracted to *him*? What if she didn't enjoy being around him as much as he liked being around her?

"Okay," she said.

"Okay, what?" he asked. Apparently he'd zoned out and missed something important.

She rolled her eyes and shook her head slightly. "The concert. I'll go with you."

He loved the slight sarcasm in her voice. It was pure McKenna.

"Right. Good. I'll pick you up at eight."

"You mean you'll knock on my door," she teased.

"Yes." He started to say more, like *How about we go out to dinner first? Swanky restaurant, candlelit table in the back corner?* But he stopped himself. "Eight o'clock."

She nodded, and he wondered: How the heck did she stay so cool? He was burning up.

He couldn't concentrate for the rest of the day. When the

bank finally closed, he wasted no time getting McKenna to the car, though he was too caught up in his thoughts to make conversation.

"I'll see you tonight," she said at her door.

"Yeah." But first he needed to get a grip.

Once inside his apartment, he changed into his running clothes and snuck out the front of the building so McKenna wouldn't see him. Running off the energy pulsing through him was the only way he'd be able to keep it together tonight. As soon as he was outside, he ran like a grizzly was chasing him.

When he got back, he stood in the shower until the water turned cold, then toweled off, wondering what to wear on a non-date date. He dressed in black jeans and a black dress shirt before going next door to get his . . . *McKenna*.

She opened the door looking super cute in a flowery dress, dark leggings, and short boots. She saw him staring and said, "Tori's clothes. She let me borrow them when we were at the homestead."

"They look nice." He should've said *she* looked nice, but he'd already bungled it. "Ready to go?"

She grabbed a jacket and they headed out.

Once they were in the car, he spoke. "I know I didn't say it earlier, but I think what you did with the foreclosures is remarkable. Truly above and beyond. I wanted to say thank you on behalf of the bank." He'd received three more calls this afternoon praising the bank's compassion and McKenna's ingenuity.

"That's good to hear. I was beginning to think that I shouldn't have made the effort, given how you were acting about it."

"Sorry for my attitude. But in the future, we really have to discuss these things first. Understood?"

She frowned but nodded.

McKenna didn't seem to like answering to anyone, and for some reason, he found that attractive.

It didn't take long to get to the venue, but finding a parking spot was another story. By the time they made it inside, the place was packed with people dancing to the warm-up band. He hadn't been to this place before so he didn't realize how few seats there were.

"Do you mind standing?" he shouted in her ear, and inhaling a good whiff of her apricot shampoo. It was intoxicating, but not as much as the feeling when she turned to answer in his ear.

"Not at all. Standing is fine." She swayed to the music, already getting into the swing of things.

They'd only just gotten here, but he was already having a great time. The song ended and everyone clapped. The drummer started a hard beat and the MC came on stage, the light pulsating to the drum. With a lot of fanfare, he announced the main event and Last Call ran out on stage, kicking off with their most well-known song. The crowd went crazy and McKenna was pushed backward into him.

He caught her around the waist and pulled her against his chest for support. He leaned down and shouted into her ear again. "If it's okay, I'm going to hang on to you so you don't get tossed around."

In response she leaned into him, or maybe it was the crush of the crowd that forced her back, but either way he was happy. Holding her in his arms as the melody of one of his favorite love songs played . . . was the best feeling in the world.

The next two hours flew by, and before he knew it, the band had finished and the lights came up. People began shuffling slowly toward the exits. Luke kept a hand around McKenna's waist so as not to lose her in the crowd.

Once outside, they moved apart, and he felt cold without having her near.

"Great concert," she said. "But I think my ears will be ringing for a week."

"Yeah." He felt awkward, wishing he could put his arm around her shoulder while they walked to the car.

"Hey, thanks for keeping me safe in there. That guy in front of me seemed determined to knock me off balance."

Darn it, he felt like an idiot for imagining it to be more. "It was my pleasure," he said.

Once the car was going, he turned on the music because he didn't know what to say. When they got back to the apartment building, he held the door wide for her, knowing there shouldn't be a good-night kiss at the end of this *non-date* but unwilling to foreclose the possibility.

They were silent as they rode up in the elevator and said nothing to each other as they walked down the hall toward their apartments.

She turned to him. "Thanks for inviting me. I had a really good time."

"I had a good time, too," he said lamely.

"'Night." She let herself into her apartment. He watched the door close and then he went down the hall to his place.

As he unlocked the door, he heard a creak and a slam.

"Wait," McKenna called. Her boots were missing and she came running toward him with only her tights covering her feet.

"Listen, I'm sorry I assumed earlier that you were asking me out on a date. I feel so silly now."

Before he could reply, she leaned up, kissed his cheek, then was gone again, running back to her apartment.

He reached out as if his arms would stretch that far, but she was already back inside. And he was left alone and confused.

What did it mean . . . a kiss on the cheek? Was she telling him that she liked him and wanted more, like he did? No, she'd just made a point of saying they weren't on a date. But if that was the case, why kiss him at all? How frustrating that she'd run right back to her apartment. If she'd stayed, he would've pulled her into his arms and given her a proper kiss good night. Bank rules be damned.

But he wasn't dumb. The bank was his life, his future.

He and McKenna apparently were only meant to be friends. Since a romantic relationship wasn't in the cards, at least they could be buddies.

But he had enough pals.

And he didn't think he could stop his stupid heart from pining after her anyway. Was it too much to ask to change how things were? Was there a way to change the future? A future where he wasn't her boss . . .

Chapter 14

THE WOMEN'S WARRIOR Weekend finally rolled around. Jesse shoved his backpack in the truck and drove to Tori's cabin.

She opened her door the moment he stepped out of his vehicle, and Scout ran to greet him.

"Come on in," Tori said. "I'm almost ready." She disappeared back inside.

He flashed back to her large suitcases at the airport and cringed at the thought of what she was going to bring with her now. *It's not my problem*, he told himself.

"Are you sure it's okay if Scout spends the weekend with Hope and Donovan?" Tori was gazing at Scout as if she didn't trust anyone but herself to take care of him.

"They assured me that Boomer was looking forward to it. Donovan has years of experience raising dogs, you know, and he says it's good to keep them socialized."

"Okay. If you think Scout will really be all right." She leaned down and gave Scout a kiss. The puppy reciprocated by giving her a kiss on the cheek.

Jesse couldn't believe he was jealous of the dog.

To keep from watching her pack her things, Jesse looked at the calendar he'd tacked on the wall. He had put it there as much for himself as for her, as he'd been counting the days. They'd both been looking forward to the Women's Warrior Weekend, but for different reasons. The next two and a half days would give him a reprieve from Tori. Yes, she was attending, but he wouldn't be her teacher. She would be another instructor's problem. Jesse had done some finagling to make sure of it by asking Luke to steer McKenna in choosing the sisters' courses. Actually it was more like he'd pleaded until Luke finally complied, with a heavy dose of ribbing.

But Luke didn't understand how torturous it was to be with Tori, day in and day out. She made him laugh. She made him crazy. She made him feel *too* alive, feel too much of everything. All of it was unfamiliar and uncomfortable, and honestly, he didn't know where to put those emotions. The bottom line was that Jesse needed time away from Tori to gather his wits because spending every day with her had driven him to distraction.

He'd worked hard to keep his distance, but he still felt drawn to her. Was all his hard work in vain? But this weekend, others would be responsible for Tori's education and give him the break he needed.

Suddenly the image of another man leaning over Tori, guiding her, popped into Jesse's head, which didn't ease his mind either. "I'll just pray that she's only assigned female instructors."

Tori looked up from her overpacked suitcase. "Did you say something?"

"No. Sorry. Just thinking aloud." He changed the subject by pointing to her things. "I'm certain you're not going to need a blow dryer."

She touched her hair. "I just wanted to try something different. When we were at the Hungry Bear on Wednesday, I saw this really cute style on the cover of *Country Woman* magazine."

"Your hair looks fine the way it is," he said, more gruffly than he meant to. Every time she came out of her shower at

Piney's, Tori had a different 'do going on with her bobbed hair.

Tori gave him a stubborn and determined smile before turning back to her suitcase and placing a curling iron in there, too.

"What I mean is," he started, "I like your hair the way it is." Heck, he liked her hair whether it was long or short; even a crew cut would be fine. *Tori was Tori*, no matter what her hair looked like. "We better get going."

She shut the bulging suitcase but couldn't close the zipper.

"Here. Let me," he offered.

She stood back while he compressed the suitcase into submission. When it was zipped, he picked it up without mentioning the impressive weight and looked around. "Is all the food locked up tight? I don't want our bear friend to stop by for a snack."

"Yes. All the food has been barreled and locked down."

"Woodstove?"

"The fire is out. I even poured a couple of mugs of water on it to make sure it wouldn't come back to life after I left."

"Then we're ready to go." He held the door open and she walked out.

As they made their way to the truck, he heard himself say, "You know, you can always use my mom's house to do your hair, if you want." Now where had that come from?

"Thank you. I might sometime."

She opened the passenger door and Scout jumped inside, looking ready for a road trip.

"Don't get too comfortable, boy," Jesse warned. "You're not going to the WWW."

When they arrived at the lodge, Tori took Scout to the door while Jesse stayed by the truck. He waved to Hope but took the moment to get a grip before the long drive to Anchorage.

When Tori was settled in the truck and they were back on the road, he asked, "Have you been camping before?" He glanced over to see her brow wrinkle.

"Once. McKenna made me. She loves to camp."

"How did it go?" But he already knew by the expression on her face.

"It was a complete nightmare. Cold, wet, and miserable. The worst part was that there were rocks—sharp ones—right under my sleeping bag. I swore I'd never go camping again."

"And yet . . ."

"This time I'm on a mission," Tori said determinedly. "And you said there were cabins."

"Don't expect the cots to be comfortable, though," he warned.

"I won't," she said. But then under her breath she added, "I don't expect anything to be comfortable anymore."

Without stopping to think about it, he reached over and squeezed her hand. "It's all going to be okay. I promise." He quickly let go when he realized he didn't want to.

For a moment the space between them felt awkward, but then she spoke. "Tell me about *your* worst camping experience."

He chuckled. "Luke and I decided to go camping in early March, thinking we were tough enough to withstand the cold weather. We were ten. My brother, Shaun, was so mad we wouldn't let him come along."

"Why not?"

"He was only a baby, eight at the time."

She joined him in laughing.

Jesse continued. "My mom and dad were against us camping alone but let us go anyway." He could see Tori's disapproval in his peripheral vision. "In truth, I believe my dad followed us."

"What about Luke's parents? Did they try to keep him from going?"

"Luke doesn't have a mom. Never did really, unless you count my mom. Luke's dad wasn't really good at being a dad either and never really kept track of what Luke was doing."

"That's sad," Tori said.

"Don't feel sorry for Luke. He was the most popular guy in school. He got all the girls. He was great at sports. And look at him now. A successful bank manager? Nah, Luke's parents weren't much, but Luke certainly turned out okay."

"So what happened on this camping trip?" she prodded.

"It was a comedy of errors. First, we got lost trying to find the trail up the mountain, but just when we were getting panicked, we picked it back up. While we were hiking, we ate all our food—M&Ms, Cheetos, Little Debbies. You know, those Swiss Roll cakes that Piney has at the store? So when we found what we thought was the perfect camping spot, we had nothing to eat."

"What about water?" Tori asked.

"Yes. That was one thing Mom and Dad made us carry with us."

"So you were hungry . . ." she prompted.

"And cold. We couldn't get the tent to stay up; it kept blowing over. Then it started snowing. When we couldn't get a fire going to save our lives, we shoved all our gear into our backpacks and headed home."

"What did your parents say?"

"Dad told us to clean our gear and put it away. Mom put supper on the table without a word. I noticed my dad's boots and jacket were covered in snow—that's why I think he was keeping an eye on us."

"And after that? Did you and Luke go camping again?"

"All the time, but much better prepared, believe you me. That trip taught me a lot. I think we became pretty good mountain men."

"You certainly look the part," she said shyly.

He glanced over and saw she was blushing. "Rough edges, I know. But being a mountain man has served me well all these years."

"And Luke? Does he still camp and go hiking?"

"You bet. He's still an outdoorsman through and through."

"He doesn't look it, though."

Jesse felt a twinge of jealousy. "So you're into the businessman type?" Why'd he say that? He shouldn't care what she liked.

She was silent for a moment, as if pondering the question. She shrugged. "Honestly? I don't know anymore."

Then she did the darnedest thing. She reached over, took his roughened hand again, and squeezed it. The shock of her touch and the pounding of his heart had him nearly driving them off the road. But he pulled it together. Just like he'd been pulling it together the last several weeks, every day an exercise in mental agility, dodging and fighting against his growing attraction to Tori.

He pulled his hand from hers and gripped the steering wheel. Why did she have to go and do that? He pressed down on the accelerator to get them there faster. Yes, a weekend away from Tori would do him good.

They didn't talk again until they pulled up to Luke's apartment building.

"Is this it?" Tori asked, a little wistfully.

"Yes," Jesse said.

"It looks nice."

He wanted to contradict her and tell her that living on a homestead beat a concrete building every day of the week. But he didn't. "I'll text Luke to let him know that we're here."

A few minutes later, Luke came to the back door and held it open.

They both got out. A second later, McKenna appeared beside Luke, but, unlike him, she tore through the door and ran down to envelop her sister in a massive hug.

That was when Tori realized what she was wearing. "We're going to look like twins."

"I love my new vest. Thanks for sending it, sis."

"Thank Jesse. He's the one who mailed it off."

"Come in and see the apartment," McKenna said. "It's a twin of Luke's."

Tori raised her eyebrows.

"Stop giving me that look. Luke said the apartments are identical."

"So you've had him over?" Tori asked.

"Of course not." McKenna looked guilty and Jesse didn't believe her. "Luke's my boss," McKenna added, as if that explained everything.

Jesse saw Luke frown and wondered if he should ask him later what McKenna's dodgy explanation was all about.

Luke followed them down the hall. "Before we leave, I have something for the sisters. Step into my apartment and I'll get it." He gave McKenna a look as if to say *Compare apartments for yourself.*

McKenna went in first. "What is it?" she asked eagerly.

"A present from your uncle."

Luke handed them each a box. "Satellite phones so the two of you can keep in touch. They came with this note." He picked up the paper and read, "'Thirty minutes a month. Use them wisely.'"

"That's a minute a day, Tori," McKenna said cheerfully.

But Tori disagreed. "Maybe a minute every other day."

"How's that?" McKenna said.

"I should save some minutes in case I have an emergency and need help."

McKenna looked chagrined. "You're right. I should've thought of that." She gazed admiringly at her sister.

Jesse was proud of Tori, too, for thinking like a homesteader.

But it was Luke who spoke. "That's exactly how a homesteader should think. Good for you, Tori."

Jesse was annoyed. He should be the one complimenting Tori, not Luke. "Let's get going," he said gruffly.

"Come see my place, Tor." McKenna and Tori took off down the hall.

Luke turned to Jesse. "Why are you glaring at me?"

"Nothing. Let's go."

Soon, they were in Luke's car—men in the front, women in the back. The men were silent, but the sisters couldn't have cared less. They were happily chatting away and catching up. Thirty minutes later, they were pulling into camp, which wasn't far from Anchorage.

Jesse felt nostalgic as they drove down the tree-lined road. He and Luke had been volunteering at WWW for ten years, and one summer they had even attended church camp here. The dark wood cabins surrounded by trees were like familiar old friends, and he felt like he would be able to breathe soon . . . as soon Tori was out of the car and out of sight.

Luke pulled into the parking lot, where other campers were unloading their camping gear. He spoke over his shoulder. "I'll show you where to check in. Then Jesse and I have to meet up with the other instructors, okay?"

"Okay." Tori looked around as if she'd never gone to summer camp before. Though Jesse could give her the grand tour, he was only her homestead teacher, nothing else.

"Come on," Luke said. "I'll introduce you to the leaders staffing the registration table."

Jesse stayed where he was as Luke walked Tori and McKenna over to meet Darla, Maeve, and Jason—three other regulars at WWW. They were from different areas of the state, and he only saw them on these weekends, but they all felt like a little family.

But as soon as Luke left the St. James sisters at the registration table, Big Dan sauntered over to them. *Big Dan!* Big Dan was an unscrupulous instructor who took advantage of the Women's Warrior Weekend to flirt and to gather phone numbers.

Acid built up in Jesse's stomach. What if Tori and McKenna weren't immune to Big Dan's charms? All the other women buzzed around Big Dan as if he were flypaper.

Luke returned. "What's wrong with you? You look like you want to throw a punch."

Jesse pointed to Big Dan. "Aren't you concerned about McKenna?"

Luke looked at the women gathering around the monster bodybuilder. "I'm not worried. McKenna seems to have a pretty good crap detector."

But at that moment, McKenna laughed at whatever Big Dan had said, making Luke glower. Big Dan wrapped an arm around each of the St. James sisters and squeezed. "How about I escort you to your cabin?"

Jesse didn't hesitate, hollering, "Dan? You're wanted in the mess hall."

Big Dan turned around. "Yeah, sure, fine. Tell 'em I'll be there as soon as I get these lovely ladies settled into their cabin."

"Totally smooth," Luke said sarcastically under his breath.

"Me or him?" Jesse countered. "Never mind. I don't want to know."

TORI SHRUGGED OFF Big Dan's gargantuan arm. "Excuse me. I have to get my bag."

McKenna didn't look any happier at being pawed either, and she rid herself of this Big Dan guy, too. "You better get to the mess hall. It sounds like you're needed. We can find our cabin on our own."

Dan winked at them. "Okay, I'll see you later."

"Not if I see you first," McKenna said under her breath as Dan lumbered away. "Can you believe that guy? Let's get going."

"Wait." Tori wanted to stay right where she was because three women had approached Jesse and Luke. She was feeling a bit territorial and worried those women were on the hunt for the perfect mountain man. "What do you think they're up to?" she said, gesturing toward them.

"Up to no good, by the looks of it." McKenna's frown seemed to be focused on Luke.

A redheaded woman laid a hand on Luke's arm and laughed as if he'd said something incredibly funny.

McKenna dropped her bag and started toward them, but Tori pulled her to a stop. "Think this through. Maybe it's harmless flirting." Or maybe it wasn't. The most amazing thing was that Tori had never seen her sister jealous. She started to poke fun at her, because even though McKenna had said she was impervious to good-looking men, apparently her declaration didn't apply to Luke. But in the next second, Tori wasn't laughing. Her blood was boiling. A tall woman with black hair leaned in playfully toward Jesse, which made Tori want to swat her away . . . with a bat.

"I know what to do." McKenna locked eyes with Tori but hollered to the men. "Jesse, Tori wants you to show us to our cabin."

Tori glared at her sister. "What are you? Three years old?"

"Older than you," McKenna said. "Look. It worked."

Jesse had left the group and was stalking toward them.

"Luke?" Tori called. "McKenna needs help carrying her bag."

McKenna pinched her.

"Ouch. It worked, didn't it?"

Luke smiled, left the trio behind, and joined them. "I'm happy to help. And thanks for rescuing me. New campers," he said, as if that was explanation enough.

"Oh, it must've been awful for you," McKenna cooed sardonically.

Jesse took the map from Tori and pointed. "Your cabin is right here." He motioned to the east. "Go down this trail. You can't miss it."

Luke picked up McKenna's duffel. "Come on. We'll show you."

McKenna reached out. "I can get my own bag."

"Let him do it," Jesse said, "he likes to show off his muscles."

Tori watched as McKenna's eyes found said muscles and got so distracted that she didn't fight with Luke over the bag again.

They made their way across the parking lot and down the trail.

"Truthfully," McKenna said to the guys, "how do you handle all the attention from the women here? Or is that the reason you volunteer?"

"Hardly," Luke said. "We volunteer because we like to give something back to the community. Some of the women get a little flirty sometimes, but it's harmless. And it's only two and a half days." He hitched a thumb at Jesse. "This one, though, ignores the women altogether."

Good, Tori thought.

"Have you ever been tempted?" McKenna persisted. Tori wanted to know this, too.

"No," Luke said, causing Jesse to scoff. "Okay, maybe a little. But I view these women like students . . . or people I work with."

At that, McKenna snatched a glance at Luke, a glance filled with knowing disappointment.

The walk through the woods was peaceful. The trees canopied the trail, making it feel like a forest tunnel. Tori snuck a look over at Jesse. He quickly looked away, which made her wonder if he'd been gazing at her, too.

The woods cleared and Luke aimed a finger at the water ahead. "The lake is over there. That's where you'll learn water safety and canoeing. That trail leads to another camp just like this one."

Ahead of them sat six identical cabins arranged in a semicircle around a grassy area, each one about the same size as Tori's homestead.

"What's that?" McKenna asked, pointing to the building that was larger than the cabins.

"That's the restroom."

"Please tell me there's running water?" Tori asked, hoping against hope.

"Yes," Luke said.

"Hot water, too?" Tori ventured.

"Yes," Jesse answered.

Tori whooped. "I may spend the whole weekend there."

"How about you put your things into the cabin first?"

"Sure, smarty pants." Then she remembered her blow dryer and curling iron. "What about electricity?"

Jesse shook his head. "Sorry, princess, not in this camp."

McKenna opened her mouth as if to let him have it for being snarky, but Tori touched her arm and shook her head, and McKenna calmed.

"Your cabin's that one, the third on the right." Jesse pointed.

A short distance away sat another, larger cabin.

"What's special about that big cabin? Why is it all by itself?" McKenna asked.

"Counselor's cabin when the kids are here," Luke said. "But while you ladies are here, that's where your camp leader will take up post."

"Luke says Annabelle is your leader," Jesse said. "She's an excellent teacher and has been doing this longer than Luke and me."

"Annabelle works at the bank," McKenna told Tori. "She's friendly."

Luke opened their cabin door and let Tori and McKenna enter first. There were three bunk beds, making the occupancy six. A small open closet, with a wood divider vertically down the middle, sat next to each bunk bed, clearly too small for Tori to hang the five outfits she'd brought for the two and a half days.

Jesse lifted Tori's suitcase a little higher. "Which bunk do you want?"

Tori deferred to her sister. "Any preferences?"

"Let's take the one in the center," McKenna suggested.

Jesse set Tori's luggage by their closet. "We have to get back to receive our marching orders. Can you two make it back to the mess hall by yourselves? Or should I send someone to fetch you?"

Surely he wouldn't send Dan.

"We're good," McKenna said. "See you two later."

Luke set down McKenna's duffel and said, "So long. We'll see you at the welcome, but we probably won't see much of you this weekend. Annabelle usually has everything under control and doesn't use floaters like the other instructors do."

But thirty minutes later, when Tori walked into the mess hall with her sister by her side, she couldn't help but scan the large room for Jesse. He was standing at the front, frowning, with his arms crossed over his chest.

"Wow," McKenna said. "Your boyfriend looks mad enough to wring someone's neck. Is he always that ticked off at the world?"

"First, he's not my boyfriend. He's my homestead teacher. And secondly, I've never seen him look so angry."

Signs were posted around the room. Their instructions were to find their clan, Timber Wolf, and gather around that table with other members of their camp.

Jesse's gaze fell on her and his brow furrowed even more. He looked even grouchier than when Big Dan had been trying to chat them up.

A Mother Earth–type woman took front and center, raising her hand. "I'm Amy, your camp director, and I want to welcome you all here for the Women's Warrior Weekend. The folks in the brown shirts by me are your instructors, coaches, and trainers for the weekend." She introduced each one, and each raised a hand when called.

Tori leaned over and whispered to McKenna. "Did I miss where she introduced Annabelle?" Which wouldn't be surprising as Tori had her eyes—and brain—trained on Jesse.

"No, Annabelle must be running late," McKenna said.

The director looked back at her staff. "Go join your clans for the weekend."

Jesse rolled his eyes, dropped his arms, and walked toward the tables. Tori wondered which table of women would have the honor of spending time with him this weekend . . . and jealousy reared its ugly head as she scanned the other tables for the trio of women who were talking to him earlier—and found they were behind her, gathered at her own table!

Tori looked up to see where Jesse had gone and found that he was headed toward her! And Luke was right behind him.

Chapter 15

LUKE SMILED WHEN he should've felt bad that Jesse was so miserable. But, hey, Luke won the coin toss, which made Jesse the leader. Luke looked forward to being an assistant for a change, as he spent his life at the bank as the one in charge. He took the seat across from McKenna.

She leaned on the table. "What's wrong with Jesse? And where's Annabelle?"

"Annabelle's kid got strep throat. And Jesse's annoyed that he had to take her spot as leader of the Timber Wolf clan."

"Does he always get this upset when there's a change in plans?" McKenna asked.

"No," Tori answered for Luke. "At the homestead, our plans change all the time and he adjusts quickly."

"It's bigger than that," Luke added. "He had a vision for what this weekend was going to look like. He's perturbed things won't go as planned."

"Then why are you smiling?" McKenna asked.

"It's about time someone forced this butterfly from his cocoon."

Tori opened her mouth but Jesse began to speak.

"Hey, everyone, I'm Jesse Montana, here to take Annabelle's place as clan leader for Timber Wolf Camp." He jutted his thumb at Luke. "This is Luke McAvoy, *my helper*." He glanced around. "I recognize a few faces here. Raise your hand if you've previously taken part in the Women's Warrior Weekend."

Four people raised their hands, and Luke waved back. But that was when he noticed that the three women who'd stopped him and Jesse earlier were smiling at him. He wasn't looking forward to being thrown together with them for the next few days, because McKenna hadn't been thrilled that the ladies had done a little harmless flirting earlier. Maybe he'd have to act like Jesse and not be as friendly as normal. He glanced at McKenna and saw her eyes were shooting daggers at the three . . . which, weirdly, raised his spirits.

His spirits were also raised at the prospect of spending time with McKenna. But the truth was she would probably be too busy with her classes to even notice that he was there helping.

Jesse was wrapping up his speech. "I hope everyone is ready to learn."

Luke jumped in. "And have some fun."

"Yes. Right. Now, a quick note about the logistics of the mess hall." Jesse explained that they were expected to dine together as a clan, and how everyone was required to bus their own tray, one clan at a time. "Just remember that all the instructors and kitchen help are volunteers and are here out of the goodness of their hearts. So don't expect to be pampered." Jesse's eyes scanned the women but didn't land on Tori. Luke wasn't surprised, since Jesse had been talking up her accomplishments.

"Right after dinner, we'll gather at the far corner of the mess for our first-aid class." He pointed to the north side.

The dinner bell rang and the tables at the end of the room rose and walked toward the kitchen to pick up their trays. During their meal, Tori and McKenna spoke animatedly to each other. The room buzzed with excitement, everyone anxious to get on with the weekend. As each table stood and cleared their places, Timber Wolf waited patiently as they were second to last.

But as they rose, there was a commotion in the kitchen. Camp director Amy, who had been calm and collected before, ran from the kitchen with blood on her hands. "I need help!"

Jesse was the first one to her, with Luke right behind him. "Where did you cut yourself?" Jesse asked.

"It's not me," Amy said. "It's Nicole. She's nearly sliced her finger off prepping for tomorrow."

Jesse turned to speak to Timber Wolf clan. "Come with me. First aid is hands-on tonight."

They all ran into the kitchen to see two volunteers supporting Nicole, who clutched her hand. Blood pooled on the stainless-steel counter in front of her and dripped onto the floor. Luke grabbed the first-aid kit from the wall and went to them.

Jesse leaned over Nicole but spoke to Timber Wolf clan. "The first thing we do is remain calm. Who can tell me what the second thing is?"

"Stop the bleeding," answered the black-haired woman who'd flirted with him earlier. "I'm a nurse," she added, looking around at the others.

Luke pulled out a large sterile pad and handed it to Jesse.

"Sorry. It's going to hurt," Jesse said gently to Nicole. He glanced up at the clan. "Apply pressure and do not look at it for five minutes. Even if it soaks through the pad. Just keep pressure on it. What's next?"

"Call 911," McKenna said with her phone already out, looking as if she'd had to make that call a time or two. "I'm on it."

Tori grabbed a chair and helped Nicole sit. She was white as the stack of clean dish towels resting on the shelf.

"What's next?" Jesse asked.

"Clean the wound," one woman said.

Jesse shook his head. "Not yet. Let's remove any jewelry

near the area so if there's swelling, blood flow will continue and not cause nerve damage." He nodded to a different woman. "Can you slip off her ring?"

The woman gently slipped the ring from her finger. "I'll find a baggie to keep it safe."

Methodically, Jesse walked the women through the proper steps, making each take part in the triage of the patient—cleaning the wound with soap and warm water, bandaging the wound, and applying ice—even mopping up the blood on the floor so no one would slip. Luke noticed that Tori seemed to be in the thick of it, every step of the way.

Twenty minutes later, the ambulance arrived and Nicole was passed off to the professionals.

Jesse rounded up the clan and praised them for keeping their heads. "Let's head back to camp, where we'll continue your first-aid class."

"How about McKenna and I stay behind and disinfect the kitchen?" said Luke.

Jesse looked at him with an eyebrow raised.

"We'll wash the dishes, too."

Jesse nodded. "Okay, then." He led the others from the kitchen, with Tori giving McKenna a backward glance.

"So," McKenna started, "why did you volunteer me instead of the redhead who has the sexy eyes? She was definitely giving you the green light." She paused. "Oh, right. You couldn't have her dirtying her hands with all this." Like a model from *The Price Is Right*, she swept an arm wide at the mess in front of them.

Before he could respond, McKenna stepped around the corner, returning with a mop and bucket in hand. "Okay, I get it. Uncle Monty told you how I took over kitchen duty when we were in Morocco. The paid help came down with a bug and I stepped in. It was no big deal."

"Yeah, something like that." Luke couldn't tell her that she hadn't come close, partly because he wasn't sure why he'd volunteered her to hang back either. The only thing he knew was that he wanted to spend time with her.

He disinfected the counter and she bleached the floor. When they were done, she went over to the industrial dishwasher.

"We definitely didn't have one of these in Morocco. Do you know how to work it?"

He pulled the suspended water hose down and showed her how to use it. "Just give the dishes a little rinse. Then load the tray into the bin." He added more trays. "Then slide it into the dishwasher and pull down the door to close it." Immediately the dishwasher came on. "It will do a wash cycle and hot-water rinse, which will sanitize the trays and dishes. Just be careful you don't burn yourself as you pull out the bin." Within thirty seconds, the cycle was done and he lifted the door to remove the bin. "Do you want to give it a try?"

"Sure. Move over and let me drive."

He smiled at her confidence and her competence as she worked the dishwasher like a pro. Of course, he couldn't help but stand over her while she worked.

But standing near her was stirring up strong emotions he didn't know he had. He blanched as he remembered that Montgomery's ban on fraternization within the bank was crystal clear. But Luke's brain felt foggy as she stood right in front of him with her barely shoulder-length feathered hair swaying side to side as she worked. She didn't wear makeup and didn't need to. She was a natural beauty in mind, body, and spirit. He wanted to pull her into his arms, but instead, he walked away.

He now understood what Jesse was going through. This feeling shook the steady ground Luke stood on. He wanted to run for the hills to put distance between himself and McKenna, and at the same time, he wanted to take the leap and make all kinds of declarations to the world. Jesse had been smart about wanting to put distance between himself and Tori. If only Luke had known what was going on and done the same with McKenna.

But somehow, it was too late for that now.

BACK AT TIMBER Wolf camp, Jesse announced that first-aid training would resume at the campfire in twenty minutes. All the ladies walked away, chatting . . . except for Tori.

"Is something wrong?" he asked.

"Do you know when Luke and McKenna will be done? Better yet, how about I head back to the mess hall and help out? Many hands make light work."

"I don't think so, Miss Philosopher. Surely they won't be long." Jesse pulled out his phone and texted Luke: Hurry back.

"The whole point of coming on this trip," Tori said, "was to spend time with McKenna."

"I thought the whole point was to learn new wilderness skills." He stared at her; she was caught in her own web.

"You know what I mean. Of course, I need to learn new skills . . . but I've missed my sister."

Tori's vulnerability had a way of making him feel weak, and right now, he felt as helpless as a newborn pup. If only he could wrap her in his arms and comfort her, it would fix everything and make him feel powerful again. "I know you've missed McKenna. She's basically all you talk about. If it's any consolation, I texted Luke and told him to hurry." He decided to change the subject or else he wouldn't keep the promise he'd made to himself, the one where he would put his feelings for Tori behind him. "You seemed pretty levelheaded during the medical crisis back there in the kitchen."

"Practice makes perfect," she said lightly.

Suddenly Jesse realized that he'd veered into dangerous territory again. Her asthma attack and all the emotion of the event rushed back—the fire, smoke, panic . . . it consumed him. He had to put it aside and focus on her. "So were you the practice?"

"My mom, too."

He nodded in understanding. She'd told him about her mom and the fatal asthma attack the first night at the cabin.

"Our therapist says that's why McKenna and I can remain calm during a crisis. We were conditioned at a young age." She shrugged as if it were no big deal. "As I said, practice makes perfect."

But it was a big deal, and Jesse couldn't help himself anymore . . . he pulled Tori into his arms, hoping the tree branches shrouded them from peering eyes. "I wish you'd never had to go through it, though."

She pulled away. "People are coming."

Yes, two women had stepped out of their cabins and started in their direction. He turned around and saw three more coming out of Tori's cabin. They would all get the wrong idea if they saw Jesse and Tori together. Hell, he had the wrong idea, too.

"It's not a big deal," Jesse said gruffly. "It was just one friend comforting another." Yeah, it was bull. He'd crossed the line again and given Tori another round of mixed signals. What the hell was wrong with him?

TORI CHOSE A log from one of the many surrounding the campfire ring and took a seat. She wondered when McKenna would get back from cleaning up the kitchen. The other Timber Wolf campers selected their spots, too, and waited while Jesse lit the kindling and logs in the firepit.

He passed around a handout to all. "Here are some notes about first aid. Be sure to study this later." He looked over at the nurse. "Though some of you clearly won't need it."

The kitchen accident, it seemed, had been an excellent icebreaker, for the clan chatted animatedly like old friends now. As Jesse went over new information, questions flowed freely about when to use a tourniquet, how to treat a burn, and what to do about back injuries.

McKenna and Luke showed up about thirty minutes into the lesson. She sat next to Tori on the log.

"What did I miss?" she whispered.

"Nearly everything," Tori whispered back.

"Can I get a volunteer to be the patient so I can show you how to wrap a sprained ankle?" Jesse asked. McKenna shoved Tori's elbow, which vaulted her arm into the air, but another woman—medium height, blond, busty—jumped up and ran to the front before Jesse could make his selection.

"I'll do it!" She was hopping and hobbling as she tried to pull off her shoe and sock as she went. It's a wonder she didn't break a limb in the process.

Jesse wrapped Busty Volunteer's ankle, and then he showed them how to make a sling out of a long-sleeved shirt. When he'd completed both tasks, he thanked the woman and gestured for her to go back to her place.

Jesse held up the handouts again. "Every one of you should take a CPR class and get the first-aid manual recommended on the last page. Also, make sure you put together a comprehensive first-aid kit for yourselves at home. There's a list of items on page three or you can buy a ready-made kit. Just remember, you can never be overprepared here in Alaska." He glanced at the counselors' cabin like he was ready to escape. "We're done for the night. If you like, you can hang out at the campfire for a while." He pointed to the container beside him. "The last one to leave, use the bucket of water to put it out. Just keep in mind that we expect you to be up early in the morning." He looked over at Tori. "Have a good night's sleep."

It felt like he was speaking only to her. It was what he said through the door as she dropped the slat into place every night. She wondered if he was thinking about it, too. But in the next second, she was sure he wasn't. He wasn't a sentimental fool like she was. And he didn't have a crush on her like she did on him. So why had he given her that nice hug earlier? More than nice.

McKenna looped her arm through Tori's. "Stop staring at the pretty man and let's get to our cabin."

Walking in front of them, Busty Volunteer was talking. "I heard that Jesse is going to be on a TV show." She glanced back at them. "What do you know about it, Coppertone?"

Tori touched her face, pretty sure her spray tan was faded by now.

But the woman went on. "Is Tall, Dark, and Hunky your boyfriend or something? We all saw you two together."

Tori started to object but then remembered it wasn't a good idea to protest too much. "We're friends." That was the simplest honest answer. But her silly heart wanted more.

"What's she talking about?" McKenna looked piqued.

Now Tori worried that she'd given something away with her tone. She tried again. "He's my neighbor. He's helping me on my homestead."

"Lucky duck," the nurse said. "I'd sure like to have those biceps hanging around. I'm Sheena, by the way. This is Bea and that one is Talia."

So Busty Volunteer was Talia. And Bea was the short one.

"Nice to meet you," Tori said.

"Nice to meet you." McKenna followed suit, though Tori was sure she didn't quite mean it. After they introduced themselves, they explained that they were spending a year in Alaska, as they all entered their cabin.

"What about the other one?" Bea pointed an accusatory finger at McKenna. "Why'd Luke choose you to help clean up the kitchen?"

"I'm irresistible?" McKenna said.

Tori rolled her eyes and told the truth. "Luke is McKenna's boss."

"Is he single?" Bea asked.

"Yeah, I want to know that, too," Talia said.

McKenna straightened her shoulders and said with conviction, "I believe he's taken."

Tori muttered, "That's news to me."

McKenna shushed her. Later Tori would prod her sister into telling her what was going on.

"What about Dan?" Bea inquired. "Is he available?"

"He's all yours," Tori and McKenna said simultaneously, then laughed.

"What's wrong with Dan?" Sheena asked. "He was very nice."

"He's not my type," McKenna said.

"Not my type either," Tori concurred.

"I have to ask—where did you get your vests?" Talia asked.

"Yeah, I was wondering that, too," Sheena chimed in.

"Tori is a clothing designer for the discerning outdoors woman."

Tori nearly choked on thin air. And before she could stop McKenna from lying more, her sister continued.

"She made these two vests so we could show them off this weekend and start taking orders. Limited availability. When they're gone, they're gone." McKenna sounded like a senior marketing manager. "What do you think?" She pranced in front of them and spun around in a circle like the cabin was a runway.

"You're a clothing designer?" Bea asked.

Tori shook her head, but McKenna answered, "Yes. A very talented one."

"How did you come up with this?" Talia moved closer as if to get a better look.

Tori glanced at McKenna to see if she was going to field this one. But when she remained silent, Tori told the truth. "I didn't want to wear what looked like men's clothes just because I'm in the wilderness."

McKenna slipped off her vest and held it out. "Look. It's very functional. She put in all kinds of pockets."

The three women passed the vest around, gushing, which was very embarrassing—not to mention Tori was feeling guilty for judging these three earlier. They weren't that bad.

"You could make a fortune with this," said Talia.

I doubt that, Tori thought.

"Can we get on your list? One for each of us." Sheena turned to her friends. "My gift to you, my bestest friends forever!" The other two women squealed and thanked her profusely . . . and Tori hadn't even agreed to make them vests yet.

"Yes, of course, we'll add you to the list," McKenna said with more confidence than Tori was feeling. "Keep in mind that her clothing is in high demand and there are people in front of you. I'll need your payment up front and I'll write you a receipt, of course." McKenna was acting like this was a real business. "Make sure I get your sizes and your contact info so I can put you in the system."

What system? Tori glared at McKenna, hoping she could read her mind.

"I'll do it now." Sheena pulled a notepad from her backpack and ripped a piece of paper from it and wrote something on it. She pulled out her checkbook, too.

"You ought to see Tori's other designs," McKenna said, really running off the rails now. "She's come up with a whole line of clever and stylish wear. She's certainly making me look better when I'm hiking on the trail."

"Oh?" Sheena looked intrigued. "Do you have pictures of your designs with you?"

"No," Tori lied. Her sketchpad was in her suitcase, along with her colored pencils.

"My email address is on there." Sheena smiled broadly, and Tori softened even more toward her. "Shoot those images to me. If they're as nice as your vest, I'll want to order more things from your collection."

What collection? She only had drawings of clothes and hats she'd like to make for herself. She made a noncommittal sound.

"I'll make sure to send you pricing, too." McKenna took the notebook paper from Sheena. "Remember, designer clothing doesn't come cheap." She tore the end off the contact list and wrote something on it before handing it back to

Sheena. "Make the check out to Tori St. James for the amount listed."

Tori glared at her sister as she grabbed her toiletry bag. "McKenna, walk me to the restroom."

"Sure. Let me get my stuff."

As soon as they were outside, Tori laid into her. "What is *wrong* with you? Why would you tell them that I'm a designer? I don't have the credentials to back that up. I only have a few scribbles in my sketchpad."

"You're selling yourself short. These vests are a work of art, and those three"—she jabbed a thumb back at the cabin—"have the good sense to recognize it."

"Please tell me how I'm going to get vests done for them when I already have so many to do for the Sisterhood of the Quilt."

"You're going to hire some of the ladies in Sweet Home. I'm sure there are women there who could use the work. Just think, you could be providing jobs for stay-at-home moms or people who need to earn a little extra in retirement."

Tori rolled her eyes and stomped away, speaking over her shoulder. "You forget that I don't have any money!"

McKenna caught up and wrapped an arm around her. "That's all about to change. Sheena's check will be waiting when we get back. You'll cash it at the bank before you return to Sweet Home."

"You're nuts," Tori said.

"You'll see that I'm right about this."

"Let's change the subject." Tori was frustrated because her sister was so exasperatingly annoying. But later, she'd regret not savoring every minute with her. Tori held the door open to the facilities.

"I forgot to tell you that Uncle Monty sent me a gift card to a salon." McKenna laughed as if that were the most hysterical gift ever, but then sobered when she looked in the mirror. She held her hair back from her face. "I wondered if Luke said something to him. Like I wasn't sophisticated enough for the bank."

"Surely not." Tori messed with McKenna's hair, too, positioning it this way and that, trying to decide on the best style. "It was probably Peggy's idea."

"Maybe this weekend you can give me an idea of how I should get my hair cut and fixed. You've always been so good with stuff like that. And I'm complete rubbish at it."

"Sure. I think you just need it shaped a bit. Before I head back to Sweet Home, let's pick up a couple of magazines and flip through them. You've got great hair—so thick, and a beautiful color. You might as well get it cut to show off your gorgeous face." Tori looked at her own hair. It had always been lighter than her sister's, but in a few months, all her highlights would have grown out and her hair would be closer to the color of McKenna's dark honey. Tori wasn't upset about going to her natural color, though. She retrieved a headband and facial scrub from her toiletry bag. "It's nice Uncle Monty sent the gift card."

"And you the solar panels and generator," McKenna added.

"It makes me feel like—"

"Like he's right here with us?" McKenna finished.

"And that he still loves us."

"But wouldn't it be even better if he just called—"

"Or wrote us a note?"

"Yeah," they said together wistfully.

Tori turned to McKenna. "So tell me about Luke. What's going on with you two?"

McKenna blanched, but then recovered, rolling her eyes. "Nothing's going on with us. What about you and Jesse? Have you been k-i-s-s-i-n-g?" she singsonged.

"Same as you," Tori lied as she tossed water on her face. "Nothing going on."

"Yeah."

When Tori looked up, McKenna's expression said she knew Tori was fibbing, too.

She paused—as close as they had always been, it was weird that they were shutting each other out now. Tori couldn't figure out what was going on with herself, let alone decipher why McKenna was being closedmouthed. Yes, Tori could rectify it by telling her sister that she had feelings for Jesse, but what good would that do? Jesse wasn't into her, and she didn't want to look weaker in McKenna's eyes than she already felt.

"Any more asthma attacks?" McKenna studied Tori's face as if waiting for her to lie again.

"No," Tori said. "In fact I haven't used my inhaler in almost two weeks."

"That's wonderful news. Just so you know, I threatened Jesse when I was at the homestead, telling him he better tell me about any breathing issues . . . or anything else that goes on."

Tori hugged her. "Always the big sister."

THE NEXT MORNING, Jesse and Luke waited for the campers at the trail. Tori, McKenna, and their three bunkmates were the first to show up. Though he shouldn't be, Jesse was especially glad to see Tori this morning. Surely it was because he'd gotten used to seeing her first thing every day.

He couldn't help but smile at Tori and McKenna. "You two look pretty tired."

"Thanks a lot," Tori said.

Luke elbowed him. "Never say that to a lady."

"We're all tired," Sheena piped in. "Those two kept us awake, yapping and giggling for most of the night."

McKenna smiled at her. "I seem to remember you three joining in."

"Anyway," Jesse said, "we've got a big day. Make sure you get plenty of coffee at the mess." By the time he'd finished, the rest of the women from Timber Wolf camp were headed in their direction.

Breakfast and cleanup went much smoother than last night, with no near digit dismemberment, thank goodness. Afterward they headed to the meadow where the field dressing class was set to take place, which Jesse would lead.

He stopped at the edge of the meadow. "A little introduction. It can be nerve-racking when you see a buck or a bull moose. After taking your shot, especially if you're lucky or skilled enough to bring down the animal, the adrenaline is really pumping. At that moment, take a breath and remember these rules: first, stay alert and make sure no other apex predators are around. Second, approach cautiously and make sure the animal you shot is in fact deceased. Finally, I personally say a prayer of thanksgiving for the bounty that will feed my family and me in the coming months. Then I get to work. Just remember that field dressing is messy and smelly, so prepare yourselves, okay?"

The group was silent. "Come on." He led them into the meadow to Luke, who was standing over the body of a black bear. Jesse continued, "There are a lot of YouTube videos on how to field dress an animal, but it's very different in person. Watching a video won't give you the experience of dealing with real blood and guts. You have to look at it as a job . . . the job of survival for those of us who live a subsistence lifestyle. It's important to use every part of the animal. Nothing should go to waste." He looked directly at Tori to make sure she understood, and she nodded.

Slowly he talked them through each part of the harvesting, and gave a turn to all those who were brave enough to take the knife—including Tori, he was proud to see.

He answered questions and then showed them how to wrap the meat to drag it out of the meadow, making sure they all had a turn to see how tough it could be to heft the meat home.

The next class was meat processing, which was the natural next step after field dressing. The women all seemed more at ease with processing and packaging than with field dressing. He kept reminding his group that if they were lucky enough to bag a big-game animal, their efforts would be rewarded with a full freezer at the start of winter. "As for this meat here today, it's going to the local food bank."

After they broke for lunch, Jesse and Luke started a lesson in orienteering, while distributing a compass and map to each camper. After they presented the basic instructions and passed out a handout with an exercise on it, Jesse said, "Let us know if you need further help."

Tori immediately raised her hand.

"Luke, can you see to Tori?" Jesse said, delegating to his assistant.

"I can't." Luke grinned broadly. "I'm needed over there." He pointed to a group of women who had their heads down, studying the handout, and clearly needed nothing at the moment.

Fine. Reluctantly, Jesse walked over to Tori. "What do you need?"

"I know this is important and I want to get it right. Can you explain again about how to use the dial?" Her eyes held all kinds of earnestness.

He had no choice. He leaned over to position the compass on the map to demonstrate how to use it. He was so close he could smell her shampoo . . . and whisper sweet nothings into her ear, if he was so inclined. The experience was pure torture, and for a moment he forgot why he'd walked over. To make things worse, she had no idea the agony she was causing him.

This weekend should've been a reprieve from his beguiling student, but instead, it had turned into more of the same. With his voice feeling thick and sounding hoarse, he showed her how to do the first few steps on the handout and quickly stepped away.

ON THE SECOND night of the Women's Warrior Weekend, Tori was wiped out . . . in a good way. Sharing this experience with McKenna had been fun. McKenna seemed pleased that Tori had graduated from being a *sissy city girl*—McKenna's words—into more of an outdoorswoman, for which Jesse deserved all the credit. But Tori couldn't tell

McKenna the truth because she wouldn't be able to hide how much Jesse meant to her.

Tori climbed up into bed and stretched out while McKenna leaned against the top bunk and said, "We haven't talked about it, but you do realize that the matchmaking event is next weekend?"

"Yeah." Tori was dreading it. "Piney said we're all expected to help get the lodge ready." Tori had been dragging her feet, not signing up for any specific duty, but sooner or later, Piney or Hope or someone else in Sweet Home would call her on it. Being part of a small community had been just as much of an adjustment as living on the homestead. Tori couldn't blend into the woodwork anymore if there was something she didn't want to do—anonymity didn't exist in a close-knit community. Her life now was as transparent as glass.

"You know what I think?" McKenna said.

"What?"

"I should visit my sister in Sweet Home next weekend."

"Definitely."

"Maybe Piney and Hope could use my help, too."

Tori could always tell when her sister was holding something back, but she didn't question her. She simply said, "I'd love for you to be there." Having McKenna there next weekend might help keep Tori from doing something rash, like spiking the punch with Dulcolax. "Can you give me a hint of what you're thinking?"

McKenna gave her a hug. "Don't worry. We'll be there to keep them from doing something stupid." She didn't need to identify *them*, as Tori was thinking the same thing about Jesse and Luke.

THE FINAL MORNING of the warrior weekend started with fishing at dawn. At the lakeshore Luke passed out thermoses of coffee, to much appreciation. Within the first few casts, McKenna rose to head of the class, as she had a real knack for landing her fly and bringing it in. But Tori held her own during the lesson on how to gut, scale, and cook their fish over the campfire.

While the campers sat around the fire and ate, Jesse and Luke stood off to the side and assessed.

"McKenna is quite the fisherwoman," Jesse remarked.

"Yeah. I'm proud of her, though I had nothing to do with her skill. Not sure why I feel this way."

But Jesse had the same feeling a few hours later, when his phenom hit the mark with nearly every pull of the trigger.

"Wow," Luke said. "Tori got another bull's-eye. She's one heck of a shot! You said she was good, but you didn't say she was this good."

"I know." Jesse couldn't stop grinning. "She has natural talent. The real test will be taking her on a big-game hunt." He had a feeling she was going to do fine. Yet he couldn't help but wish he had a full year with her—all four seasons— to teach her everything. Even *that* didn't feel long enough. He hated that he would have to leave her soon. *But why?* he asked himself. The answer was daunting and made him uneasy. He'd never felt this way about a woman before.

Before Jesse knew it, WWW was over. The weekend had been a success for the women warriors. But Jesse hadn't come close to attaining his goal of forgetting about Tori. If anything . . . he wanted her even more.

Chapter 16

TORI WAS SO happy to be home in her own bed with her dog cuddled up beside her that she woke up smiling on Monday morning. Scout had been so excited to see her that when Hope brought him out on his leash to greet her, he kept knocking himself over with how hard his tail was wagging. Silly dog.

"Come on, sweetie. Lots of work to do today." She quickly dressed and had some chores done before Jesse pulled in.

She went out to meet him, but he didn't leave the side of his truck. "Come on and bring your dog. I thought we'd run over to my house and I'd teach you how to milk a goat."

"But I don't have a goat. Just chickens at the moment."

"A trial run to see if you'd like to have one of your own."

When they arrived at the Montana homestead, Jesse guided her directly to the barn. "Mom's still asleep," he said, taking Tori to the milk stand. In no time, he'd taught her how to milk the sweetest little goat.

When they were done and walking back to the truck with the container of milk, Jesse's mother appeared on the porch and gave a friendly wave. Even though she moved slowly, she looked remarkably better, Tori thought.

"So nice to see your mom," she said when they'd climbed in the truck.

"Thanks, she's doing really well. Her recovery is making it easier for me to leave for the show, you know?"

Yeah, Tori knew, and was happy for him. But not so happy for herself.

Back at her homestead and after depositing the fresh milk in the cold-hole, Jesse grabbed a shovel from the back of the truck. "I'll start digging the root cellar." They'd cut the hole in the floor last week. "What are you going to do?"

"I need to weed the garden. But shouldn't I help you?"

"There's only room for one to dig. Besides, it's back-breaking work." He gave her one of his radiant smiles with a teasing glint. "You'll appreciate my hard work come winter."

She smiled back. "Thank you for being my homestead hand." Really, she didn't know what she was going to do without him.

After weeding the garden, Tori went to the meadow on her own to practice shooting. When she returned, Jesse was laying in the first boards to the wall of the root cellar. "The hole needs to be deeper, but that's a start. We should get to Home Sweet Home Lodge."

When they arrived, she and Jesse parted ways as he went to find the guys. While the Sisterhood of the Quilt helped Kit get ready for the bachelorettes, Tori worked on vests and pumped people for information about the Real Men of Alaska venture. Apparently in Scotland, Kit had been combining her matchmaking service with fishing trips for the men and quilt retreats for the women, and she said she was thrilled to be offering it here in Alaska, too.

Donovan, Jesse, and Rick were also helping with setup and putting together a fishing adventure on the river out behind the lodge. Hope pointed out to Kit that if her bachelorettes wanted a break from sewing—or an opportunity to check out the eligible men in action—all they needed to do was step outside and sit in one of the rockers on the back porch.

Meanwhile, Jesse came by each morning and he and Tori had coffee, and then they spent a few hours gardening, fishing, or digging the root cellar. Around lunchtime, they would head to the lodge. Piney basically forbade Tori from doing anything but work on the vests for the WWW women. How did Piney know about the paying customers? McKenna told Luke, Luke texted Jesse, and Jesse blabbed to Piney. Piney, in turn, had assigned Aberdeen, Lolly, and Paige to help Tori work on her orders.

"Our gals can wait on their vests," Piney insisted. "The first rule of business is to keep the customers happy, especially the *paying* ones. So get your paying orders done first, then work on the Sisterhood of the Quilt vests."

With the help of the other three Sweet Home seamstresses, Tori was able to get the WWW vests shipped off quickly and then get back to the vests for the Sisterhood of the Quilt.

During breaks from sewing, Lolly hauled Tori off to the kitchen to practice baking, something Tori enjoyed very much . . . especially the eating part of the lesson. Jesse benefited, too, as they usually had leftovers in the morning with their coffee.

On Friday, Tori and Jesse remained at the homestead all day instead of going to the lodge. Even though they had completed the root cellar, things weren't working smoothly between them. Granted, Tori had been hyperfocusing on Jesse's every word and action, looking for signs that he was excited about meeting a bunch of luscious women this evening.

"Why are you frowning at your lunch?" He sounded like he was itching for a fight. "Your soup is going to get cold if you don't start eating."

"I can't believe you're making me live without a microwave." She might be looking for a fight, too.

"I'm not making you do anything. You've been cranky all day. Didn't you sleep well last night?" he asked, kind of angrily.

"Slept like a baby," she said sarcastically.

"Well, all I have to say is that you're in a mood." He took a swig of water as if her mood were of no consequence.

She might as well put it out there. "I bet you're looking forward to this evening. Thrilled to meet a bevy of new women?"

"Tori, do I seem thrilled?"

"I don't know."

He looked irritated. He looked like he was in pain, too, which honestly made her feel better.

He scooted his chair back and stood. "Let's finish up and get the logs split. After that, I'll run you in to the Hungry Bear, if you'd like. Come on, Scout."

It was considerate of him to remember that she'd need a shower before McKenna arrived later this afternoon.

Satisfied—at least for the moment—Tori stood, too, and followed Jesse to where they'd left the logs from yesterday's haul. For the next hour, physical labor relieved some of her pent-up stress and she felt better. But Jesse seemed to get crankier by the minute.

When the last log was stacked, he grumbled, "Let's get to town."

When they walked into the store, Tori grabbed a Snickers bar and tossed it to Jesse. "This should help with your *hangry* issue."

Frowning, he caught it, and instead of tossing it back, he tore the wrapper open and took a bite, looking as pleasant as a riled grizzly bear.

Tori turned to Sparkle with an eye roll. "Please put that on my bill."

Sparkle smiled and nodded as if she was enjoying the show.

But the sugar didn't quash Jesse's attitude. When she was done at the Hungry Bear, he dropped her off so he could run home and get cleaned up, too. Luke and McKenna arrived at the homestead before Jesse returned.

Scout ran out to greet them, but McKenna was also in a bad mood. Luke—who looked great in his business-casual button-down shirt and dress slacks—seemed miserable, too. Normally he was as good-natured as they come, but Tori felt certain that the long drive with McKenna had caused the distress on his face.

"Where's Jesse?" Luke asked.

"He'll be here any minute. He ran home to get primped for his date . . . or dates, as the case may be." The words tasted like vinegar. She looped her arm through McKenna's and the two of them went into the cabin, leaving Luke to wait for Jesse.

As soon as the cabin door was shut, Tori turned to her. "Jesse has been hard to be around all day and Luke seems rather unhappy, too. I think the guys have a case of nerves."

McKenna sighed. "We're all anxious about tonight."

"So . . . ? I've been waiting patiently to hear the plan for this weekend. What did you come up with?" Surely McKenna had concocted some brilliant strategy to keep the guys from being snatched up at Kit's matchmaking event. Because Tori was pretty certain that McKenna liked Luke as much as Tori liked Jesse.

McKenna groaned. "Nothing. I couldn't think of a thing. Which is so unlike me!"

"Darn it. I was counting on you." Tori's stomach churned unpleasantly. If only she weren't expected to help out tonight, Tori would hide out in her cabin under a quilt and not come out until Jesse wed one of Kit's perfect bachelorettes and whisked her off with him to his new job. "What are we going to do?"

"I don't know." Distractedly, McKenna picked up Tori's sketchpad. "What are you wearing tonight?"

Tori walked over to her makeshift closet, a bar suspended from the ceiling with chains on which to hang the clothes she'd brought with her, plus her new designs. She pulled out her new plaid sheath dress to show her sister. "Paige gave me this tartan from her stash. She said this lightweight worsted wool doesn't work in the quilts she's making these days. She's famous for her plaid quilt designs, you know. She teaches at large quilt shows and guilds all around the U.S."

McKenna rushed over. "I love that dress. It's adorable. And classy."

"It hugs all the right places, too," Tori admitted, pulling it from the hanger and holding it up to her shoulders.

"Perfect for the homesteader going to a fancy party. How do you come up with this stuff?"

"I just see it in my head and sketch it."

McKenna flipped through the drawings. "These new designs are really fantastic. I can't believe all the new outfits you've come up with in the last week."

"Yeah, going to the Women's Warrior Weekend provided some great inspiration. Did you see the hunting outfit?"

McKenna flipped back to that page. "That's really cute."

"Look at the shoulders. I'm going to add Velcro at the shoulders so you can attach a waterproof/bloodproof bib for field dressing animals."

"Ingenious."

"What are you wearing tonight?" Tori asked as she heard Jesse's truck pulling up outside.

McKenna held her arms wide. "You're looking at it."

"You can't," Tori cried. Her sister looked ready for the rodeo in jeans, a denim jacket, and a tee shirt with *Cowboy* stamped on it. Just a bit of the front was tucked into the jeans, showing off the big belt buckle. Instead of cowboy boots, though, she was wearing her trusted Merrell hiking boots.

McKenna put her hands on her hips defiantly. "I can and I will wear this. I could've gotten all dolled up, like you are. But I've decided not to compromise who I am. I can never compare to the kind of women that Kit is bringing tonight. And I don't want to. If men want those sexy supermodel types, then let 'em have 'em." Of course, McKenna didn't mention which men she was speaking of, but Tori knew exactly who.

"Rebellious. Stubborn—" Tori said.

"Yes, but I've got to be me."

"Okay." Tori hugged her. "I love you just the way you are."

"Yeah, that makes two of you—you and Mr. Darcy from *Bridget Jones's Diary* . . . who doesn't really exist."

Tori laughed and hugged her again. "You're adorable. But you need to change out of that jacket. I'll lend you one that will work better. Your hair looks amazing, though."

McKenna stepped back and smiled shyly as she touched her newly styled locks. "It's really easy to take care of. It's strange to admit it, but I really like the way it looks, too." She sounded a little distraught.

Tori smiled and shook her head. "It's okay to feel like a girl. I promise your tomboy membership won't be revoked."

McKenna gazed out the window. "A new haircut doesn't change anything."

Tori knew McKenna's last statement was about Luke and the matchmaking event this weekend. "Leave it to me." Tori was pulling something out of thin air, putting it together on the fly, actually grasping at straws. But something had to be done! Desperate times called for desperate measures and all that jazz.

"Leave what to you?"

"Tonight." The only thing Tori could come up with was to *fight for what is ours*. Then inspiration hit, or maybe it was divine intervention. She would fight, but not just for her and McKenna.

"What are you going to do?" McKenna looked concerned.

"Don't worry your pretty little haircut over it," Tori said. "I've got it handled." McKenna might not want to compete with the women at the lodge this weekend, but Tori sure would. She wasn't a supermodel, but she understood the latest styles better than most professionals. And what she needed tonight was to transform into someone formidable.

Tori slipped off her clothes to put on her new dress. For what she needed to pull off this evening, her blown-dry hair was too cute. She dug around in her cosmetics case and pulled out a tube of styling gel, something she hadn't used since she arrived. She squirted out nearly a palm full and ran it through her hair.

McKenna frowned. "What are you doing?"

"I'm going for a look." She slicked back her hair and then glanced in the small square mirror that Jesse had hung for her on the bathroom door. She retrieved her black eyeliner and dark eye shadow and generously applied them.

"You don't look like you," McKenna said. "Right now you remind me of some of those severe-looking women on the runway. Are you going for intimidating?"

"No. More of a *I mean business* look."

There was a knock at the door. "Are you ready?" It was Jesse. "Hope said she wanted you there early."

"We're coming." Tori grabbed the matching plaid buttercup purse she'd made from the dress fabric.

"You're going to shock the pants right off Jesse," McKenna muttered.

"Just trying to give him something to remember when Kit parades her model types in front of him."

Tori opened the door and stepped out. Scout barked as if he didn't know her and Jesse nearly fell off the porch. She stopped her satisfied smile from coming to the surface because she was in badass mode right now, and she was pleased that he was too stunned to do more than gape at her. Tomorrow she'd have to triple-wash her hair in the basin to get the gel out . . . but tonight, his reaction was worth it. Then she got a load of what he was wearing. Black jeans—new black jeans!—a black shirt, and cowboy boots that looked as if they were only worn for Sunday best. He actually took her breath away and for a second, she forgot why she was standing on the porch.

"You look great, Tori," Luke said from the bottom step.

"Um, thanks."

Luke leaned to the side to glance beyond her. "McKenna, aren't you going to change?"

"Nope. I'm fine just as I am."

Luke shrugged. "Suit yourself." He waited for McKenna to come down the steps before heading to his car.

They took separate vehicles to the lodge. Tori rode with McKenna and Luke. Jesse couldn't seem to find his voice and rode alone with Scout.

"Scout is going to the event?" McKenna inquired.

"He has a playdate with Boomer, Hope's dog," Tori said. "If you haven't noticed, Scout pretty much goes everywhere with me."

At the lodge, Piney stopped Tori with a suspicious, "Why are you all gussied up? You're here to help, not to be one of the bachelorettes."

"Just wanted to try out my new dress," Tori said in a chipper voice, hoping to sound like a maid who was ready to work.

Piney jabbed a finger at Tori's head. "Why does your hair look like that?" She waved her hand around Tori's face, indicating her makeup. "You were heavy-handed when you painted the barn, too. What's going on with you?"

Hope moved closer as if to displace Piney. "That dress is amazing, Tori. I love it." She spoke over her shoulder. "What do you think, Donovan? Should I order one?"

"You would look great in it . . . but I think you look great no matter what you wear." He beamed at his wife.

Aberdeen, Lolly, and Paige came into the living room.

"Love that dress!" Lolly exclaimed.

"You sure put that fabric to good use," Paige remarked, smiling broadly. "Do you have a list going for that design, too?"

McKenna, who had been right beside Tori, stepped forward and pulled Tori's sketchpad out of her bag. "Yes. Just use a clean sheet at the back. And while you're at it, take a look at her other designs that will be available soon." The three women followed McKenna to the table to see the drawings. "Of course, you'll all get the Sweet Home discount."

Tori rushed over to grab her sketchbook. "Why do you have that with you?"

"Marketing," McKenna said. "I decided while Kit had her clients here, maybe they'd like to place their orders, too."

"I'm sure their stylists wouldn't approve of my doodles."

McKenna gave her that look. "You know good and well that your sketches aren't doodles. You have a gift, Tori, and you should share it with the world. I'm here to give you a little push."

More like a hard shove from the high dive.

She reached for the sketchbook one more time but was stopped by the front door opening to reveal Kit Armstrong.

Tori braced herself, making sure her badassery was completely in place as she made her way to Kit.

"I need to talk to you," Tori said bravely. "You hurt the feelings of the single women of Sweet Home."

"Oh?" Kit gave her a worried look.

"It was inconsiderate not to ask them to be part of your event. Around here, we believe in including everyone. We're a community and we support each other." Tori motioned to the table where her sister and three of Sweet Home's finest were gawking at her. "You could've just set up something for the singles in the area. If it'd been up to me, you never would've been allowed to bring your rich, long-legged, sexy clients here."

"Ummm," Jesse cleared his throat. He stepped around Kit and placed his hand on Tori's shoulder.

She became aware that a bunch of women had come in behind Kit and were now scuttling to form a semicircle around her. Tori was confused, not sure who they were supposed to be.

The women surrounding Kit were of all shapes and sizes, mostly wearing designer jeans and silky shirts. They were clearly from out of town, but there wasn't a super-model in the lot. They weren't even particularly sexy either. Just normal people. No Botox. Not a fake boob among them.

"I-I . . ." Tori didn't know what to say.

Jesse pressed down on her shoulder to turn her around and force a retreat, rescuing her from the pitying looks that were appearing on everyone's faces. She glanced up at him to see that he was giving her a pitying look, too. "Come." As he moved her away from the door, he said lightheartedly, "Just give her a minute. I think she's a little thirsty."

The second he got her in the kitchen, Rick and Sparkle cleared out, obviously embarrassed. An uncomfortable fog surrounded Tori.

He went to the cabinet, pulled down a glass, filled it with water, and handed it over. "Drink," he said, then added, "What's going on with you? Has all that hair gel seeped into your brain?"

"I was trying to look out for Sweet Home's women." She stared down at the glass but didn't bring it to her lips.

"I don't believe that's the only thing."

"Well, it is." Finally she looked up and again saw that look on his face. "Stop staring at me like that!"

"Like what?" More pity filled his eyes.

"Like I'm the most pathetic person in the world."

"Drink your water and pull yourself together."

There was a knock on the jamb. "Can I come in?" Kit didn't wait for an answer and entered with that same worried look on her face. "Listen, Tori, you were absolutely correct. It was rude of me. I never should've overlooked the women of Sweet Home. This isn't the first time I've had tunnel vision when it comes to finding matches for my clients. And it's not the first time I've been called on the carpet for it either." She laughed ruefully as if remembering. "At the same time, I assumed all the eligible bachelorettes who wanted to be matched were already taken, as Alaska has the highest male-to-female ratio in the United States. But once again that was just me putting blinders on. Of course, there are women here who would like to get paired up." She gave Tori a knowing look.

Tori was stunned by Kit's graciousness after how Tori had acted.

"I'll make it right with the locals," Kit continued, "and do what I do in Scotland."

"And that is?" Jesse said.

"Give my help pro bono to all the singles in the area who want to find true love." Kit paused as if for dramatic effect, then added, "Starting with the two of you."

Time froze. Tori's grip on the glass tightened so much that she was surprised it didn't shatter. All oxygen in the kitchen had disappeared, too, and Tori couldn't draw a deep breath, though she felt certain she must've gasped at Kit's offer.

Jesse looked like he'd taken a fist to the chest—his eyes were bugged out, staring at Kit in incredulity. "What do you mean?" he finally said.

"That you two are a match." Kit said it like it was a simple fact.

"No, no, no." He jabbed a finger at Tori. "Tori and I have a professional relationship. Nothing more."

In that moment, Tori's heart broke into a million pieces. She willed herself not to cry. If McKenna had been in Tori's place, she probably would've punched Jesse. Clearly, Tori was not that strong.

She ran for the front door. Outside. Down the porch steps. She saw Jesse's truck and stumbled toward it, knowing he kept his keys in the sun visor. She got in, turned the key, and peeled out.

Despite herself, she laughed through her tears as she drove away from Home Sweet Home Lodge.

He'd stolen her heart.

So she stole his truck.

Chapter 17

"WELL, ARE YOU going after her?" Kit's tone said she wasn't asking.

Jesse went to the door and watched as his truck raced down the road. "She took my truck," he said in disbelief.

Luke rushed over to him. "Where did Tori go?"

"No clue," Jesse said. He loved his truck. It was the only big-ticket item he'd ever bought himself . . . and now it was gone. "Who steals a man's truck?!" But then again, he'd embarrassed Tori. It hurt to have to tell Kit that he wasn't interested in being set up with Tori, but dang it, he was leaving soon. Starting a new career. A new life. A clean slate. It made no sense to jump into a relationship with Tori now.

"We have to go after her," Luke said to McKenna. He laid a hand on Jesse's shoulder. "We'll find her. Just pull yourself together before she gets back, okay?"

Jesse shook his head but couldn't find words to express his feelings. It wasn't a good idea for Tori to come back. He'd want to pull her into his arms and tell her he hadn't meant it. Probably make a declaration that he had no right to make. Certainly kiss her. And he would never let her go. But he would have to let her go. He was leaving!

McKenna glared at Jesse as she passed by. "My sister is crazy about you. She didn't deserve that."

As Luke ushered McKenna out the door and to his car, Piney appeared. "Kit said the men will arrive any minute. I need you outside with Donovan and Rick to meet them."

Jesse came out of his fog and realized he should've gone with Luke and McKenna. Instead, he was going to be stuck in bachelorette hell for the next several hours. To be fair, the women seemed sweet and lovely. They certainly didn't deserve the likes of him. He would probably just do something to hurt them, too.

Donovan laid a hand on his back. "Come on, dude, time to meet the competition."

The chimes of the clock rang seven. The rest of the evening was going to be torture.

INSIDE HER CABIN, Tori heard a vehicle pull up. She kept pouring water over her head, washing out the gel. By the time she'd reached the homestead, she knew she would have to go back and apologize to Kit and her clients for ruining the matchmaking event. She heard someone hurrying up the steps and had no delusions that Jesse had come after her. She'd grown up too much since coming to Alaska for that nonsense.

The door burst open and Tori was glad she'd changed into a work shirt and jeans the second she got home.

McKenna rushed to her side. "Are you all right? What are you doing?"

"Where's Luke?" Tori asked.

"Waiting outside for the all clear." McKenna scanned Tori from her wet hair to her tear-streaked face, down to the hem of her jeans. "Now talk to me." Her eyes traveled to Tori's new plaid sheath crumpled on the floor where she'd stepped out of it. McKenna picked it up and hung it on a hanger.

Tori's face flushed, remembering. It had been the dumbest idea ever to try to act like a badass tonight. It had only made her downfall more shameful. Maybe if she'd been in Dallas she could've pulled it off, or maybe not. She wasn't the same person anymore. And she had the sinking feeling she wouldn't fit in with the Dallas crowd anymore either.

"I'm washing out the hair gel," Tori said. "It's not me. I'm no longer the stylish sophisticated woman I thought I was." She wrapped a towel around her head and pulled on the ends of her work shirt. "I don't fit the homestead either." She was a woman without a place in this world.

McKenna hugged her and then dragged her over to the hanging clothes. "Keep the jeans; those are cute. But pick out one of your new designs."

Begrudgingly, Tori pulled down a white blouse made out of a moose and bear print. She was so pleased that she'd thought of putting four vertical pleats on either side of the buttons. It wasn't badass, it was classy, and she needed all the class she could get right now.

"That's adorable." McKenna dug around in her bag. "Here're your short boots. They will pull it all together." She laughed. "I bet you never thought you'd be taking fashion advice from me."

Instead of seeing the irony in it, Tori gave her sister a sad smile before changing into the homestead chic blouse. She idly thought that "Homestead Chic" would make a clever label for a line of cute clothes for the homesteading woman.

Tori combed her hair without looking in the mirror and was sure she looked more like a blond Orphan Annie now than a badass bombshell. "I'm ready."

"No, you're not." McKenna grabbed a washcloth and wet it. "Fix your makeup."

Tori glanced at her reflection in the mirror. "I look like a sad goth clown."

"Yeah, but a little soap and water can fix it."

If only she could fix her shredded heart as easily.

When Tori stepped onto the porch, Luke graciously didn't comment on her appearance.

"Back to the lodge?" he said cheerily.

"Yes," McKenna answered, but then she frowned. "Thanks for bringing me. I never would've found the homestead on my own. I hope you didn't miss out on too much socializing." She didn't sound all that sincere.

"No problem." Luke turned to Tori. "Do you want me to drive the truck and you two follow me in the car?"

"No. I'll drive back."

"Okay. You lead the way." He opened the passenger door for McKenna.

"I'll ride with Tori," McKenna said.

"No. Go with Luke. I'm fine. I'll see you there." Tori needed to be alone. She wished she'd learned how to meditate, because her nerves were like downed electrical wires, jumping and twitching all over the place. She said a prayer of peace as she drove slowly back to the lodge.

When she got there, she couldn't even pull into the driveway as it had gotten so packed. She parked Jesse's truck on the road with the others and turned off the ignition. In the rearview mirror, she saw Luke and McKenna parking directly behind her. Luke had lost his prime parking spot by coming to get her. Just another person she'd let down tonight . . . besides herself.

Reluctantly, Tori got out of the truck and looked at the lodge with trepidation.

McKenna ran over to her and wrapped an arm around her shoulders. "I'm right here."

She knew coming back to apologize was the right thing to do, but if it weren't for the need to absolve herself and return Jesse's truck, she wouldn't have come.

Once inside, Tori saw dozens of faces, both familiar and unfamiliar. But she didn't see Jesse in the gathering.

Kit pushed through the crowd to her side. "Are you okay?"

Tori deflected. "How's it going?"

"We're taking a five-minute break. We just finished the first icebreaker."

It's a shame the bachelors hadn't been there for Tori's epic fit; it would've given the two groups something to talk about.

Kit reached out and gently touched Tori's arm. "How *are* you?"

"I'm fine. I came back to apologize for being ridiculous and making a spectacle of myself."

Kit shook her head. "It wasn't your fault."

"No, I was rude. And I need to apologize to your clients, too."

"No need. We had a quick chat, and they were all concerned about you. You see, my girls have all been in awkward situations while looking for love, so they completely understand. Once you talk to them, you'll see that they're a group of smart, somewhat shy, but lovable women who have a tremendous amount of empathy." Kit squeezed Tori's arm. "I'm so sorry for putting you and Jesse in that uncomfortable situation. I stuck my nose where it didn't belong. Unfortunately it's an occupational hazard."

"Actually," Tori said, "you did me a huge favor. Without you, I'd never know exactly where I stood with Jesse. He's been all over the place with me." Tori thought about the amazing kiss he'd laid on her. "Or maybe I've just been misreading his actions." Maybe he kissed all his friends that way. "Anyway, thank you."

Kit's eyes flitted to a spot above Tori's head.

"He's right behind me, isn't he?"

"Yeah. I'll let you two talk. I have to set up for the next icebreaker." Kit gave her a fierce hug and whispered into her hair, "Let me know if I can mediate." She let go and left her alone with Jesse.

Before Tori turned around and faced him, she dug in her pocket and produced his keys. She held them out, not meeting his eyes. "Thanks for letting me borrow your truck."

"We should talk," he said.

"We have nothing to talk about," Tori said, trying to sound casual. "You were clear earlier. I get it." She walked away, which was good timing, because Kit was summoning everyone into the living room.

"Tori, come here." Kit waved her over.

"Do you need drinks or snacks brought in?" Tori asked, ready to play hostess, the reason she was supposed to be here.

"We need you to fill in to make an even number for the next game."

Tori backed away. "Oh, no, I'm fine being the serving wench."

But Kit took her arm and held on tight while she explained the next activity. "This game is called Quotes. Everyone will come pick a quote from the hat here on the coffee table, then the women will line up across from the men. You'll each have sixty seconds to discuss your quote with the person across from you. I'll ring a bell when it's time to switch to a new partner."

Tori begrudgingly took a quote from the hat and lined up with the other women . . . only to see who her partner was . . . and try to step away.

But Kit was there to stop her. "It's time to break the ice," she said quietly but firmly. And then to the group, "Has everyone read their quote?"

An affirmative murmur rose as Tori opened her paper to read the quote but mostly to avoid the inevitable . . . Jesse's gaze.

The words were a familiar quote from *Little Women*, a quote that Tori had memorized long ago and had discussed in a comparative literature class in college. But now it felt personal.

"Okay, start," said Kit.

The words on the paper gave Tori the courage to look up and face Jesse.

"I'll go first." She held up the paper. "It's a quote from Louisa May Alcott's *Little Women*."

"Go on," he encouraged, not breaking eye contact.

"'I am not afraid of storms, for I am learning how to sail my ship.'"

"And what does it mean to you?"

"It couldn't be more pertinent to what I'm going through right now. I came to Alaska kicking and screaming, and it's been really, really tough, but though I might be battered and beaten, I've faced the wind and the waves, and with every accomplishment I feel better, more confident."

He nodded. "I can see that about you."

"So, this quote means a lot to me. It's a reminder not just to be brave but that I *am* brave." The hitch in her voice said she was still a work in progress. "What's your quote?"

He sighed as if he didn't want to tell her.

"Go on," she said.

"It's from Shakespeare . . . um, *Romeo and Juliet* . . ."

He looked at her as if to say *Do I really have to do this?* But then he squared his shoulders and read, "'Parting is such sweet sorrow . . .'" He paused there as if the weight of the quote had stopped him in his tracks.

Then he continued on with the rest: "'That I shall say goodnight till it be morrow.'"

"Apropos, don't you think?" The universe had a cruel sense of humor. But she was proud of the nonchalance in her voice, as if it meant nothing to her that he was leaving soon.

He stepped forward and tilted his head. "Listen, Tori, about what I said to Kit—"

Kit rang the bell.

Tori was grateful and slapped on a fake smile. "Gotta run. I've got another bachelor to impress."

Her flippant words earned the hard frown that he gave her. But Tori was newly determined to chat up all the cute Alaskan men there that weekend. Not to make Jesse jealous, of course, because they only had a *professional relationship.* But Tori could take this opportunity to set her sails toward new horizons, meet new men, start moving on, and begin the process of mending her broken heart.

Yeah, sure she could.

Without a backward glance, okay maybe a little glance,

Tori made her way to the next man in line—Larry the lineman. Larry was a big, burly, slightly balding teddy bear, as sweet as they come, but he wasn't nearly as sharp as Jesse and didn't understand the comparison she was making between homesteading and sailing a ship. Next was Arthur, a history professor from a community college who was so full of himself that Tori didn't get a word in edgewise. While switching to the next guy she caught a glimpse of Jesse with *his* speed date, Aberdeen. He was giving her a genuine smile, and Aberdeen was grinning back as if she'd won the prize boar at the county fair.

"Hey," Luke said, drawing her attention. "I'm your guy on this round. Do you want to skip out on the rest of it and sneak hot cocoa out on the back porch?"

"You're a lifesaver." She saw that McKenna was currently paired with Larry and they were laughing merrily. Luke glowered and guided Tori out of the living room into the kitchen.

They filled their mugs and headed outside. "Are you okay?" she asked.

"This is not my cup of tea," he said.

"More of a hot chocolate man?" she asked, saluting him with her mug.

He laughed. "Yeah, something like that. Why did I ever agree to this speed-dating weekend?"

"Temporary insanity?"

"You nailed it." Luke glanced back at the door. "McKenna seems to be enjoying herself."

"You should've nabbed McKenna and brought her out here instead of me. Let her know how you feel," Tori suggested. "I can go get her for you."

"Nah. She's mad at me. Wouldn't talk to me the whole way here. It's not my fault Jesse made me sign up for this matchmaking thing. I felt trapped, but she blames me. The only time I could get her to communicate today was when we went to look for you. Do you want to tell me why you ran?"

"No. It doesn't matter now. Ancient history."

"Okay." He took another sip of cocoa.

The door opened and an indignant McKenna marched onto the porch. "What's going on out here?"

"Oh, I was just heading back inside. Too cold for me," Tori said, though, really, the weather was mild.

McKenna tapped her arm. "Hey. Take a look at the paper on the table, sitting beside your sketchbook."

"Why?" Tori asked.

"You have a bunch of new orders . . . from Kit's clients. They must be anticipating their new Alaskan lifestyle with their rugged men. Also more orders from the local women."

Tori was flabbergasted. "McKenna, stop doing that! How am I supposed to work on orders when I have a homestead to run?"

"You get help," Luke interjected. "A lot of homesteaders have jobs, too. You'll hire locals to get the orders done. McKenna and I can find you a lawyer to talk to about setting up an LLC. I can give you my CPA's number and you can talk to her about sales tax and deductible business expenses and stuff like that."

Was Tori really going to do this? "I'm not a designer," she tried again.

"Your customers think otherwise," Luke said.

"Besides," McKenna added, "you've always had a real passion for clothing people . . . like the women at the homeless shelter?"

Tori gasped. "You knew?"

"I caught on," McKenna said. "I saw you buying clothes that you never wore. You always had a glow about you after you'd been to the shelter, too. Wayne finally told me that he dropped you off there at least once a month."

"Wayne"—Tori's driver—"shouldn't have blabbed where I go."

"I threatened to rat him out for using the car for his many dates if he didn't tell me where you slip off to sometimes. Sorry about that." McKenna hugged her. "You've got a talent, Tori, and a big heart. It's okay to turn your passion into a business. Let's go inside now. You're right; it's chilly."

Tori shoved her mug at McKenna. "Why don't you stay here and keep Luke company?"

"I don't think so. He better get back inside, too. I'd hate to get in the way of all the women stumbling over themselves to talk to him."

"We'll all go in," Luke said angrily, turning on his heel. "Apparently, I have fans waiting."

For the rest of the evening, Tori tried unsuccessfully to ignore Jesse.

She forced herself to chat with three other men from Sweet Home. McKenna, on the other hand, flirted outrageously with all the men, which seemed to enrage Luke even more.

When the evening was over, Tori stuck with McKenna and Luke drove them back to the cabin. It felt like the first step of her life without Jesse, without depending on him, without him constantly by her side.

But she was unprepared when Luke came by to pick them up the next morning with a troubled look on his face.

"What's wrong?" Tori asked.

"Jesse's gone."

Chapter 18

LUKE STOOD IN the doorway of Tori's cabin, looking really sorry about the news he'd just delivered.

"What do you mean, gone?" Tori asked. And why didn't Jesse stop here to say good-bye?

McKenna handed Luke a cup of coffee. "Sit and tell us what happened."

Luke did as instructed. "Jesse received a text last night from the assistant to the executive producer of his show. They've bumped up the production schedule and needed him at headquarters immediately. Jesse left this morning for Knoxville."

"But he has a commitment to Tori. Uncle Monty isn't going to like that he skipped out on her," McKenna said.

"He emailed Montgomery. Apparently being called away was a possibility all along, according to Jesse. It was something he and Montgomery had discussed beforehand."

"So how long did Jesse say he was going to be gone?" McKenna asked.

"He didn't. I don't think he even knows."

"What about Patricia?" Tori said, feeling truly concerned. "She needs him."

"She's doing much better. But Jesse did call Piney and asked her to look in on her while he is gone."

But he didn't think to tell me he was leaving. As the news sank in, Tori became more miserable. She dropped onto the bed and Scout automatically jumped up to join her. She gave him a squeeze. "Your daddy's gone."

Luke lifted one eyebrow and Tori glared. "Scout is Jesse's dog, isn't he?"

She looked down at the large puppy sprawled across her lap.

"It seems as if Scout is your dog, too," Luke said.

"He's my buddy." She laid her head against Scout's.

Luke drank the rest of his coffee. "We better get going."

McKenna ruffled Scout's fur and then helped Tori to her feet. "You okay?"

"I'm fine." Or she would be. She was on her own now. And like Jesse always said: she would need the Sweet Home community, now that he was gone.

She grabbed the Alaska cross-stitch project and shoved it in her bag, hoping to get some time to work on it today.

When they arrived at the lodge, Luke went down to the river to fish with the guys. Tori and McKenna went to the sewing studio to join the Sisterhood of the Quilt, who were hosting Kit's clients. Paige was standing at the front of the room, giving instructions on how to make her Plaid Flag quilt with four stars and stripes, perfect for July fourth.

"I'll teach you a shortcut on how to make stars," Paige said. "First, Piney and the ladies have already cut strips, so come on up and choose your colors. Just shout if you need any help picking your fabrics."

Tori loved Paige's plaid flag wall hanging, but she was more interested in taking a closer look at the new orders for clothes, or working on the cross-stitch project for Patricia, anything to keep her mind off Jesse being gone. "You go on," she told McKenna. "I have plenty to do here."

"Are you sure?"

"Have fun."

Piney, with Hope in tow, appeared at Tori's sewing station. "I see you have a lot of orders. I took the liberty of finding you a few more seamstresses. A couple of Ella's high school friends—"

"Are very good at sewing," Hope cut in, "extremely precise, especially Uki and Ruthie. Do you mind using them on weekends and after school?"

"Of course she doesn't mind," Piney answered for Tori. "Sally would like to sew for you, too. She's a good seamstress and would rather sew for you than go back to work at the salmon jerky factory after the baby is born. It's an hour's drive away. Working from home or here at the lodge will be perfect for her."

Tori was overwhelmed with gratitude. "Thank you so much. I wasn't sure how I was going to do this on my own."

"I can help, too," came a voice from the doorway.

Tori turned to see Patricia walking toward her. She had more color in her face than the last time she'd seen her and she was much steadier . . . and heartier-looking, too.

"Hope picked me up and brought me over." Patricia gazed around the room. "I've missed coming here. It feels like old times." She beamed at Tori. "Give me a task. I'm eager to be busy."

Tori didn't know if it was a good idea to put Jesse's mom to work, but she wasn't going to argue with her. Better to let Piney step in and be Sweet Home's pit bull. But Piney remained quiet. "What would you like to do?" Tori asked. "Basic sewing, or maybe help me figure out workflow?"

Patricia smiled. "I'm pretty good at strategic planning. I've had a lot of practice, many years running a homestead."

Tori patted the seat beside her and then slid the notebook over. "Take a look and tell me what you think." She glanced up at Hope. "I'm thrilled to enlist local help."

"But you're thinking even bigger," Hope said, as if she'd read Tori's mind.

"Perhaps." Tori didn't want to get ahead of herself, but her mind was racing. "What if we expanded to hire other women in Alaska who want or need to work from home?"

Hope seemed excited. "A real cottage industry."

Piney jumped back into the conversation. "If we use people we don't know, how can we be sure they sew well enough for Tori's company?"

Tori started to object and say she didn't have a company, but Patricia spoke.

"That's easy: a test garment, let's say a vest. You ship the supplies to potential workers—fabric, pattern, thread, accessories—and give them a deadline to meet." Patricia looked up at Piney and Hope. "If the vest comes in on time, you can decide whether the quality is good enough to hire the person for the company."

This was the second time in the last minute that they'd referred to Tori's hobby as a company, and she had to put a stop to it. "I don't have a company. I'm just making some clothes."

McKenna sidled over. "Sorry, little sister, you're wrong."

"And I love your idea that all the clothes would be home-made here in Alaska," Hope said. "What a great hook for the business."

"Perfect branding," McKenna added.

Alaska Chic, Tori thought. Not *Homestead Chic*. Or maybe Homestead Chic could be a particular line under the Alaska Chic brand? Other ideas popped into Tori's head: Hiking Chic, Backpacking Chic, Hunting Chic, the possibilities seemed endless . . . all under the Alaska Chic umbrella! Excited, she reached into her bag for her sketchbook.

"What are you doing?" McKenna asked.

"Writing down ideas." She looked up and smiled. "Do you really think this is going to work?"

"Yes!" "Yes!" "Of course!" exclaimed Kit and her clients, who apparently had been listening in. A few even said they'd like to get in on the ground floor of the company by investing. Tori was overwhelmed by the support and felt like she'd made a new circle of friends.

Patricia was a great help when it came to building a production timeline, and Hope and Aberdeen made sure Kit's clients were perfectly measured for the clothes they'd ordered.

"You should start a database." McKenna pulled out her phone, swiped a couple of times, and then showed it to Tori. "There's a spreadsheet app on your cell you can use until you can download it to your computer."

Tori wasn't sure she had enough power to run a computer . . . not that she even had a computer at the homestead.

At some point Piney came over and encouraged Patricia to go home and rest. "Lolly's offered to drive you. I know you've had a grand time, but too much of a good thing won't do your recovery any good."

"Thank you for all your help," Tori said warmly.

"It was my pleasure." Patricia smiled at her, but she was looking a little tired. "I just pointed out a few things, really."

"You did more than that. You saved me a lot of time."

Unexpectedly, Patricia pulled Tori in for a fierce hug. Tori was hesitant to hug her back, afraid she might break her.

Then Patricia surprised her by whispering in her ear. "Give Jesse a call. Tell him how you feel." Then she let go and looked searchingly at Tori. "Okay, sweetheart?"

"I can't," Tori said softly.

"If you won't do it for yourself, then do it for me. I want to see him happy."

"See who happy?" Piney asked.

"Uh—" Tori groped for an answer.

"Scout. I think Tori should bring him by to see Checkers. I'm sure the puppy is missing his mama."

Patricia was definitely sharper than Tori right now, which was Jesse's fault. With him gone, she was completely unbalanced.

Patricia gripped her hand. "Let's talk soon."

Tori nodded and gave a little wave as Piney gently ushered Jesse's mom out the door.

Tori barely noticed as the rest of the day flew by, and too soon, it was time for dinner speed-dating with a side of moose steaks, garlic mashed potatoes, and salmonberry pies.

Kit peeked into the sewing studio, where Tori was still working, alone. "Are you ready to join us?"

Tori glanced up from the tall table in the center of the room. "I'm going to pass. I'm working on patterns to fit everyone. Thanks again for measuring your clients. The website will eventually have a way for women to upload their own measurements so they can get a personalized fit." Tori couldn't believe what was coming out of her mouth. She was talking like she had an actual clothing company with an actual website. She scribbled a note to herself: *Find someone to build website.*

"I'll have a plate brought back to you," Kit said.

"McKenna? What's she doing?"

Kit grinned. "Flirting with Larry."

"And Luke?"

"He looks ready to murder poor Larry."

McKenna really shouldn't be toying with Larry to get back at Luke. And it didn't even sound like her good-hearted sister. What had gotten into her? Oh yes—love. It clearly caused its own kind of madness.

Tori forced her gaze down to the roll of paper in front of her, determined to put her mind back on work. She was glad she had the distraction of a project . . . actually a lot of projects. Still, Jesse's face floated through her thoughts . . . as it did every other minute. She just couldn't help but wonder where he was now and what he was up to. How could she still long for him when his feelings for her couldn't be clearer? She wasn't even worth his time to say good-bye.

An hour later, Luke came back to the studio.

"I'm ready to take you and Miss-Flirts-a-Lot back to the cabin. Are you ready to go?" He seemed down, really down.

"Yeah. I'll be right there." Tori didn't ask where

McKenna was because she could guess . . . systematically making her way through all the bachelors to torture Luke.

When Tori got to the living room, McKenna had cornered some guy whose name Tori couldn't remember. "Let's go home, sis. I'm beat."

Reluctantly McKenna said good-bye to the man, who in turn looked relieved. Luke was definitely annoyed and didn't say a word as he drove them back to the cabin.

Scout hopped out first and Luke walked them to the door. He waited silently while Tori lit the lantern. As soon as she had the light going, he said good night, nothing else.

When McKenna didn't respond, Tori said, "Thanks for the ride, Luke. Good night."

The second she heard him step off the porch, she turned to McKenna.

"What is wrong with you? He likes you, McKenna, and for two days you made him miserable. Do you care for him or not?"

McKenna turned toward her duffel bag as if she were more interested in rooting around in it than what Tori had to say. "Even if I do like him—and I'm not saying that I do—we can't date."

"Why not?"

"I read the employee handbook. *No fraternizing.* Luke cares more about his banking career than he does breathing, and I would never do anything to come between him and his *great love*."

"Are you certain?"

"Yeah, I'm certain. So you see there's no reason to discuss it further."

"Then why have you been throwing yourself at every Y chromosome at the lodge?" Tori asked.

McKenna hung her head. "I don't know. I'm just so angry at the whole situation." She turned around and faced her. "It's just so rare for me to meet a man I think is truly interesting, and *of course* he's off-limits."

"Well, I think you should apologize to him in the morning," Tori offered.

"Yeah, maybe I should." McKenna stepped closer. "And you and Jesse?"

"There is no *me and Jesse*. He made it clear how he feels . . . or doesn't feel, in this case. Jesse and I are nothing to each other."

"But—"

Tori cut her off. "It's for the best. I have a new business to focus on, which will take all my time and energy." Her business would be enough. Plus, she had the homestead.

The big question now was how could she do both, especially when she was all alone? Yes, she had help sewing, but she still had a load of chores to do every day. Maybe she'd have to choose a capable man from the magazine under her bed after all.

The next morning after church, Luke chauffeured them to the lodge for brunch. Tori went in alone while McKenna stayed behind to speak with Luke. Five minutes later, she came inside by herself.

"Well?" Tori asked.

"I told him how it is. I think he's a great guy but I'm not interested," McKenna said.

"That's not even close to the truth!" Tori countered.

"That's all he needs to know. It'll be easier for him this way, easier for him to move on."

Tori opened her mouth to say more but her sister held up her hand. "Let it go."

Tori was at a loss how to fix those two, unless Luke was willing to give up his job, which, according to McKenna, would never happen. Besides, Tori realized, she shouldn't try to fix others when she couldn't fix herself.

A few minutes later, Luke entered the lodge, his silver-blue eyes filled with sadness. Tori was glad that she wouldn't be in the car when he and McKenna made the long haul back to Anchorage that afternoon.

At brunch, Tori took notes on everyone's favorite colors

and what prints they might like for their clothing. They'd make the final fabric choices online before she started cutting.

After brunch, a few bachelors and bachelorettes took a walk around the perimeter of the lodge, looking like they were making plans for the future. Aberdeen was smiling and having a lively conversation with Larry, making Tori wonder if those two might see each other again as well.

An hour later, a van arrived to take Kit's clients to the airport. The men said their good-byes, too. Luke approached McKenna and Tori.

"We have to hit the road," he said without a glint of good humor. "Tori, would you like for us to drop you at the cabin or are you going to hang around here for a while?"

"I better stay and help clean up." Also, she could make use of the abundant electricity, since she had a limited amount at home. She pulled McKenna in for a hug and whispered, "Be nice to Luke. He's hurting."

"What about me?" she whispered back.

"You're stronger than he is."

McKenna nodded and pulled away. "We'll be in touch about the LLC."

"And the CPA," Luke added.

"We're really doing this?" Tori couldn't keep the bewilderment and excitement from her voice.

"Yes, *you're* doing this, Ms. Designer." McKenna blew her a kiss and was gone.

Tori went to the kitchen, intending to wash dishes, but Piney and Miss Lisa shooed her away.

Hope squeezed her arm. "Get yourself in the studio. The Sisterhood of the Quilt has decided that you have important work to do. As soon as we're done, we'll join you."

But when Tori and Scout got to the studio, the first thing she did was pull out her phone and make sure it was connected to the Internet. Despite Patricia's insistence, Tori stopped herself from calling Jesse . . . even though she was desperate to hear his voice.

Instead, she wrote Uncle Monty an email about McKenna, Luke, and the infernal employee handbook, which eclipsed the silent treatment she'd been giving her uncle. The thing is, once Tori got started, she couldn't stop. She asked him to tell her and McKenna sometime about his adventure in Alaska. She had so many questions. She told him how she was mentally preparing herself for winter, how she'd learned it was important to have plenty of food stored up. Then it was as if the floodgates were opened. She told him about her passion for designing stylish clothes that were perfect for being outdoors. About sewing with the Sisterhood of the Quilt. About how much she loved Alaska and the tight community she'd found, or more accurately, how he'd sent her to the right place. She didn't mention her broken heart, only the good things, and thanked her uncle for giving her Sweet Home. She hit send and was wiping away the tears as the other women came through the studio door.

The Sisterhood of the Quilt worked the rest of the afternoon before Lolly, her sister Jilly, and Paige drove Tori and Scout back to her cabin.

"Sparkle said Rick will come by and get you around noon tomorrow," Lolly reminded her.

"I'll be able to help with your orders for a few hours, then, too," Paige added.

"Thanks! See you." Tori waved good-bye to her friends and turned toward the cabin.

How many times had she taken seeing Jesse here for granted? Having him show her how to care for this beautiful place? Too many to count, and now she was alone.

She looked down at Scout. "But I have you, and we don't have time to feel sorry for ourselves, do we? Jesse is gone and that is that." She frowned at the dog. "We didn't do any of our morning chores, and while it's still light, we better get to the spring for our water. Then we need to tend the garden and carry firewood inside, in case it gets chilly tonight." She also wanted to head to the river to see if the fish were biting. "I thought you and I could have fresh fish for a late supper."

But when she and Scout went into the cabin, she stopped short. Two large jugs and three pails of water were waiting for her. She looked around to see if Jesse was going to jump out and surprise her, but no one was there. There was no note either. But there was more . . . a container of fresh vegetables sat on the counter; she recognized the Swiss chard and green onions from her garden. They had all been washed and were ready to eat.

She wondered what other surprises she might find. She spun around, and sure enough, firewood was stacked neatly next to the woodstove.

"What's going on here?"

But Scout's happy panting was no help.

"How about I change out of my Sunday clothes and then you and I head to the river? After that, we'll get back to work on the Alaska cross-stitch project for Patricia." It was nearly done.

Scout barked and their plans were laid.

For the next few days, Tori split her time between the homestead and sewing clothes at the lodge, and ended her day by working on the cross-stitch. She was thrilled with herself when it was completed. She wrapped it with tissue paper and couldn't wait until she could gift it to Patricia.

With Piney as an HR director, Tori's number of employees ramped up fast. Every evening, Tori would arrive home to more completed chores. Piney finally told her in confidence that some of the women who were sewing for Tori had sent their husbands to do a few things for her as thanks for the work. Piney had been firm that Tori not say anything to anyone about it. "They just wanted to show their appreciation for the employment."

"But—" Tori tried.

"But nothing," Piney said. "Let it go."

Patricia walked into the sewing studio then, looking

even better today than over the weekend. Patricia raised her eyebrows in question.

Tori knew what she was asking and answered by shaking her head no. "Come here, though. I have something for you."

Patricia seemed surprised when Tori pulled out the present. "For me?"

"Yes." Tori looked around first and then lowered her voice. "But only on the condition that you won't bug me anymore about Jesse."

"I make no promises." Patricia tore into the little package and held up the cross-stitch. "Oh, Tori, it's perfect. I love it." She stood up. "Look, everyone, what Tori made for me."

Tori blushed as the Sisterhood made a big deal over her little bit of a project. But she had to admit that she was proud. "I thought about putting it in a frame or maybe making it a pillow, but I didn't know your preference."

"Help me pick out some fabric from the wall and I'll make it into a pillow right now. Thank you so much!" She pulled Tori in for a hug. "You would make a wonderful daughter-in-law," she whispered into her hair.

Tori shook her head no and blushed even more.

Every day from then on, Patricia would complete her ritual—ask if Tori had called Jesse—and Tori would silently answer no. But Tori thought about him nonstop. It was hard to resist hitting speed dial on her sat phone when she saw a cloud in the shape of Alaska that she wanted to show him. Or to tell him how good she was getting with a crossbow. Or when she'd cooked a nearly perfect roast. She didn't get to tell him about the first large fish she caught, scaled, gutted, and cooked, all on her own. Or how she wished he'd been there to see the deer walk into her yard while she was sipping coffee on her porch. Sure, she could have used the dog as an excuse—Scout clearly missed him, because he ran outside whenever a vehicle pulled up, his tail wagging as fast as a hummingbird flapping its wings. The simplest truth, or more accurately the complete truth, was that she missed Jesse with all her heart.

Tori poured hot water into her mug for tea, thinking her familiar sad thoughts. *Patricia can hound me all she wants, but I know Jesse doesn't want to hear from me.*

A noise outside had her running to the door. Every truck sounded like Jesse's, but this one was much larger than a pickup. Scout barked furiously at the strange vehicle.

The truck parked and three men got out. The driver came toward her with a clipboard. "Tori St. James?"

"Yes?" She tried to keep the suspicion from her voice.

"We have a delivery for you." He hitched a thumb at the guys behind him who were unloading.

"What is all this?"

He showed her the clipboard.

Uncle Monty had sent her a large freezer for putting up food for winter, a new computer, and a super-sized generator.

EVERY DAY TORI woke early with Jesse's voice ringing in her head. *You have to prepare for winter.* And every morning since the freezer had arrived, she grabbed her rod and reel, leashed her trusty sidekick Scout, and headed for the river. Then later, after she finished with the daily sewing at the lodge, she would return to the river and cast her line again, grateful for every fish. She was surprised at how quickly she was now able to ready the fish for the freezer. Which made her miss Jesse even more. If he were here, he'd think of funny things to say about her talent with fish guts, or praise her for her skill at chopping firewood. More than anything, she missed his smile.

She shook her head and put her mind back to what had to be done. The fish were great, but she would need a moose, too, in the fall. Darn Jesse for not being here to teach her. She had practiced shooting with his big-game firearm, a Marlin 1895 lever-action rifle that he'd lent her, but they hadn't been out hunting for real. Who, then, would help her get a moose?

Of course, she could ask any one of the Sweet Home residents, but she already felt like a bother, as a rotating crew kept helping out on the homestead. A couple of Sweet Home men had even come to her place to double-check that the delivery guys had installed her new generator correctly. Yesterday Hope had insisted on lending Tori one of their cars. "Use it for whatever you need. Since you're Patricia's neighbor, it would be great if you checked in on her every day. Now that Jesse isn't here, I worry about her, even though she does seem to be doing well. You don't mind, do you?"

"Not at all. Happy to do it." As long as there was a moratorium on Patricia nagging Tori to call Jesse. "Thanks for the use of the car." And thank goodness McKenna had thought to have the bachelorettes pay up front so Tori could afford gas for her borrowed wheels.

"Come on, Scout. The day is flying by and we have to get to the lodge to sew."

Scout barked.

"You're right. We'll check on Patricia first." Tori cleaned up and changed before driving over to Jesse's house. Strangely, when she knocked at the door, no one answered. Tori knocked again. Scout whined and scratched at the door.

"Come in," Patricia said weakly.

Tori eased open the door and saw that Patricia was stretched out on the couch with a wet washcloth on her head. Checkers sat dutifully by her side. Tori rushed to Patricia. "Are you okay?"

Patricia stretched her hand out toward the coffee table. "My phone . . ."

"Do I need to call the doctor for you?" Tori's heart sped up. She wished Jesse were here.

"No. But can you call . . ." Patricia's voice trailed off.

"Who?" Tori grabbed the phone. "Who should I call?"

Patricia's mouth stretched into a smile. "Jesse."

Tori breathed a sigh of relief and frustration. She snatched the washcloth from Patricia's eyes. "How could you! You scared me!"

"Well, I'm impatient." Jesse's conniving mother sat up and patted the couch beside her. Patricia took Tori's hand and squeezed. "Take it from me," she said, looking serious now. "You've only got one shot at life. You should grab happiness while you can."

Tori pondered for a moment what happiness even looked like now. At one time, it was working at the women's shelter, or partying at clubs, or just hanging out with McKenna. But happiness had changed over time. First it was learning and working side by side with Jesse. Then, happiness came in the form of the Sisterhood of the Quilt and the rest of Sweet Home. Now, her happiness was compounded by building her own company and working on designs for outdoorsy women. But Patricia wanted more from her, and Tori shook her head in defeat. "If I call him, do you *promise* not to pester me anymore?"

Patricia shrugged. "That depends on whether you tell him the truth."

"And that is?"

"That you love him." She squeezed Tori's hand again. "You've given me hope that if something happens to me tomorrow, Jesse will have you to make his life whole and happy."

Tori shook her head. "He's made it clear that our relationship is strictly professional."

Patricia laughed . . . Tori thought it was a little insensitive to laugh at her pain. "My son is as stubborn as the old mule in the barn. He knows you're his soulmate . . . and for some reason he's as scared of true love as he is of losing me."

None of that made any sense, but at the same time, Patricia's words rang true.

Patricia continued as if Tori had been unmoved. "Listen, I feel certain that Jesse is your soulmate, too. Call him. Tell him everything that's in your heart."

Reluctantly, Tori pulled her hand away and reached in her vest pocket for her own phone. "I'll do it, but it isn't going to work."

"I'll go in the kitchen to give you privacy." Checkers and Scout followed her.

"Thank you." But Tori shouldn't be thanking her at all. This call that Patricia was forcing her to make was only going to embarrass Tori more . . . and open the gaping hole in her heart even wider.

She walked over to the window and sighed heavily before selecting Jesse's number from her favorites.

He answered right away. "Is everything all right?"

"Fine." *Except your mom is being a pill.* But Tori remained quiet on that subject. "When are you coming home?"

"I think two days or so." He paused then, "Why?"

Patricia leaned into the living room. "Tell him."

Tori put her hand over the phone. "He'll be home in two days. I can talk to him then."

Patricia hit her with a hard stare, which gave Tori a peek at what it might have been like to have Patricia for a mother—she was hardheaded and strong, which she would have to be to raise two homesteading boys, according to what Jesse had told her.

"Talk to me about what?" Jesse said. "Is Mom okay?"

Tori rolled her eyes. "She's a pain in the neck," she said loudly enough for Patricia to hear.

"What do you need to tell me? I have a few minutes," he said quietly.

"Hold on." Tori took the phone outside, shut the door behind her, and stood on Jesse's porch. But then she couldn't speak.

"Tori? Are you there?"

"I'm here." She really didn't want to do this. But she

should get it over with. After all, his rejection of her would be easier to take over the phone than it had been in person.

"I know you've been clear that we only have a professional relationship—teacher to student. But . . ." This was so hard! Best to just blurt it out. "I have feelings for you." He was silent, and she rushed to walk it back. "Probably because I was so dependent on you for survival and I'm isolated and you were the only guy around."

"Thanks. That's really flattering," he deadpanned.

"Or maybe it's that I've been a fish out of water." Which only made her want to tell him about fishing. "Or it could be that your mom has this crazy idea that I'm your soulmate." Tori couldn't believe she'd used the S-word—a stupid notion that Patricia had put into her head.

Once again, there was no sound on the other end of the line. She pulled the phone away from her ear to see if the call was still connected. It was. She didn't know what to do, so she waited. It was too late to ask the question burning in her heart: *Can you love me back?*

She couldn't take it anymore. "Are you still there?"

"We can talk when I get home in a couple days," he said gruffly.

In other words, *This is awkward*. She hung up.

She'd made things worse. And now they probably couldn't even be friends anymore. She wanted to blame Patricia, but her heart was in the right place, and everyone got it wrong sometimes. Heck, Tori's heart had been completely mistaken from nearly the first moment that she met Jesse. To imagine Jesse would ever love her back was laughable.

The front door opened a crack. "So? How did it go?"

Tori couldn't face Jesse's mom. "It's all good."

"Did you two get things worked out?"

"Sure," was all Tori replied. She didn't say the rest.

Jesse was coming home, but Tori was going to be gone when he got there.

Chapter 19

JESSE HUNG UP, feeling a sense of dread and urgency. Something in Tori's voice, especially there at the end, told him he shouldn't wait two days to get home. He had to bug out now. He pocketed his phone and went to find the show's producer to tell her he had to go home. Besides, the production company had basically finished with him a few days ago; he was only hanging around to watch other shows being filmed so he could learn about story structure, even though they'd offered to send him recordings if he had to leave.

Well, he had to leave now!

When he first met Tori, he never imagined she'd be so brave. Braver than he was. She had just admitted having feelings for him. And somewhere in the disastrous phone call, she'd used the word *soulmate*. He didn't believe in soulmates, especially after what happened to his brother Shaun and his fiancée. Broken up after four years together. But Jesse did believe in Tori. He flagged down the producer and told her he had to head out.

Back at the hotel, he threw his clothes into his backpack and wished he'd said more to Tori, kept her on the call until he could form meaningful sentences, but he just couldn't talk about his feelings over the phone. The only thing he knew for certain was that he had to see her. Had to let her know . . .

"Oh, man." He stopped in the middle of shoving a pair of jeans in his bag. "I have feelings for her, too."

Another leveling thought hit him. Without a doubt, he'd give up this dream job for Tori. Once he saw her again, he was sure he wouldn't be able to leave.

That niggle of urgency in his chest was now full-on panic. "I was a complete ass. What if she's moved on by the time I get back to her?"

His phone dinged that his Uber was here. He zipped his backpack and rushed out, frantic to be home. On the way to the airport, he tried over and over to reach Tori, but his call only went to voice mail.

Thirteen hours later, he stepped off the plane and followed the signs to the shuttle bus. With each passing hour, he got more clarity, and he didn't like what he saw. He'd been chicken and had blown it with Tori. Thirty minutes later, he threw his backpack into the passenger seat of his truck, jumped behind the wheel, and hurried out of the parking lot. As soon as he was able, he pressed the accelerator, but the engine couldn't keep pace with the beat of his pounding heart.

When he finally arrived in Sweet Home, he thought he might be able to breathe, but apparently that wouldn't be possible until he saw Tori and pulled her into his arms. He'd barely put the truck in park and shut off the ignition before he was out and running for the cabin. "Tori! Tori!"

It was eerily quiet—Scout didn't bark, Tori didn't step out on the porch to welcome him home with her smile that lit up his world.

Just silence.

He ran up the porch steps and rushed inside. The interior was unnervingly still. He placed his hand on the woodstove and found it cold. "She didn't sleep here last night. Back to Dallas?" But the four walls couldn't tell him where she'd gone.

He started calculating how long it would take him to return to the airport and fly to Texas. But then his rational brain kicked in. *She must be at the lodge sewing.*

He ran back to his truck and drove like a speed demon to Home Sweet Home Lodge. Hope took her sweet time answering the door when he pounded on it.

"What's going on?" she said, motioning him in.

"Is Tori here?"

Hope shook her head. "We haven't seen her. Your mom said Tori was busy with the homestead."

"When was that?"

"Yesterday. Apparently, Tori had your mom drop her off at the cabin and then Patricia drove the car to the lodge."

His mouth went dry and his stomach dropped. He was keenly aware that every minute meant Tori was getting farther away. "Is it possible someone gave Tori a ride to the airport?"

"Why would she want to go to the airport? This is her home now." Hope gave him a worried look as if she were more concerned with what he'd done than any trouble Tori might have gotten into.

He couldn't answer her, couldn't tell her what a coward he'd been on the phone with Tori yesterday.

Hope must've taken pity on him because she said, "Let me call Piney." She pulled out her phone before he could decide whether that was a good idea.

With that one call, all of Sweet Home knew Tori was gone. For the next ten minutes, Hope's cell phone rang nonstop, but no one knew if Tori had left Alaska.

After the eleventh call, Jesse had to do something. "I can't sit around here and wait."

Hope pulled her phone away from her ear and spoke to Jesse. "What did McKenna say when you called her?"

Crud! In his exhaustion, he'd missed that important detail. "I'll do it now and let you know."

He went to his truck and called Luke.

"Are you back?" Luke asked.

"Have you heard from Tori? Is she there with McKenna?"

"Not that I know of," Luke said. "Hold on." There were footsteps and then he could hear Luke whispering to Tori's sister, knowing she was out on the bank floor. Jesse's spirits lifted. Maybe McKenna knew where Tori was. Maybe she was with her in Anchorage.

Jesse could hear McKenna whispering and then Luke came back on the line. "Neither one of us has heard from her. What's going on?"

"She's missing!" Jesse regretted it the second he spoke, because McKenna's gasp could be heard clearly. "You had me on speaker?"

But Luke didn't answer. McKenna did. "We're leaving for Sweet Home. Now."

LUKE DROVE LIKE a madman, trying to get to the homestead as fast as he could, trying to get McKenna to Tori. Anything to wipe away the worried expression on McKenna's face. Anything for her!

The last three weeks had been hell. He kept playing it over and over in his head, wishing now he'd done something differently. He should've tried harder—made McKenna engage with him, or he with her—but since the matchmaking weekend, she had shut him out. No companionable jogs in the evening. No Wednesday night pizza and a movie. She'd even bought a bike, which she used to get to and from work. Anything to avoid him, apparently.

At the bank, she'd been businesslike, professional, and he missed her sassing him. He glanced over at her now and saw she was still chewing her lip, something she'd been doing for the whole trip.

He let out a pent-up breath. "Before we get there, I have something to say."

She looked over at him, seeming almost startled that he was in the car with her. "You haven't really spoken to me in the last three weeks."

"You were clear when you said I wasn't your type. You said you were letting me down easy. What was I supposed to say?" He was so exasperated with her. "Scratch that. It doesn't matter. What I want you to know is that I've tried to put you out of my mind."

She stared at her hands in her lap. "And?"

"It's not possible. Have you missed me, too?" he asked, not caring one iota that his voice held an earnestness that made him seem vulnerable.

"Of course I've missed you." She turned to look out the window.

"Running isn't the same without you. I've missed our weekly movie night." He missed how they chatted about their day. Or how she would report any new discovery that she made about Alaska. "I'm crazy about you, McKenna. That's something you wouldn't let me say before and I thought you should know it now."

She didn't scoff so he went on.

"I've never met anyone like you. There's something so very special about you and all that you do. You care so much for others. Look what you did for the people who were about to lose their homes and businesses. I see the other things that you do, too. The sandwiches you've been giving to the less fortunate on the street. The time you take to speak to the elderly. You have a big heart, McKenna St. James." He paused because he wanted to get the next part right. "I was just wondering if there is room enough in there for me, too?"

She kept her gaze out the window and swiped at a tear. "It doesn't matter now."

"It does."

He reached over and took her hand. And since she didn't

jerk away, he brought her hand up to his lips and kissed it, while keeping his eyes on the road.

"This changes nothing."

"I'm in love with you, McKenna. Nothing would make me happier than if I could go running with you every evening, climb every mountain in Alaska with you on the weekends, spend our days laughing together—or arguing—until death do us part."

"Stop." She pulled her hand away. "We can't be together, Luke."

"If it's about company policy, we'll figure it out. Let's run off to Vegas and get married. That would solve everything."

She glared at him, tears spilling down her cheeks now. "Getting married will solve nothing. It doesn't even matter that I love you back. There's something you need to know."

"Did you just say that you love me?" His chest was pounding and he wanted to reach for her hand again, but she was wiping away the tears.

She pressed her palms against her eyes for a moment before looking over at him again. She must've willed herself into being composed. "I told you it doesn't matter."

He knew he was grinning like an idiot who'd won the lottery. *She loves me!*

"I'm leaving the bank and Anchorage, and moving to Sweet Home to be with Tori. She needs me." Her voice hitched. "But we have to find her first."

He took her hand then, and wrapping an arm around her shoulder he pulled her closer. She leaned into him across the console and cried into his chest.

"We're going to find her." If it was the last thing that Luke did.

JESSE PULLED UP to his mom's cabin, grabbed his duffel, and went inside, only to be surprised to see his mom at the bookshelf with a dust rag in her hand . . . just like old times.

"You're home!" She rushed over and hugged him. "Tori said you weren't going to be here until tomorrow." Her expression changed and she said, "What's wrong?"

"Tori's gone."

His mom shook her head. "Oh, surely not. Someone probably picked her up and took her to the lodge. The only reason I didn't go today was so I could get things straightened up here for you. Why are you home early?"

He took the dust rag away from her. "Sit down and rest."

"I'm tired of resting. I'm restless. Now tell me what's going on."

He looked down at his boots. "I was worried about Tori. She didn't sound right when she called."

"I know. She seemed uncannily calm after she talked to you."

"You were listening?" He was mortified.

"I wasn't listening in. But I knew she was calling you. Afterward she said she had things to do at the homestead and couldn't go to the lodge. So I dropped her off at the cabin and went on without her."

"Yeah, that's what Hope said, too. Are you sure she didn't say something else to suggest where she was going?"

Patricia wrapped an arm around him. "Come sit down. You look dead on your feet. I'll fix you a hot cup of tea. Then you and I are going to figure out where she's gone."

Jesse did as his mom wanted and drank tea. While they waited for Luke and McKenna, Jesse made his own calls to everyone in town, but no one had seen Tori.

Finally, he jumped to his feet, unable to sit any longer. "I'm going back to Tori's cabin. Tell Luke to meet me there."

"Okay," Patricia said. "If you can, keep me updated."

"I will." Before he left, he took three long strides across the room and kissed his mom on the cheek.

At Tori's cabin, he did a more thorough search and went through her full rack of clothes, where all her wilderness wear was still hanging. Clothes she wouldn't need in Dallas. Like she didn't need him.

Next, he checked the contents of the cold-hole; everything seemed to be in its place, but he couldn't be sure. He'd been gone over three weeks. Inside he stared at the hanging clothes again. Maybe when McKenna got here, she would be able to figure out if anything was missing. He took another look around the cabin and this time—he didn't know what compelled him—he looked under her bed. There were Tori's three large suitcases. Reassuring, but puzzling. If her suitcases were here, then she hadn't left for Dallas. Was it possible she'd been kidnapped or attacked by a wild animal?

At the sound of a car pulling up, he ran outside, surprised how quickly Luke and McKenna had gotten there. McKenna got out of the driver's side and hurried toward him, her eyes red as if she'd been crying.

"Well?" she said. "Any word?"

"No," Jesse said. "It looks like her things are still here. But no one knows where she's gone."

Jesse followed as McKenna rushed inside, where she made straight for the clothes rack. "Her hunting vest, cargo pants, and the new shirt she designed with all the pockets are all missing."

Luke stuck his head in the door. "Any ideas in here?"

McKenna told him about the missing clothes. "I'm going to take a complete inventory of the cabin."

"We'll be outside, looking for clues," Luke said.

Once they were out of earshot, Jesse asked, "What is it?"

Luke pointed to the trail. "Relatively fresh tracks—human and dog."

"When you say *relatively fresh*, do you mean she left this morning?" Jesse asked.

"Not that fresh. She didn't leave this morning. Probably yesterday."

McKenna stepped outside and called to them, "I don't

see the new backpack she made for herself. She must've taken it with her."

"Luke found her tracks," Jesse said.

"Luke did?" McKenna asked, incredulously.

"Sure. He's the best tracker I know."

MCKENNA FELT REASSURED and at the same time confused. She caught up with Luke as all three of them hurried down the side of the hill, following the tracks. "Suppose you tell me why you hid the fact that you're really an outdoorsman."

Luke shrugged. "I wasn't hiding it. I love everything about the outdoors." He pointed. "I think Tori headed toward the river." He took McKenna's hand and started walking faster.

The thrill of holding his hand, mixed with the guilt of feeling euphoric while her sister was lost and alone and maybe hurt, made McKenna stumble over a log. Luke's hands caught her arms and he righted her. It seemed like he'd been righting her since the day they met.

He brushed a leaf out of her hair and they continued.

"I've come to a decision," he said. "What if I moved back to Sweet Home, too?"

"I won't let you do that. You love being the manager at the bank."

"No. I love you."

And she loved hearing him say it. But it also made her sad because they couldn't be together.

"Here's the thing," he said as he moved a branch out of the way. "Lately it's been hard to stomach being a hard-nosed banker. I've known it for a while, but you helped me to see more clearly that profits aren't everything. Especially at the expense of people." He squeezed her hand. "You've changed me, McKenna. I certainly didn't think I'd ever want to return to Sweet Home and the homesteading life, but it sounds like the most perfect thing in the world to me now, as long as you're there."

"But . . ." She didn't know exactly how she would make a living. She'd probably have to learn to lead a subsistence life like Tori. Eventually she'd get paid to manage Tori's budding clothing business, but not at the start. Not to mention the biggest changes. "You have to know that when I leave Anchorage, Uncle Monty will cut me off, which means I'm kissing my substantial inheritance good-bye."

Without a word, Luke pulled her into his arms and kissed her hard before pulling her down the trail again. "I don't love you for your money, you silly woman. I love you for who you are."

McKenna loved him, too, but she was sure Luke was kidding himself if he thought he could leave banking behind.

Luke pointed at a broken twig on the side of a tree. "Jesse, over here. Tori went this way." Luke took off again, glancing over at McKenna with his all-is-well grin filling his face.

But McKenna only felt dread. Whether it was from Tori or the future, she didn't know. It felt as if nothing was ever going to be okay again.

Chapter 20

TORI GLANCED DOWN at the tub full of fish that sat in the middle of the canoe. She was so proud of herself for picking this spot without anyone's guidance, as Jesse had never taken her this far downstream before. She was still breathing hard from wrestling in the last fish but glad for the exertion. "You know, Scout, for a minute there, I was worried I wouldn't be able to haul it in by myself." She was sure the dog had found her efforts hilarious to watch. Now she gazed with deep satisfaction at all the fish. "We'll definitely be set for winter."

She still couldn't believe that she'd run away to camp in the woods, but it served dual purposes. One was to fill the freezer, but, more importantly, she wouldn't be around when Jesse got home tomorrow.

She never dreamed she'd catch this many fish so quickly. Now her plan to stay out here for several days would have to be revised. She would need to take the catch home today, fill the freezer, and be gone again before Jesse returned. But truthfully, would he even notice she wasn't around? Probably not.

The problem with heading back to the cabin was that she would once again see Jesse everywhere she looked. At the log piles, the cold-hole, the spring, standing over the wood-stove, and especially on the front porch.

But those days were over. No more Jesse. Her focus now was on preparing for winter, and this fishing camping trip was just the thing.

Then it hit her. Since she'd gotten to Alaska, she hadn't thought too far ahead, only the next day or the next week, always ready to bail. And now she was preparing for winter? She laughed. "It seems the idea of staying the whole year has snuck up on me, buddy." She patted Scout's head and he panted back at her with his Scout-y grin. "I'm sure going to miss your daddy, though."

Cut it out, she told herself. Right now she had bigger fish to fry . . . so to speak. She grabbed the rope she'd tied to the tree and pulled herself back to shore, deciding along the way to break camp and choose a new fishing hole. She'd leave the rest of the fish alone in this area as a thank-you for the bounty they'd given her today and pick a new spot to set up her tent for the night.

Back at camp, she loaded her things into her backpack, took down the tent, and stored it all in the overfull canoe.

"Come on, Scout. You get in, too." Eagerly the dog followed her onboard. "Got a lot of fish to clean." But not near the cabin. In case a bear smelled the fish blood and innards, it was best to keep all the guts away from where she lived.

Tori was exceedingly proud of herself as she pushed away from shore. She was taking care of business like a real homesteader. But once she was out in the middle of the river, she realized she didn't have enough strength to paddle against the current. She'd been so proud of herself, doing this fishing trip alone—gathering all the camping and fishing gear, setting up her tent, making a fire, and sleeping alone in the tent overnight. Paddling downriver yesterday had been a breeze and it never occurred to her what force it would take to make it back upstream with such a heavy load. Frantically, she plunged her oar into the water, over and over, but only lost ground, ending up farther downstream from where she'd set up her campsite. The more she tried, the more frustrated she became. She wanted to cry.

But she didn't. She was going to find a way to get out of this mess. She began paddling for shore again, relieved when she made it there without tipping over. She dragged the canoe—and a barking Scout—as far as she could up on the pebbly shore and looked around for inspiration.

Unencumbered, she could walk all the way back to her cabin, but with pounds and pounds of fish to carry? She certainly couldn't drag both the canoe and its contents home in one trip.

She scanned the surrounding woods and spotted some small trees growing near the edge of the river. Jesse had taught her to always look to the land to solve problems, and Tori knew what she had to do. She pulled her hatchet from her backpack and went to work. Chopping down even little trees was hard work and time consuming, but eventually she had enough to lash together for a sled. She was grateful that Jesse had insisted she always carry paracord with her.

When the sled was done and the fish were tied down, she pulled the canoe all the way out of the water and leaned it against a tree. Later she'd have to figure a way to get the canoe upriver.

She glanced over at Scout as if he had the answer. "Come here and let me put your leash on." Then an idea came to her. She would bring a long rope back with her to tie onto the canoe and float it upriver by walking along the edge. But for now she only needed to worry about getting her catch back to the homestead and into the freezer.

If Scout were older, she might have hooked one side of the homemade sled to him and the other side to herself, but as it was, she was on her own, with Scout as moral support. She slipped her backpack on with the cord tied to it and began dragging her fish toward home.

The terrain was rough and the trek arduous, but Tori kept telling herself that she was a strong Alaskan homesteader now and this was what homesteaders did. Homesteaders took care of what they needed to take care of and didn't give up when things got tough. Though a part of her wanted to sit down and have a good cry, crying like a baby would serve no purpose, only use up energy. As it was, she needed every ounce to get back to the cabin.

Suddenly the crunching of twigs and a huffing noise sent adrenaline flooding her system. She stopped to listen, but Scout went crazy barking and pulling. Thank goodness she'd attached the leash to her belt. When she heard more huffing, almost directly behind her, the hair on her arms stood up. With one hand, she reached for the sling holding her rifle, and with the other, she grabbed the bear spray in her holster, mentally walking through the training Jesse had given her. If the bear that was tracking her didn't become disoriented from the fog of bear spray, she would have to use her rifle. *Take even breaths*, Jesse had said. *Everyone gets nervous, but try to remember to keep calm.*

Slowly Tori turned to see the bear—a grizzly, like the ones she'd seen in the movies. But there was no trainer standing by to control it. There was only Jesse's voice in her mind: *You've got this, Tori. You're an excellent shot.* She raised the rifle.

A SHOT RANG out. Jesse whirled sideways to look at Luke, knowing he recognized the sound of his Marlin. There was a second shot. "This way."

All three of them took off in the direction of the rifle shot. Jesse's hammering heart nearly beat out of his chest as he bounded through the woods to get to Tori. *Maybe she's just shooting for target practice.* But his gut knew differently. Suddenly everything between him and Tori was clear, and with every footfall, the issues he'd struggled with since meeting her disappeared and the pieces fell into place. When he got to Tori, he wasn't going to hesitate to tell her how much he loved her. That he wanted to spend the rest of his life with her. He just needed to find her safe and sound so he could convince her that they belonged together. Yes, the new job was an exciting opportunity, but he'd give everything up for Tori. Everything!

"Tori! Tori!" Jesse yelled.

"Tori! Where are you?" McKenna joined in.

TORI DECIDED NOT to take any chances and pulled the trigger one more time. The bear spray and warning shots had the bear running in the opposite direction, but he could just as easily turn around and come back to steal her fish . . . or take a bite out of her. She hoped this final shot would discourage the beast from following her home.

The danger seemed to be gone, but she wasn't taking any chances. Though Scout was nearly the size of a full-grown dog, she snatched him up and ran, with her sled jostling behind her. Suddenly Scout began squirming. "Stop that. I'm not letting that nasty bear have you for an afternoon snack." Despite her best efforts, Scout bolted from her arms, and in the process broke the belt loop that held his leash. But instead of heading back in the direction of the bear, he raced ahead of her, leading the way. "What's gotten into you!"

Then she heard it. Jesse's voice, calling her name! Suddenly she wasn't winded from pulling the heavy sled over uneven ground. She was Wonder Woman and the sled weighed no more than a bag of cotton balls. "Jesse! Jesse!"

Scout was barking happily as he disappeared over the hill. And then she saw her rugged mountain man. The backpack slipped from her shoulders and she raced up the incline toward him as he recklessly two-stepped it down the embankment toward her. It wasn't like the movies, where the couple ran toward each other through an empty field of grass. They were hurdling logs and ducking low-hanging branches to get to each other—it was a true Alaskan scene.

At that moment, she didn't care that she'd made a fool of herself by telling him her feelings. She wanted to shout her love to the sky. To the river. To all of Alaska . . . because she was alive and he was here.

There was so much to tell him, too. He'd helped her to fall in love with homesteading. Alaska had given her purpose. And she couldn't wait to tell Jesse about the work she'd done on her new clothing line since seeing him. And how her little business might help other women throughout the state.

She moved the last branch and Jesse was there, pulling her into his arms, as Scout jumped and barked at their feet.

Jesse stopped to cup her face with his calloused hands. Oh, how she loved his hands. "Tori, thank God. What happened? You're shaking. Are you all right?"

"Grizzly," she got out.

He scanned her from head to toe and then, apparently satisfied, he pulled her in for another tight hug. She savored it, savored him, never wanted him to let go.

"Tori!"

McKenna had appeared at the top of the embankment and was coming toward her. It didn't seem real. Maybe the bear had killed her and Tori was in heaven, because the two people she loved most in the world were here with her in the middle of the forest. Then she noticed that Luke was right behind McKenna. "How did you two get—"

McKenna threw herself at them and wrapped her and Jesse in a hug. "You're okay!"

"Yes. I'm okay. But why are you here and not in Anchorage?"

"We came to find you," Luke answered.

"We all came to find you," Jesse interjected.

"But why? I was just camping. I'm fine." She remembered the last five minutes. "Except there was the bear."

McKenna pulled Tori away from Jesse and clutched her arms. "I'm never letting you out of my sight again. Do you hear?"

"That's ridiculous," Tori said, feeling for the first time as if she were on equal ground with her sister. Living on the homestead had done that. It made her grow up, made her independent, and gave her a world of confidence. "I love you, McKenna, but you're too overprotective. I think I've proven that I can take care of myself." Shirking off the *fragile* mantle was freeing, and for the first time, Tori owned her own power.

McKenna looked down as if just noticing the leaves beneath her feet. "It's not just for you, you know?"

"What's not for me?"

"The reason I don't want you out of my sight. I miss you so much. I would've thought you knew the truth by now."

"What truth is that?"

"That I need you more than you need me," McKenna admitted.

"You're being silly. We need each other equally."

McKenna hugged her again. "Regardless, I'm leaving Anchorage and moving to the homestead with you."

Tori looked at Jesse over McKenna's shoulder. He was gazing at her, too. "Let's talk about it after we get back to the cabin, all right?"

McKenna let go. "Okay."

"In the meantime," Tori said, "I have a sled full of fish to get back to the homestead and it would be great if I had help getting them in the freezer."

Luke took McKenna's hand. "We'll get the fish. You talk to Jesse."

Tori smiled at their clasped hands. "I like you two together."

As they walked away, Tori went to Jesse and took his hand, intertwining her fingers with his. She felt brave, brave enough to do the unthinkable. She brought her eyes up to meet his before she spoke. "When you leave, Jesse Montana, I want to go with you. I don't care if you don't love me just yet. I have enough love for the both of us until you come to your senses." It wasn't hard to swallow her pride when she loved so deeply. And part of being the new Tori was asking for what she wanted . . . what she needed.

His eyes smiled first before he broke into a grin. "Coming face-to-face with a bear has made you feisty."

"So what do you say? May I?"

"Give me a second to say what I have to say first."

Only moments ago, her heart had been jumping for joy, but now it stilled and dropped to the ground.

Then he pulled her into his arms and kissed her. She wrapped her arms around his neck and kissed him back. When they pulled away, she nuzzled into his chest.

"I certainly enjoy your nonverbal communication, but I gotta know what's what." Her heart wanted to know because being in his arms was giving her hope.

He kissed the top of her head, not letting her go. "I came home a day early because there's something I need to tell you that couldn't wait. Not even another day."

She felt giddy. "And what's that?"

"I love you, too, my homesteading woman."

Tori pulled back to see his face and saw him smiling with love in his eyes . . . for her! "But what if I gave up homesteading to have my own clothing line for the outdoors woman?"

"I love that Tori, too. The truth is that you can be whatever you want, and I'll still love you. Forever."

"Yeah, well, you might think differently when you find out that I'm going to lose my inheritance."

He hugged her tight. "What do I care?"

"I've got to call Uncle Monty to tell him that I'm breaking my deal with him by leaving the homestead. That is, if you let me go with you."

Jesse shook his head. "You're not going anywhere with me—"

His declaration had her soaring heart nose-diving again. "But—"

"Let me finish," Jesse said. "You're not going anywhere with me unless we get married first."

"Me? Married? To you?" She sounded like a simpleton.

"Yeah. I just decided."

"You did?" She was nearly speechless.

"You see, I had planned to give up the TV show so I could stay here in Sweet Home, close to you. But you, once again, surprised me with the brilliant idea of you coming with me. We'll still base out of Sweet Home, of course, which doesn't give us a lot of time to get started on our own cabin."

"Wait." Her head was spinning. "Cabin?"

"Well, if McKenna is moving to your homestead, then we should find a place on my family's land to put down roots." He gave her a quick kiss as if he couldn't stand not kissing her for another moment. "I know all your requirements. You're going to need a large studio for your clothes business, storage, and a shipping area, too. You'll need plenty of electricity to run the sewing machines and room for your crew."

"If I had my inheritance, I could just rent one of the buildings in town to run the business so my 'crew' won't have to make their way out to the homestead."

"That's an excellent idea," Jesse exclaimed. "You certainly have a head for business." He kissed her again as if this time it were a reward. "I bet we can rent you a building in town for a song and a dance, and I'll be able to cover it so you don't need your uncle's money." He stopped and gazed at her then. "Will you be able to run your business while you're with me filming on location?"

"I don't want to be separated from you again. But if I need to spend time working in Sweet Home, we can be apart for a little while, right?"

"Yes. I'm confident we can survive you being a successful business owner."

Luke and McKenna had almost caught up to them. Luke was wearing Tori's backpack and they were each pulling a rope attached to the sled.

"You two get everything worked out?" Luke asked.

"You can say that," Jesse answered for them. "We're getting married."

"Married?" McKenna exclaimed with some puzzlement in her voice. "How long were we gone?"

Jesse laughed. "How does July fourth sound for a wedding date? My birthday."

Tori smiled up at her fiancé. "Really, huh? No discussion on that either."

"Okay, you choose the date, but remember I'm an impatient man. I want to start our lives together as soon as possible."

"But how?" McKenna said. "What about your clothing business? What about the homestead? What about Jesse's new job?"

Tori smiled up at her soon-to-be husband. "We don't have all the answers, but we'll figure it out as we go. Right, Jesse?"

"Right."

McKenna looked stunned. "You can't make life decisions without weighing all the options."

Tori looped her arm through McKenna's. "It turns out that we've both given it a lot of thought. Give Jesse your rope. I'll tell what we're thinking so far."

"Excuse me," Jesse interrupted. "Where's the canoe, Miss Homesteader?"

"I had to leave it down by the river. I'll go get it tomorrow." Tori wasn't looking forward to going back for it . . . especially if the grizzly might be waiting for her.

Luke handed his rope and backpack to Jesse, and then put his hands out to Tori. "Can I borrow the rifle? I'll go back and get the canoe now."

"Thanks." Tori handed over the rifle but saw the worried look on McKenna's face. "Don't worry, big sister. Luke knows what he's doing." She glanced over at Jesse and he nodded reassuringly. "Come on. Let's get back to the cabin."

On the way, Tori shared their tentative plans. By the time she was finished, McKenna was on board to help run her business whenever Tori was away. When Luke made it back to the cabin and McKenna told him what Tori and Jesse were up to, he also offered to help in any way he could.

Tori was suffused with love for these amazing people in her life.

"What about Scout?" McKenna asked. "Can he stay with me on the homestead?"

"I don't know." Tori would miss him so much.

But Jesse answered, "Thanks, McKenna, that would be great. Some of the places we'll be filming the show are pretty remote and wild."

Tori leaned down to kiss and hug Scout. "Don't worry, good boy, you're going to love living with Aunt McKenna while I'm away." Then she turned to Jesse. "Can McKenna and I borrow your truck? We need to run into town and find a place to make a call to Uncle Monty's lawyer."

"Isn't it kind of late?" Luke asked.

"We'll leave a message," McKenna answered. "We both want to get this over with."

Jesse kissed Tori. "We'll work on the fish while you're gone."

"Are you sure?" Tori asked.

"It's no problem. Plus, Luke is an excellent cook, so dinner will be ready when you get back."

McKenna gaped at Luke. "Really? You cook, too?"

Luke smiled. "You learn to cook when you grow up on a homestead."

McKenna shook her head. "I feel like I'm only just getting to know you."

Luke leaned over and gave her a quick kiss on the lips. "We have plenty of time. But wouldn't it be great to have a double wedding with your sister and Jesse?"

McKenna paled. "I don't think so."

Once in the privacy of the truck, Tori faced McKenna as she turned the key. "I like the idea of a double wedding, too, don't you?"

"Don't start on me," McKenna said. "I love Luke—"

"I can tell," Tori interrupted.

"But . . ." McKenna sighed. "I can't see it working out. Luke is talking like he's leaving the bank for my sake, but that's not really going to happen. The bank is part of who he is."

Tori reached over and squeezed her sister's hand. "Don't give up hope. Besides, you just admitted there's still so much to learn about him. So maybe he'll surprise you yet."

McKenna shrugged, and didn't say anything the rest of the way into town.

"There's pretty good cell reception behind the high school building," Tori said, turning the truck into the parking lot.

When she put the truck into park, Tori pulled out her phone and dialed.

Terrence picked up on the first ring.

"Um, this is Tori St. James. I expected to leave a message."

"Working late," Terrence explained. "Is everything all right?"

"Yes, very much so." But a glance at McKenna told Tori she was only speaking for herself.

"What can I do for you?"

"Can you pass a message along to our uncle? Can you let him know that McKenna and I love him, but we don't need his money or the inheritance anymore?"

Terrence was silent for a long moment. "Are you sure?"

"If it's okay with Uncle Monty, McKenna and I would still like to have use of the homestead. Oh, and to answer the question he's sure to ask, please tell him we both found something more valuable than money."

"And that is?"

"Hard work and self-worth." Tori didn't add *love*, but she was thinking it. "Would you let Uncle Monty know?"

"Certainly."

"Thank you, Terrence." She knew this would be the last time she would need to speak with him. "Take care. Bye."

Tori ended the call and turned to McKenna. "It's done. Are you still okay with it?"

"Yes. You and I are going to work things out on our own. It's hard to fathom, but it seems we're actually more suited to Alaska than Dallas."

Tori laughed. "Who knew, right?" She thought of the many reasons why Alaska was the perfect place for them. Alaska made them wiser and more centered. They'd learned new skills and tapped into old talents. And not least— because their men were Alaskan. But Tori didn't dare say that out loud because McKenna would argue.

A sense of urgency came over Tori. Before it was too late, she needed to ensure that her sister had a happily-ever-after ending, too.

Chapter 21

TWO DAYS LATER, Tori awoke to a vehicle pulling up outside the cabin. She tossed her pillow at McKenna, who was camping out on an air mattress on the floor. "The guys are here." As Tori threw on her clothes, she heard a second vehicle pull up, too, and wondered why the guys were driving separately today. Was Luke heading back to Anchorage? She hoped he hadn't given up on McKenna.

Fully dressed, Tori opened the door with a big smile, anxious to see her man. But to her surprise, Jesse's truck was parked near a sleek black Range Rover.

The doors opened and a man and a woman got out . . . Uncle Monty and Peggy!

Tori hollered over her shoulder, "McKenna, get out here," and ran down the steps to hug her uncle. "We've missed you!" she said.

Uncle Monty didn't seem as happy to see her as she did to see him. "You girls had better explain yourselves."

"Uncle Monty!" McKenna exclaimed from the porch. "What are you doing here?" She ran to get her hug, too.

Tori broke away and gave Peggy a hug. "How are you, Peggy? How has the trip around the world been going?"

Peggy gave her a genuine smile with deep crinkles

around her eyes. "Lovely. However, when Monty got that call from Terrence, we quickly said good-bye to Rome. He's worried about you two." Peggy gently pushed a stray curl behind Tori's ear. "Your new haircut is darling. I bet it's easy to take care of."

"It's been perfect for the homestead." In that moment, Tori couldn't remember why she and McKenna hadn't liked Peggy. She'd always been sweet to them, in fact, more motherly than anyone else Tori had known besides their own mother.

Jesse and Luke joined them, and Tori introduced Peggy.

Uncle Monty surveyed the homestead. "I see the last generator arrived safely."

"It's been a godsend," Tori said, giving him another hug. "We have so much to tell you. But let me go make some coffee for all of us. Jesse, do you want to help?"

He grinned and followed her inside. The moment they were through the doorway and out of sight, he pulled her into his arms and kissed her senseless. "How are the wedding plans going?"

"I'm ready as soon as your birthday gets here." Tori had sketched a wedding dress that wouldn't take long to make. The only holdup might be getting the fabric to Sweet Home in time. But for the first time in her life, she didn't care what she wore. She'd be happy wearing a pair of jeans and one of McKenna's old chambray shirts if she needed to.

Reluctantly they pulled apart and started the Mr. Coffee machine Hope had given her the last time she was at the lodge. The lodge no longer needed it, as the cabins had been upgraded to Keurigs.

They returned outside with the coffees. Uncle Monty and Peggy were settled on the steps, while McKenna and Luke sat on the porch with their legs dangling over the side.

"Wouldn't you two be more comfortable in the chairs?" Tori asked as she handed the two elders their mugs.

"Is it true?" Uncle Monty said to her, ignoring her question.

"Which part? That I'm engaged?" She beamed up at Jesse. "That we're getting married July fourth?" Peggy's eyes went wide, and Uncle Monty's mouth popped open.

McKenna laughed. "We hadn't gotten to that part yet. I told him the latest about your company. About how you're going to rent one of the buildings in town and that I'm going to help you manage Alaska Chic."

Tori settled in beside Uncle Monty and took his hand. "Your experiment was a success." She smiled over at Peggy. "I suspect you helped him to come up with it."

Peggy nodded. "Just a nudge. I explained that he'd seen to your formal education but he'd done nothing to prepare you for the world."

"I'm very grateful," Tori said.

"Me, too," McKenna agreed.

Tori continued. "Back in Dallas, I didn't know that I could be more than I was. Apparently, trial by fire was just what I needed." She turned back to her uncle. "Please don't worry about us. Both McKenna and I know what we're giving up. Our new life in Alaska is everything we ever wanted."

"Stop." Monty put his hand up. "I might as well tell you what I did. My company has been looking into buying the bank in Sweet Home, and the board of directors thinks it's an interesting investment considering the improvements the town has made in the last year, such as reopening A Stone's Throw Hardware & Haberdashery and Home Sweet Home Lodge." He stared at McKenna. "In a nutshell, I want you to run it. A small bank is a great place for you to start managing. Luke here says you have a real knack for helping people. How about helping the people here in Sweet Home and the surrounding area?"

"I–I—" McKenna stuttered.

Uncle Monty gave her one of his reassuring nods. "I believe you can handle both the bank and some of the details of Tori's new business, can't you? Since you were a little girl, I knew you had your great-uncle's management acumen." He laughed.

"And any questions you may have, I'm sure Luke will be willing to help. Just give him a call."

"Sir," Luke broke in, "I'm going to be resigning my position at the bank in Anchorage—and as soon as a new manager is in place, I'm moving back to Sweet Home."

"Why in heavens would you want to do that?" Monty sounded astonished. "We have plans to move you up in the corporation."

Peggy reached over and took Monty's hand. "Dearest, I believe he wants to be where your McKenna is."

"What?"

"Yes. I want to marry your niece . . . as soon as she figures out that she can't live without me. Because, sir, I can't live without her. And I want to help the families around Sweet Home, homesteaders who are having a rough go of it, like me and my dad did when I was a kid."

Monty turned to McKenna. "You're welcome to hire anyone you like to work at the bank. I suggest you hire that young man."

McKenna gave Uncle Monty a huge hug.

Luke squared his shoulders and cleared his throat. "Does that mean we have your blessing to get married?"

McKenna shot him a look. "You should get *my* blessing first."

Uncle Monty put his hand out and he and Luke shook. "You're going to have your hands full with this one."

Luke beamed. "I wouldn't have it any other way."

Monty turned to Jesse now. "So . . . you want to marry Tori?"

"Yes, sir. I know I should've asked your permission first, but when a man is consumed with love like I am, well, the niceties go by the wayside."

"Not all the niceties, I hope," Monty said sternly.

"No, sir. I know it's a little late, but may I marry your niece?"

Tori laid her head on Uncle Monty's shoulder, knowing he had a soft spot in his heart for his two girls.

Uncle Monty cleared his throat. "Yes, well, I guess. You have to promise to always be good to her, to treat her like gold." His gaze went to Luke. "That goes for you, too."

"Yes, sir," they both agreed together.

"Well, then, we have a couple of weddings to plan," Peggy said, as joyfully as if she were the mother of the brides.

"We would love your help," Tori said, reaching for Peggy's hand.

McKenna took her other hand. "Yes, that would be wonderful. Apparently I'm going to be busy getting the bank up and running, and Tori's business, too." She laughed and then gazed up at Luke. "I definitely didn't see my life turning out like this."

Jesse came and stood next to Tori, laying his arm around her shoulders.

"Oh, and girls," Uncle Monty said, "you aren't cut out of the will."

"And?" Peggy prompted.

Monty pulled out two envelopes. "You can have your credit cards back."

THE NEXT FEW weeks were a whirlwind of arrangements, which Peggy orchestrated and Uncle Monty paid for. At dinner one night, he filled Tori and McKenna in on his time in Alaska—the good times, the antics, and the rough times—and how hard it had been to leave a place he loved so much. But with his father's death, he'd been duty-bound to return home and take his dad's place in the company. Uncle Monty was now standing at the back of the Baptist church, ready to give Tori and McKenna away. Tori had designed herself an A-line dress that a woodland fairy might wear, with loads of white chiffon petals cascading down to her toes. It was whimsical and she'd never felt prettier. McKenna had wanted to wear something practical, but when Tori showed her a drawing of a flirty V-neck, tea-length dress with a satin belt atop a tulle skirt that would swish like a bell, McKenna had given her an emphatic thumbs-up. She looked incredibly beautiful in it, and it fit her to a T. Tori could never have pulled off completing the dresses in time if it hadn't been for the Sisterhood of the Quilt stepping in to ease the load. They'd made the wedding dresses a community project, creating a memory she would hold in her heart forever. How did she ever get so lucky?

But the bigger question was how did the Sisterhood complete their matching wedding quilts in time for the rehearsal dinner last night without Tori even having a clue? From a distance, their quilts looked like a large log cabin, but up close, there was a theme playing out on each row. One row had bear appliques with bear paw blocks on each side. Another row had fish, a canoe, and a fishing pole. Another had a vegetable garden and what looked like her cold-hole refrigerator. McKenna's quilt had some variations, like a bicycle block, a building with *Sweet Home Bank* written on it, and a block that looked like running shoes. At the top of both log cabins was a star. Tori could tell a lot of love had gone into making the quilts and her heart swelled every time she thought about it. The quilters had even made a little Log Cabin dog quilt for Scout, which had the silhouette of a bear in the bottom right corner.

The double ceremony was substantially boosting Sweet Home's local economy, for Uncle Monty had flown all of their friends up from Dallas to witness their happy unions. Plus all of the Sisterhood of the Quilt was there with their hankies at the ready. Jesse's brother, Shaun, had arrived from Houston that morning and was sitting with Patricia in the front row. Tori knew because she'd peeked into the sanctuary.

Peggy handed Tori and McKenna their white composite bouquets—bouquets made to look like one large flower. They were simple and elegant, which seemed to fit both of them now. "Your uncle is waiting for you. I'll see you both in there."

"Are you ready, sis?" Tori asked.

"You bet," McKenna answered.

They stepped out of the small classroom and met Uncle Monty at the back of the church. He was quite dapper in his black tux and white boutonniere. They each kissed him and then looped an arm through his.

The church was packed to capacity, and beautifully decorated with bouquets of baby's breath and forget-me-nots attached to each pew. Tori's heart was bursting with love as she walked down the aisle, her eyes on Jesse, who was waiting for her at the altar, smiling, his eyes locked on her in return. She sneaked a peek at McKenna, who was equal parts tears and smiles for Luke. The rest of the ceremony felt like a dream—clasping hands, repeating vows, exchanging rings, and finally, *You may kiss the bride*. Tori couldn't have imagined a more perfect wedding.

At the reception, Uncle Monty took his champagne flute to the front of the crowd. "Thank you all for coming together to witness the weddings of my nieces."

"Hear, hear!" many shouted.

"First, I'd like to start off with a toast to my girls, McKenna and Tori. They have been the most wonderful gift, and I can't imagine my life without them."

"We're the lucky ones," McKenna hollered back, making the old man smile.

He raised his glass. "To McKenna and Tori."

"To McKenna and Tori," the group said together.

Tori glanced over at the family photo with her mom and dad that she and McKenna had placed there so her parents could be part of this day, too. McKenna leaned into her. "They would be so happy for us."

"I know."

Uncle Monty turned to the head table. "While I'm up here, I would like to say something else. I have a special wedding present for you girls."

The wedding had been enough, Tori mused, but apparently Uncle Monty wasn't finished.

"McKenna," he began, "although Tori took the homestead and made it a home, I am gifting the homestead property to you. Tori, is that all right?"

"Absolutely! I hope McKenna and Luke are as happy there as I've been." Tori and Jesse had already picked out the site to start building their own cabin—a little spot nestled among the trees, a place of their own, but only a few minutes' walk to Patricia's house. They hoped to make some headway on their cabin before they left to film Jesse's show in four weeks.

"And for you, Tori," Uncle Monty said, "I bought the lease on the old Tate building across from the Hungry Bear. I know it needs work, but I'll have it remodeled any way you like. I hope it will be a good home base to get Alaska Chic off the ground."

Overwhelmed, Tori mouthed *thank you* and McKenna reached over and squeezed her hand.

"Lastly," Monty continued, "to Sweet Home, I want to thank you for taking my girls in and for treating them as your own. You gave them the same love and welcome you once gave me. I can't imagine a better place for my girls to call home. Thank you." He raised his glass. "To Sweet Home." Everyone clinked glasses and drank.

Tori kissed her new husband and said, "McKenna and I need to speak with Uncle Monty."

"Don't be gone long," Jesse said. "The dancing's going to start any minute."

Tori gave him another quick kiss, grabbed her sister, and headed for Uncle Monty, who was taking his seat at the neighboring table.

Tori wrapped her arm around McKenna's waist and said, "I'm glad you came to your senses and married Luke. You look very happy."

"It was never a question of loving him," McKenna said.

"I just didn't want him to give up on his big-city dream because of me, if that was what he really wanted."

"But what he wants is you."

"He's what I want, too." McKenna's smile was so bright. As bright as their futures, Tori thought.

They each took a seat on either side of Uncle Monty, and he looked from one to the other in confusion. "Why aren't you girls with your men?"

"We need to talk to you," McKenna started.

Tori picked up from there. "We think it's time, Uncle Monty."

His bushy eyebrows crashed together. "Time for what?"

"Time for you to make an honest woman out of Peggy," McKenna said.

Tori didn't give him time to respond. "We love her, Uncle Monty, and want her to be part of the family officially."

"Oh, that." Uncle Monty reached into his suit jacket, pulled out a box, and set it on the table. "What do you think about me giving her this ring at the end of the evening?"

Tori and McKenna squealed in unison.

"Oh, Uncle." Tori hugged him.

McKenna laughed. "No longer the bachelor."

Peggy was coming over—probably to see what the commotion was about—and Tori scooted the box back to Uncle Monty to hide.

But McKenna stopped her by snatching it up. "Can we ask her?"

"Oh, can we?" Tori added.

Uncle Monty sighed. "You know I can never say no to you girls. Go ahead."

Tori met Peggy and pulled her over to the table.

"What's going on?" she asked.

Jesse and Luke were making their way over as well. "We have a little announcement to make" was all Tori would say until her husband was by her side. She couldn't believe she was married!

"Can we join the family meeting?" Luke asked as he wrapped an arm around McKenna.

Jesse pulled Tori into him, too, and kissed the top of her head. "You were gone too long."

"Go on," Uncle Monty said, the laugh lines crinkling around his eyes. "Say what you need to say, girls."

McKenna took Peggy's hand and pulled her to her chair. "You have to sit for this."

"Sit for what?"

Uncle Monty took Peggy's hand and kissed it. "The girls have an important question to ask you."

McKenna opened the ring box. "Peggy, will you do us the honor—"

Tori took over. "Of becoming part of our family?"

Peggy's mouth dropped open. "Is this for real?"

Uncle Monty leaned over and gazed into her eyes. "Darling, will you marry me?"

At that perfect moment, the music started to play, and Peggy said, "Yes. Yes, of course, Monty."

"Let's give them a minute alone," said Jesse, pulling Tori out on the dance floor.

But Tori cranked her head around to see Uncle Monty and Peggy kissing, which filled her heart with joy. Luke was dragging McKenna out on the dance floor, too, twirling her as they went. That brought Tori joy, too.

Then she looked into Jesse's eyes. She could see everything in their depths. She saw his love for her, his kindness, his steadiness, but most of all she saw her future.

He tipped her chin up. "I love you, Mrs. Montana."

"Mrs. Montana . . ." she said in wonderment.

Then he leaned down to kiss her, and all her thoughts melded into one. The best day. The best place. The best life.

Keep reading for a preview of

Happily Ever Alaska

Coming soon from Jove

LOLLY CROCKER STEPPED outside to get her mail, glad for the warmer days of July and to be free of a jacket. A group of her home ec students would arrive any minute at her humble abode on the cheap side of Sweet Home, Alaska, population 573. Over summer break, Lolly was giving baking lessons based on *The Great British Baking Show*, a favorite binge for both her and the girls who were in her class at Sweet Home High. Today's bake was macarons, a treat that Lolly loved. Which was perfect—it was her thirty-fourth birthday. She'd returned to her hometown around this time last year to take a position teaching family and consumer science, but since the end of school she'd basically been holding her breath. Rumor had it that non-core subjects like hers might be cut from the curriculum in the fall. But as each day passed and the new school year drew nearer, she felt more confident. No teachers had been laid off, according to the grapevine, which was more accurate than the nightly news. And yet, Lolly couldn't breathe easy until the school district sent her a new contract. Hers must've fallen through the cracks. On Monday, she planned to call and find out what the holdup was. The first day of school was in one month and four days. Surely it was just an oversight.

As she reached for the mailbox handle, a blue Ford pickup pulled in beside her. Newlyweds Jesse and Tori Montana grinned at her as they disembarked.

"Hey, Lolly." Tori gave her a hug with a gift bag in hand.

"How is your staycay-honeymoon going?" But Lolly needn't have asked. They both seemed to be floating on air.

"We've made progress on our new home," Jesse said, "and when Shaun gets back, it'll go much quicker." But as soon as he said it, he seemed to regret mentioning his brother.

Probably because he'd seen Lolly blanch.

Shaun Montana was Lolly's one mistake in a long line of breakups. She had quite the record of dating good guys and then cutting them loose. A couple of times—okay, three—she'd even been engaged. Each time, when her stomach started hurting, she knew without a doubt that Mr. Right-this-time hadn't really been right after all, and she broke it off.

But Shaun was different.

Lolly looked up into Jesse's face and realized the air surrounding the three of them was wrought with awkwardness. "Sorry? What did you say?"

Looking embarrassed, Tori held out the gift bag. "No worries. I brought you a present."

Lolly accepted the bag. "Present? For what?" What she really wanted to ask was *When is Shaun going to be back in town*? Lolly had seen him at their wedding, but only from a distance, as if he was trying to stay away from her on purpose.

Jesse came around from his side of the truck with their dog, Scout, following him. "You did an amazing job on our wedding cake. You really made the log cabin come to life, not to mention the miniature of Scout. We wanted to thank you."

Lolly reached down to pet their labradoodle, a good

friend and playmate to her own Bichonpoodle, Thor, who right now was in her fenced backyard. "No need to thank me. The cake was my present to you." She smiled at the two of them. "Really *I* should be thanking *you*. I love baking, but I seldom get the opportunity to use my decorating skills, especially on a cake of that magnitude . . . and McKenna's cake, too, of course." Tori and her sister had had a huge double wedding with people coming from all over. McKenna and Luke's cake was shaped like a map of Alaska, with the town of Sweet Home in 3D on top.

"Go ahead and open your present." Tori seemed excited, so Lolly reached in and pulled out the gift: an adorable reversible apron—one side masculine, in a print of rustic wood and animals, and the other side decorated with forget-me-nots and fireweed. "Thanks, I love it! You know how crazy I am about flowers."

"It was Jesse's idea to make it reversible."

"Guys like to cook, you know," he put in.

"Well, I'm honored that you would gift me with an original Alaska Chic design," Lolly gushed. Tori's new clothing company was all that people were talking about in town these days. "Are you going to make a whole line of kitchen and home products like potholders, dish towels, and coasters?"

"I never even thought about it," Tori said, "but I'm sure if McKenna were here right now, she'd say '*Absolutely!*'"

Lolly held the apron to her chest as if to model it. "I'm going to treasure this forever." What a nice, unexpected birthday gift.

"Oh, before I forget," Tori added, "Piney said to tell you that we're all expected at the lodge at seven for an impromptu meeting of the Sisterhood of the Quilt."

Lolly shot her a suspicious look. Their quilting group had a standing date to sew together the first Saturday of every month. Yes, they gathered at other times, usually to make a comfort quilt, and sometimes for celebrations, but . . . "What's the reason for tonight's meeting?"

Tori winked at her. "No reason. No reason at all. But

Piney did want you to whip up one of your special cakes and bring it with you. You know, the one with the three layers—yellow, pistachio, and chocolate?"

Lolly shook her head. So Piney wanted Lolly to make her *own* birthday cake for the surprise party they might or might not be throwing for her. "Sure. I have all the ingredients." She'd been planning to make a small version for herself anyway. "Is there anything else that Piney needs me to bring?"

"Do you have extra birthday candles? Piney said she didn't have enough at the store."

Lolly laughed. "I'll see what I can dig up."

Jesse laughed, too. "Don't you just love living in Sweet Home?"

"I wouldn't want to be anywhere else," Lolly answered honestly.

Tori gave her another hug. "See you tonight."

"See you tonight." Lolly waved as they pulled away. She'd nearly forgotten why she was standing by the road, but now she opened the mailbox and pulled everything out. The first envelope held a birthday card from her best friend, Paige, who was in Denver teaching a series of workshops for various quilt guilds. The second bore the return address of the school district. *Finally,* she thought. But it seemed too thin to be her contract.

She slipped her finger under the flap, tore open the top, pulled out the letter, and read: *We regret to inform you that we will not be renewing your contract for the upcoming school year.*

Lolly looked around as though someone might be watching and know her shame. The school she loved so much didn't love her back enough to have her for a second year. She read the note again, this time to the end. Budget cuts, nothing to do with her, blah blah blah. But still . . .

What was she going to do?

Well, her students were going to be here any minute so

there wasn't time to call Paige to grumble about her downfall.

Lolly frowned at the cottage she shared with her sister. Jilly, a traveling nurse, was gone most of the time, and had been thrilled when Lolly moved home to do all the cooking and split the rent. But how could Lolly do her part when she wouldn't have a paycheck come August 1?

"So much for being excited about being back home," Lolly muttered to herself. It was very late—in fact, too late—to find a job for this school year, but she'd have to try anyway.

Then reality set in.

She'd have to move.

She'd have to come up with the first and last month's rent.

She'd have to leave Sweet Home, when she'd only just gotten back.

As she started to head inside, sixteen-year-old Ella Stone pulled up in her Subaru Outback filled with her friends Lacy, Uki, Ruthie, and Annette, right on time. They scrambled out of the vehicle with loads of enthusiasm, but then Ella stopped short.

"Is everything all right, Ms. Crocker?"

Lolly dug deep and produced a smile. "Yes, all good. Thor has been waiting for you. He's in the back. Do you mind letting him in? I'll be just a minute."

"No problem." The girls laughed and hurried inside, leaving Lolly a moment to pull herself together. She wished she had time to think things through, but the girls and macarons were waiting. Lolly tamped down the sadness and disappointment and went to her front door, feeling like she'd mastered her emotions. Then she reached for the doorknob, and—

Oh, crud. I have to face the Sisterhood of the Quilt tonight. Maybe between now and *then* she could pull herself together.

In the kitchen, Uki, Annette, and Ruthie were busy digging through the cabinets and setting out bowls and measuring cups while Ella and Lacy sat in the window seat. Ella had Thor in her lap and Lacy held the recipe card, but she wasn't reading out the ingredients. Instead, Lacy wrapped an arm around her best friend's shoulder while Ella complained.

"I can't believe Mom's going to have a baby!" She whined. "At her age!"

Her comment struck a chord with Lolly, who was a year younger than Ella's mother, Hope. Lolly always assumed she'd have a husband and kids by this age. If only she'd been able to follow through with at least one of the engagements, then maybe she'd have a couple of kiddos by now.

Lacy squeezed Ella. "C'mon, I promise your mom and dad won't forget you after the baby is born."

Ella hung her head, which told Lolly that Lacy had pinpointed the problem. Lolly knew this feeling all too well. She'd felt the same way when her little sister, Jilly, was born, when Lolly was ten. Happily, they'd always been friends, despite having opposite personalities. And though Lolly occasionally nagged her wild-child sister, they were super close now that they were adults.

But Lolly would hold off on giving advice. She knew it was important, as the adult-in-charge, to be invisible and let the girls talk this over among themselves.

"Having a little sister or brother is cool," Uki piped in. "They look up to you and think you know everything. I bet you'll like it."

"Except when it's time to change the poopy diapers." Ruthie screwed up her face as if she'd had experience with little ones.

"The crying all night can be annoying, too." Annette had a nephew who was two or so. She glanced over as if just noticing Lolly was in the kitchen. "What should we do first?"

"It looks like you've made a good start. The ingredients are in the pantry, as you know. I thought we might co-work in the space today. While you work on the macarons, I need to make a cake for the Sisterhood of the Quilt."

Uki smiled broadly. "Yeah, we heard. Happy birthday, Ms. Crocker." The other girls joined in with their best wishes, too.

Their sweetness really lifted Lolly's spirits. As did the sweets they were making. Somehow, sifting flour, mixing batter, and pulling baked goods from the oven was the best medicine, always making life more enjoyable. And in this case, perhaps, bearable.

"What would you like for your birthday?" Ella asked.

To have my job back. But of course, Lolly kept that sentiment to herself. "How about some help chopping up the pistachios that are in the freezer? And to be honest, eating the yummy macarons you're baking will make my birthday week brighter."

"We're on it." Ruthie went to the freezer.

They spent the next couple of hours chopping and stirring and beating. Baking seemed to make even Ella forget her troubles, and helped Lolly shove down the thoughts taunting her about her uncertain future and lack of employment . . . well, mostly.

As the last batch of macarons came out of the oven, her cell phone rang. "Hey, Piney. What's up?"

"Do you have some of those chocolate chip oatmeal wonders in your freezer that you could share with me?" Piney asked. "I forgot to turn on the oven again and my cookies won't be ready for the lunch crowd."

"I have several dozen." Lolly was beginning to wonder if Piney was being forgetful on purpose. This was the fourth time this month she'd asked at the last minute for baked goods for her Hungry Bear Grocery-Diner.

"Can you run them up to me? I'm all alone at the store and can't get away."

Lolly glanced at the girls, who were flipping through Lolly's cookbooks. "Sure. I'll be right there."

"You're a lifesaver," Piney said.

Lolly hung up and turned to her students. "Piney needs me to bring cookies to the Hungry Bear. Do you mind if I'm gone for a few minutes?"

"We've got it under control, Ms. C," Ruthie said, always so full of confidence.

"I know you do." Lolly went to the freezer and pulled out containers holding three dozen of her favorite cookies. She didn't shove them in her Hungry Bear upcycled grocery bags right away, but opened a container and pulled out a pancake-sized cookie for herself. *Delivery tax*, she thought. She'd worry about the calories later. The extra pounds she'd put on this last year were a nuisance, but she chalked them up to starting a new job. Still, she'd have to start paying attention soon. She couldn't eat anything and everything the way she could in her twenties. Today, though, this cookie was more than a craving; it was therapy. She needed it to counteract the lousy news that had come in the mail. "Can you keep an eye on the chocolate cake? I should be back in about ten minutes."

Ella looked at the clock and nodded. "Will do."

"Don't worry," Annette said. "We're on it."

Lolly hurried out the door with the bag looped over her shoulder. Normally, a good brisk walk to the Hungry Bear was rejuvenating, but this walk only gave her mind time to dwell on what she'd lost. Her livelihood, and possibly her hometown, since she'd more than likely have to move. She took another bite of the cookie and hurried on to rescue Piney.

AS SHAUN MONTANA drove from the airport in Anchorage to Sweet Home, he kept checking his rearview mirror, as if his past were hot on his trail. He had been scheduled to leave Houston tomorrow, but when he got the chance to get out sooner, he took it. Too many bad memories in Texas.

He laughed to himself. *Yeah, like Sweet Home holds no bad memories.*

Well, in thirty more miles he'd be home. Thirty more miles until he could put the last four years behind him.

Yes, he'd briefly returned for his brother's wedding, driving the 4,200 miles in his Toyota 4Runner, loaded down with all his worldly goods so he could get a jump on moving home. He'd had to immediately fly back to Houston to train yet another new person before leaving for good. After handing off the final project yesterday, he caught an earlier flight back to Alaska.

He told himself that leaving Houston early had nothing to do with hearing about Tanya's engagement to her ex-boyfriend. He didn't understand how he'd been so naïve. It had taken her two years to say yes to Shaun's proposal, then another year of dragging her feet. When he finally pushed her to set a date, she said they were in two different places and she wanted to take a break. Now all of a sudden she was marrying her ex?! Shaun usually saw only the good in people, but all signs pointed to the fact that Tanya had stepped out on him.

Maybe now you'll change your ways, huh? For someone who was supposedly smart—he was a software developer for the petroleum industry—he sure was dumb when it came to relationships. Shaun had fallen in love too many times. He'd just never done the casual thing, for which he blamed his parents; they'd had a real, lasting love until the day his father died. Shaun always assumed he'd have that, too: a partner to share everything with. His parents made it look easy. Yet the women he dated never seemed to want the same things he did: a home, family, roots. The result? His heart had been trampled again and again.

The way he saw it, he could either sign up to become a monk or learn how not to get so attached to the opposite sex. He was still on the fence about which way to go.

In the meantime, he had plenty to do to keep him busy. He needed to get up to speed on what had to be done on his mom's homestead before Jesse and Tori left town to film the new *Homestead Recovery* show on HGTV. Plus, Jesse needed help finishing his cabin, which should be a fun project. This was all good. Shaun would be too busy to go into town often. He'd make sure of that. Town was where he might see Lolly Crocker, the first person to stomp on his heart. The last thing he needed was to run into her day in and day out. It was bad enough seeing her at Jesse's wedding.

Shaun couldn't help but gawk at Lolly as he made his way down the aisle. She looked even more beautiful than when they dated in high school, and he'd had to work hard to keep from staring at her. But remembering how she'd coldheartedly broken up with him made it easier. Back then, Shaun had thought the two of them would be together forever. That he'd follow her to college after he graduated the following year. That they were strong in their love. But, boy, was he wrong. After dumping him, she'd left him standing on her front porch while she went inside without a backward glance and turned off the porch light.

If only he'd been able to turn off his feelings for her as easily. And seeing her at the wedding made all those old emotions come flooding back. The anger, the feeling of betrayal . . . how stupid he felt for loving her more than she loved him.

Of course, in the end, Shaun really should be thanking Lolly. He didn't follow her to college but instead went to far-off Texas for school. There, he found a new life, one without her. Only once had he asked his mom about Lolly.

"She got her teaching certificate and took a job in Oregon. She wasn't right for you, Shaun. It's for the best."

Once again, Shaun wondered why his mother hadn't warned him before the wedding that Lolly was back in Sweet Home. Or Jesse—although his older brother had already left home when the whole thing with Lolly went down and didn't really know how badly she had skewered Shaun's heart.

Shaun had given Lolly a wide berth at the wedding reception, which may have been a mistake. Maybe he should've walked right up to her and shown her that she meant nothing to him now but ancient history. That he never thought about her. That he never asked himself *What if?*

But he hadn't, so he'd have to continue to keep his distance from her. Lolly was where it all started. She was where he'd gotten off track and the reason he kept repeating the same mistake in relationships over and over again. Falling for the same type of woman—heartless. It was past time to learn from his mistakes. Stay away from Lolly-type women and from Lolly herself. This would be the only way he could move on and not repeat the past.

At last the population sign for Sweet Home appeared and prompted him to slow down as he pulled into town. Out of the corner of his eye he saw a flash of movement as someone stepped out into the road from between two cars. Shaun threw on the brakes and came to a screeching halt. At a glance he took in wide eyes, an apron and, over the woman's shoulder, a grocery bag, the kind Piney sold at the Hungry Bear. And was that a cookie in her hand?

Without thinking, he jammed the SUV into park and jumped out shouting, "Are you crazy? You could've been killed!"

"Sorry. Distracted." She bit her lip and brought her blueberry eyes up to meet his. That's when it registered whom he'd almost run over.

"Lolly Crocker!"

"It's good to see you, Shaun."

Ready to find
your next great read?

Let us help.

Visit prh.com/nextread

Penguin
Random
House